WAITING

for the

MONSOON

WAITING *for the* MONSOON

THREES ANNA

TRANSLATED BY
BARBARA POTTER FASTING

First published in English in 2012 by House of Anansi Press Inc.

Publication of this book has been made possible with financial support from the Dutch Foundation for Literature.

This edition published in 2012 by
House of Anansi Press Inc.
110 Spadina Avenue, Suite 801
Toronto, ON, M5V 2K4
Tel. 416-363-4343 Fax 416-363-1017
www.anansi.ca

Distributed in Canada by
HarperCollins Canada Ltd.
1995 Markham Road
Scarborough, ON, M1B 5M8
Toll free tel. 1-800-387-0117

House of Anansi Press is committed to protecting our natural environment. As part of our efforts, the interior of this book is printed on paper that contains 100% post-consumer recycled fibres, is acid-free, and is processed chlorine-free.

16 15 14 13 12 1 2 3 4 5

Library and Archives Canada Cataloguing in Publication

Anna, Threes, 1959–
Waiting for the monsoon / Threes Anna ; translated
by Barbara Potter Fasting.

Translation of: Wachten op de moesson.
ISBN 978-0-88784-257-3

I. Fasting, Barbara II. Title.

PT5882.1.N63W3313 2011 839.31'37 C2011-902443-8

Cover design: Alysia Shewchuk
Cover images: Woman: Luca Zampedri/Getty Images; Fabric: Gallo Images/Getty Images; Ornamental details: HiDesignGraphics/iStockphoto
Interior image: Jasmine flower: Gizele/Shutterstock
Text design and typesetting: Alysia Shewchuk

Canada Council for the Arts Conseil des Arts du Canada

We acknowledge for their financial support of our publishing program the Canada Council for the Arts, the Ontario Arts Council, and the Government of Canada through the Canada Book Fund.

Printed and bound in Canada

MIX
Paper from responsible sources
FSC® C004071

To my dear father, who never had to fight in a war.

1995 Rampur ~

IF HER SOUL had been as spotless as her lawn, she would not have died that year. She was like the old Lloyds. For years it was the only electric lawnmower for miles around: the fact that it was still functioning was thanks to the brand and not to love.

The machine hummed softly as she pushed it along. On the horizon the sky began to colour, and the electrical cable came to the end of its reach. With a jerk, Charlotte steered the Lloyds to the left and began to push it in the direction of the house. This was even more arduous, since it was uphill and she had to be careful not to run over the cable. She was panting. Again she had barely made it. In the distance she heard the bus starting up for the first run of the day. In one of the houses at the bottom of the road a light came on; the crickets had fallen silent and the birds were still in dreamland. India was slowly awakening.

Charlotte pushed the Lloyds into the shed and began to rein in the cable, which consisted of a series of extension cords strung together. Every time she had gone to New Delhi the gardener asked her to get an extra cord, so that he could go farther down the hill. Until one morning six months ago, when he didn't wake up.

She had been jealous of the *mali*'s peaceful death. It was still dark when they came to get her, just like now. Against the back wall of the shed, next to the old Lloyds, stood his simple bed, knocked together out of wood and rope. The old man was out on the bed: he was wearing a long white shirt, his hands were folded on his chest, and his feet were slightly apart. His rib cage was visible through the thin material and his eyes were closed. It was as if he were praying. "You have a better god than I do," she'd whispered.

After breakfast, three of the gardener's nephews whom she'd never seen before had arrived to claim their uncle. Charlotte was always amazed at how fast news spread. The men rolled the body in a length of cloth and placed it on a bamboo stretcher. All of his earthly possessions were rolled up in another cloth and disappeared into a small bag. After Charlotte gave them money for the cremation, the men left, the body rocking slightly between their shoulders. The following week she had tried to sell the bed, but no one was prepared to pay money for the wooden affair in which the *mali* had died.

She put the bundle of extension cords on the rickety bed. It was time for tea, before the sun began to scorch the land and only the cuckoo was willing to sing. In the kitchen, a building some twenty metres from the main house, a light went on. Charlotte snuck up the monumental staircase and quickly went inside and back to her bedroom. She didn't want Hema to see her in her old work trousers.

The butler's real name was Hemavatinandan, which she found difficult to remember. So for twenty-nine years she had called him Hema, which was a girl's name. But Charlotte, whose full name was Charlotte Elizabeth, didn't know that. Just as she didn't know that Hema had waited in the kitchen until she was finished mowing the lawn and putting the mower away before he turned on the light. He had made the necessary preparations in the dark, knowing that she would ring the bell for tea as soon she was back in her bedroom.

Charlotte kicked off her slippers and got out of the trousers. She was still wearing her cotton nightgown. With a sigh she crept under the mosquito net and back into bed. The bedroom windows and shutters were wide open, and the sheets finally felt cool to the touch. Within a quarter of an hour the sun would make its appearance, cruel and merciless. She dreaded today, as she dreaded every Tuesday, and more than ever during the hot months. She pulled the cord hanging next to the bed. Outside, the sky had turned pink and the birds under her window twittered as a light morning breeze swept the last breath of nocturnal air from the room. She stretched and waited for her tea.

IN THE KITCHEN, the bell sounded. Hema wiped the sweat from his forehead and laid the Calor gas bottle on its side. The fire beneath the kettle had already gone out twice, and he didn't have a spare bottle.

He'd tried to start a fire in the old fireplace in the corner, but the coals wouldn't catch. Moving quickly, he went out to the shed. He pulled the battered portable stove the gardener had used from under the bed, and took it with him into the kitchen. Most of the English households had long since installed electric furnaces, but Charlotte had informed him that she didn't like the taste of food that was prepared on such a modern furnace. Hema had no idea how she could taste the difference. He placed the tray with tea things next to her bed and poured her a cup.

"Didn't you hear the bell?"

"Sorry, Charlotte memsahib." He bowed his head. "Gas cylinder empty and no new cylinder."

"But there are still coals?"

Hema nodded as he closed the bedroom shutters.

"The old *bobajee* always cooked on coals," came the reply from the bed. The fact that the old cook never kindled the fire himself but always called on the gardener for help was something else that Charlotte did not know. She took a sip of her tea and smiled. "Fortunately, your tea tastes better than the old *bobajee*'s."

Hema pulled the curtains across the shutters and the room was completely dark again. There was a rumbling sound, a light bulb was illuminated, and the fan on the ceiling began revolving. Charlotte looked at the man's back as he walked over to the window again.

"Ma'am?" Hema smoothed the curtains with his hand.

"Yes?"

"Can I buy new gas bottle?"

"Why don't you use the coals?"

Hema bowed his head low. "Yes, ma'am, but very busy."

"I know, Hema, but I would still prefer that you finish the coals before buying a new bottle."

The old man walked to the door in his bare feet, his head still bowed, as he mumbled, "Of course, Charlotte memsahib, of course."

Charlotte closed her eyes. The first of the morning heat

seeped through the cracks in the shutters and entered the bedroom. She heard Hema open the bathroom door and turn on the faucet.

"You won't forget to shut the upper windows in the nursery?" she called after him.

THE CLOCK ON the landing struck six. A pigeon scurried around outside the attic window, searching for a way to get in, and Hema took the key that was hanging from a nail next to the nursery. Everyone tried to make the most of the early hours of the day, before it got so hot that no one wanted to move. Charlotte opened her eyes and saw that there were blades of grass clinging to her feet. She hoped that Hema hadn't noticed. There were a lot of things Charlotte didn't know, but she was certain about one thing: Hema's eyesight was still excellent. She reached under the mosquito net in the direction of the bedside table. Opening the drawer, she rummaged around among the medicine bottles, handkerchiefs, and various odds and ends until she found a small box in the corner. It was made of wood and had once been baby blue; now it was grubby and the paint was peeling. Charlotte picked it up and pulled it under the mosquito net. She hesitated for an instant, about to put it back. But then she opened it quickly: in the box lay a cigarette and a lighter. Her nostrils quivered slightly and the tip of her tongue flicked across her upper lip. The noises in the house died down, and outside the birds had ceased their dawn chorus. Slowly she brought the lighter to the tip of the cigarette, but just before lighting it, she paused. She took a deep drag on the unlit cigarette, filled her lungs with air, and then exhaled large imaginary smoke rings. She relaxed and flicked the ash into an imaginary ashtray next to her on the bed. She took another drag, deeper than the first. Then she pursed her lips and slowly blew out the smoke. The day had begun.

CHARLOTTE HEADED DOWN the hill on her old Raleigh. Her hair and skirt billowed and her speed made the sand swirl around her. At the bottom of the path there was an old sign so rusted that no one knew it was a right-of-way sign. She crossed the road without looking to the right or left. A truck filled with watermelons was coming around the corner. The driver swore at her, but she didn't hear him, since by that time she was already passing the vegetable stall, where a bandy-legged man was busy piling tangerines into a great heap. He raised his hand in greeting. She waved back at the man, who was good at repairing tire punctures. Her bike slowed, not because she braked, but because the hill had become a flat road leading to the outskirts of the city. Beads of sweat formed on her forehead, her skirt clung to her legs, and her breathing accelerated. The dust that lent the air its greyish tinge clung to her skin. She could feel her knees creak and cursed the rattletrap she was sitting on. A car honked, and Charlotte glanced in the direction of the driver. Behind the chauffeur she saw the wife of Nikhil Nair, attired as always in pink, waving in her direction. Her lips were moving, but her voice was inaudible: no one would dream of opening a car window unless it was absolutely necessary. Charlotte lifted one hand from the handlebar and waved back. For a brief moment she hoped that the wife of the district director of the Eastern Indian Mining Company would offer her a lift, but the car drove on and she breathed in the exhaust fumes it left behind.

If she hadn't had stomach troubles three weeks before, she wouldn't have missed the talk by the professor from Calcutta at their regular Tuesday-morning get-together. He had impressed on the ladies the importance of daily exercise in the battle against cellulitis. "Aha," said one of the ladies, "hence the bicycle." The others nodded. None of them had understood why Charlotte, who always drove to the meeting, had sold the Vauxhall and from then on came by bike. The car disappeared into the distance. She didn't know what make it was, but that it was new, big, and expensive was no secret. What was a secret, however, was the fact that Nikhil Nair wanted to buy Charlotte's clock, the large standing clock that had stood on the landing since her earliest youth. Her grandfather had carried it on a tandem bike as he crossed the Khyber Pass, with his wife walking behind him. Again a car horn sounded; this time it wasn't a club member who honked, but the driver of the truck with watermelons. Charlotte glanced in passing at a storefront clock. The meeting would be starting in ten minutes. Today's speaker was a doctor, a fingernail specialist. As a child, Charlotte had seldom been given fresh milk, and she was convinced that that was responsible for her weak nails. Today she had carefully filed her nails and painted them bright red, the only colour she had on hand, knowing that the club members would be certain to examine each other's hands with extra interest.

Suddenly a cow crossed the road. Charlotte barely managed to avoid the animal as it trotted off in the direction of a wooden cart with a large iron drum, parked at the side of the road. The cow began to butt the drum with its horns. A small boy sitting on the rim shouted something to the animal, dived into the water, and emerged with a bucket of water, which he poured over the animal's head. The cow opened her mouth. The water sloshed down her throat and she drank greedily. In the distance Charlotte heard a piercing noise that was coming steadily closer. Her heart always missed a beat at the sound of a fire engine siren. She breathed a quick prayer that it wasn't a big fire and that no one would die, especially not the firemen. The siren ebbed away and she was glad there was no sign of the large, red fire engine. The boy climbed out of the drum with a second bucketful of water and poured it into the animal's open mouth. Charlotte was thirsty, too. When she arrived at the club, there would be a pitcher of ice water alongside the coffee and tea.

She pedalled under the archway. The guard was sound asleep in the shadow of the guardhouse. In his hand he held an empty cola bottle, and beside him, under a blue and white umbrella, the secretary's dog lay panting next to a water bowl. The lawn of the New Rampur Club was yellowed and arid, and the stream that once ran through the terrain had disappeared. The eucalyptus trees that lined the long driveway cast shadows on the road, providing a modicum of cool shade. Before her stood the clubhouse, built in classic English country style and surrounded by enormous old plane trees. She heard a car approaching behind her and moved to the side of the road. The widow Singh's 1957 Ambassador went by at top speed, her elderly chauffeur at the wheel. Charlotte did not raise her hand, since the widow never waved. She was asleep. She was always asleep, in the car and during the presentations. Whenever she sat still for two minutes, her head would drop forward, and she'd begin to snore softly. Charlotte appreciated the breath of air created by the speeding car.

THE BUILDING THAT housed the New Rampur Club was — to put it mildly — due for renovation, and the library was in even worse shape. Most of the thousands of books it housed had been attacked by small black beetles, and the mice had also helped themselves. Moreover, as a result of repeated leaks during a monsoon, the closely packed books on the topmost shelves had been transformed into lumps of pages pasted together, and they gave off a stale, musty odour.

The Reverend Das, who was not often seen at the club, entered the library with a weighty pile of books. He had lost all of his hair at the age of twenty, and it was perhaps for this reason that his vanity was reflected in his moustache, which was very large and dyed black. He went over to the reading table, shoved the women's magazines aside, and replaced them with his own books. The door to the room reserved for the ladies was half open and he heard the chatter from the Tuesday-morning club as the members introduced themselves to the guest speaker. Without even glancing inside, he closed the door softly. Peace and quiet returned to the darkened library.

The minister began arranging his books. Above his head, the fan whirred at full speed, and the sole remaining fluorescent tube wheezed softly. Five months ago, he had himself been the guest speaker at the ladies' club meeting. He preferred not to recall his talk on the subject of good causes. He had spent weeks working on his presentation; he collected begging-letters from all over India, which he kept in a plastic folder. He told the ladies about child labour, rural poverty, ritual killings, and the sacrifice of widows, but they decided that their annual club dues would go to a lapsed nun from

Calcutta who wanted to set up a dog pound. The Reverend Das had no idea how the lapsed nun's letter had got into his folder. He had never seen the application and suspected that the epistle — which was full of grammatical errors — had somehow been slipped into his folder when he wasn't looking.

Dusty and perspiring, Charlotte walked into the library. She had hoped to freshen up in the change room at the tennis court, but it was occupied, so she washed her hands and face in the ladies' room, ran a comb through her hair, and brushed most of the dust from her dress. She was surprised to find Reverend Das at the table with ladies' magazines. It was rumoured that he had become a member in order to keep a closer eye on his parishioners. Seeing how furtively he was going through the reading material on the table, the evil tongues may well have been right.

"Good morning, Mrs. Bridgwater. How are you today?" he inquired, in the same booming voice he used in church. The thought struck him that she was still worth looking at, despite her age.

"Thank you, Reverend Das, a bit warm but in good health. And yourself?" Charlotte was about to walk away, but the clergyman stopped her.

"Are you familiar with this book?" He pressed a book into her hands. The title was *The Lord, My Shepherd Even When It Rains.*

"No, but we could certainly use some rain. And some cool weather." Charlotte walked over to the whirring fan and stood directly under it.

"It's an excellent book. I just finished it. You must read it." He lowered his voice. "It describes the problems of an immigrant family with . . . er . . . their demented father."

The clergyman had been carrying a pile of books the last

time Charlotte ran into him. He had tried to interest her in the story of a woman of easy virtue who became a missionary in Africa. She told him she only read real literature, which prompted an interminable oration on the importance of devotional reading material, and he wouldn't let her go until she promised him she would read it. So Charlotte accepted the book he handed her.

"Very interesting." She turned it over and skimmed the back cover.

The clergyman looked at her red fingernails. "What did you think of that other book?"

"Quite unusual." It was none of his business that it was still lying — unread — in a pile of books in her living room. "If you don't mind, I came for the Tuesday-morning talk. I think they've already started," she said as she tried to walk past him.

Reverend Das nodded but did not step aside. He pointed to the plaque above the door. "Your father . . ."

Charlotte looked up at the row of names on the wall. Her father had prided himself on the fact that he had financed the construction of the library, and she was glad he had never seen how dilapidated it had become. The clergyman moved closer to Charlotte; she tried to step back, but the table with the women's magazines was in the way.

"Mrs. Bridgwater . . ." He was wheezing slightly. "I am collecting money for the restoration of this library. You do know that we have an extensive collection of religious books here?" He pointed to the high shelves behind her, full of books that for the most part hadn't been borrowed. "I thought it would be splendid if . . . as a kind of family tradition . . . out of respect for the work your father did back then . . . you could make a donation."

The then minister had paid a visit to Charlotte's father shortly after the death of Mathilda Bridgwater and asked him if he would consider building a library in memory of his wife. The military man had stared at him for a long time with a hard look in his eyes — it was so long that the clergyman began to feel uncomfortable and finally mumbled that a bookcase would also be very much appreciated.

Victor Bridgwater approved of the idea of something to do with books, since his wife had died holding *Gone with the Wind* in her wasted hands. He muttered that he would support the new library provided that all the religious books were kept on the topmost shelves. The minister was euphoric. He was unaware of the fact that those shelves would be so high that no one could reach them, and his entire collection would remain unread.

"I'll give it some thought," said Charlotte, after a slight hesitation. The minister stepped aside, and she entered the room bearing the sign LADIES CLUB.

1934 Rampur ~

THE MUSIC REACHES her from below. Charlotte is squatting next to the large standing clock, which has just struck nine. All of the candles in the enormous chandelier above the stairwell are alight. Below, in the marble hall, the British officers who are stationed at the army base nearby are arriving. They are in gala uniform, each with his wife, attired in a magnificent ball gown, on his arm. The Indian servants are wearing brand-new uniforms: yellow jackets and navy blue trousers with gold piping. The door of one of the bathrooms opens and a woman with elaborately coiled blond hair steps onto the landing. She's wearing dangling earrings and her lips are deep red. She giggles when an officer with a chest full of medals offers her his arm and leads her down the stairs. Charlotte hears her father's voice behind her and slips back into the nursery. She closes the door, careful not to make any noise. On a mat next to her bed lies her ayah, Sita, sound asleep. They played together all day, but while she was singing a lullaby for Charlotte, the young Indian girl fell asleep herself. Charlotte creeps past her. The balcony doors are open. She glances over her shoulder, but Sita doesn't stir.

Peering over the balcony, Charlotte sees the driveway, which is illuminated by torches, and shiny automobiles parked next to the house. On the broad flight of stairs leading to the front door, men in blue jackets and gold caps are stationed on either side of the red carpet. They are carrying plumes, which the guests pass under, and just before the guests go through the door, two servants throw rose petals before their feet. The sweet scent rises to the balcony. Charlotte wishes she were already grown up.

Behind her she hears her father's voice again. She ducks down, but then realizes that he is in her mother's bedroom, next to the nursery. Charlotte crawls over to the open window and looks over the windowsill and into the yellow room. Her mother is sitting at her dressing table, wearing a long, pale green dress and a gold tiara in her hair. She's painting her lips red with a brush.

"Mathilda, you look perfect." Her father, in full regalia, is standing near the door. He taps his sable against the sole of his boot. There is a medal on his chest.

"Almost, Victor, almost," her mother says with a smile as she carefully alters the contour of her lips. "Do you like this colour?"

"It's the same colour as the uniform jackets of the Irish Guards."

"Yes. Scarlet. Would you hand me my black gloves?"

"These?"

"No, Victor, the long ones."

He tosses them to her.

"Ah, my gallant knight." She smiles and pulls on the close-fitting gloves. Then she stands up, walks over to her husband, and puts out her hand. It seems to Charlotte that he is about to salute, but then he takes Mathilda's hand and leads her out of the room.

Charlotte waits until her parents are gone and then creeps through the open balcony door into the room. Once before, during a violent thunderstorm, when Sita was spending the night with her own family, Charlotte sneaked into the yellow room. Her mother didn't wake up, and Charlotte fell asleep pressed against that warm, unfamiliar body, longing for Sita's arms around her.

The room smells sweet. There are dozens of bottles on the dressing table. Charlotte picks up a small green one, pulls out the stopper, and puts it to her nose. Then she closes her eyes and inhales the pungent scent. It smells like her mother after she returned from Delhi wearing the blue sun hat. She picks up another bottle and opens it: this one smells like her mother about to leave for church. The next one reminds her of a garden party, and a pink bottle smells like her mother decked out in her jewels. *Being a grand lady is the best thing there is*, she decides.

Suddenly she's jerked from the stool. She sees her father's image in the mirror, next to her own. She hadn't heard the door open. He picks her up and carries her over to the large wardrobe. He opens it, shoves her inside, closes the door, and turns the key. Charlotte hears the bedroom door open and shut. She sits there, surrounded by her mother's sweet-scented clothes. She starts to cry. *Sita, please wake up and let me out. I'm afraid.*

1935 Rampur ~

AT THE BOTTOM of the stairs stands a chest. It's been there for weeks. No one dares touch it, since Major Victor Bridgwater is away and the chest arrived the very day that Mathilda delivered her first son. She has been able to leave her room the last few days, but she hasn't given orders for the trunk to be moved. Although the unwieldy wooden object is sitting smack in the middle of the hall, no one has complained. For the first few days the servants would sneak a look at the object on their way upstairs with clean nappies and hot compresses, curious about the seals and stamps on the cover and convinced that it must have something to do with the newborn baby. But ever since Charlotte told Sita, the nursemaid to whom she confides everything, that it contained a machine that can take over their work, everyone is afraid of the trunk.

The old butler, bearing a large teapot on a silver tray, sees one of the sweepers shoot past the trunk at a considerable speed. "Stop!" he orders.

The *mehtarani*, a young woman in a colourless sari, gives him a guilty look.

"Why haven't you swept the dust from the trunk?"

"But, sir," the woman whispers, "then he'll break loose!"

"Who?"

"The iron beast, sir."

Although he would never admit it, the butler is also afraid of what's in the trunk. He heard it from the *bobajee*, who had heard it from his *masalchee*, who talked to a coolie who's acquainted with a friend of the coolie of the principal official at the post office: the trunk contains a machine that can walk and talk. The coolie saw how the official opened the trunk to verify that it contained exactly what the customs papers said it contained. He recounted how his boss had uttered a cry and slammed the lid of the trunk down, after which he ordered it to be transferred as quickly as possible to the general, who is actually only a major.

"There's dust on the chest. Memsahib is going to complain."

"I have three small children," the *mehtarani* wailed. "The youngest is not even weaned."

"If you don't dust the chest, you can leave."

"I've worked for the general for five years, and I've never forgotten a single corner. I even sweep under the low cabinets every morning, and on the day my father was cremated I came to sweep and also the day after I had my last baby. How many of the other sweepers can say that?"

"Dust the chest."

"It'll be my death, sir," she blubbered. "Can't we do it together?"

"I don't sweep. Butlers never sweep."

"But please, sir, couldn't you stand very close to me while I do it?"

"Memsahib just called. I have to go upstairs."

The *mehtarani* begins to sniffle, wringing the broom made of dried grass between her hands.

"And don't break the broom."

"What's going on?" Mathilda looks over the balustrade at the two servants standing next to the chest.

"Nothing, memsahib, nothing."

"I thought I heard someone crying."

The butler, a middle-aged man who previously worked for other English army families, has been with the Bridgwaters for the past six months. He looks up. "No, memsahib. There's nothing wrong."

The *mehtarani* runs from the hall with her head down; the butler smoothes the pleats of his uniform.

"Oh, that's all right then. You know I can't abide the sound of crying." Mathilda turns to go back into the nursery, where Sita is changing the baby's diaper, but before she enters the room, she calls out, "And will you see to it that the chest goes to the shed? My husband is coming home tomorrow to his son, Donald." She stresses the word "son."

The butler stares at the chest, which is as tall as he is and resembles an upright coffin. There is lettering on one side, but he has never learned to read. He thinks of his father, who after the Great War was given the task of capturing a tiger for the London zoo, along with a Scottish officer named Macintosh. It wasn't difficult to find a tiger and kill it. Macintosh had already killed some forty tigers. But this one had to be taken alive. They built a chest and set a trap. With the raging tiger in the chest, they drove to Bombay, where they were to deposit the beast in the hold of a ship. During the five-day car journey to Bombay, his father lost first his forefinger and later his entire right hand, because Macintosh refused to help him feed the animal. The butler looks at his own attractive hands with their long fingers. . . . Not a scratch to be seen.

THE ENTIRE STAFF is assembled in the kitchen, a stone building with a roof made of palm leaves. Forty Indian men and women, each and every one in uniform, are packed together in the narrow space, looking at the butler with shocked faces.

"Anyone who's afraid can leave now," he says.

No one moves a muscle. The servants are terrified of the butler. Everyone knows that he comes from heroic Kashmiri stock and that an English zoo once named a tiger after his family. But they are also struck with fear when they think of the general, who is arriving home tomorrow.

"Pick up the poles."

The servants walk back to the house carrying the long poles. The butler, a worthy descendant of his forebears, has explained to them how they are to transport the chest. They will lay the poles on the ground, tip the chest over using another pole, and then carry it to the shed as if it were a stretcher.

"Quiet now, or you'll wake the baby." The butler opens the door.

In the hall stands Victor Bridgwater, his swagger stick still under his arm. Next to him stand his five-year-old daughter, Charlotte, and his wife, Mathilda, with the baby in her arms. The chest is open.

"General! You're here already?" the butler stammers, surprised that he didn't hear him coming.

"With my hands still covered in blood!" Victor booms. "What's the meaning of all those poles? Is this how you protect my son?" He laughs heartily and turns to his wife. "Your troops would appear to be more competent than mine, Tilly."

Mathilda glances uneasily at the group of dark-skinned men and women holding their sticks, relieved that her husband has returned just in time. But why are all the servants suddenly carrying poles? She clutches her newborn baby tightly to her breast.

Victor pushes the lid of the chest aside and says, "Have any of you ever seen an electric lawnmower before?"

~

THE GENERAL IS standing at the top of the stairs. The toes of his boots extend over the edge of the top stair. At the bottom, Sita is holding the howling infant in her arms. Next to him stands his wife, Mathilda. Charlotte, who spent all afternoon playing with Sita and her dolls, slips noiselessly over to her mother's side and searches for her hand, which she holds hidden in her skirts. Excruciatingly slowly, her father's white-gloved hand goes up. He points his swagger stick at the outer door, where the butler is standing with an umbrella. Everyone stares at the motionless stick. The only sounds are the crying of the baby and, in the background, the monotonous strokes of the sweepers' brooms in the salon.

"But, *sarkar* . . ." The words issue haltingly from Sita's mouth as she gently caresses the wailing baby. "*Chota-sahib* is so little."

The swagger stick seems to grow larger. Sita, in her faded sari, walks hesitantly toward the large grey pram with its hood and lace trim, all the while comforting little Donald with her caresses. The baby stops crying. The young woman, still a girl herself, transfers the baby to her other arm. Charlotte's sigh of relief is audible. She knows that Sita will protect her little brother, as she has always protected her. Outside there is a loud thunderclap and the sky breaks open. The baby starts to cry again. Charlotte finds her mother's hand and squeezes it hard. There is no response.

The swagger stick motions briefly in the direction of the pram and then points again to the outer door. Sita puts the baby in the pram. He starts to cry even harder. She goes to pick him up again, but a sound from the top of the stairs stops her. The butler opens the outer door. The rain pelts down on the tiles. Sita rocks the pram gently back and forth, in the hope that the cries will subside, but the opposite is the case when a flash of lightning illuminates the hall, followed by a deafening peal of thunder. For the second time, Sita slowly pushes the pram with the screaming baby outside. As the first raindrops hit the hood, she stops.

"The middle of the lawn," orders the general.

The girl cautiously pushes the carriage down the stairs. She tries to cushion the jolt at each stair, as she used to do with Charlotte, but the child's cries grow even louder. Once on the path, she looks back. Behind her the door is already closed. In despair, she walks onto the grass; the rain is pounding down with tremendous force. She slides the baby as far under the hood as possible, so that he doesn't become soaked, but on the inside the sound of the rain must be deafening. In front of the salon window stands the broad figure of the general, who has just returned from a mission during which he made short work of a group of Indian protesters whom he regarded as mutinous slaves. Sita stops in the middle of the lawn. She bends over the pram and tries to quiet the baby. She knows that she must now leave him alone, otherwise the general will come storming outside and she will lose her job. She caresses the child once more and pulls the sheet over him as best she can. The lashing rain continues unabated. She walks away, leaving the pram in the middle of the lawn. Out of sight of the window, she crouches down near a bush full of winter roses. She hears the cries over the peals of thunder.

Charlotte runs back to the nursery. Looking out the window, she sees Sita sitting next to the bush, not far from the lonely pram, ready to jump up at any moment. "Don't cry, don't cry," she whispers to her baby brother. "If you go on crying, he'll leave you out there for hours, just like he did with me."

1995 Rampur ~

ALL THE WOMEN gazed in bewilderment at the secretary of the New Rampur Club. No one said a word. Only once before had he walked into their midst unannounced, after Mr. Chatterjee — the owner of two fashionable ladies' apparel shops in the town centre, but a poor tennis player — hit the ball straight through the windowpane of the "Ladies Club." Now the secretary was standing before them again, wiping his brow, while the women stared at him. The ceiling fans were going at full speed.

"Are you sure?" The query was launched suddenly from a corner of the room.

The secretary nodded. He was surprised by the identity of the speaker, seeing that the wife of Alok Nath, the goldsmith, invariably spoke in an inaudible whisper because she thought it sounded aristocratic.

"What?" said the widow Singh, who was sitting next to the wife of Alok Nath and was awakened by the unexpected sound of a voice next to her.

"That's impossible! Quite impossible! On my way to the club I dropped off a very expensive length of pink Chinese silk." The corpulent wife of Nikhil Nair, district director of the Eastern Indian Mining Company, was on her feet, glowering at the secretary. "He walked out to the car with me to get the material, and there was nothing wrong with the man."

The secretary then turned to the wife of Ajay Karapiet, who ran the town's biggest hotel as well as two cinemas. "Your husband just called. He told me that your daughter went to the workplace with a piece of brocade and that just as she was about to hand it to him, his eyes began to roll and he slowly collapsed, without making a sound."

"With the brocade in his hand?" shrilled the wife of Ajay Karapiet.

"I have no idea," said the secretary. "Your husband didn't say anything about that."

"I brought him a length of material, too," said the woman who was married to a coconut oil manufacturer.

They were all talking at once. In the previous weeks each of them had delivered a length of cloth to Sanat the *darzi*, one more costly than the other. Only Charlotte and the wife of Adeeb Tata, the local landowner and a distant relative of the immensely wealthy Ratan Tata, had not given the tailor their material — the wife of Adeeb Tata because she had already bought a dress in Paris, and Charlotte because she didn't have any fabric yet.

"He said I could pick up my dress the day after tomorrow. It still has to be embroidered."

"Does anyone know if he has a successor?"

"What am I supposed to do now?"

Many of these women wore a dress or a *salwar kameez*, in contrast to the ladies of the Wednesday-morning group, who wore saris. The garments, all made by Sanat, were indistinguishable from one another. This was not surprising, since they were all based on the same pattern. The only difference was that some had long sleeves, others short, and the neck was either square or round. That is why the embroidery, the buttons, and the lace were so important: together with the material itself, it was the details that made all the difference. The bicentennial of the club was coming up soon and it was going to be celebrated in style. Small wonder that the ladies had gone to such pains to find an exceptional piece of fabric. Charlotte had heard that some of them went all the way to New Delhi or Bombay to ensure exclusivity. It was obvious that this group of middle-aged women would like nothing better than to set off en masse to the workplace of the recently deceased tailor in order to check on the safety of their fabric. However, that would not be appropriate. They would have to wait until after the cremation and the subsequent farewell rituals. Their concern that the costly fabrics were in danger of mysteriously disappearing or shrinking in size was not entirely unfounded. The wife of Nikhil Nair suggested they post a guard at the door, but the other women felt that the family of the tailor might interpret that as a motion of non-confidence. The wife of the goldsmith knew the wife of the tailor's cousin, and she could ask him to keep an eye on things, but the wife of the builder who had submitted the proposal to renovate the club reported that in his youth the tailor's assistant had been involved with the police. The wife of the police commissioner knew nothing about that but promised she would ask her husband to look into it. The widow Singh had dropped off again, and was snoring softly.

The nail specialist was still standing in front of the group holding a plastic hand on which each finger displayed a different nail problem. But he was already surreptitiously sliding the carrying case closer with his foot. The fan turning rapidly above his head no longer provided cool air, and he wanted to go home. He surveyed the flushed faces of the women. They couldn't get enough of the discussion about the deceased tailor and the problem of what they would wear to the party. Although he had hundreds of tips for festive nails, he could not get his audience to listen. His gaze came to rest on the only European woman in the group, and he wondered how she had become a member of a club for Indian ladies. There were almost no British citizens left in his country, which had shaken off the yoke of the Raj several decades ago. Her dress was just as unappealing as those of the other women, except that hers bore a Scottish tartan pattern while all the others had opted for a floral or botanical design. Clearly the late tailor was no great talent when it came to the design and fabrication of women's clothing.

"I know a very good tailor," he said suddenly.

It was a while before the message got through to the women, but then they began bombarding him with questions. Where did the man live? Was he expensive? Had he ever worked with Chinese silk before? Did he have more than one pattern? What was his family background? Did he have his own sewing machine? When could he start? etc.

"I've never met him myself," the nail specialist stammered.

There was a collective sigh of disappointment.

"But my first cousin on my father's side says he's an absolute master." The man looked at the group of women in their tent dresses. "He has several different patterns and apparently he's not expensive. But . . ." Here he hesitated.

"What's the matter?" the women wanted to know.

"He'll only come if he really wants to."

"If he wants to," sneered the wife of Nikhil Nair.

"He's . . . well . . . different from other *darzis*."

"Like the fashion designers in Paris," cooed the wife of Adeeb Tata, who liked to remind the other ladies that she'd seen more of the world than they had.

"Yes, perhaps something like that," the nail man said as he put the artificial hand back in its case.

PANTING AND DAMP with perspiration, Charlotte parked the bicycle in the shed. The piercing rays of the sun streamed through the holes in the roof. She resolved to move the Lloyds and her bicycle into the music room as soon as the monsoon began. She seldom went in there now that the piano was gone. She shuffled off to the house, where the heat that had plagued her the entire morning was even more intense, and saw to her relief that Hema had closed the upper windows in the nursery. In the distance, the siren began to wail. And again her heart skipped a beat. She looked around to see if there was smoke anywhere, but the sky was clear and cloudless.

Inside, the heat had not been tempered by the closed shutters, curtains, windows, and doors. Charlotte turned on a lamp, set the fan on "high," and lay down on the sofa positioned beneath it. Her legs throbbed and her feet were swollen. She wished that Hema was there: he would have brought her a bucket of cold water. But the butler had gone to the town centre to shop, since she could no longer buy on credit in the neighbourhood stores. She looked at the sideboard filled with the Wedgwood china service, which had been a wedding present. A month ago, there had been a dealer prepared to buy it, but the price he quoted was ridiculously low. In the end he left with only the silver soup spoon, one of her parents' wedding gifts.

Charlotte rose from the sofa, trudged up the stairs to the bathroom, and filled the tub with a layer of water. She began to relax when her feet reached the cool water. She looked at her veined feet in the old cast iron tub. They bore clear traces of wear and tear. Her big toe toyed with the black string attached to the plug. She remembered that when Donald was little he insisted on pulling it out because he thought the string was some kind of animal. He was afraid of snakes and spiders and insects as well. It had been a long time since she'd heard from him. Her last letter, written at Christmastime, had elicited only a beautiful card with New Year's greetings, but no news. Was he still having problems with his back? And did his wife still suffer from kidney stones? The photo of his daughter, taken years ago on a trip to Disney World, was downstairs on the mantelpiece. Charlotte seldom looked at it. Old photographs made her feel sad.

The front doorbell sounded. She withdrew her feet from the water and without drying them walked into the hallway, down the stairs. When she opened the door, she was momentarily blinded by the glare of the sun, and it was a while before she could see the man standing in front of her.

"Mrs. Bridgwater?" he asked in a nasal voice.

Charlotte nodded.

"Will you sign here?"

Absently, Charlotte signed her name, and the man left without saying another word. He gunned the engine as he drove off, scattering pebbles in all directions.

She tore open the envelope, even though she was already aware of the contents. The only thing she didn't know was the exact amount. She put on her glasses, glanced at the figure under the line, and with a sigh placed the letter in the dresser drawer with the other bills. She closed the drawer, but then opened it again, fishing around until she found the business card. She walked over to the telephone next to the dresser and dialled a number. Someone answered immediately. Charlotte's first impulse was to hang up, but instead she said in a low voice, "This is Mrs. Bridgwater."

On the other end of the line someone began to talk very fast.

"Yes, the big house on the hill," Charlotte said. "Come by when you have time."

1936 On board the King of Scotland

ON THE QUAY Mathilda waves to her daughter, Charlotte, who is standing at the railing far above her. The little girl does not wave back.

"I'll write to you every week!" her mother calls.

Charlotte keeps her lips pressed tightly together.

"And don't open your birthday present until the day itself, promise?"

The box, which her mother handed to her just before she boarded, is on the bed in her cabin. She threw the doll — which has real hair and a white dress — into the corner so hard that the head broke off. The ship's horn sounds and a thick cloud of black smoke rises from the smokestack.

Charlotte feels the ship start to move. She clutches the railing with both hands and looks at her mother, who is waving vigorously. She can't hear her voice because of the horn blaring out its farewell.

"Oh, there you are!" An older lady with a shawl in her hand comes over to her. "Where were you? I couldn't find you anywhere. I don't want you to leave the cabin without my permission." The lady puts her hand on the girl's shoulder. She is still staring at her mother in the distance, still silent. "Go ahead and cry if you want to. Everyone cries the first time. I've seen children try to climb over the railing, but the captain stopped them by shutting them up in a cabin at the bottom of the ship. He didn't let them go until Bombay was out of sight." The woman starts to wave her shawl. Charlotte sees her mother take out a handkerchief and start to wave even more vigorously. "You can call me Auntie Ilse. Come on now, wave to your mother. You see? She's waving, too. When you say goodbye, you're supposed to wave. Come on now, wave!"

Charlotte grasps the railing even more tightly; the horn is bawling its farewells and the ship is starting to move. The passengers around her call out, "See you soon," "Goodbye," and "Until next year."

The woman she's supposed to call Auntie Ilse drops her arm. "Well, if you're not going to wave, then neither am I. I don't even know your mother. Come along, we're going to get something to eat." She walks in the direction of the dining room, but Charlotte remains at the railing. "If you're going to act this way the whole time, I'll have to ask the captain to lock you up somewhere in the bottom of the ship." Charlotte lets go of the railing and follows Auntie Ilse.

Down on the quay, Mathilda is crying.

~

IT'S DARK OUTSIDE. Charlotte opens the door and looks into the corridor. There's no one there. Quickly she slips out of the cabin. She's holding a bundle in her hand. She runs up the stairs and pushes open the heavy door. It's quiet on the promenade deck. Everyone's in the huge auditorium, where they're showing a movie that Auntie Ilse doesn't want her to see. She walks along the railing in the direction of the stern, where she sees the English flag waving. Today is her birthday. At breakfast the people at her table sang "Happy Birthday." The chef brought out a cake with six candles on it, and she had to blow them out all at once, which she did, and then Auntie Ilse gave her a scarf she had in her suitcase and after dinner she was allowed to see the wheelhouse but she didn't enjoy that because the captain was there too and she was afraid he'd lock her up in the bottom of the ship if she did anything wrong. She walks toward the stern, clutching the bundle to her chest. Two sailors are standing at the bottom of a flight of stairs, smoking a cigarette, but they don't notice her. There's no one on the afterdeck. She walks over to the railing and looks down. Far beneath her, the sea is foaming. The water is white, and by the light of the moon she can make out the trail they leave behind.

"Shouldn't you be in bed?"

She gives a start and turns around. There's a man standing behind her, his black hair waving in the wind.

"Or did you think the film was scary, too?"

Charlotte shakes her head.

"What's your name? I'm Ganesh, named after the god with the head of an elephant. I'm lucky I didn't get such a long nose." He laughs.

"My name is Charlotte Elizabeth, just like my grandmother who's dead."

"Oh, that's too bad! Do you miss her?"

"No. I never met her."

Ganesh squats down and looks out to sea with her. A gull dives into the water and comes up with something in its beak.

"She walked over a mountain with my grandfather and our big clock, then she got an infection on her foot because it was so cold that they couldn't stop to rest. They had to keep walking and her whole foot went black and had to be cut off, otherwise she'd die. But then she died anyway, but my father didn't cry."

"You come from an adventurous family. Too bad I can't say the same about mine. For centuries they've lived in the same little town at the foot of the Himalayas. I'm the first person in my family to travel."

"Why?"

"I got a scholarship to study in England, so I can become an engineer."

"I have to go to school, too. A boarding school, because I'm six."

"Are you really that old?"

Charlotte nods her head fiercely. "I'm travelling alone," she says firmly. "And I didn't cry."

"That's brave of you. I did."

"Did your father let you cry?"

"No, but I did it in secret."

"All alone?"

Ganesh nods.

"I sometimes cry when I'm alone, but nobody knows," Charlotte says softly.

"I won't tell anybody," Ganesh whispers and locks his lips with an imaginary key.

Charlotte smiles.

"Why are you up this late?"

The smile disappears from her face. Again she presses the bundle to her body and looks out to sea.

Ganesh waits.

"I have to bury her."

"Who?"

Charlotte opens up the cloth that holds the doll with the broken neck.

"Are you going to throw her into the ocean?"

Charlotte nods. "Auntie Ilse says that if I die at sea, they'll put me on a plank and throw me into the sea, because otherwise I'll start to smell and the other people will get sick."

"She could be repaired."

"No."

"Do you want me to try?"

"No."

"Are you sure?"

Charlotte shakes her head but gives the doll to Ganesh, who gingerly takes it from her.

"What a lovely doll."

"It's a stupid doll."

"She has real hair."

"She's stupid."

Ganesh examines the broken doll. "Shall I try to fix her?"

Charlotte doesn't reply.

"If it doesn't work, then tomorrow we can drop her into the sea, together, with a real wooden plank. But if we manage to fix her, then you can give her a name. A really pretty name."

"What's a pretty name?"

"Maybe something like Khushi. That means 'happiness.'"

1901 Khyber Pass ~

HE IS FRIGHTENED. Very, very frightened. William Bridgwater, a young and ambitious road builder who comes from a family of teachers in Ipswich, has made the mistake of his life. He has fallen in love with Elizabeth Charlotte Elphinstone, daughter of the wealthy director of the New Indian Railway, and she with him. They are not just in love, they are head-over-heels in love. For more than six months they have taken advantage of each and every opportunity to meet in secret. The garden of her house is walled, but among the bushes at the back there is a small opening, which William has enlarged. Elizabeth is not allowed to leave the house on her own, since her father is afraid of assaults by members of the Afridi tribe, who continue to oppose British plans to build a railroad through the mountains. Last night, as the first snow of the season was falling on the tents of the railway workers, Elizabeth Elphinstone stood in front of the opening in the wall, showed him her belly, and announced that she was pregnant.

William doesn't get a wink of sleep. The tent that he shares with another engineer stands on the edge of their encampment. After breakfast he writes a letter to his parents telling them that he is going on a long journey. After pushing the letter through the opening in the red box that serves as a mail pickup, he makes it known that he will be away on business for several days. He then leaves the camp, carrying a suitcase. Once outside, he makes his way through the bushes to the path leading to the garden behind Elizabeth Elphinstone's house. He doesn't want to be seen with a suitcase.

Near the opening in the wall he sees a boy with a standing clock. William gives a start. All those months he had managed to avoid her overprotective father and today, of all days, he's been discovered. The boy sees William and raises his hand. Only then does he see that it's Elizabeth."Are you ready?"

She nods.

"Are you sure you're not going to regret this?"

She shakes her head; a wayward curl escapes from under her heavy cap.

William pushes the curl back under the cap and strokes her cheek with his finger. "Come, shall we be off?"

Elizabeth points to the clock.

William looks at her in astonishment.

"It's the only object of value I have."

"A clock! We can't take a standing clock with us."

"Well, you told me to take my valuables with me. This clock was a present from my grandfather."

"Don't you have a necklace, or a ring or something?"

Elizabeth shook her head. "All I have is this clock. And my belly."

William looks at the clock in desperation. It's taller than Elizabeth herself.

"If I can't take my clock along, then I'm not going," she says firmly.

"But how?"

She points to the hole in the wall. Following her gaze, William sees a bicycle among the bushes.

"It's stuck," Elizabeth says.

"But a bicycle isn't big enough to carry a grandfather clock."

"It's a tandem."

William starts to pull. There's a sharp crack, a large chunk of stone breaks away from the wall, and he falls flat on his back in the snow, tandem and all.

~

HE PULLS THE blanket over her. It's cold and dark. The icy wind blows more and more snow onto the mountain.

"Are you hungry?"

Elizabeth nods. William pulls a piece of chocolate out of his coat pocket and gives it to her. They don't speak. They're too tired and too cold. William kisses her softly on the mouth. She kisses him back. He can taste the chocolate on her cold lips. They huddle close together.

"If only we could make a fire," Elizabeth whispers.

William points to the clock, which is firmly tied to the side of the bicycle with two ropes.

"No, not the clock. It's for Victor."

"Victor?"

"That's his name," she says, and puts both hands on her stomach.

IT IS STILL dark. William pushes the handlebars of the bicycle while Elizabeth pushes on the back. The clock is on the left and the suitcase on the right. William wants to get past Fort

Maude before it gets light. It's been calm there ever since Afridi tribesmen set it on fire and the British army left, but his mind is still not entirely at rest. The highest point of the pass is now in front of them. Elizabeth sings lullabies softly and William gives thanks to the Lord for this woman. Tonight, when they get to Jamrud, he'll see to it that she has a warm bath and a warm bed. He'll make sure that the mother-to-be wants for nothing. He knows a hotel where they can have a good meal.

It starts to snow again. The wind is stronger and fiercer now, blowing the swirling flakes through the opening between the mountain walls. They trudge on, without speaking, the clock and the suitcase between them.

THE STORM RAGES through the pass. Slowly, they plow their way forward. Again and again the tandem comes to a dead stop in the snow. Together they manage to push it forward. They pause, and while Elizabeth beats her arms against her sides, trying to create a bit of warmth, William tightens the ropes around the suitcase and the clock.

"The clock is the future," she whispers in his ear.

It's firewood, thinks William.

From the top of the pass, where the icy wind has blown the snow from the road, it is all downhill. They attempt to get on the bicycle, but it proves impossible with the clock and the suitcase already on it.

1901 *Jamrud* ~

ELIZABETH ELPHINSTONE IS running a high fever. She's lying in a small attic room in the house of an old coppersmith, who doesn't speak a word of English. They spent three days in a hotel, but the owner became more and more curious about Elizabeth's condition. William had to find someone who was willing to help them. The new room is small and has no windows, but it is warm and dry.

Elizabeth has not eaten in days. Nothing but a little tea and the soup that William feeds her. The clock stands in the corner of the room. William hates the clock. If it weren't for the clock, they could have navigated the pass more quickly, and Elizabeth wouldn't have fallen ill. The clock strikes twice. William brings a spoonful of lukewarm soup to her mouth. Suddenly her face is contorted.

"Don't you want any more soup?"

She shakes her head and tries to speak.

William puts his ear close to her mouth.

"It's starting."

"What's starting?"

"The baby."

William looks at her in disbelief. Elizabeth nods weakly. He jumps up and calls out that he's going to get help, but before he reaches the door he runs back to the bed.

"What do you need?"

"You."

"But I don't know anything about how babies are born. I'll ask the owner if he has a sister, a mother, someone who knows about babies."

"Don't leave me alone."

"I have to fetch someone. A woman. I don't know what to do."

Elizabeth's face is twisted in pain. William runs out of the room, down the steps, across the courtyard, out the gate, and into the street. He sees men in long coats. Nowhere does he see a woman. He runs down another street, he peers into tunnels and alleyways. Wherever he looks, he sees nothing but men. He runs back to the house. In the courtyard he knocks on the owner's door. The man with the long red beard opens the door. He drags the man up the stairs by his arm. Elizabeth is lying in bed, moaning softly. In desperation William points to her distended belly.

THE WOMAN IS wearing a long black dress and a headscarf. After sending William out of the room, she bends over Elizabeth. The owner brings buckets of hot water up the stairs. William sets them down inside the room but is immediately sent away again. He sits down at the top of the stairs. He hears Elizabeth's weak cries.

The clock strikes nine. The woman comes out of the room. Her hands are covered in blood. William races in. Elizabeth is lying on the bed, deathly quiet, in a pool of blood. On her belly lies a baby covered in blood, still attached to the umbilical cord. His eyes go not to the child, but to the woman with whom he hoped to grow old, the woman he had intended to worship for the rest of his life. He knows at once. It is over. She has left him. He walks out of the room, and behind him he hears the baby's first cries.

1936 On board the King of Scotland ~

CHARLOTTE BRIDGWATER STARES in amazement at her arms.

"Auntie Ilse! Look! I have pimples all over my arms!"

"That's gooseflesh," says Auntie Ilse. "It's because you're cold."

Charlotte runs her hand over the pimples. She's never been this cold before. But once, when she was in the kitchen with Sita, she put her hands on a block of ice, so that it gradually turned to water.

"Go back to the cabin, put on two shirts and two pairs of underpants on top of each other," orders Auntie Ilse, who's wearing a woollen sweater and a tartan skirt.

Charlotte tries to push the pimples back into her skin.

"Stop playing with yourself and put on your scarf. I didn't give it to you for nothing."

The girl walks down the deck with Khushi, who is also wearing a scarf around her neck. She sees Ganesh standing at the door to the dining room.

"I have gooseflesh." She proudly shows him her arm.

"You see? I was right. When you get to England, you'll see that everyone's wearing a scarf."

"You're not."

"I was born in the snow. I don't mind the cold."

"Is it always cold in England?"

"No, only in spring, autumn, and winter. In the summer it slowly starts to warm up, and sometimes people even go around without a coat."

"I don't have a coat."

"Didn't your mother pack a coat in your suitcase?"

"I guess she forgot."

"How about a sweater?"

Charlotte shook her head.

"Do you want to borrow one of mine?"

Charlotte skips around in a thick green woollen sweater — on her, a short skirt. Ganesh's grandmother spent a good many hours working on it. The sleeves are rolled up and he has tied a string around her waist. Ganesh is proud of the result. Charlotte looks like his little sister. When would he see her again? Would he ever see her again? On board not many people talk to him. Most of the passengers are British couples and military men heading home on leave. They play bridge and midget golf, or drink whisky at the bar, none of them things he's used to doing to pass the time.

"What shall we play?" Charlotte puts her doll on a chair and looks at him.

"Do you know blow-blow-I'll-catch-you?"

"Is it scary?"

"Sometimes. If you play it at night, when there's no moon."

Ganesh spreads his arms as far as he can and bends over, while holding his head up. "Choose a wind."

"A wind?"

"Yes, a hard wind or sharp wind, fat wind, soft wind, warm wind, cold wind, tickle wind, swivel wind, morning wind, or winter wind."

Charlotte looks at him open-mouthed. "Do you know that many different winds?"

"In the mountains we have lots more winds. Feather wind, sand wind, snow wind, race wind, quiet wind, bride's wind, summer wind, dive wind, clap wind, fall wind, push wind, north, west, east, and south wind, and of course the dream wind. There are lots more, but those are the most important ones. First you choose a wind and make it blow. The other person has to guess which wind it is. If you guess right, you have to grab the wind and make a new wind blow. Do you get it?"

Charlotte nods. "I'll go first." She spreads her arms wide,

bends from the waist, narrows her eyes to slits, and whooshes around the deck.

"Hard wind?" Ganesh shouts.

She goes on blowing.

"Sharp wind? Race wind? Whirlwind?" Ganesh shouts the names of all the winds he knows, but the little girl isn't satisfied with any of them.

"No, no," she shrieks.

"Night wind . . . dry wind . . . fleece wind . . . devil's wind . . . sun wind . . . ?" Ganesh calls out the names of more and more winds.

"It's a really easy one."

"Top wind?"

She shakes her head.

"Finger wind . . . sulphur wind!"

She runs around him in circles, she laughs, arms wide open, her head bowed. "Wrong, wrong, all of them wrong. And all of them right."

"That's impossible."

"It's the wind of India," she crows, "the wind that blows around our house just before the monsoon!" She hurtles past. "Now that you know the answer, you have to catch me."

Ganesh runs after her, arms wide apart and head low, his steps becoming longer and faster than hers. With a sweep of his arm, he lifts her from the ground and swings her around and around. They're going faster and faster. And laughing harder and harder.

There is a hair-raising scream, and two hands pull her down. Charlotte lands on the deck with a smack. She cries out in pain. Auntie Ilse grabs her hand and jerks her to her feet.

"Help! HELP!"

People come running from all directions, shouting questions.

"He, he . . ." Auntie Ilse points to Ganesh. "He tried to steal my child!"

Two men grab him by the shoulders, drag him backwards, and push him against the wall. A tall man with a moustache punches him in the stomach. Ganesh doubles over. A man wearing brown boots gives him a kick.

Auntie Ilse pulls the sweater over Charlotte's head and throws it over the railing.

A shower of blows rains down on Ganesh, mercilessly, without stopping. "Brown rat, you'll pay for this." He doesn't feel the blows, he doesn't feel anything. All he hears is Charlotte crying.

1936 Grand Palace ~

THE MAHARAJA'S SEVEN daughters are gathered together in the silver room on the first floor. They are all attired in costly saris and jewels. Chutki, the youngest daughter, is bothered by the weight of the gold chains around her neck, wrists, and ankles, and the nose ornament, which her eldest sister had insisted upon, is uncomfortable. The girls peek through the openings in the heavy gold brocade drapes. Beneath the window, four-year-old Chutki sees her father's snorting elephants. They are decked out in jewels and expensive draperies, but they don't seem to mind. Seated on their backs are her uncles and other important men attired in glittering robes. All around the square in front of the palace where they live, musicians with gold turbans and large copper horns are stationed a metre apart. One of her sisters points to the left, where the village chiefs of their district are assembled on the stairs. And on the right the Royal Guard stands in readiness, wearing full dress and mounted on her father's jet black horses. Directly in front of her she sees the long driveway flanked by men in red britches. They stand perfectly still, each holding a shield in his hand. The road itself is covered with carpets, and in front of the great gate there are gold bowls filled with burning incense. The heavy scent penetrates the room.

Everyone is awaiting the arrival of Victor Alexander John Hope, the second marquess of Linlithgow and viceroy of India. In an hour Chutki, her sisters, and her mother, the maharani, are to have tea with the wife of the viceroy and her three daughters. Her father, Maharaja Man Singh, a great admirer of hunting and Sherlock Holmes novels, does not want his daughters involved in matters of state, only his sons. Chutki is jealous of her four brothers, who are wearing their official outfits, with new turbans. Her eldest brother, who is twelve, even has a sabre on his belt. The boys have already gone hunting and have seen their father shoot a tiger. Downstairs in the pink marble hall, next to the room where the reception will take place, her father's passion for hunting is clearly visible. The walls are covered with the stuffed heads of bisons, lions, tigers, and deer. And above the fireplace hangs the head of an elephant; the tusks are inlaid with gold, and on the forehead of the elephant there's a medallion with a photo of her great-grandfather encircled by diamonds.

Outside, the horns resound. Through the opening between the curtains she sees a long line of large black motor cars, rolling slowly across the carpets in the direction of the Great Gate. The roll of drums drowns out the horns. One of the elephants trumpets.

In the corridor she hears her father's dry cough. Chutki knows that cough well: she has it, too. As well as the permanent sore throat and the difficulty swallowing. No one understands why Chutki and the maharaja have chronic laryngitis while the other members of the family do not. They all live in the same palace and their food comes from the same kitchen.

For weeks now everyone in the palace has been especially busy. Extra palm trees have been planted near the Great Gate, and around the temple there are three new marble fountains in honour of Chutki's grandfather. Outside, cars are stopping. Chutki hears the large drum being struck and the sound of the trumpet, which means that her father has appeared on the steps. And when she hears the double horn, she knows that the viceroy is about to get out of his car. Chutki takes a sip of water, swallowing with difficulty. Her throat hurts. The servants know that she must always have a glass of water within reach; even on a day like this, they have not forgotten. Chutki watches. She doesn't enjoy talking. Talking hurts.

THE VICEROY AND the maharaja are seated opposite one another at the long table. It is not the first meeting between the two men. They were officially introduced upon the viceroy's arrival in India and met again at his inauguration in April. Now, as then, the maharaja is ill. For the fifth time, his hand unconsciously goes to his swollen throat and he coughs: a dry, raw sound.

"I know a very good physician," says the viceroy.

The maharaja nods, slightly taken aback by such a personal remark.

"A young man from Manchester," the viceroy continues. "He's made throat problems his specialty."

The maharaja coughs again; the servant standing behind him immediately pours cold water into his glass. He takes a sip and has to swallow several times. Never before has a viceroy adopted such a personal tone. The maharaja dislikes talking about his health, especially to an Englishman. "Please do not be concerned," he says in a hoarse voice. "It's just a slight irritation. I believe it's what you call 'a frog in the throat.'" He puts his glass down on the silver plate with slightly more force than necessary. It is clear that the subject is closed. "Are you fond of hunting?"

The viceroy's eyes take on a gleam. "I've been told that you have the largest continuous hunting ground in all of India."

The maharaja smiles deprecatingly. "I believe there are some four thousand tigers in my area."

The viceroy emits a good-natured grunt of approval. "Do you shoot elephants, too?"

"Only when they attack one of the villages."

"Like that elephant in the hall?"

"That one didn't die during the hunt. It was my grandfather's favourite elephant." The husky voice of the maharaja becomes still softer. "That's the elephant he rode when he went hunting. Nowadays I use horses. Elephants make it difficult to take immediate action. Hunting is speed, don't you agree?" He begins to cough.

The servant quickly exchanges his glass for one containing a brown liquid. The maharaja takes a sip and swallows with difficulty, but his fit of coughing does not abate. The viceroy is concerned and looks around him. The servants, a number of whom are standing against the wall, look straight ahead, except for the man in the green turban, who is positioned behind and to one side of the maharaja. Now the servant steps forward and hands the maharaja something from a small box, which he deposits behind a back tooth. Slowly the coughing subsides. The maharaja is wheezing and his eyes are moist.

"Shall I ask the throat specialist to drop by sometime?"

They hear screams from outside. An elephant trumpets. The man in the green turban runs to the window and then hurries back to the maharaja. He whispers something in his ear. Maharaja Man Singh stops coughing. After a quick glance to identify the source of the shrieks, he looks at the viceroy. Then he leans toward the man in the green turban and says something in a language the viceroy does not understand. The maharaja begins to cough again. As he struggles to suppress the coughing, he wheezes, "Would you like to shoot an elephant?"

The viceroy swallows. "An elephant?"

The maharaja motions toward the window, which is immediately thrown open. The sound of screaming enters the hall. From all directions men rush in, some of them carrying guns. The disciplined order that reigned supreme only a short time ago has disappeared, and servants are running and calling out. Still coughing, the maharaja motions to the viceroy to come outside with him. In the square in front of the palace an elephant is lashing about with his head and trunk. He is surrounded by men with sticks and ropes. The chair on his back has slipped to one side and a man in a long purple coat is trying desperately to hang on to one side as the elephant lithely flings his trunk backwards. Maharaja Man Singh is handed a spanking new hunting rifle, which he immediately passes on to the dumbfounded viceroy.

Victor Alexander John Hope, the second marquess of Linlithgow and viceroy of India, regularly hunts in England,

and has even taken part in the royal hunt. He considers himself a brilliant horseman and he is much enamoured of pheasants and hares. But the mad elephant fills him with fear.

The maharaja begins to cough again. This time he seems about to choke. The viceroy grabs the gun.

"Between the eyes," the maharaja groans.

"But the men around him?"

"Aim between the eyes," he pants, in between bouts of coughing.

The viceroy looks through the sight. The man atop the elephant falls to the ground, and the elephant tries to trample him underfoot. The man's long purple robe prevents him from rolling away. A small boy with a stick jumps in front of the animal, but he receives such a hard blow from the trunk that he flies through the air. The elephant turns around and flexes his trunk. Then he scrapes the ground with his tusks and sweeps the man away. The man's coat is torn and his leg is hanging at a strange angle. The viceroy's finger curves around the trigger. He sees only the wrinkled bulge between the two small eyes. The elephant raises his head again and tosses his trunk high into the air. He screams. The viceroy draws his lower lip into his mouth, narrows his eyes to slits. The moment the trunk comes back down, he shoots. The bullet whizzes through the air and enters the forehead of the elephant. It is as if the animal feels nothing: he bellows and trumpets. Turning around, he tramples the man again. A boy with a rope lashes the elephant and tries to pull the man to safety, but the animal sweeps the boy away with a single blow. Fearfully, the viceroy stares at the beast. He knows for certain that he hit the elephant squarely between the eyes. Next to him, the maharaja's coughing fit continues. Between two attacks, he croaks, "Well done."

The viceroy is puzzled. The elephant turns in the direction of a man on horseback who is approaching from behind and, lowering his head, batters the horse, which starts to rear. The elephant throws his head and legs into the air. His trunk brushes the stars. The maharaja points. The elephant begins to wobble. He reels. He screams. He tries to find support somewhere. His knees are knocking. His head swings from left to right. He trumpets one last distress call and collapses, as if in slow motion. The ground shakes. The men rejoice. The viceroy looks proudly at the maharaja, who asks, still panting, "What did you say the name of that throat specialist was?"

The viceroy turns to him in surprise. "The throat doctor . . . ? Oh, his name is Peter Harris."

1942 Queen Victoria College ~

Dear Donald,

I wish you a Happy Christmas. Did you get a letter from Father? I thought maybe he only sent one letter, and that it went to your address. If so, would you forward it to me? Everything's fine at school. Since the war, there are a lot more children from India. Which is nice, since we all agree that it's very cold here. After the summer vacation I'm moving to a small dormitory. They say it's much nicer. And we get to stay up an extra half-hour. Have you asked if we could meet sometime? Mrs. Blackburn, our director, says that if the war doesn't flare up again, we could arrange something during the summer vacation. Will you remember to send me Father's letter?

Bye,
Your sister Charlotte

1995 Rampur ~

CHARLOTTE LAY ON her bed "smoking." The fan above her head rotated, while outside the nocturnal crickets chirruped. All the windows and shutters were wide open, and on the desk stood a lighted candle, which illuminated some sheets of paper covered with calculations. A few crumpled wads lay on the floor. There was dance music coming from an old transistor radio, and her toes kept time with the music. In her younger years she would have jumped up and danced around the room. Now only her toes could not resist the temptation. She longed for the cool that night would bring, but it was long in coming. Her thin nightgown clung to her breasts, and there were drops of perspiration in the furrows on her forehead. "Dream wind" . . . the expression suddenly popped into her head. Dream wind . . . that was one of the winds the man on the boat had told her about. Auntie Ilse, the woman she was travelling with, had forbidden her to ever speak of him again or even think about him. As a six-year-old, she had done her best. But the image of him — his face covered in blood — still appeared in her dreams, and she often woke up crying. She thought of the doll she'd called her "lucky girl." Auntie Ilse had thrown it overboard, because *he* had repaired it. Charlotte was not allowed to think about *him*, but no one said she couldn't think about the winds. Lying in her bed in the cold dormitory at boarding school, she had tried for years to recall the long list of winds. She'd forgotten many of them, but she could still recite the most important ones. The soft wind and the hard wind. The warm wind and the cold wind. The morning wind and the evening wind. The quiet wind and the race wind. The summer wind and the winter wind. The northern, western, eastern, and southern winds. Her favourite was the dream wind. She looked at the figure of Ganesh, the god with the head of an elephant, which she'd bought years ago when she was feeling so terribly lonely. She had never understood what he meant by a dream wind, until this moment. She felt the beginning of a gentle breeze, starting in her toes, which were still keeping time to the dance music. Suddenly something swirled upward past her legs, her pelvis, her spine, and then her throat. She opened her mouth and felt the wind escaping. She was momentarily confused, thinking she was exhaling imaginary smoke, but it was a different air stream, a cool, sultry breeze. She put the cigarette back in the wooden box. A second gust of dream wind escaped. Charlotte sat up. She didn't understand what was happening. Again she opened her mouth, wider this time. Holding her hands in front of her mouth, she felt the cool air passing over her skin. It gave her goosebumps. She pursed her lips and blew the cool wind toward her feet. The music on the transistor radio was interrupted by a news bulletin.

She drew the mosquito net aside and got out of bed. On the radio a man announced that tomorrow the temperature would hit forty-two degrees. She sighed, and again a stream of cool air escaped. She walked out of the room in her bare feet.

She held the lighted candle and a bunch of keys, which jangled softly. She walked past the large grandfather clock, which was ticking away, and went to the door of the nursery, where she stopped and listened. All was quiet. She walked over to the staircase on her tiptoes. The steps creaked and the creaking sound mingled with the singing of the crickets in the garden. The gigantic chandelier with holders for hundreds of candles hung in the spacious hall; it was years since it had been lit. She opened the door and went into the music room. The windows were shut. Seeing that nowadays no one ever entered the room, it was better to keep them closed. She took one of the keys from the bunch and opened a cabinet. The cool breeze that had accompanied her until she got to the stairs was gone. A cold sweat covered her skin. It did not occur to her to return to the hall and call up the dream wind again. The candlelight slid across the floor. Startled moths, black beetles, and hundreds of ants had taken possession of the cabinet. Charlotte let the insects go — the house was full of them — and continued her search.

A pile of photo albums lay on the top shelf; they were wrapped in plastic bags to discourage unwelcome guests. She ran her fingers over the spines as she tried to decipher the dates by the light of the lone candle. She pulled out an album dated 1936–1939, and turned to the table. But the piece of furniture that had always stood under the window had disappeared, along with the sofa her father had ordered from London. She swept the dust from a section of the floor, put the photo album down, and knelt in front of it. She removed the plastic wrapping. The cover was worn, the purple velvet now brown and threadbare. She opened the album.

There was a photo of her mother in a floor-length dress,

with a tiara in her hair, next to another woman, also wearing an evening dress. The caption under the photo read CHRISTMAS AT THE CLUB. She turned the page: her father with his shotgun, in uniform, one foot resting on a dead deer, behind him two young boys in *longhis*. The caption underneath, in the same handwriting, read OUR HERO. Charlotte recalled the blond officer in 52 company who, after a few too many *burra-pegs*, almost proposed to her. He was the one who told her that it wasn't her father who killed the deer, but two Indian boys. "With their bare hands," he had added with a chuckle. The pages that followed were filled with photos of her mother in evening dresses or on the tennis court, and occasionally there were photos of her father with his men, in the mess or out hunting. She also found two of her brother, Donald. One, with Sita, bore the caption JUNIOR WITH THE AYAH, and the other was a formal portrait, of her brother together with her parents in front of the house, which had hung over her bed in England for years. There was no photo of her or the ship that had brought her to England. Charlotte could not remember ever examining the album so carefully. She had always assumed that somewhere there was a photograph of the large black ship. She took another album down from the shelf: THE WAR. A beetle scurried away and moths circled the candle. These photos were much smaller, and featured men in uniform who meant nothing to her. They were seated around tables, smoking cigarettes, or shaking hands. And there was one of her father, which showed someone pinning a medal on his chest. Not until the last page did she find the sole photograph of herself, taken the year after the war. The caption read WEDDING PETER HARRIS AND CHARLOTTE BRIDGWATER OCTOBER 1946.

HEMA LAY ON his mat in the kitchen. He had collected kindling and lit the coals, since there was no more kerosene. He had already prepared the meal and done various other chores. It had been dark outside for hours. He looked hungrily at the small pan with rice, dal, and vegetables. He wondered why memsahib didn't call him. In many of the houses at the bottom of the hill the lights were already out. Perhaps something had happened and she wasn't feeling well. She was getting on in years, and such incidents were becoming more and more frequent. He jumped to his feet. Why hadn't he thought of that before! Perhaps she'd taken a fall, hurt herself, and was unable to get to the bell. The bell had been out of order before, probably because the general gave the rope such an almighty jerk. Hema ran across the grass in his slippers, heading for the big house. The moon had just begun to rise. He could have kicked himself. He didn't want to admit that he had fallen asleep, and he had no idea how long he'd been napping. Maybe she had called and he hadn't heard her. Hema had been hired all those years ago because it said in his letter of reference that he never slept and always answered a call immediately. Since there were no longer any other servants and he was well over seventy, he often nodded off. His cousin on his mother's side had told him it was simply part of growing old, but that was something Hema wouldn't admit to.

By order of memsahib the side door was open, because it was better for the circulation of air. The salon was empty, and she wasn't in her father's old study either. Hema rushed up the stairs, his knees creaking as loudly as the steps. He stopped in front of her door and coughed. He knew that she hated being disturbed. The thought that she might have fallen or had another attack of malaria — or something worse — made him knock softly on the door. Not long ago he had awakened her: she had merely fallen asleep, but he thought she'd stopped breathing. She was furious and told him never to wake her again. If she was dead, it wouldn't make any difference anyway. With the image of her lying on the floor in the back of his mind, he knocked again. There was still no sound. He walked over to the old nursery. The door was locked. He took the key from the nail, inserted it in the lock, and cautiously turned the handle. He listened. It remained still. He carefully opened the door and crept in. He didn't like the sour odour that hung in the room, but memsahib had forbidden him to open the large windows. Quietly he moved on. When he got to the balcony door, he inserted a small key in the lock and managed to open the door without a sound. Quickly he slipped outside, onto the balcony, and into the night, shutting the door behind him. By the light of the rising moon, he walked over to the window of Charlotte's bedroom. All her windows and doors were wide open, and the curtains swayed slightly. He went down on his knees and crept farther. The bedroom itself was pitch black. He peeked over the edge of the windowsill and heard the whirr of the fan above her bed. No matter how hard he listened and strained his eyes, the mosquito net made it impossible for him to tell whether she was in the bed or not. By the light of the moon, he saw that there were crumpled pieces of paper on the floor. He crept to the door and stole inside.

The fragrant scent of memsahib Charlotte permeated the room. Hema loved that scent, and he inhaled softly. On all fours, he moved closer to Charlotte's bed. He had to take care not to disturb the wads of paper. If she woke up now, he was sure she would fire him. Without a sound he crept closer, taking care to avoid her slippers, and looked through the mosquito net. The bed was empty. He looked under the bed, behind the chair, and in the bathroom. There was no sign of an indisposed woman. He crept back to the balcony on his creaking knees, forgetting that he could just as well have gotten up and walked. Not until he reached the door of the former nursery did he grasp the doorknob and pull his stiff old body up to a standing position.

Hema was not thinking of the pain in his back, his worn-out knees, or his torn nails. He was worried about his memsahib Charlotte. More and more often she was short of breath when she returned from the club: at her age, the cycle ride in the blazing sun was brutal. Why didn't she just hail a rickshaw for a few rupees, like he did? The lunch he'd prepared had remained untouched. The doorbell rang. She said she wasn't hungry. She told him to go ahead and eat, and save what was left. Hema had gone to the door. The caller was a man he had seen before. He had straight hair that hung over his eyes and he was wearing an expensive shirt. He said that his name was Arjun Soumitra, but Hema suspected that that was not his real name. Memsahib had told him to take the visitor into the salon. But Hema had left him standing in the hall while he hurriedly unrolled the large carpet. For some time the Persian rug had been kept rolled up in plastic behind the sofa and was brought out only when there were guests, which was a rare occurrence. He placed the table in the middle of the rug and ushered the man in. The man walked straight over to memsahib's dresser and picked up one of the large bowls, which were her pride and joy. Hema had coughed discreetly, but the man continued to examine the porcelain. Hema wasn't sure whether it would be right to leave him alone in the room. Just as he had been about to go and fetch memsahib, she walked into the room. She had greeted the man amiably and sent Hema out of the room.

Noiselessly Hema made his way across the nursery floor, after which he locked the door and hung the key on the nail. He went down the stairs and halted in the middle of the marble hall. He listened and heard the house creak: no matter how hard he tried to combat them, more and more insects were gnawing their way through the dry wood of the walls and appearing in the most unexpected places. He heard sounds coming from the piano room. The door was closed, as memsahib had ordered. He knocked and walked in.

Charlotte was standing on a wobbly construction consisting of a chair and a stool. She seemed relieved to see Hema. "Take a candle and give me a bit of light."

Hema, who was used to his employer's whims and was much relieved that she wasn't lying dead on the floor, picked up a candlestick and held it aloft.

"Higher," said Charlotte from her unsteady perch. She had a pair of scissors in her hand and she cut a gem from the red lampshade that hung from the ceiling. "The last one," she said with a sigh.

1936 Grand Palace ~

THE LITTLE GIRL lies on the white table in front of him. Slowly her eyes close and her breathing becomes heavier. Every day for the past week Peter Harris has examined Chutki, the youngest daughter of the maharaja. Despite the fact that she continues to complain of a sore throat, difficulty in swallowing, and breathing problems, she is strong and healthy. He has studied all the possible causes, just as he would have done in his hospital practice at Long Millgate. There is no doubt that chronic inflammation of the larynx is the culprit. It is a miracle that it hasn't spread to the bronchial tubes and the lungs. He runs the back of his tweezers over her skin, but the girl does not react. The chloroform has worked faster than usual due to the high temperature in the room. Back in the slums of Manchester, he always had a fully equipped operating room at his disposal, but here the drip hangs from the ceiling on a string and the operating table has been adjusted to the right height by means of blocks sawed to measure that morning. The maharaja would not allow him to take the girl to the hospital in Delhi, where he has worked for the past four months. Maharaja Man Singh, who is suspicious by nature, keeps walking in to see what the surgeon is doing with his daughter. Peter has forbidden him to enter the room during the operation, after delivering a lecture on bacteria and the risk of infection.

Peter presses the back of his hand against the girl's forehead and prays that all will go well, that he will be able to meet the high expectations, and that there will be no permanent scar on her neck, so that when she marries, she will wear the family jewels with pride. Peter suspects that the maharaja is using his daughter as a guinea pig. This powerful man will agree to be operated on himself only if she recovers. Glancing at the rickety construction supporting the table, he regrets that he did not insist that the operation take place in an official hospital. But then Peter nods to Aziz, his assistant, and with even more precision and concentration than usual, he tilts the girl's head backwards. During the mirror examination he saw just how serious the condition of the larynx was. Aziz paints the girl's throat with an antiseptic and covers it with a cloth. There is an opening in the cloth on the exact spot where the young throat specialist will make the incision.

THE MAHARAJA, WHO is not accustomed to taking orders, strides out of the palace. He would rather have gone straight to his study to oil one of his guns, but he is unable to concentrate on anything but Chutki. Although she isn't his favourite daughter, she's a good dancer and he doesn't want to lose her. He slows his pace as he approaches the stables. He has not yet met the taxidermist whom he summoned from Bangalore. The abattoir, which on his father's initiative was covered with Delft blue tiles straight from Holland, and where the English throat specialist declined to operate, has for several days been the domain of the man charged with mounting the elephant head for the viceroy. Maharaja Man Singh has already decided that he will only make the viceroy a present of the head if he survives his coming operation. The heavy door of the abbatoir creaks open. There are large hooks hanging from the ceiling and draining racks along one wall. The elephant's head lies on a large round table in the middle of the high-ceilinged room.

The taxidermist, who is kneeling on the ground, does not look up when the maharaja enters. The Indian prince waits in amazement. In his palace, people jump to their feet as soon as he appears. For a moment he considers dismissing the man, but instead he sits down on the long wooden bench against the wall. He watches as the blade of the scalpel slowly sinks into the elephant's neck. Then the head is quickly separated from the body, together with the accompanying loose ends. The maharaja puts his hand to his throat. With great precision, the razor-sharp knife slices through the thick grey hide.

THE GIRL MOANS softly. Doctor Harris finishes bandaging her neck. Gradually he becomes aware of the sounds from outside. He is thirsty. His trusted assistant is already at his elbow with a glass of water, which he downs in one gulp. He's done it. Chutki will never be an opera singer, but provided she doesn't whisper, cough, clear her throat, or drink too much water during the coming forty-eight hours, she will be able to speak without pain and her sore throat will be a thing of the past. The men sit down and watch as the little girl slowly wakes up. *A daughter,* Peter thinks to himself, *that's what I want, too.*

~

HE LONGS FOR the peace and quiet of his room. The interminable dinner is by no means over: new dishes filled with unfamiliar fare are continually being brought in. The *punkah-wallah* pulls impassively on the rope, and above their heads the enormous fans are doing their work. Peter Harris is not used to Indian food. His landlady in Delhi served only English fare, and the spicy dishes paralyze his taste buds and set his mouth on fire.

The maharaja, a bandage around his throat, claps his hands and the various conversations fall still. "Harris sahib," he begins with a slight bow in Peter's direction. "My voice is still weak, but my happiness is great." He snaps his fingers.

The man in the green turban comes forward. He is

carrying a walnut chest, which he places at Peter's feet. Softly the maharaja begins to speak, choosing his words with care. He praises Peter for his great expertise and the British people for their advanced developments in the field of medical science. Peter gestures deprecatingly and smiles in embarrassment. But the maharaja, clad in a silk suit, dismisses the surgeon's modesty, stressing that he will be in his debt for all eternity and expressing the hope that their paths will often cross. While the gift that his youngest daughter has selected is in no way comparable to what the doctor has given him, he hopes that this token of esteem will be accepted.

Chutki, who is sitting next to her mother and for the first time in her life has been allowed to attend a dinner, points to the chest: "Open it!"

Peter Harris, somewhat flustered by all the attention, lifts the lid. On a black velvet cushion lies a magnificent crystal lampshade. Sparkling rubies hang at a distance of one centimetre apart, each on its own fine gold chain.

1995 Rampur ~

HEMA DID NOT trouble himself with things that were beyond his field of vision. He never went near the top of a cabinet, did not like attics, and was not in the habit of looking up at the ceiling. Which explains why he never noticed that every once in a while a ruby disappeared from the lamp in the deserted music room. Charlotte, who had always acted in secret for fear someone would find out about her treasure, was no longer worried, now that she had cut off the last of the jewels. While she had to maintain the large house and pay the usual living costs, like all the other women who belonged to the New Rampur Club, she wanted a new dress for the upcoming festivities.

Hema helped her down from the wobbly structure, and as he picked up the photo albums from the floor and returned them to their plastic jackets, he inquired if she wanted her supper. The house search he had just carried out had not dulled his hunger. Charlotte shook her head and told him she wanted to get some sleep, which was not entirely true. She was still elated about the successful sale of the Wedgwood service and the costly ruby in her hand.

The dealer who had come to look at the Wedgwood had initially been uninterested, even condescending. Floral motifs were old-fashioned and unpopular, the white was not as creamy as it should be, and over the years the porcelain seemed to have lost its transparency. Charlotte could not have said exactly what was going through her mind when she took the topmost plate from the pile and fixed the dealer with a piercing look. She had placed the plate casually on her outstretched hand, as if it wouldn't bother her if it fell and broke. "My good man," she had said, "you obviously know very little about valuable china services." He had laughed scornfully. Still balancing the plate on her open palm, she had delivered a brief lecture on the qualities of the costly ceramic. She had explained how it was possible to make the material hard and translucent at the same time, that bone ash was added to the clay of the original Wedgwood to make it even stronger, that it was odourless and tasteless, that even after lying at the bottom of the sea for a century it had barely discoloured, and that if he was not prepared to make her a reasonable offer, he could leave the house immediately, since her situation was not as hopeless as he seemed to think. And still staring him straight in the eye, she had spun the plate in her hand. The buyer could not take his eyes off the plate, which began to twirl faster and faster. Then Charlotte tilted her hand and it described a graceful arc in the direction of the floor. But before it could hit the ground, the buyer had taken a dive toward the plate and managed to catch it.

"Wedgwood doesn't break that easily," Charlotte said. Now she was the one laughing.

He had hurt his knee when he dived for the plate. But it was worth it. He knew that he could charge a lot more for a complete service than for one that was missing a plate.

"Well?" Charlotte took the plate from his hands and placed it carefully on the stack. "You know my price."

The man walked back over to the dresser, rubbing his knee. He picked up the plate again, held it up to the light, and squinted.

Was it his lank hair, his neat suit, his taut lower lip? Charlotte couldn't say, but she had never driven such a hard bargain. In the end he paid her three times his original offer. Charlotte knew that he already had a buyer, and probably in Rampur. She just hoped it wasn't one of the ladies from the Tuesday-morning club.

~

THE AIR CONDITIONER hummed. The wife of Nikhil Nair, the district director of the Eastern Indian Mining Company, and the wife of Ajay Karapiet, whose husband owned a hotel and two cinemas, were having tea in Nikhil Nair's beautifully decorated sitting room.

"One-third Assam, two-thirds Darjeeling," said the wife of Nikhil Nair.

"I should have guessed! You always have such delicious mixes," squeaked the wife of Ajay Karapiet, who took much more milk in her tea than the wife of Nikhil Nair.

"That manicure doctor with the plastic hand . . . has he contacted you about the tailor?"

"Didn't I tell you?"

"You never tell me anything."

"I'm sure I told you."

"Are you suggesting that I'm becoming forgetful?" snapped the wife of Nikhil Nair.

"He's agreed to come."

"When?"

The wife of Ajay Karapiet sighed. "I don't know."

"Why don't you know?"

"Because the nail doctor didn't know."

"He can ask, can't he?"

"He says the tailor is on his way."

"Why isn't he here yet?"

"I don't know."

"You never know anything."

"Well, I know that he's coming, don't I?"

The wife of Nikhil Nair took a bite of her biscuit. The crumbs fell onto her lap. She was crazy about the biscuits that her cook baked for her every other day. She'd eat at least two whenever she got the chance — and that was reflected in her figure.

The wife of Ajay Karapiet didn't like the biscuits. They stuck to her dentures.

"Did you get that piece of brocade back?" the wife of Nikhil Nair asked her friend.

Again the wife of Ajay Karapiet heaved a sigh. "What's left of it."

"What do you mean?"

"I have a feeling that someone's cut off a piece."

"I have the very same feeling. I'm positive I gave him five metres of that expensive pink Chinese silk. Yesterday I had the girl measure it, and she says it's only four and a half metres."

"And I'm missing a metre."

"Are you positive?"

The wife of Ajay Karapiet nodded.

"If the new tailor is just as big a cheat as Sanat was, then . . ."

"Darzi Sanat was honest. It's that servant of his who's a cheat."

"The new *darzi* . . . where is he going to work?"

"In Sanat's workplace, of course."

"The workplace belongs to a bookbinder now."

"That's not possible."

"What will you do with the cinemas when your husband dies?"

The wife of Ajay Karapiet had once confided to the wife of Nikhil Nair that she hated films but that her husband must never know. She lowered her eyes, ignoring the question. "Perhaps an exception can be made, so that he can work at the club."

"Of course! In the shed next to the tennis court. I'll call the secretary right away." She picked up the receiver. "When does he arrive?"

"I already told you."

"No, you didn't."

"He's on his way."

~

Charlotte was wearing a low-cut evening gown made of pale green silk and had a gold tiara in her hair. As she descended the staircase, her train glided over the carefully polished steps. Her earrings caught the light from the candles in the chandelier. Classical music wafted in from the salon. She was beautifully made up, and her scarlet lips glistened. At each step she took, the music from the salon swelled. In the hall there were servants in livery. Each of them held a tray bearing a pair of evening shoes. Her bare feet, with their scarlet toenails, were visible beneath the hem of her gown. Each servant had a different pair of shoes on his tray: there were various colours and styles, but all of them had very high heels. Charlotte sat down on a chair on a low platform and extended her foot. The first servant knelt before her and put the shoe on her foot. It was too small. Then the next servant knelt down: he had exquisite golden mules on his tray. But they didn't fit her either. Another servant knelt down. This one held out a pair of shoes with glass heels. Her foot slipped effortlessly into the shoe.

"How dare you!" bellowed a voice from above.

Charlotte looked up at her father, who stood at the top of the stairs in his uniform. Before she could say a word, the general called out, "Slut! You have sullied the reputation of the family!"

Charlotte awoke with a start from her dream, bathed in perspiration and tangled in the sheet. She freed herself and got out of bed. Going into the bathroom, she held her wrists under the faucet. The water streamed with force over her hands. Her nails were still scarlet. She looked into the mirror and saw her sweaty, sleep-worn features. She splashed water over her face and dried herself off. Walking across to the nursery in her bare feet, she stopped to listen. In the distance, crickets were chirping, but otherwise all was quiet. She went back to her room and lay down under the mosquito net. Above her head, the fan was still whirring. She lay still, with her eyes open. Very slowly a tear formed, rolled down her cheek, and dropped onto her pillow. It was absorbed by the pillowcase, which had already survived a thousand washings.

1946 Bombay

ALL AROUND HER, people are hugging and kissing one another, shedding tears of joy or sadness. Her eyes dart from left to right. Where is her father? Or has he sent someone else, someone who won't recognize her? Her little blue hat is askew and she's hot. After ten years in England, she is no longer used to the oppressive heat. She wipes her forehead and adjusts her hat. She is standing next to her trunk. Men with red cloths wrapped around their heads walk back and forth, balancing suitcases and crates on their heads. She's already sent three of them away. Charlotte has no idea where to have her suitcase taken. She has only one address in India and that is her parental home in Rampur, a two-day trip. She listens to the characteristically accented English, which she hasn't heard for so many years, and watches the affirming nodding of heads. Nearby stands an English soldier, a captain, whose uniform inspires confidence. Could he have been sent by her father? She catches his eye and smiles somewhat awkwardly. The handsome captain looks down and blushes.

There is almost no one else left on the quay but Charlotte and the captain. The former boarding school girl walks over to the officer.

"Have they forgotten you, too?"

The man smiles shyly.

"Me, too."

They stand side by side, without speaking. The last of the lading is tackled from the ship, divided up, and loaded onto handcarts.

"Do you know Bombay?"

"I've been here once, but that was before the war," are the first words spoken by the man, who is older than Charlotte.

"Me, too. When I had to leave," Charlotte says softly. The memory of the last time she saw her mother appears clearly in her mind. The waving hand, the handkerchief, her slight figure. "I'll write every week!" she had called out. But there were no more monthly letters. Six months later she received a letter from her father announcing that her mother had died suddenly. "I was in England," she says. "At boarding school. I wanted to go back, but my father thought it would be better for me to spend the whole war in England."

The man nods. He pulls out a pack of cigarettes and offers her one. She looks around somewhat nervously and takes a cigarette from the pack. He gives her a light. Charlotte breathes in the smoke.

They smoke in silence and watch as the last handcar rolls down the quay. The doors of an enormous shed are closed with a chain and padlock. A barefoot boy walks by with a crate of carrots on his head, singing as he goes. In the distance a ship's horn sounds, and overhead a flock of twittering birds flies by. It's the first cigarette she has smoked since leaving England. She hopes that she'll never have to return to that country, where it rained constantly, the houses were cold and dark, and no one ever laughed.

"Are you hungry?"

"Yes, a bit," Charlotte says. She skipped breakfast because she was so excited to be back in India at last. She picks up her suitcase and says, "But I think I ought to go by the shipping office first. Otherwise, when my father gets here, he won't know where I am."

Behind the counter sits a greying man in thick glasses, surrounded by thousands of fat folders full of yellowed pages. "Put a note on the bulletin board," he says, pointing to a large notice board near the entrance. It is already plastered with messages from lost travellers and those who came to meet them. Charlotte adds her message to the others.

THEY WALK ALONGSIDE one another. The captain, who has a slight limp, carries her suitcase. He's afraid to look at her, and vice versa. She notices that he is missing a little finger, but outside of that she finds him quite attractive. He has dark eyes, a straight nose, and a cleft chin like Cary Grant. She's aware of a delicate scent she has never smelled on a man before. Not that she's had much opportunity to compare men's scents at boarding school: the regime was too strict, except perhaps for the long, lonely school vacations.

The summer before, she roamed the grounds of the school alone, which is how she met Perry, the gardener's son. He taught her to smoke and to ride a bicycle, until she took a fall and skinned her knee. Mrs. Blackburn, the principal, didn't believe her story about stumbling over a curb, and forbade her to leave the school grounds. But Perry knew a lot more places within the boundaries of the school grounds than Mrs. Blackburn, and smoking a cigarette together became part of their daily routine. Until the gardener caught his son giving

Charlotte kissing lessons. He was afraid of getting the sack, and sent the boy off to stay with an uncle fifty kilometres away. The rest of the vacation was just as lonely and monotonous as all the others for the past nine years. During the day she read, or hit balls against the wall of the school. In the evening she ate alone in the deathly still dining hall, beneath an enormous painting of Queen Victoria. Charlotte had never really understood why she couldn't spend a month or so in India, or stay with an aunt or uncle in England, but her father had written to tell her that he had no relatives in Great Britain, and that her mother's sister wanted nothing more to do with the family after her mother died of black water fever. Charlotte did try to contact the aunt in Glasgow, but the operator told her the number did not exist, and that no one else was registered under that name.

"Shall we have something to eat here?" the captain says, pointing to a rather sober establishment on a corner.

"As long as there aren't any portraits of Queen Victoria, I'm not bothered."

"The last few years there have been fewer paintings of the royal family around," the captain says in a serious tone.

She's beautiful, he thinks, with her long hair. Her eyes twinkle, her lips are perfect, and her laugh is bell-like. She looks around her as if everything is new to her, and she has a question or a remark about everything she sees.

"I've missed India," Charlotte says, as she helps herself to lamb curry and rice.

"Yes, a lot has changed," the captain observes as he fills their glasses with cold water.

"According to my father, everything has remained the same."

"What does your father do for a living?"

"The same as you, he's in the army. He's just been promoted to lieutenant colonel. And what do you do?"

"I'm a surgeon." He toys with his food. He isn't hungry. "When war broke out, I was called up," his voice softens, "like most of the British men here. They made me a captain immediately because I'm a doctor. I was sent to Burma." He looks out the window, absently stirring the curry with his fork.

"That was when your leg . . . ?" she says softly.

The captain nods his head, and his gaze wanders back to the window. He doesn't see the horse and cart passing. A man with a handcart shouts something to a mate, a hawker tries to peddle his flowers, and in the distance a tram goes by. He doesn't see any of this. "The war was cruel," he says, his voice almost inaudible.

"My name is Charlotte," she says.

He starts, then straightens up. Putting out his hand, he says, "My name is Peter. Peter Harris."

THEY WALK BACK to the harbour together. At the entrance to the shipping office, they look at each other, and then quickly look away again. The office is closed. Charlotte knocks, but there's no sign of life inside. She looks through the window and tries to make out whether her note is still hanging on the notice board.

"Do you suppose he found it?" She straightens her hat. "If he was here, that is . . ."

Again the captain carries the suitcase with all her belongings. *Where am I supposed to go?* she thinks. Donald is still at boarding school in the north of England and Mother is dead.

Charlotte realizes that she has no idea what her father looks like. Perhaps he was there that morning but they didn't recognize each other. Every year, at Christmastime, he sends her a copy of his temporary address. First there were various army missions, and later on he was sent to the front. Under the address he had written, in his precise hand, MERRY CHRISTMAS, FATHER. Is he bald? Maybe he has a beard or a moustache. Does he wear glasses or is he perhaps missing an eye? She doesn't know. After she received that one photograph taken in front of the house when Donald was two, she received no other pictures. She has longed to return to Rampur, but suddenly she no longer knows why. There is no one there that she knows. There's no one waiting for her. Years ago she prayed and begged to be allowed to come home. It wasn't that boarding school was all bad, but she always dreamt of India.

She has no idea where the captain is taking her, and she doesn't want to ask. She wants to keep on walking beside him. As long as she's walking beside him, she's not alone.

HE WAS RIGHT. She was standing on the exact spot he had indicated and she was wearing a blue hat. Except that her dress had circles on it instead of stripes. Peter didn't believe the maharaja's astrologer when he told him that his wife would be waiting for him at the harbour, wearing a striped dress. He laughed and said that he didn't have a wife, and wasn't in love. After the horrors of the front, all he wanted to do was enjoy the quiet and luxury which the maharaja had promised him. After consulting his calculations, the astrologer concluded that this was his only chance. He was to put on his uniform again and not waste any time, since the day after tomorrow the stars would be in the right position. So without even informing his host, the maharaja, he threw a few things into a valise and headed for the station. It was all totally counter to his inclinations, but the astrologer had insisted, and in the end he managed to make the night train to Bombay. He spent the whole night and the following day on the train, going over the scenarios, thinking up ways he could make contact with an unknown woman, and then discarding them again. He approached the harbour terrain without a plan and filled with apprehension.

He had spotted the blue hat when he was still some distance away. The woman proved to be a young beauty who had only just turned sixteen, and he fell in love with her as if he had been hit by lightning. In love . . . he had never imagined that it could happen again. He hears that she is out of breath, and he slows down. It feels right that she's walking next to him.

THE HOTEL IS on a narrow street. Peter doesn't know where that special hotel is located where British girls travelling alone spend the night, so he takes her to his hotel, where Charlotte registers and asks for a room with a bathtub. She gives him a quick smile and walks down the corridor with the key in her hand. Peter has no idea what to do next. He has never seduced a woman before. He's only been in love once, when he was just about her age, and the girl didn't even know it. He was going to tell her the day he left for India, but she didn't show up. He cycled over to her house and waited there for hours, but he never summoned the courage to ring the doorbell. He must not allow such a chance to slip by a second time.

At the end of the corridor there is an outdoor café. He moves his chair to a spot where he has a view of the corridor, and orders a whisky. He wants to be there for her if she can't sleep or feels like company. He wants to be able to comfort her if she has a bad dream. He wonders if she realizes that the India she is returning to is a totally different country than the one she left as a young child. Does she know that the power of the British is waning, and that the army is being deployed to put down riots organized by freedom fighters? He believes in an independent India, but now that he is in uniform again, he does not dare say so out loud.

HE AWAKES WITH a start. Charlotte is sitting next to him, wearing a long white nightgown. The doors leading to the corridor are closed. The stars twinkle above.

"I couldn't get to sleep," she says.

"Have you been here long?"

"You snore," she says with a giggle.

"Do I snore?"

"Very softly. No one else heard you, only me. And you wiggle your nose while you're asleep."

"My nose?"

Charlotte wiggles her nose up and down very fast.

"No, I don't."

"Yes, you do."

"You look like a rabbit." He chuckles.

"You're the one who looks like a rabbit, not me. I was just imitating you."

"I don't believe a word of it."

"It's true." She smiles. "And you talk in your sleep, too."

Peter looks at her in amazement.

"You said you liked the girl in the blue hat."

Peter looks at this girl who is flirting with him so openly and innocently. Does she realize what she's doing? Should he stop her, send her back to bed, and then take a cold shower? She puts her hand on his hand. She runs her forefinger over the spot where his little finger should have been.

"Did it hurt?"

"Not at first. But it did later on."

"And now?"

His whole body aches. His heart is beating a mile a minute. He closes his eyes and feels her finger glide across his hand. She must stop.

TINY DROPS APPEAR over his dark eyebrows. His lips open ever so slightly. Charlotte sees how his nostrils quiver. Her forefinger moves across his arm. Is this what Mrs. Blackburn was protecting her against all those years? This delicious sensation? Charlotte is no longer thinking about school, or her father, or Rampur, or sleep, or tomorrow. For the first time in ten years she is happy.

1995 Rampur ~

CHARLOTTE HAD BEEN planning to hail a rickshaw for the Tuesday-morning meeting, since thanks to the sale of her china service, she finally had cash on hand. But when she saw the electricity bill, she'd grabbed her bike and decided that she would have to economize even more.

Behind her someone honked. Without looking around, she raised her hand. The driver did not pass and continued to honk his horn. Charlotte's hair clung to her forehead, and when she looked over her shoulder, it interfered with her view of the traffic behind her. That morning the thermometer had hit forty-seven degrees, and the air was like treacle. The driver in the car behind her continued to honk, and Charlotte stopped.

The wife of Nikhil Nair beckoned to her. Charlotte leaned her bicycle against a tree and walked over to the car. The door opened.

"Jump in!" came the order from inside the air-conditioned car.

Charlotte entered the cool interior.

"Akhilesh, go lock the bike," said the woman in her pink trouser suit to her chauffeur.

"Please, ma'am, the key." He reached out his hand to Charlotte.

At the club she always parked the Raleigh near the entrance, and at home in the shed. "The bike doesn't have a lock," she said.

"Then I needn't have bothered to stop," muttered the buxom lady.

"Is there something wrong?" Charlotte inquired, revelling in the cool of the car interior.

The wife of Nikhil Nair rolled her eyes dramatically and waved her hands to reinforce her story. "You know that the nail specialist was going to arrange everything. Well, the man never called back. It appears that he's arriving this week. We figured that since it's going to benefit all of us, the shed next to the tennis court at the club would be a good place, seeing that the old workplace has already been rented out to a bookbinder, but now the secretary says that the shed is to be used to house the books, since the library is going to be refurbished in the next few weeks, in connection with the fete, since there will be important guests there, and he says that in honour of your father the library must be preserved in a proper state for the sake of future generations. The Karapiets' extra room in the servants' quarters is occupied because they've just taken on a cook with five children. Yesterday I spent the whole afternoon calling around. Time is getting short. He's already on his way here, and we still don't have anything, so we thought that — since you have so much space — you might have room for him." Panting, the woman put her hands to her bosom.

"Room for whom?"

"For the tailor."

"In my house?"

"Not in the house, of course, but there must be servants' quarters?" The wife of Nikhil Nair, and everyone else, knew that except for Hema, Charlotte no longer had any personnel, while in the past there must have been at least forty servants, many of whom lived on the premises. The wife of Nikhil Nair saw the hesitation on Charlotte's face and said, "Of course, he'll be paying rent."

Charlotte wanted to ask how much he would be paying. But because she knew that was what the wife of Nikhil Nair wanted to hear, she replied that she would think about it. She stepped out of the car and into the suffocating heat.

IT HAD ALREADY occurred to Charlotte that taking in lodgers was an honourable way of making money, but after the fiasco with the couple from Kerala who were schoolteachers, she hadn't tried it again. Of course, two teachers who were constantly at each other's throats was not the same thing as a tailor. Charlotte thought back to the evening when she drove by the workplace of the old *darzi* around eleven o'clock at night. She had remembered that she had a length of cotton in the car, and when she saw a light burning, she stopped and knocked on the door, assuming that he was still at work. A little girl opened the door, and behind her a whole family was lying asleep on the floor. Sanat jumped to his feet when he heard her voice, and with a smile he took the piece of material from her.

"I make beautiful dress, ma'am," he had said, "round neck — sleeves short?"

She really wanted a square neck and long sleeves, but she had nodded and gone home. That evening she walked through all the unused rooms in their spacious house and decided to take in lodgers.

But the idea of a tailor coming to live and work on her property simply did not suit her. It would mean that all the women in the club would come to her house for fittings, and naturally they'd all stay for a cup of tea. The last thing she wanted was all those inquisitive female eyes in her house. There was already enough gossip about her — and besides, she had just sold her Wedgwood cups.

SHE PARKED HER bicycle near the entrance to the club. All her brooding about the tailor had almost made her forget about the oppressive heat, but when she saw the wife of Nikhil Nair standing near the entrance with a hopeful expression on her face, the heat engulfed her like an oppressive blanket.

"Everyone thinks it's a wonderful idea!" called out the wife of Nikhil Nair.

She didn't know where the other women had come from, but she was suddenly surrounded. The wife of Ajay Karapiet clapped her hands and called her their knight in shining armour. The widow Singh smiled at her encouragingly. The wife of Alok Nath, the goldsmith, pressed the length of material she had bought for a new dress into Charlotte's hands, as if she were the tailor, and the wife of Adeeb Tata said that her Paris dress had to be shortened. The women were all talking at once. The enormous sense of relief was palpable. Charlotte, by contrast, broke out in a cold sweat. She had to put a stop to this. She had to explain that this was not what she wanted, that she was too busy, that her house was not suitable, that the servants' quarters were home to scorpions and snakes and close to collapse, and that there was no way she could house a poor tailor.

She was ushered inside as if she was a hero. Someone handed her a glass of cold, sparkling lemonade and a home-made biscuit. The women gave themselves over to speculation about when he would arrive: one person said today, another thought it would be tomorrow, but it was clear to everyone that he could not be far away.

1937 Queen Victoria College ~

CHARLOTTE IS COLD. She wears two pairs of pyjama pants to bed, one over the other, and a heavy woollen sweater. That's not allowed during the day, so she puts on an extra woollen shirt under her school uniform and wears a pair of tights.

The cold didn't seem to bother her friend Iris, who often forgot to put on a coat.

"There's snow in the air," says Iris.

Charlotte looks up at the steely skies and shivers. "I don't see any snow."

"You can't see it, but you can smell it."

She sniffs. It smells the way it always smells: like coal-fired heaters and the pine trees next to the school. Smells she associates with her first six months in England, when almost no one talked to her and she spent entire afternoons alone in the library, reading. Now that she and Iris are friends, school isn't that bad. The two of them make fun of the gym teacher's nose and Miss Brands, who teaches handicrafts and always has spots on her skirt. "I've never seen snow," she says.

"Don't they have snow in India?"

"There's lots of snow in the Himalayas, sometimes fifteen metres deep, but I've never been there. India is a very big country."

"Snow is nothing but frozen water."

"Does it hurt?"

Iris laughs. "Only when you fall on your backside."

The two girls walk down the path leading to Albert Hall, where Mrs. Blackburn is going to read the Christmas story to the children in the lower grades. Charlotte's gaze keeps returning to the sky. It reminds her of the period just before the monsoon, when the clouds hang lower and lower and the sky turns a darker shade of grey.

The girls are already seated on benches around an empty chair in the middle of a room with a high ceiling. On the walls there are paintings of old men, and a fire is burning in the fireplace. Everyone's chattering away and the smell of freshly baked biscuits hangs in the air. Charlotte and Iris find a spot near the windows. Outside, the first flakes start to fall: on the path, on the grass. Then there are more of them, and they're larger. It's magical. The trees in the field are gradually covered by a blanket of snow, and the huge Victorian school building on the opposite side of the road disappears from sight.

"Isn't it beautiful?" Charlotte whispers.

Iris smiles.

Mrs. Blackburn walks into the room with a large book under her arm. The girls stop chattering and get to their feet. When the headmistress sits down, the girls follow suit. The teacher places her hands on the book and looks at her pupils, one by one. She smiles, but her fingers are drumming on the book. The girls are as still as mice. Again Charlotte's gaze wanders to the window. She is witnessing a miracle, one that's totally new to her. It's more magical than the fireworks during Diwali, and more exciting than the Holi festival of colours. Behind her, a buzz of activity is audible as a cook wearing a starched apron comes in with a steaming pitcher and begins to fill the beakers. Mrs. Blackburn puts her purse on her lap and begins to search for something inside.

"They're not here," says the headmistress.

"What?" asks the cook.

"My glasses." Then she looks at the girls opposite her, who try to avoid eye contact.

Outside, it's bitterly cold. Inside, the room is filled with the aroma of hot chocolate.

Iris sees the longing in her friend's eyes and gives her a nudge. "Do you want to go?"

Charlotte nods dreamily.

The girl sitting next to Charlotte notices and she starts nodding, too.

"You?" asks a classmate with her hair in a bun, sitting on the other side of the girl.

"Does she want to go?" her neighbour, a girl with a ponytail, asks the girl with the bun.

"No, not me. She's the one," says Charlotte's neighbour.

"Ma'am! Charlotte wants to go!" calls out the girl with the ponytail.

Charlotte hasn't the faintest idea what the question is or why everyone is pointing at her.

The headmistress comes over to Charlotte. "I'm glad you're willing to go. Just run over to my house and ask the housekeeper for my reading glasses. I left them lying on the hall table." She holds up a monocle, and then turns to the rest of the class. "I'll make do with this, for the time being."

The girls laugh.

Charlotte is standing on the doorstep in front of the huge old door and she stretches out her hand. The snowflakes fall onto her palm and immediately melt. She licks up droplets of water. It tastes like ordinary water. She puts out her hand again, higher this time. The flakes on her hand melt, but those on the sleeve of her grey coat don't. She inhales the air. The lantern illuminates the entrance, but the path in front of Albert Hall is invisible.

Cautiously she places one foot on the virgin snow. She can feel the cobblestones underneath the layer of white. One step at a time, she follows the hedge in the direction of the school building. She can just make out the contours. The night seems brighter than usual. The flakes that blow into her face feel cool and wet. She sticks out her tongue and tries to catch them. They blow into her eyes and stick to her eyebrows. She keeps walking, occasionally looking back to see what's happening to her footsteps. The hedge is no longer there, and she has no idea whether she is still on the path. The headmistress's house is on the road behind the sports field. Since she can no longer distinguish the path, Charlotte decides that she might as well take the shortcut over the hill and along the park until she gets to the tennis courts. She is struck by how quiet it is. There's no one outdoors and the only sound is the crunch of snow under her feet.

She starts up the hill. She almost loses her footing with every step. She didn't expect it to be so slippery. She has to use her hands to make any headway. The snow is cold, but that's the only way she can continue climbing.

At the top of the hill there's a strong, cold wind, and flakes of snow blow straight into her face. Her hands and feet are ice cold. Charlotte remembers the story about her grandmother, whose feet were frozen during a snowstorm, and who died without anyone shedding a tear for her. Would the girls in her class cry if they found her dead in the snow? Iris would, she hoped. But she wasn't sure about the others. Provided they were able to find her, that is. She sees that the snow has now covered everything. She wishes she had the big clock with her, just like her grandmother. Then she could hide inside it, to get out of the snow.

Charlotte starts down the hill; she falls, slides, scrambles up, stuffs her hands into her pockets, but has to take them out again to get back on her feet. She can't see a thing. The world around her is white and black at the same time. The other girls are drinking hot chocolate and listening to the story of Mary and Joseph in the stable. Charlotte has no idea where she is and doesn't know whether to go right or left, forward or backward. She'd like to find a spot and stay there, but the thought of her grandmother's blackened frozen feet and her death, propels her onward. She peers ahead, but the snow that blows into her eyes is piercing.

Then she bumps into something. A tree, a pole, a wall? It turns out to be a tree, which means she has reached the park.

She must take care not to go into the park but to follow the road leading to the tennis courts. She trudges on, one step at a time. Her hands and feet are numb. If only she'd followed the path with the lanterns. She shields her eyes with both hands and peers into the distance. A light is burning. She begins to run in that direction, but the first long stride sends her sprawling, and she hits her knee on a branch hidden under the snow. She cries out, but there's no one to hear her. She slips and slides toward the light. Sometimes it's there, sometimes it disappears. She rubs the snow out of her eyes. She totters. The smell of a smoking chimney comes wafting in her direction. That means she's close to a house and warmth and people. She sees a lighted window. She pounds on the door with both fists. She hears someone coming. The door opens and a pair of hands pull the snow-covered girl into the hall and close the door behind her.

Shocked, the woman looks at the blue lips and red eyes of the unrecognizable child. "What on earth were you doing outside alone?" she says sternly. "Have you lost your senses?"

Charlotte feels the warmth of the hall and the woman's hands as they unbutton her coat, and she smells the aroma of stew. She thinks of her grandmother, whom she never knew, and her father, who always said, "A true Bridgwater doesn't cry." Suddenly she realizes that her father has no idea what snow is like, and cannot understand how much it can hurt. And that he couldn't know that his mother didn't cry, because he was still a baby when she died. "I came to get Mrs. Blackburn's reading glasses," she sobbed.

1946 Bombay ~

He looks lovingly at the most beautiful woman he has ever seen. Since the day before, they haven't spoken a word. They have only made love. Peter feels that he has known her for years, that there is no need for her to speak, to tell him who she is, why she is here. Her long hair glides over her shoulders as she looks up at him and smiles.

She strokes his leg. There is a large scar below his knee. With her fingertip she gently traces the ragged, swollen line of the poorly healed wound. She senses that it is a miracle that he still has that leg, that it is painful, that he doesn't want to talk about it, that she mustn't ask him any questions, that he will tell her about it when he's ready.

There is a knock at the door. They look at each other questioningly. The magic of the past night is suddenly gone. Shyly, Charlotte wraps a bath towel around her naked body. She pulls the curtain aside. The morning light, which for hours has been trying to creep into the room, finally appears, making a sparkling entrance. Quickly Peter draws the sheet over himself. Charlotte walks to the door. She looks back at him, smiles, and turns the key.

The door is pushed open, knocking her backwards. She immediately recognizes the uniformed figure who steps into the room.

He looks at her, is momentarily at a loss for words, and then recovers himself.

"Charlotte?"

She nods.

"How you've grown."

She is conscious of her breasts and thighs, which are still fiery. "Did you get my note?"

Now he is the one who nods. He doesn't know what to say. His daughter is not the girl he expected to find. Before him stands a beautiful woman. She looks like Mathilda, the same eyes and narrow lips. For an instant he thinks that he could fall in love with her if he didn't know who she was. Charlotte runs a hand through her hair, just like her mother used to do, and smiles shyly. *How beautiful she is!* Then he takes a step forward, into the room, and his eyes go to the bed. His mouth falls open and his swagger stick shoots upward. Suddenly, from nowhere, the adrenaline races through his body. He searches for words, drops of saliva appear on his lips, his nostrils flare.

Charlotte pulls the towel around her tightly, and a cold shiver passes from her feet and up her spine, leaving behind a trail of gooseflesh. The overpowering scent of their love-making fills the room, and vague memories of long ago fill her with dread. The light, which a moment before had come dancing into the room, shines hard and ruthlessly. The bed is a tangle of pillows and sheets. The floor is littered with garments. At her father's feet lies the captain's cap. She knows intuitively that he has to control himself to keep from trampling on it.

Peter, naked and vulnerable, looks at the man standing in front of him. Even without the lieutenant colonel's uniform he would have known instantly that the soldier with the swagger stick was her father. He pulls the sheet up to his chin. He can't take his eyes off the man by the door. He knows for sure that he's seen him before, but can't remember where. Then he feels a sudden stab of pain, and beneath the sheet his whole body convulses. He gasps for air.

The father and the daughter do not notice. They see only each other.

Victor looks at the fine hairs on her neck, damp with perspiration, and is aware of a rutting smell combined with the intoxicating aroma of his daughter. His blood charges through his body. He hears his own breathing and feels sweat on his palms.

~

THEY HAD GOTTEN up early, put canteens of water in their backpacks, and set off up the mountain. Seldom did they spend more than a half-hour together: the duration of the evening meal. Victor looked at his father's back, and saw his large steps. When he asked his father if he could slow down a bit, the answer was, "We're not a couple of old ladies."

They were standing close to the edge; below them was the abyss. The toes of William Bridgwater's boots extended over the edge — an edge so sharp that it seemed to have been sliced off with a knife. They surveyed the panoramic view and the clouds above.

"Son," his father said after a while. "This is the mountain."

"Which mountain, Father?"

William spread his arms wide, as if he was showing his son his future land. "The mountain that was the death of your mother."

Victor looked around. It was an ordinary mountain, no steeper or more terrifying than other mountains.

"We loved each other, Elizabeth Charlotte Elphinstone and I. We were made for each other." His father's personal revelations made Victor feel uncomfortable. He wanted to walk on, but it was clear that his father expected him to listen. "Did I ever tell you that we weren't married? That we simply did not have time to get married? And yet God knows that she was my wife, and that I have always been faithful to her."

Victor, who had just turned sixteen, had shaved that morning, for the very first time. He looked at his father and saw that there were tears running down his weathered face.

"She was beautiful . . . so beautiful . . . my dear Elizabeth . . ." William Bridgwater turned to his son. The tears were flowing even faster now. "Son, if you hadn't been born prematurely, she would have lived."

Victor thought he must have misunderstood his father's words. Until then he had assumed that his mother had died of cholera, malaria, or some other deadly disease. His father never talked about his mother. Victor knew only that the grandfather clock had belonged to her and that she wanted him to have it.

His father looked up at the sky. The sun was just emerging from behind a cloud. He let out a bestial howl and jumped.

Victor saw him take off, like an elegant swimmer diving into a river: his arms straight in front of him, alongside his head, and his legs extended. The wind froze the echo, which seemed to last forever. Until the body dashed soundlessly against a rock, rebounding in silence into the depths, leaving behind a faint, red trail and coming to a stop hundreds of metres below.

After a half-hour it had still not moved. Victor turned around and walked down the path.

~

VICTOR LOOKS FROM the naked man under the thin sheet to his daughter and says, "You're getting married today."

1947 Ganga Yamuna Express ~

Dear Donald,

I have wonderful news to report. I'm married! The fact that you're only now hearing the news isn't strange, since we didn't have a party. We've only known each other for a short while, but Father thought it was better to get married right away. My husband's name is Peter Harris. He's a surgeon and he also fought in the war. It's lovely to be back here, although I'm still not used to the heat. It's a shame we couldn't see each other before I left. I had hoped so much that we could meet, but the man I talked to on the telephone said that the road to your school had been washed away. Didn't that mean a lot of inconvenience? Now that you're twelve, do you get to transfer to a smaller dorm, like I did back then? Or don't they have them where you are? Right now I'm sitting in a first-class train carriage. It's a real luxury, and servants come by to ask if there's anything you want. I had quite forgotten what it was like to have servants around all the time. At my school we had to make our own beds. Do you have to do that where you are? Shall I ask Father if you can come to India this summer? Maybe we could pay for the trip. I'll talk it over with Peter. Could you have a photo of yourself taken? All I have is that photo back when you were really young. I want to show Peter who my brother is, although I don't really know either, since it's been so many years since I last saw you. Father hasn't changed at all, except that he's a bit older and has more stripes on his uniform, but he's still wearing the same boots. Peter and I are going to live in New Delhi, since that's where he works, in a hospital. I've never been to Delhi, but it's supposed to be a really beautiful city. It's not easy to write when the train's rocking back and forth, so I'll close now.

Bye-bye,
Your sister Charlotte

1995 Rampur ~

A PICKUP TRUCK was heading up the driveway. There was a table in the bed of the truck that looked exactly like the one Charlotte had sold four months earlier. She didn't recognize the man at the wheel, and waited in the salon for Hema to come and tell her who he was. The truck stopped near the entrance to the kitchen; the driver hopped out and went inside. He re-emerged about ten minutes later, together with Hema. He lifted the table out of the truck, leaned it against the outside wall, and drove off. Hema went back into the kitchen. Charlotte picked up the phone and called him. She was not used to things happening without her knowledge.

"Who was that?" she asked Hema when he walked in.

"Mr. Sukumar. With a table."

"I didn't order a table."

"You didn't, memsahib?"

"No. Why should I buy a table if we don't need one?"

"He said, 'Table for memsahib.' I thought it was okay."

"Well, it's not."

The phone rang and Hema answered it. "Mrs. Nair," he said with his hand over the receiver.

Charlotte sighed and took the receiver.

"Has it arrived?"

"What?"

"The table."

"Oh, did the table come from you?"

"No, it's not mine. I borrowed it from the wife of the chief of police. She has generously offered to lend it to you temporarily."

"I don't need a table."

"No, but the *darzi* does."

Charlotte was about to protest, she wanted to tell Mrs. Nair to mind her own business — and that she had plenty of tables — but then she realized that she had sold almost all of the tables in the house.

"You don't mind, do you?"

She asked herself how the wife of Nikhil Nair knew that there were no longer any large tables in the house. What else did the woman know? Now she understood her husband's interest in the clock, and her proposal to have the *darzi* live on Charlotte's premises. "No," she said, "but I haven't decided if I want the *darzi* to work here."

The wife of Nikhil Nair sighed. "You're not going to leave us in the lurch, are you? You can't do that. Where else can he go? We're counting on you, and so are the Wednesday-morning ladies and the ladies who play tennis on Friday. And it appears that the ladies who seldom come to the club also want new evening dresses. The organizing committee called me especially to let me know. It's unthinkable that the celebrations can't go ahead because there are no accommodations for a simple *darzi*."

"I don't think that would happen," said Charlotte, who considered the wife of Nikhil Nair a difficult person who always exaggerated. However, she added, "But very well."

The wife of Nikhil Nair cheered, and in the background Charlotte heard the wife of Ajay Karapiet call out, "Hurrah!"

"On one condition." Charlotte tried to make herself heard. "That people don't come to the house. That would be much too upsetting, you must understand that."

"Yes, yes, of course. We won't disturb you, quite understandable. We'll be no bother to you. No bother at all," the wife of Nikhil Nair assured her, and hung up the phone.

1995 On the way to Rampur ~

IF HE HAD known that his name was Madaṇ and that his parents would not have parted with him for the world, he would never have been cycling to Rampur with a sewing machine on the back of his bike. His tires were almost flat and the bicycle pump he had borrowed and forgotten to return was broken. The road to Rampur was full of potholes. It was used by hundreds of trucks, which sent clouds of diesel exhaust fumes billowing into the air, as well as by ownerless cows that chose to relax and chew their cud on the cracked asphalt, rickshaws carrying women who were busily fanning themselves as they headed for the market, taxis whose drivers couldn't advance a single metre without honking their horns, men pushing handcarts piled so high that they couldn't see the road in front of them, cavorting children, buses determined to pass every vehicle ahead of them, old people sauntering in the direction of the temple to say a prayer, mopeds so heavily laden with buckets and tubs that the drivers were invisible, goats — as well as chickens, crows, and rats — searching for something tasty in the omnipresent street litter, open car windows and drivers seeking a breath of fresh air. And cyclists like Madan, who had piled all their earthly possessions on the back of a bike in the hope that they could earn more in the next town. The car wheels often grazed the colourful wares of the street vendors. It was a question of give and take. The road belonged to everyone.

Calmly, Madan pedalled on. A cousin of the family for whom he'd made bridal outfits the previous week had heard from his wife, who had heard from her brother, a doctor who specialized in nail problems, that in Rampur a *darzi* had suddenly died and there was an important party coming up. An important party meant new clothes, and new clothes meant work and food.

Madan loved the tailor's trade as if it were a woman. A length of cloth sliding through his fingers excited him: the nap of the velvet, the sheen of raw silk, the texture of diamond cloth.

A lorry sprayed pitch-black smoke in his face: bitter, half-burned diesel oil. His eyes, nose, and throat smarted. Madan tried not to inhale until the lorry had passed him, but an ambling cow brought traffic to a standstill. The driver leaned on his horn as the cow bent her head to the ground and snuffled around in a mound of rubbish. Madan got off his bike, trying to manoeuvre it backwards, together with its awkward, top-heavy load. It was not easy, since the surface of the road was full of ruts, which became deeper each year after the monsoon and were never repaired.

A man with the physique of a boxer was standing by the side of the road, seemingly unaffected by the clouds of exhaust fumes. He looked in the direction of Madan, who was unable to back up. "Need some help?" he asked after a while.

Madan nodded, relieved. Hands the size of coal scuttles picked up the bicycle and lifted it over the cracks and fissures, manoeuvring between two rickshaws and a honking taxi, and put it down on the cement stoop alongside the road. Madan smiled his gratitude to the stranger and took back his bicycle. He couldn't lean it against a wall, and if he let go of the handlebars, it would fall over backwards, so Madan simply nodded again to the man and walked on, pushing his vehicle past the small shops, each with its own profusion of articles displayed out front. He had to keep his hands on the handlebars, so there was no need to restrain his lightning fingers when he passed a crate full of shiny apples.

1946 Grand Palace ~

THERE WAS ONLY one extra dress in her suitcase, in addition to her school uniform. It was pink, with stripes, and that was the dress she was married in. Father said it was nonsense to buy a wedding dress, and Peter wore his uniform. Few words were spoken, and it was all over before she knew it. She did not remember the details of the train trip, alongside the quiet captain whom she could now call her husband. The journey ended at a small station where a luxury car was waiting for them. In silence, the chauffeur has taken them to a palace that is even larger than her former school, the renowned Queen Victoria College.

She is led into the *zenana*, where women in nightgowns and colourful saris are lounging or lying on beds. Every movement produces a tinkling sound that emanates from the bracelets on the women's wrists and ankles. There are single and double beds, three-quarter beds, children's beds, and even two four-poster beds, as well as sofas for reading. Everywhere she looks, Charlotte sees women, girls, and young children. There is no discernible order or system. Peter has remained behind with the maharaja; they greeted each other like old friends. Charlotte, who is accustomed to a dining hall with long wooden tables, where girls in grey school uniforms speak diffidently and at a whisper, stares in amazement at the chaos that prevails in the women's quarters. The women are lounging on couches and beds covered in costly fabrics; some are doing each other's hair or makeup. In one corner three girls are reading a book together, and a grey-haired old lady is sound asleep in a bed in the middle of the immense room while a female servant fans her with a fan made of peacock feathers.

A girl, only a bit younger than Charlotte herself, puts out her hand and says, "My name is Chutki."

"My name is Charlotte." She shakes the girl's hand.

Several women join them. The news that Peter Harris has married a young Englishwoman in Bombay came as a shock to everyone except the maharaja, who merely nodded, mumbling that his astrologer was the best.

"Are you really and truly married to Dr. Harris?" says a heavily pregnant woman in perfect English. She proves to be the wife of the maharaja.

"Yes," says Charlotte softly. She can scarcely believe it herself.

This produces an animated hum of voices throughout the room. The women crowd around her. One woman picks up her hand and points to her finger — no ring.

"We haven't had time," says Charlotte.

There is a hiss of disapproval. A man who cannot buy jewellery for his wife is not a man.

"Doctor Harris is a good man," says a woman with a large nose-piercing.

"He's a *handsome* man," says a girl with full, red lips.

"He thinks too much," opines a woman with dark-ringed eyes.

"We thought he would never get married," contributes an older woman wearing a red sari.

"Was it a big party?" someone asks in a low voice.

"We didn't know anything about it," another woman says, crestfallen.

"We would all have come," says the woman with the nose-piercing, and others echo her words. The element of reproach is unmistakable: Harris sahib got married and they were not invited!

A cry sounds. The women turn around and look at the heavily pregnant maharani. Wide-eyed, with her hands on her stomach, she is standing in the middle of an ever-widening puddle. The other women rush over to her. They are all talking at once, in a language Charlotte has never heard before. The moaning wife of the maharaja is led away. Female servants are summoned, the pool of liquid on the floor is carefully mopped up, and flower petals and drops of essential oil are strewn on the spot, while two women go over to the wall altar by the door and break into song and the woman with the nose-piercing pulls her sari over her head and crawls onto a bed. Chutki is the only person still standing next to Charlotte. She takes her hand and leads her away.

THEY WALK THROUGH corridors and large rooms. Charlotte has never seen such a gigantic building. Each room is more luxuriously furnished than the previous one. Everywhere deathly quiet servants dart off when they pass by. Charlotte would have liked to stop and watch, but the girl walks on. They go up a flight of stairs that takes them to another corridor. Upstairs there are all sorts of rooms and halls with costly furniture and wall decorations. They stop in front of a large wooden door and then enter the room without knocking.

Along the walls there are shelves filled with costly fabrics in magnificent colours. A man is sitting on the floor in the middle of the room; in front of him is a hand sewing machine. The man is turning the wheel and sewing. Chutki says something to him and points to Charlotte.

He gets up, walks over to where Charlotte stands, bows his head, and greets her with his hands in front of his chest: "*Namasté.*"

Charlotte returns his greeting. He takes the tape measure hanging around his neck and stands behind her. He takes her measurements without touching her, but with great precision.

"What is your favourite colour?" asks Chutki.

In the past few years Charlotte had scarcely worn anything but her school uniform, which — like everything in England — was dark and dreary. Now she is overwhelmed by the brilliance of the fabrics around her: blue, purple, green, yellow, red, pink, and orange in all shades. There are both solid and patterned fabrics. Some with embroidery, miniscule beads, or sequins. She looks around her at the shelves filled with dazzling fabrics. So many piles, so many colours, so many shades . . . Would Peter prefer pink? Or blue? He said he liked her blue hat. And what colour would she look best in? At school no one ever talked about colours. Her head starts to spin — until she sees a roll of pale green silk under a pile on the topmost shelf. It looks just like the evening dress her mother once wore, floor-length with a low-cut neckline. Charlotte points to the top shelf. The *darzi* follows her gaze and his stick goes to the pile. Charlotte nods enthusiastically when the tip of the stick reaches the green fabric. The man takes a ladder and climbs to the top. He pulls the roll out from under the pile and drapes it over his arm. The long, supple length of fabric reaches to the floor. Charlotte lets the material glide through her fingers.

"Do you like this one?" Chutki asks.

"Is it really all right?"

"Gaurav makes all our clothes. Just choose something. Father would do anything for Doctor Harris."

"Why?" Charlotte asks softly, and again she realizes how little she knows about her captain.

"Doctor Harris is a good doctor, he knows everything about throats. We were always in pain and now we have no more pain, and Papa can even sing again, but only when I dance."

"Did he operate on both of you?"

Chutki nods enthusiastically. "Here in the palace. Papa didn't want to go to a hospital, and Papa always does everything just the way he wants. Now he wants you to have an evening dress."

At the top of the ladder the *darzi* waits patiently, with the long, pale green length of silk over his arm.

"Is this the one you want?" Chutki asks.

"Yes," says Charlotte with conviction. She wants to look just as beautiful as her mother.

THE WOMEN'S QUARTERS are empty. Only the old woman in the bed in the middle of the room is still there, but she's asleep. Her *punkah-wallah* is also dozing off. Charlotte walks over to the table next to the window and pours herself a glass of water from an insulated flask. Peter told her that he had something important to discuss with the maharaja, but she has no idea how long their discussions will last. The water is delightfully cool and quenches her thirst. Outside she sees that a car has just arrived. Two servants hurry out to the car carrying parasols. A man with a case gets out. He goes into the palace and everything is quiet again. On the vast lawn in front of the palace a crow pecks listlessly in the grass, and in the room a fly drones. Charlotte walks over to the open door on the other side of the room and peers into the narrow corridor. She doesn't know where Chutki has gone. Some distance away she hears noises and women's voices. She walks into the corridor, her footsteps muffled by the high-piled carpeting. She hears a cry. Charlotte starts and doesn't know if she should turn around and go back or keep on walking. At the end of the corridor a woman wearing a nurse's cap and a white apron appears, carrying a large pan of sloshing water. She disappears into another room. The cries mingle with women's voices: it sounds as though they're cheering someone on. Charlotte feels like an intruder, and yet she cannot withstand the temptation to get closer to the maharani in labour. The cries and groans increase in volume, as do the encouragements. Then it is still.

She peers into the room. A nurse is holding up a baby covered in blood. Her eyes are turned away from the newborn, but when she catches sight of the pale English girl in her pink striped dress, she gives a start.

Charlotte sees the pitiful creature she's holding in her hands: a wizened little face with closed eyes, two wet legs with tiny feet, a piece of the umbilical cord and, underneath, the scrotum.

The nurse lets out a scream and ducks behind a folding screen.

Another woman glares at Charlotte and roars, "You're not allowed here! Go back to the big room!" She gestures toward the end of the corridor.

"I'm sorry, I . . ." Charlotte stammers and turns around.

"Is she gone?" groans the maharani, still covered in blood.

"Yes," says the woman who sent Charlotte away.

"What was she doing here?" she sobs. "Why didn't someone stop her?"

"Chutki was supposed to stay with her, but she disappeared."

"Did she see it?" the mother asks, in between sobs.

The woman with the nurse's cap bows her head contritely. The mother begins to shriek again, and covers her face with her hands. The other women come running with wet cloths and water, and light incense sticks around the bed, murmuring that they will do extra *pudja*.

"Why my child?" the mother sobs. "Why?"

The nurse casts a worried glance at the others and motions them to leave. "Do you want to see it?"

The maharani moans. "If you all close your eyes."

From behind the screen the nurse again produces the baby, provisionally swaddled, without looking at him. The other women also avert their eyes.

The maharani takes the child in her arms and pulls aside the swaddling cloth. "A son," she says, and her lip trembles. Her glance goes from the little penis and the rust-coloured scrotum between his legs to the tightly closed eyes and balled fists. "You, my son, will never find happiness."

The baby opens its mouth and begins to wail.

1995 Rampur ~

Hema swept the area adjacent to the kitchen where the *bobajee* and his wife had lived. The room had not been used in years: the windows were grey with dust and the shutters were jammed. Memsahib never entered the servants' quarters, and this building was exclusively his domain. He knew that rooms that weren't visited regularly contained secrets. Every time he pulled aside a chair or box, he expected to find a snake or a scorpion, but the only inhabitants were a colony of giant ants that had set up house in the wall under the window, black and green beetles in the cabinet, and the pink dust larvae that had almost devoured the mattress. He dragged the remains of the mattress outside, threw burning coals onto it, and covered them with an old newspaper. The mattress immediately caught fire and the entire nest was exterminated. He swept the beetles outside and poured boiling water into the ant nest. The insects ran off in all directions. Hema, a devout Hindu and strict vegetarian, abhorred this massacre. In the past the *mali* had carried out such chores, but now they were among his duties. Hema was pleased that someone was coming to live in the servants' quarters, even though it was only a tailor, who did not fall under his jurisdiction. He missed the responsibility and the prestige he had always enjoyed. Being boss over a household that didn't include other servants was like being "a farmer without land," the neighbours' butler had once said to him. The arrival of the tailor would mean more visitors, although he understood from his memsahib that she was not planning to receive any of the ladies in the big house. That would entail too much commotion. He washed his hands under the faucet, filled a bowl with yogurt from the refrigerator, stirred in some sugar, and took it with him to the nursery.

CHARLOTTE PUT DOWN the telephone. The wife of Adeeb Tata was leaving for their summer house in the hills this weekend. She wanted to deliver an ironing board for the *darzi* before she left this evening. If at all possible, the members of the club all moved to the high hills in the summer, to escape from the blistering heat. As this was something Charlotte could no longer afford to do, she spent many hours a day lying listless and bathed in sweat on her bed in the darkened house. Every morning, after sunrise, Hema closed the windows and shutters, so that the all-devouring sun could not enter the house. Charlotte watched the hypnotic rotation of the fan above her head. Her thoughts turned to the aged *punkah-wallah* she used to have, who had to wave his *punkah* without a break. He often fastened the string to his big toe, and sometimes he fell asleep. If the general caught him sleeping, he knew he was in for a rude awakening. He'd threaten the man with immediate dismissal, whereupon the slightly built Indian began to pull the cord as if possessed, and the room gradually became cooler. But after lunch, when stomachs were full and the temperature reached its zenith, everyone fell asleep, including her father and the *punkah-wallah*. Her eyes closed and the memories became dreams.

From a thousand metres under the surface of the sea, a sound came bubbling up, a sound that awakened her. It was a while before she realized that she was not inside a submarine, and that the doorbell was ringing. She listened, wondering who was crazy enough to be standing at her front door and ringing the bell at this time of day. The wife of Adeeb Tata would never come before dark. The doorbell sounded again. Despite Hema's reputation, she suspected that at this particular moment he was fast asleep, like everyone else. With a sigh, she crept out from under the mosquito net. The heat had taken over the house and now lay over her like a clammy blanket. Her limbs failed to respond, as if bewitched by some magic formula. Slowly, she made her way to the staircase. The clock ticked languidly, and even the wooden banister was sweating.

When Charlotte put her hand on the door handle, every fibre in her body seemed to shout, *Don't open the door! Don't open the door!* She turned the knob and, with an effort, pulled open the creaking door.

The bright sunlight blinded her and the scalding air billowed into the house. She was about to slam the door when she saw the contours of a body. Her reaction was totally opposed to her own rules — never invite a stranger into the house — but she said, "Come inside. Quickly!" She took a step backwards, into the shadow. The figure on the doorstep, who by that time must have been almost charred, stepped inside. She slammed the door. She couldn't see the person she had just let into the house. It was dark in the hall, and the glaring sun had left flecks of white light in her eyes.

THE SECRETARY OF the club had told Madan that he would be working in the big house on the hill, beyond the main road. He had left his bicycle standing against the wall of the New Rampur Club, in order to take a midday nap like everyone else. But the gardener made it clear to him that only club members were allowed on the grounds, so Madan got onto his bike and pedalled off at a speed that suggested that the broiling sun didn't bother him.

The last part of his journey, up the slightly sloping hill, was tough, but the colonial house with its thick walls and closed shutters beckoned. Madan loved houses — after years of sleeping on the street, in constant fear of being robbed, he found that he slept differently with walls around him. While he was on the street, he had never dreamt. He slept only a few minutes at a time and woke often to check on who or what was there before dozing off again. With walls around him, sleep took him to unfamiliar lands and people he didn't know. At the bottom of the stairs he leaned his bicycle, with the sewing machine on the back, against a small column that had lost its statue, and walked up to the large door.

From a distance the house had looked quite distinguished and prosperous, but now, as he went up the stairs, he saw that the marble steps were cracked and there were chinks in the walls. He pulled the bell and heard it jingle inside. Madan liked bells and closed doors. They, too, gave him a sense of security. He knew that somewhere in the house a servant would awake from a dream, unable to fathom why anyone would be ringing the doorbell at this time of the day. It would be a while before it dawned on him that it was the doorbell that was ringing, so Madan pulled it again, to wake the servant from his dream. After a while he heard a shuffling sound and the door opened.

He started. Before him stood a small white woman with grey, curly hair. Her eyes blinked against the fierce glare, she was barefoot, and she had apparently just been awakened from a deep sleep. She was fragile and pretty, almost as if she were made of glass. Beckoning, she told him to come inside quickly.

Madan had never been inside the house of a white person before and he wasn't sure what to do, but the woman was already shutting the door again, so he stepped over the threshold.

Slowly, among the flecks of light in her eyes, the figure of an Indian man took shape: he was forty or thereabouts, and his hair stuck out in all directions. His forehead was sweaty and there was dust from the roads clinging to his face. He was wearing a magnificent green shirt. He didn't look at all like the men at the bank or like the court usher. She wasn't expecting a buyer out to make a killing, and the man didn't have a basket of fruit or other wares with him. He couldn't be a servant or a coolie who worked for one of the club ladies, since they were always simply dressed and never came to the front door. He held his right hand over the left and stared shyly at his shoes.

"Would you by any chance be the tailor?" she asked suddenly.

Madan nodded, still staring timidly at the ground.

"It's not this door," she said in a clear voice. "You have to go down to the kitchen. There's a room prepared for you."

Madan knew English, but the woman spoke much too quickly, so that the only word he caught was "tailor." She walked down the marble hall to a small door near the stairs; opening the door, she beckoned to him. She went ahead of him in the direction of the outside door. At the end of the corridor, the blazing sun shone through a windowpane. Madan saw the female contours of her body through her thin clothing. He quickly cast his eyes to the floor, feeling as if he'd been caught looking. The woman pushed open the glass dividing door and walked into a little hall, where a bucket and a broom stood.

"Hema!" she called in the direction of a small building he hadn't noticed while he was cycling up the hill.

HEMA, TOO, WAS rudely awakened from his afternoon nap. He was at a wedding feast and was just about to bite into a crisp pastry when he heard his memsahib's voice. He sat upright, and heard his old bones creak. He crawled from his mat and went to the door. Outside he saw her walking with a man. A man who had a light tread and was wearing a magnificent green shirt and white trousers. Who was he? Hema had never seen him before. He wasn't from the bank: he knew all of them. Suddenly Hema felt a pang of anxiety. He must be another buyer. Memsahib wanted to sell the stove, and from then on he'd have to cook over coals, or — even worse — the man had come to buy the whole house . . .

They entered the kitchen. "This is the tailor. Will you show him his room?"

This man could not possibly be a tailor. Sanat, the old *darzi*, and the *darzi* in his native village never wore such beautiful clothes and didn't walk the way this man walked. The motions of his hands were strange, too. As if he were constantly smoothing something. Hema was overcome by an uneasy sensation.

"Welcome," he said amiably in the local language as he opened the door.

1947 New Delhi ~

THE SITTING ROOM is muggy and, in her recollection, much warmer than it used to be in the big house on the hill. After spending the morning at the hospital, Peter is napping on the sofa under the window, as he does every day after finishing lunch and reading the newspaper. Charlotte, who regards afternoon naps as something for old people, usually sits outside on the veranda with a book. But today it is so hot that she has been driven indoors. She looks at the man she is doing her utmost to love. Above his head hangs the crystal chandelier with the red stones. The sparkling rubies scatter tiny droplets of light that pass across his face. His hair is stuck to his forehead and his breathing is deep and irregular. Charlotte wishes she could look inside his head to find out what he's thinking, what he feels and dreams. They have been married for six months and still he has told her nothing about the wound on his leg or his missing finger. She knows that he was born in Manchester, that he went to university in Leeds and then returned to Manchester, where he completed his doctoral research in the back streets of the city, that he left for India immediately after getting his degree, that he worked in the same hospital where he is presently employed, until the war, when he was called up and sent to Burma. Peter refuses to talk about the war. The only thing she has ever gotten out of him is that he was in the jungle for a while and that he never wants to go back.

His fingers flex in his sleep, as if he is trying to grasp something. Charlotte goes over to him and, very gently, places the back of her hand on his forehead. He starts, and his fingers begin to move faster. Quickly she withdraws her hand. Then his feet also begin to twitch.

"Hush, my darling," Charlotte whispers, "it's me."

He awakes with a cry and stares at her, panting and distraught. His hands are clenched into fists and he's trying to swallow. She strokes his hand. The panting subsides and a spasm of fear passes over his face.

"Did you have a bad dream?" As always, she waits for the moment when he will tell her what happened in his dream. He doesn't know that she watches him for hours on end while he's asleep, that she sees how he waves his arms and kicks his legs about, shouts and cries. Charlotte has never before seen a man cry before. Her father taught her that crying is a sign of weakness and that one must never shed a tear in the presence of others.

"My father is going to be in Delhi next week. And he's finally coming to see us." Peter's muscles immediately tense under her caressing hand. "Don't you want him to come?" she asks in surprise.

"Of course I do," he says. He gets up, in order to escape the touch of her hand.

"But if you don't want him to?"

"Why should I not want him to come?"

"I got that impression."

"No, of course not. When is he coming?"

"He didn't say." Charlotte looks at Peter.

He pours himself a glass of whisky and finishes it in one draught.

~

The table is set with the Wedgwood service, a wedding present from the maharaja, and the cook has done his very best. Peter is slicing the roast beef. A good piece of roast beef is not easy to come by in a country where beef is seldom if ever eaten.

"You ought to have that knife sharpened," says Victor.

Peter nods and goes on slicing. The warm juices flow from the meat onto the wooden plank.

"A knife like that will ruin the meat."

Charlotte looks at her father, who, from the moment he walked in the door, in uniform and with a swagger stick under his arm, has provided a running commentary on everything his son-in-law has done. Peter, who is wearing civilian clothes, goes on slicing the meat without looking up. The silence is uncomfortable and Charlotte casts around for a neutral topic of conversation.

"You were in Burma, too, weren't you?" her father says out of the blue.

Charlotte sees how Peter stiffens. He tries to continue, but the knife sticks in the meat.

"What unit were you with?"

"The fourteenth," Peter murmurs.

"So," says Victor, with a look that says nothing but suggests a great deal. "Did you cross the Irrawaddy River, too?"

Charlotte, who is just as interested as her father, looks at her husband. She sees the colour drain from his face as he stares at the roast beef in front of him with fear in his eyes. Very slowly, he nods.

The old man stares into his son-in-law's face, which he has not seen since the meeting in the hotel room and the accelerated wedding ceremony. He is searching for something he recognizes.

Then Peter puts down the knife, turns his hand, and shows Victor the missing little finger.

Now it is the old man who turns pale.

"Will you have some roast beef?" his son-in-law whispers, and holds out the platter with the sliced meat. His hand is shaking. Victor cannot take his eyes off Peter's mutilated hand.

"It's really excellent beef, Father," Charlotte says, when she sees that her father has not served himself.

~

Dear Donald,

I wish you a happy birthday and hope that this year it's really going to work out and you can spend your vacation here. I've talked it over with Father, but he's afraid that you'll miss too much school if you take two extra months off. I told him that a lot of children whose parents live in India take longer vacations, but he still didn't think it was a good idea. But I'm not giving up. It can't be good when you never get to see your family. Later, when we have children, I'm never going to send them to boarding school. Not even if they turn out to be really difficult children. Here in Delhi everything is much bigger than in Rampur. The roads are wide and there are lots of big buildings. Would you do me a favour and have your picture taken? I guess you forgot. I'll enclose some extra money in the envelope. Part of it is for your birthday and the other part for the photo. I would love to see you again. I think that Father would, too, so could you have two prints made? Sometimes I can't even remember what you look like. When I went away, you were a year old, and now you're thirteen. Maybe I won't even recognize you when I come to pick you up! I hope we'll soon be seeing each other.

Your sister Charlotte

1995 Rampur ~

ALONG WITH THE ironing board, the wife of Adeeb Tata had left behind a list with the names of all the women who wanted to make use of the services of the new *darzi*. Naturally, the name at the top was that of the wife of Nikhil Nair. Charlotte knew that she had drawn up the list and passed it on to the wife of Adeeb Tata.

She called Hema and asked him to send the tailor to her. He stood near the door, his head bowed slightly. "What's your name?" she asked.

He took a business card out of his chest pocket and handed it to her. Charlotte had never heard of a tailor who presented his card at the first meeting. Wholesale buyers had cards, and businessmen, and the men at the pawnshop, but not artisans or manual workers. It was a simple card bearing the text:

MUKKA — TAILOR

"Mukka. Is that your name?"

Madan shook his head no.

"Can you read? What a stupid question: of course, a tailor with a card can read."

Madan shook his head.

"That's all right," said Charlotte, relieved that there was at least one thing about this man that was normal. She took the list and began to read out loud. "You'll start with Mrs. Nair; she lives behind City Hall in a big house with a red front door. Then you go to Mrs. Singh; she lives two streets behind Mrs. Nair. There's always an old Ambassador parked in front of the house, with her chauffeur. After that, you go to . . ."

Madan listened to the warm, soft tones of the woman's voice. He didn't know her name, since she hadn't introduced herself. He peeked at her face from under his eyelashes: she was wearing reading glasses, and she moistened her lips with the tip of her tongue while she read from the piece of paper.

And again it was there, his first memory, which kept returning at the strangest moments. For a long time he had thought it was a dream, but the emotions and the images that he saw before him were so lifelike that he had concluded that they must be real. He was in pain, a lot of pain, and he'd fallen asleep. At the very moment he woke up and opened his eyes, he looked straight into the face of a white woman, a beautiful woman, who was like a princess. He felt her warm arms close around him, and her red lips had kissed him. She had smelled like jasmine.

"Can you remember all that?" Charlotte asked.

Madan's daydream evaporated. He hadn't caught a word of what she said, and had no idea where he was supposed to go. But he nodded.

"You start with Mrs. Nair in the house with the red door. You show her the list, and she'll help you with the rest."

Madan stood up, took his leave with the usual slight bow, pressing his hands together in front of his chest, and departed.

THE HAND-SEWING MACHINE, a heavy black Singer, was sitting on the table in the middle of the room. Next to it lay a large pair of scissors and a piece of chalk, as well as a small bottle of sewing-machine oil that the *darzi* had used that morning. On the floor lay a sleeping mat and a sack with a few clothes. Hema stood next to the ironing board. He looked around the room, which was otherwise empty. The man hadn't uttered a word, merely nodded or shaken his head when he asked him a question. Hema had hoped that something of the old atmosphere would return to the kitchen, now that he was no longer alone. But he felt uncomfortable in the company of the *darzi*, whose name he still didn't know. Not that the man bore him any ill will. On the contrary, he was quite friendly and smiled the whole time. But Hema was always eager to hear stories and gossip from other cities and villages.

The bell rang. Hema hurriedly put his *beedi* out in the ashtray, a habit that memsahib did not approve of. Then he picked up the bowl of yogurt and walked over to the big house.

Madan rang the bell next to the red door. A uniformed servant opened the door. He gave the man his card. The man read it, glanced up at him in surprise, and let him in. The hall was full of antique furniture, each piece with its own pink satin cushion. Madan waited by the door as the servant disappeared behind one of the hanging carpets. The house was delightfully cool inside. On a small table next to the door there was a silver vase with a few flowers. Nearby stood a candelabra, also made of silver. He heard someone walking upstairs. Next to the candelabra lay a silver comb. Madan could not keep his eyes off the precious objects. He thrust his hand deep into his pocket and stared fixedly in another direction. A plump woman in a bright pink dressing gown entered the hall. She was holding his card in her hand. Her eyes went from him to his card and then back to him.

"Can you hear?" she asked, after some hesitation, but in a loud voice.

Madan nodded

"Oh, thank heavens." Then she turned and started down a hallway, saying, "Follow me."

The room they entered was spacious and even cooler than the hall. On the table lay a length of pink Chinese silk.

"I want this made into an American evening gown," said the wife of Nikhil Nair in a loud voice.

With a thrill Madan picked up the material and ran it through his fingers.

After the sale of her china service, Charlotte had filled the empty spot in the sideboard with the unread books from Reverend Das. She shook her head in irritation. No matter what she tried — rearranging the sideboard, having tea, tallying up her loans, thinking about the monsoon that should already have started, or about her father — her thoughts kept returning to the silent tailor. The telephone rang and the widow Singh asked her what time the *darzi* would be at her place, since she wanted to play mah-jong at the club. She'd only just hung up when the wife of the police commissioner was announced and entered the room carrying an ironing board. The woman looked around inquisitively. Charlotte had told her that there was already an ironing board, and that the tailor was doing the rounds of the houses, taking everyone's measurements.

"My place as well?" asked the wife of the police commissioner, and hurried back to her car.

Charlotte had barely closed the door when the telephone rang again.

"My, what a strange man," said the wife of Nikhil Nair. "But I'm glad he can hear."

"What do you mean?" asked Charlotte.

"Because he's dumb."

"Dumb?"

"Yes, didn't you know?"

"No," said Charlotte in amazement.

"It's on his card. *Mukka* means "the mute." But he can hear. Did you notice how he handled the material? I've never seen anything like it, they say that the blind have extra senses, maybe he does, too, now if only he knows something about sewing, I have a very costly length of cloth, you'll keep an eye on things, won't you, he seems quite respectable, but you never know, and it is already half a metre shorter than it was . . ."

He can't speak. The thought echoed through Charlotte's head. Stupid of her not to have realized earlier. The milkman's eldest son was dumb, and he did the rounds with his brother. He was a tall, lanky boy, and when he was trying to make something clear, he would resort to high-pitched, bestial sounds. For a long time she had thought the boy was retarded, until one day he helped her to get her car started when it was acting up again. The retarded beanpole was suddenly transformed into a clever deaf and dumb boy who needed to make only a few adjustments under the bonnet of her car to get it started again. She'd been ashamed of herself, and she gave him a generous tip.

Charlotte pulled the bell above her bed.

Hema came into the room with a cup of coffee.

"Did you know that he can't speak?"

"Who, memsahib?"

"The new *darzi*."

"No, ma'am, he doesn't talk."

"Thank you for the coffee."

She wished he'd leave the room. Today, everyone got on her nerves.

CHARLOTTE HOPED HEMA hadn't noticed that she'd been up in the attic, rummaging around among broken chairs and torn boxes. Somewhere there was a bag with a length of fabric, she was sure of it. Everything of any value had been snapped up by the first wholesale buyer. Back then, it didn't occur to her that he would not be the last.

That was the month the cyclone raged over Andhra Pradesh, taking more than ten thousand lives, many years ago now. On the radio she heard how the miserable huts were swept away and how the rivers had overflowed their banks. There were dead bodies everywhere, floating on the surface, but people still waded through the water with the last of their possessions on their heads. She had an attic full of stuff that no one used anymore. Initially, she wanted to give it all away, until the man from the bank arrived with the letter that changed everything. After that she had opened all the envelopes and kept track of all the bills. On the advice of the man at the bank, a wholesale buyer had come and taken everything away. First from the attic, later the rooms on the first floor, and ultimately the ground floor. She had become a master at rearranging furniture and accessories in order to disguise the empty spaces. She knew she could get used to anything. And once in a while, when no else was around, she played Schubert or Mozart. She placed her fingers on the edge of a table and closed her eyes. And as she played, she listened to the music in her head. That brought her some solace.

She slid two boxes apart and saw the bag with the length of silk. It was still there!

1952 Bombay ~

EVERYWHERE THERE ARE people shouting "*India zindabad*! *India zindabad*!" Madan looks around, wondering where the others have gone. They were there a minute ago. All around him, he sees nothing but men's legs, all going in the opposite direction. No one pays any attention to him. Then he catches sight of his sister's blue coat. He tries to get closer, but then the blue disappears among all the legs. Every time he thinks he sees someone he knows, he is shoved aside by some man shouting enthusiastically. He is in pain. The unknown legs propel him forward, but he wants to go back. He wants to find his sister. He's reeling on his tiny legs. Everything hurts. A fat man in a brown *longhi* passes him. He is drawn to the man, with his solid build and measured tread. He feels safer behind the big man, who smells like horses. The little boy follows him without the man noticing. Suddenly the man stops and bends forward. Madan presses his whole body against the man's back. He's frightened by the wild cheering and the dancing throngs. "*India zindabad*!"

Madan sees that the man is drinking water that's spouting from a pipe. He's thirsty, too. When the man walks on, Madan tries to drink, but he can't reach the pipe. He stretches out his hands and manages to catch a few drops, which he licks from his hands. He wants more water, but he is pushed aside. He turns around, but the fat man in the brown *longhi* is gone. Now a man with a black beard is holding his mouth over the spouting water. Madan looks at him, in the hope that the man will pick him up, so that the water will spout into his mouth, too. But the man growls something at him in a language he doesn't understand. Madan is pulled backwards and carried along by the thousands of legs around him. There is no sign of his sister.

THE THRONG OF people begins to thin. The men fan out into the side streets and the shouting ebbs away. Again Madan sees a car go by, and a horse and cart. He's tired and in pain. Across the street, under a tree, he sees a boy drinking out of a bottle. Madan crosses the street without looking. A car honks angrily. Madan doesn't hear it. All he sees is the boy who's drinking water. He goes up to him and points to the bottle.

The boy, who's slightly older and taller than Madan, looks up. "What do you want?"

Madan stands motionless.

"Go away." The boy takes another swallow. "Get out of here, I said!"

He doesn't move. "Have you ever been kicked?" The boy looks at the small figure standing in front of him. There's blood all over his shirt. He has a wound beneath his chin; it's covered by a bandage where something glitters. He isn't wearing pants and his feet are bare. His lips are dry and there is fear in his dark eyes.

"I suppose you want a swallow."

Madan nods.

"And then you can piss off." The boy gives him the bottle and Madan begins to guzzle it down. "Hey, you're not supposed to finish it."

Madan goes on drinking.

"Did you hear me?" The boy snatches the bottle from his hands. "Are you deaf?"

Tearfully Madan stares at the half-empty bottle in the boy's hand. He is already walking away.

When the boy looks over his shoulder, he sees that Madan is following him.

"Scram," he says, and again he makes a dismissive gesture with his hands to reinforce his words.

Briefly Madan stands still, but when the boy walks on, he continues to follow him. The boy crosses the street and so does Madan. He tries to ignore the wound and the pain. His little legs avoid the potholes in the street, he jumps over a sewer pipe in a narrow alley, and he has to climb over a wall. He feels that the wound in his throat is bleeding again.

The boy stops at the entrance to a park. Slowly Madan walks in his direction. "Are you still thirsty?" the boy asks.

Madan nods. The boy gives him the bottle and he pants as he drinks.

"Hey, leave some for me."

Madan hands him the bottle.

The boy finishes what is left and asks, "What's your name?"

Madan doesn't answer.

"If you want to be friends, then you have to tell me your name."

Madan starts to cough, bringing forth only a few hoarse sounds. He points to the bleeding wound under his chin. The boy stares at him in amazement. Madan tries again, but cannot produce anything intelligible, only groans.

"Can't you talk?"

Tears appear in his eyes.

"Are you going to start bawling?"

Madan shakes his head.

"Go ahead and cry, if you want. You're still a little kid."

Madan gives the boy an angry look, shakes his head, and holds up six fingers.

"You're six."

Madan gives him a proud look and nods.

"And I'm eight." The boy sits down on the ground, under a large tree, and motions to his newfound friend to come and sit next to him. Together the two of them watch some boys who are playing cricket nearby.

"My name is Samar, and I'm going to call you Mukka." He looks at Madan. "Is that okay?"

1995 Rampur ~

CHARLOTTE EMPTIED THE bag with the length of silk onto the coffee table. The fabric, which once, long ago, had been destined to become a ball gown, disintegrated at the slightest touch. Peter had finally promised to go dancing with her. But every time they were invited to a dance, he found a compelling reason not to attend and begged off at the last minute

— there was an emergency at the hospital, a terminal patient unexpectedly began to hemorrhage, he had to go to Bombay on short notice, or he himself was suddenly struck down by a severe headache and stomach problems. Once she was so angry that she called a taxi and went by herself, but the gossip that made the rounds later was so nasty and malicious that from then on she accepted his excuses and stayed home.

She gathered up the scraps and threads and stuffed them into the bag. As the remains of a fantasy faded away, she resolved that, no matter what, she would attend the festivities attired in a beautiful gown.

Suddenly she felt the presence of someone on the other side of the door. She was certain of it. Someone wanted to enter. She hadn't called Hema, and he knew that he was not allowed to disturb her unless she summoned him. She jerked open the door.

There stood the tailor, head slightly bowed, his hand poised to knock. He bowed his head even lower, making apologetic gestures with his hands.

"Why are you eavesdropping at my door?"

I wasn't eavesdropping, he wanted to say.

"I do not wish to be spied upon, and certainly not by someone who is not permitted to enter this house," she spat out.

Madan made a gesture with his right hand, as if he was turning the wheel on his sewing machine.

Charlotte was furious. She pointed to the door every bit as icily and implacably as her father.

You have to help me: my sewing machine is gone. He went on gesturing with his hand, and there was panic in his eyes. *Listen to me! Listen!*

Charlotte turned and pulled the bell cord. She would ask

Hema to send the man away. It had been a bad idea from the beginning, and now that he refused to leave the salon, she could not stand his presence on the premises one more minute. If the women were determined to have new dresses, then they would simply have to find a workplace themselves. She didn't even have enough money for a new piece of fabric, let alone a ball gown. What was taking Hema so long?

The tailor was still standing on the threshold, desperately making turning motions with his hand.

"Is there something wrong with your sewing machine?"

Madan nodded violently, his hair flying in all directions.

"Is it broken?"

He threw his hands into the air, to make it clear to her that the machine had disappeared.

"Is it gone?" she asked in surprise.

He nodded and showed her his empty hands.

"And you don't know where it is? It's no longer in your room next to the kitchen?" No one except Hema ever entered the servants' quarters. She never went there herself: that would have been unseemly. "Have you looked everywhere?"

Madan had looked everywhere. He had walked into the room and seen immediately that his machine had disappeared. The table and the ironing board were still there, but his scissors, his chalk, the bottle of lubricant, and his Singer sewing machine had disappeared. His heart had started to pound furiously. Never before had anyone moved his most precious possession. He took exceptionally good care of his machine, as if it were his child. He had searched every room in the servants' quarters, even that of the old man who functioned as a factotum. He had raced outside in the hope that he would find him in the garden. But then he noticed that the back door of the big house was open. That's where the man was! Madan entered the big house, knowing that he was not permitted to simply walk in. That had been made quite clear to him. But the theft of his sewing machine was more important. The woman must realize that. That morning, while he was taking the ladies' measurements, he had heard that her name was Charlotte Bridgwater, that she seldom went to parties and no longer gave any, that she never received guests, and that she was an excellent pianist but had sold her grand piano.

Charlotte gave the cord another yank. It irritated her that Hema had not yet arrived. At this hour he'd normally be in the kitchen, preparing lunch. "Did you ask the butler?"

Panic-stricken, Madan shrugged his shoulders. His face was distraught as he tried to tell her that both his sewing machine and the man had disappeared.

Charlotte walked over to the window, drew the curtain aside, and pushed open the shutter. The excruciating heat and the blinding sun hit her square in the face. With one hand half shielding her eyes, she peered outside. She expected to see Hema trotting toward the house, but she saw only a bare expanse of dry grass and the odd crow pecking at the ground. That was all. Then she heard the sound of stumbling in the hall and, behind Madan, appeared the face of Hema.

"I called three times!"

"I was upstairs, memsahib."

"Is there a problem?"

"No, ma'am, everything okay."

"Do you know where the *darzi*'s sewing machine is?"

"Yes, ma'am, in the *mali*'s shed."

"In the *mali*'s shed? Why?"

"Ma'am, the shed is better for work."

"Are you out of your mind? The shed is hot and dirty! There are holes in the roof, and snakes."

"The *mali* says that it's a fine house."

"The *mali* is dead. I want you to put the sewing machine back. Now!"

Hema bowed humbly. "Of course, memsahib, of course."

Charlotte watched as the two men walked across the grass in the direction of the shed. Hema had never done anything without asking. Was he failing, too? She closed the shutters. It would be too hot to sit in the salon for the rest of the day.

1953 Rampur ~

THE BUTLER IS waiting at the station with five coolies. She's glad her father hasn't come to fetch her. She adjusts the black veil so that it covers more of her face, hoping that no one can see her eyes. Two bearers slip into her compartment, carry the dozens of suitcases outside, and then load them onto the waiting handcart. Charlotte doesn't look at them. She is interested only in the coffin that is being unloaded from the last wagon. A simple wooden casket containing Peter's body. The men tie cloths over their noses and mouths before loading the coffin onto the cart. Father told her she was hysterical, that it wasn't done, but Charlotte insisted that her husband be buried next to her mother.

She has visited her mother's grave only once before — in the second year of her marriage, during her first visit to her parental home. She walked down the hill to St. Stephen's Chapel. The cemetery was behind the church. She was alone and had no idea where the grave was. She searched and searched among the sagging tombstones and overgrown shrubs. Just as she was about to give up, she saw a stone with the inscription:

MATHILDA BRECKENRIDGE BRIDGWATER
1915–1938

She had never known exactly how old her mother was when she died. She never asked. When she saw the dates on the tombstone, she realized that she was exactly the same age as her mother was when she died. The tears welled up out of nowhere. She threw herself on the stone, encircling it with her arms, shedding all the tears she had been longing to shed, tears for the years of loneliness at school, the longing for a mother, the punishments administered by her father while she was still a child, the brother who was sent to a boarding school in a different city and whom she was never allowed to see, the war experiences that Peter refused to talk about, her childlessness . . . She could not stop the tears: they drenched the tombstone.

The cart carrying the casket is ahead of them. The butler tells the men to walk more slowly and with more dignity. Even at a distance of five metres she smells the penetrating odour of decomposition. Peter's scent disappeared long before he died. They walk up the hill leading to the big house. She is unaware of the faces at the windows of thc houses as they pass.

Dressed in black, with her face hidden, she is someone else. Ever since the night she was awakened by the horrible screams.

He was foaming at the mouth and his eyes were wide open. She tried to calm him by saying his name softly. He didn't seem to see or hear her. She had no desire to see what he was seeing, for fear of triggering the same nightmares that plagued him. His screams were growing louder and he fought off her caresses. His heartbreaking sobs were without tears. Again and again she spoke his name, as a kind of calming mantra, but she could no longer reach him. He drifted down into the merciless deeps, dragged down by sharp claws that would not let loose and had already torn him apart. From far away, there arose an imploring cry for help. She begged him to stay, not to leave her, told him that she loved him. That she would never desert him. And she was lying when she said that she wasn't afraid. His screams were louder now and definitive. The cries filled the room, the house, the street, her heart. Then everything was still.

He was gone, along with her dream of having children and finding happiness together.

THE *MALI* IS standing at the door with a bunch of flowers in his hand. He doesn't dare look directly at her face. He had never looked directly at her. He knows that she is sad, and that she is trying not to cry. They're tiny yellow flowers.

The garden is full of flowers: there's a border all along the driveway, around the house, in front of the veranda, and alongside the terraces. But Charlotte has never seen those tiny yellow flowers before. She accepts the bouquet and the *mali* shuffles back to the Lloyds, which stands in the middle of the lawn, humming softly. She goes into the house. She knows now that she will never leave.

Dear Donald,

This is a letter with very sad news. I don't know exactly how to tell you . . . sometimes I can't even believe it myself . . . but Peter is dead. He'd been ill for some time. I didn't tell you because I thought that it would pass. Even the doctors didn't know what it was. His body was healthy, they kept saying, but it was in his head. It was the war. I don't know what happened during the war, but it must have been something horrible. With Father, you never really notice that he fought in the war. Sometimes I think he wasn't even at the front, that he just told us he was, but then I realize that I'm imagining things. They didn't give him a medal for nothing. I'm in Rampur now. I didn't want to stay in Delhi or Bombay. I thought it was right to bury Peter next to Mother. Although I sometimes wonder whether it was such a good idea. Father was quite angry when I told him, but I didn't pay any attention to him. Peter was my husband. It's very sad that we didn't have children. Sometimes I feel so lonely. It would be wonderful if you could finally come to India, before you start university. I can tell from the photo that you've turned into a fine young man. It's strange to think that we are sister and brother, but I know that it's true. And I feel it in my heart. It's good for me to be with Father for a while. Will you promise me that you'll come? I can pay for your passage. I have enough money, now that I've sold our house in Delhi. So I'll sign off now, my dear brother. I hope to hear from you soon.

Your sister Charlotte

1952 Bombay ~

MADAN AND SAMAR lie close together underneath their rag. They take turns keeping watch and trying to get some sleep. Madan, who is now on watch, falls asleep. A fat brown rat sniffs at his hand. It finds the piece of bread in his clenched fist and starts to nibble at it. Madan opens his eyes, sees the rat, and screams, but the sound that comes from his throat is no more than a shrill groan. The rat scurries off. Madan looks anxiously at his friend, who's asleep, his head resting on a stone. He sits up, afraid of dropping off again. The spot they discovered, behind a wall in an empty shop, cannot be seen from the street. Madan picks up the stick that his new friend found that afternoon and grasps it tightly. He's afraid that rats can smell blood and that they'll bite him. He puts one hand on the wound in his neck, just above his chain. It still hurts, but the bleeding has stopped.

There is the sound of voices. Madan dives to the ground. Samar has told him that no one must see them. He scrambles back under the rag. Still as a mouse, he lies there next to his friend as the voices and footsteps come closer. *Keep on going, keep on going.* He edges closer and closer to his friend, pushes the chain around his neck under the bandage, and closes his eyes as tightly as he can. The men stop; they're laughing, and they speak a language that Madan doesn't recognize. He hears someone light a cigarette, the match falls to the ground and someone spits. Then they move on. He senses that Samar is now awake as well: his whole body is suddenly hard and tense. The voices disappear, and it's quiet again. The boys are afraid to move. They hold their breath and cling to one another.

After two minutes that seem to last a whole night, Samar whispers, "They're gone." He crawls out of the hiding place and looks around to see whether the street is really empty. When he crawls back under the rag, he whispers, "Mukka, we were really lucky. If the police had seen us, they would have taken us away and thrown us into jail. If that happens, we're dead."

~

UNDERNEATH THE STATION is a narrow corridor reserved for the railroad workers, but if they hold in their bellies, Samar and Madan can just manage to slide underneath the gate. After the lights go out and the men close off the entrance with a large padlock, they crawl under the gate and into the corridor. Halfway down, they discover a crate full of rags, and for the first time in weeks Madan sleeps the way he remembers sleeping — not on the hard ground, but on something soft.

He wakes in the middle of the night. Where is Samar? He looks over the side of the crate, but it's too dark to see anything. He waits and listens. He hears a few noises, but nothing that sounds like Samar breathing or peeing. Madan checks the bottle of water near his head; it's full. Did Samar get hungry and decide to go out and look for something to eat? Surely he wouldn't do that without him. Madan climbs out of the crate. *Where are you?* He feels along the ground to see if his friend is lying there. Maybe he doesn't like sleeping on rags. On the floor he finds only a few planks and a wheel. Cautiously, to avoid bumping into anything, Madan feels his way back to the exit. As he gets closer he hears more and more noises that weren't audible in the corridor. A car goes by, a dog barks, and in the distance there's the sound of a ship's horn. *Samar, where are you?* He slides under the gate on his stomach.

The alleyway on the other side of the gate is empty except for a cow chewing her cud. Some distance away, a rickshaw passes. Madan walks to the street and looks around. His friend is nowhere to be seen. He goes back to the alleyway with the gate, and slides back inside. *He's probably back in the crate.* He crawls back down the corridor until he reaches the crate. *Are you there?* He feels around. There's nothing there but a mass of rags. No Samar. He calls out: "Samar, where are you?" A high-pitched moan fills the corridor. Madan climbs back into the crate. He doesn't know what to do. He finds the bottle and takes a drink of water. He doesn't want to drink too much. When his friend comes back, he'll probably be thirsty. He puts his hand to his neck. His chain, which according to Samar is made of gold, is gone. He realizes that his friend is not coming back.

1995 Rampur

MADAN'S SEWING MACHINE was back on the table, and the rose-coloured Chinese silk was spread out in front of him. He made tiny chalk marks on the fabric and examined the result. His fingers glided over the fabric, as if it could tell him what kind of dress it wanted to be. Sometimes he pulled the material toward him and adjusted one of the chalk marks. Then he picked up the scissors and started cutting. Not slowly and cautiously, but confidently and at breakneck speed. He tossed the pieces in the direction of the sewing machine.

Hema, who was trying to rekindle the fire, glanced in the direction of the tailor in the adjoining room. Memsahib had been furious with the butler, but the mute was deliriously happy as he took the sewing machine from the shed and put it back on the table in the music room. And after lunch, when everyone else had succumbed to the paralyzing heat and sought a cool place to sleep, the mute had gone on working. Now it was almost dark, and Hema was blowing on the coals. To his relief, he saw them catch fire. He heated the blackened pan over the fire. His memsahib favoured tea the way he made it, from an old family recipe. He filled the pan with water and put it on the burner. He saw the mute sit down at his sewing machine and watched as he started turning the wheel. Like the neighbours' butler, Hema looked down on tailors. But after seeing the mute at work, he couldn't help but feel a certain respect for the man in the green shirt. He worked quickly and without hesitation, while Hema had to stop and think before each operation. The water came to a boil; he added the milk and then reached for the sugar bowl. There was very little left. He would have to ask memsahib to pay Mr. Anand the shopkeeper; otherwise he wouldn't give him any sugar. He carefully sprinkled half the sugar over the white liquid and began to stir to the rhythm of the whirring sewing machine. He heard footsteps on the path. Probably a coolie — several of them had already come by that day, sent by members of the club to deliver extra thread or trim. Some were just curious, hoping for a cup of tea. Nowadays memsahib disliked visitors, while in the past she used to enjoy it when friends came by.

Charlotte walked into the kitchen. She noted that it was unchanged, although she could not remember when she had last been there. Hema jumped to his feet and began rushing around. She told him to calm down and go back to what he was doing. Then she walked into the adjoining room, saying, "I just want to make sure the *darzi* has everything he needs."

Madan didn't hear her come in. It was only with the utmost concentration that the pale pink silk allowed itself to be formed into tiny pleats above the shoulder. With his left hand he exerted the necessary pressure, and with the right he turned the wheel at just the right speed. The "American" evening gown he was making for the wife of Nikhil Nair had nothing to do with America. He knew only that it was a country where everyone had a car and that an American had once landed on the moon, although he wasn't sure whether that was actually true. So he listened to the material and called to mind the figure of the woman who lived in the house with the red door. He would camouflage her protruding stomach and sagging breasts with the pale pink silk.

"Would you like a cup of tea?"

Madan looked up and saw Charlotte leaning nonchalantly against the door frame. She stepped into the room.

"Do you have enough light? Or should Hema see that you get a stronger bulb?"

Hema listened to the words of his memsahib with growing amazement. That same bulb had been hanging from the ceiling for years and everyone who had lived or worked in the room had made do with the light it provided. How did she expect him to come up with more light? She had sold all the extra lamps, and if he tried to replace it with a stronger bulb, the fuse would surely blow.

Madan nodded.

Charlotte couldn't tell whether that meant that he would like some tea or that he had enough light.

He pointed to the ceiling and gestured that the light was fine. She turned to Hema. "A cup of tea for the *darzi*," she said.

Hema looked at the white mass in the pan, stirring slowly. Was he supposed to give the memsahib's tea to the *darzi* or was the tea for her? And did she want her tea there or in the big house? Hema always made the tea so that there was a cup for him, too. But he was afraid to do so in front of his memsahib. He cast a furtive glance into the room and saw how memsahib picked up the fabric from the table and let it run through her fingers. Now that the piano was gone, she was usually in her bedroom at this time of day. Hema had no idea what she did there. He assumed that she slept or read a book. When it got dark and life resumed at the bottom of the hill, she always wanted a cup of tea with a biscuit. Then he opened the shutters and the curtains, so that she could enjoy the evening air and the sounds that rose from the city to the house on the hill. She said something to the mute that he didn't quite catch. Why had she come? Why hadn't she simply called him, as she always did, and asked if the tailor had everything he needed? She would — and he knew this for certain. . . . Hema gave a cry of pain. The pan was boiling over onto his hand. Charlotte came into the kitchen and saw her butler squatting next to the furnace with a small fire on the ground in front of him. "What happened?" she asked in a concerned voice. "Nothing, memsahib, the tea is hot."

"Would you bring me a cup, too?" As she strode back to the house, she made a mental note never again to go to the kitchen unannounced.

1952 Bombay ~

At first light he crawls under the gate, with the empty bottle in his hand. Yesterday he saw where Samar filled it, but without his friend, he cannot find the faucet. He knows it isn't far from the spot where they slept, but every time he thinks he's found it, it turns out to be a hollow pipe sticking out of the ground, or a pole, or a rod of some kind. But not a faucet. If he had a choice, he'd go back to the crate under the railroad tracks. But by now there would be workmen there, with hammers.

An old man with a pushcart almost runs him down and then starts cursing him. A boy carrying a crate on his head casts a friendly glance in his direction. Madan is naked except for his blood-stained shirt and the bandage. He has no idea where to go. He stays close to the walls of the tall buildings, peering into each and every alleyway, hoping to catch sight of Samar, who would know where to find something to eat and drink.

"Freshly baked cakes," a man on a bicycle calls out, "fresh cakes!"

Madan sniffs the enticing scent emerging from the crate on the back of the bike and feels his stomach contract. The man puts his bicycle on the stand and calls out even more loudly, "Cake! Fresh cakes! Bargain prices!" A well-dressed man wearing a hat and carrying a walking stick buys a bag of cakes. A woman with a long braid stops and also buys a bag. Madan approaches the seller and looks at the crate on the back of his bicycle.

"Scram," he hisses. "Get lost. You're ruining my business!"

A shiny car stops, and the window is rolled down. All

smiles, the baker sells another two bags of cakes to the passenger in the car, but as the car drives off he snarls at Madan to make himself scarce.

~

A GOAT IS greedily devouring potato peelings from a pile of garbage. A crow pecks around in the sour-smelling tip. Some distance away, four men are playing cards on an upturned bucket.

"Chai-eeeeee! Chai-eeeee!" the *chai-wallah* calls out. He swings his woven basket full of glasses around and around without spilling a single drop.

One of the card players holds up his hand. The *chai-wallah* hands each man a glass. There are two glasses left in the basket. Madan, half hidden by a pile of boxes, stares longingly at the remaining milk tea. He can already taste its creamy sweetness. The voice of the *chai-wallah* sounds again, as he is eager to get rid of the last glass before it gets cold. Madan, who hasn't had anything to eat or drink for three days, cannot take his eyes off the glasses. A man with a basket full of oranges stops. The boy watches the tea disappear into his stomach in a single gulp. Now there is only one glass left in the basket. The voice of the *chai-wallah* continues to blare through the street. Madan looks left and right. There are no police uniforms in sight. He goes up to the tea seller.

The man is so busy hawking his wares that he doesn't notice the grimy little boy looking up at him so longingly. "Chai-eeeee! Chai-eeeee!" he calls out to the mattress maker, who is busy combing out his cotton and isn't interested in tea.

"Chai-eeeee!" the *chai-wallah* calls. This time he tries to attract the attention of a sugar-cane buyer, but he has his own drink and isn't planning on spending money on tea. He calls out to the man who's repairing a punctured tire and the bricklayer carrying a sack of cement on his head. "Chai-eeeee . . ."

"Can't somebody shut that guy up?" grumbles one of the card players. "How am I supposed to think, with him bawling the whole time?"

"Chai-eeeee . . ."

Suddenly the card player turns around to face the *chai-wallah*, who is just opening his mouth again to sing the praises of his tea. Seeing the card player glaring at him, he grabs the last glass of tea and holds it up. The man shakes his head.

Madan, who is standing right next to the *chai-wallah*, looks up at the glass in his hand.

"Chai-eeeee . . . !"

"Give the tea to the kid and shut your mouth!" He tosses a coin in the direction of the *chai-wallah* and goes back to his cards.

"Him?" says the *chai-wallah* as he effortlessly plucks the coin out of the air. He looks down in surprise at the small, grimy figure standing next to him.

The card player, Ram Khan, is no longer listening to the vendor. He pulls a card from his hand, throws a king onto the pile, and exults: "Gotcha!" With a big grin on his face, he gathers the stack of cards. "Another round?"

They check the time, confer, and finally shake their heads no. The cards are gathered up and returned to the box. "See you tonight, then," says the man, who has just shoved the cards into his pocket. His words are greeted with gruff assent.

Ram Khan walks back to his shop with his stool in his hand. His workspace consists of a kind of cabinet, which is mounted on the wall, in between a man selling kitchen utensils and a coppersmith. He pulls up the cloth he had let down to protect his possessions and places his stool in front of a sewing machine. He picks up a shirt that needs mending from the pile in front of him.

Madan, who has followed his benefactor, watches as the man steps into a kind of closet. On a plank supported by two blocks of wood stands a treadle sewing machine, and behind it there's a large pile of clothes. The man sits down in front of the machine. On the back wall hang several religious prints and a pair of scissors. There isn't room for anything else. The man presses his foot down on the pedal and starts to sew. On the ground, behind the man's feet, is a small pan. Madan isn't sure whether it's empty or holds something he's saving for the evening meal. He decides to stay put and wait.

It's not long before Ram Khan notices that someone is watching him. He peers over the rim of his glasses to the other side of the street, where a young tramp is sitting and smiling at him. Ram Khan has no time for tramps; they have diseases and they steal. He knows that from experience. He gestures to the kid to make himself scarce and returns to his work. Ram Khan was wearing his reading glasses during the card game, and he doesn't recognize the boy sitting opposite him as the one he bought tea for. When he looks up again, he sees that the boy is still there. He picks up the stone he uses to sharpen his needles and throws it as hard as he can in the boy's direction. Ram Khan has never played cricket and the stone misses its target. Madan, whose hunger is stronger than his fear, stays put. Annoyed, the tailor gives the shirt a jerk, but when he presses down on the pedal, the stitching is crooked. He yanks the garment out from under the foot. Peering through his glasses he tries to pull out the stitches, but he has trouble finding the thread in the plaid fabric. Ram knows that his eyesight is deteriorating and that he needs much stronger lenses, but new glasses are expensive. If he messes up on this shirt, he won't even have enough money to buy food for tonight. With his bent fingers, he searches for the beginning of the thread. He's becoming more and more irritated by the boy's stares. He looks around to see if there's something else he can throw at him, but except for his scissors and his slippers, there is nothing at hand.

Madan squats and waits silently.

"Hey, Ram!" One of the card players walks by, carrying a heavy box. "Have you finally got yourself an assistant?"

"What?" growls Ram Khan. He has just found the beginning of the thread and does not want to look up because he is afraid of losing it again.

"Your errand boy."

Ram Khan looks up in surprise. He glances from his friend to the boy across the street. "That little rat has nothing to do with me!"

"If you ask me, he's looking for more. You'd better watch out, before you know it, he'll grab that pan from under your feet. Don't forget . . . if you feed a rat sugar you're asking for trouble."

"Give him a kick," Ram Khan snarls. "Can't you see I'm busy?"

Madan makes himself smaller but continues to stare at the tailor. He's sure that he threw the stone past him on purpose. The man with the box continues on his way, muttering to himself, and in his cubicle the tailor stares at the shirt on the table in front of him with an angry look on his face. Again his gaze is drawn to the filthy child, who continues to stare at him. The boy is wearing a grimy undershirt, and he's covered in dried blood.

Suddenly Ram Khan stands up and walks into the alleyway next to the coppersmith. Madan watches him expectantly. The tailor motions him to follow. He scurries after the man, taking small, quick steps. At the end of the narrow passageway, the alley curves to the left. It's dark, and there is a stench of filth and urine. What little light there is comes from a narrow shaft between the buildings. The man looks threateningly at the boy as he walks up to him. The street noises have disappeared. In front of a decaying door stands a bucket half full of water. Ram Khan points to the bucket. Madan's thirst has not abated after the cup of sweet tea an hour ago, and he goes down on his knees to drink.

Ram Khan gives him a kick. "Don't drink, wash!" With one hand, he grabs a rusty can out of the bucket and empties it over the child. "Wash. Your shirt, too. And when you're clean, come out to the street." He throws the can back into the murky water and strides off.

When the man is out of sight, Madan bends over the bucket and begins to drink. He slurps greedily. The water tastes strange, but it quenches his thirst. Then he throws a can of water over his head and rubs his hands over his arms.

Not clean, but at least wet, he again stands in front of Ram Khan. The man doesn't look up, but continues sewing. Madan waits stock still, watching the man's hands pull the blue cloth through the machine. It's the same shade of blue as his sister's coat. The tailor turns the material twice. Then he picks up his scissors and trims the threads. Without looking, he throws the garment in Madan's direction; the boy picks it up and sees that it's a pair of pants that may fit him.

1953 Rampur ~

"A MAN DOES not simply die. A man only dies by choice . . ."

Through her black veil Charlotte looks at her father: he is in uniform, on the other side of Peter's open grave. The casket has just been lowered and the small group of mourners, heads bowed, are listening to the general's words. Charlotte wants to protest, she wants to tell her father that he's wrong, but she knows that it's true. In this case.

"Peter Harris was a good doctor," Victor continues, looking down at the casket that holds the remains of his son-in-law, "but a wounded human being." Peter's officer's cap lies on the casket, together with a small bouquet of yellow flowers. "I never expected that you would give my daughter back so soon. But . . ." Victor picks up a handful of earth. "I promise you that I shall care for her as if she were my own wife." He throws the earth onto the coffin. It lands with a dull thud.

The others follow, one by one. Charlotte wants to put her fingers in her ears so that she doesn't have to listen to the hollow thud that sounds on the casket and its contents. The thought of burying Peter fills her with despair, now that she is closer to understanding the cries for help triggered by his dreams. Peter was wounded and terrified of suffocating in those dark depths. Why didn't she bury him in New Delhi? Why did she want him to lie next to the mother she had never known? Why hadn't she gone back to England? Why did she return to Rampur? The small group of mourners look in her direction, waiting for her to take a handful of earth and throw it onto her husband's coffin. But she is unable to move. Now she, too, feels the hand that gripped Peter's throat every night during those final months. Her mouth is dry as dust, and she feels as if the breath is being squeezed from her lungs. She gasps for air, fresh air, clean air. She has to get away from this place, away from death and gravestones. Her father clears his throat and looks at her encouragingly. No one can see her face behind the veil. The veil! It's the veil! She pulls the widow's veil from her hat and gasps for air. She feels the eyes focused on her. She bites her lip. Stooping down, she takes a handful of earth from the pile next to the grave and throws it. Half of it hits the edge of the grave; the rest lands on the grass. Fortunately, she didn't hit his coffin.

THE ASHTRAY IS full of half-smoked cigarettes, and a grey haze fills the room. She's ordered the shutters to be kept closed, and her suitcases are still standing in the corner. The old nursery hasn't changed. Her bed with the pink spread is still under the window, and her brother's bed, with the blue spread, is in exactly the same spot as it was seventeen years ago: against the wall of the bathroom. The mat Sita used to sleep on is rolled up and lies underneath the wooden bench, as if she slept on it last night. Charlotte is happy that Sita was at the funeral, even though she stood at the back and didn't speak. She was there. She had always been there during difficult times. If only she could walk into the room now, sit down next to her, and put a reassuring arm around her shoulder. The familiar scent of the coconut oil that Sita rubbed into her hair every morning comforted her. Charlotte longs for a ginger lozenge, a delicacy that the ayah drew from the folds of her sari to treat a skinned knee or a nosebleed. She remembers how the girl used to brush the tangles out of her hair at bedtime: at each stroke she whispered the name of a dream elf. But her father sent Sita away and now she is alone.

Charlotte gets up and walks over to the wardrobe she shared with her brother. It's in the same place, next to the balcony door. And the toy chest still stands in the middle of the room. She lights another cigarette. The familiar objects from her past have a soothing effect. She was flustered by the panic attack at the graveside. Is it possible that Peter's legacy consists of his own demons? She senses that what happened next to the grave was rooted in what he himself went through every night. Could he be floating somewhere above her, trying to tell her that he loves her? Or perhaps he never loved her, and this was her punishment for not having children. She hears a knock. Before she can say "Go away," the door opens.

"What a stink hole!" her father blusters. Without slowing his pace, he strides across the room and throws open the shutters. The setting sun casts its rays onto the bed. "Get out of bed and on with life, that's the only remedy. Sitting around and snivelling about someone who's not coming back won't get you anywhere." He gives the cord on the wall a yank. "I'll see that this room gets a good airing. . . . That'll chase away the worries going round and round in your head."

"Father?" There's a catch in her voice. The general stares at his daughter as if he's seeing her for the first time in her black widow's weeds, sitting on her childhood bed, a cigarette in her hand.

There's so much Charlotte wants to tell him. That the shutters must be closed, that there aren't any "worries" going round in her head, that she has to fight to keep back her tears, that Peter may have been afraid but it wasn't his fault, that she didn't know what he'd gone through in Burma but her father might well know, that she is terrified at the thought that she may have inherited Peter's terrors, that she doesn't know where to go, that there's not a single spot on earth for her except perhaps this room, which hasn't changed since her childhood, that she misses her mother, or at least she misses the time when she had a mother, that she doesn't know what the word "family" means, that she doesn't even know what it is to have a husband, that the passionate night of love in Bombay was never repeated, that she did her best to seduce him but that she never succeeded, that Peter seemed more devoted to his patients than to her, that she feels as if her youth has been stolen from her although she doesn't know by whom, that she is afraid, terribly afraid, of becoming even more lonely than she already is, that when she looks in the mirror she sees a woman she doesn't know, that she . . . "Did you cry when Mama died?"

Victor looks at his daughter in amazement. No one has ever asked him such a personal question in his entire life. He is astounded, and for a moment he wonders if he misunderstood her, but looking at his daughter's face, he knows that he heard her correctly. "Cry? Me cry?" He smiles derisively. "The man or woman who's seen me cry has yet to be born. No, Charlotte, a true Bridgwater doesn't cry. Ever." He is about to add, "Not even when he sees his father jump into a ravine," but he swallows his words. Why burden a child with futilities from the past that are best forgotten?

"I didn't cry when she died either," Charlotte said.

"You see . . . you're your father's child."

"Because I didn't know that she was dead. Because you didn't write and tell me until six months later," says Charlotte.

For a moment it is quiet. Outside a bird is singing and the shrill voice of the samosa vender sounds.

"There was no sense in writing you any sooner," says

Victor emphatically, "no sense at all." Then there's a knock. He looks in the direction of the door. "Just as it makes no sense to sit here and mope in the dark. Come in!" The last words came out louder than he had intended.

A servant in a spotless uniform enters the room. "Did you ring, sahib?"

"Take my daughter's suitcases to the yellow room."

WHEN SHE OPENS the little perfume bottle, she smells her mother's scent. Behind her, the servants are emptying the cabinets in the yellow room. Bags filled with dresses and boxes of women's shoes disappear in the direction of the attic and the nursery. The old closet is now filled with scarves and shawls her mother collected and piles of fabric in different colours. Every drawer, cabinet, and shelf is scrubbed. Charlotte cannot bear to watch. She doesn't want to cry now — fifteen years later — over the loss of her mother. Her father is right. She can't bring her back, no matter how hard she cries.

"Ma'am, should I throw away that bottle, too?" asks one of the servants shyly.

She hands him the perfume bottle, which is almost empty. Noiselessly, he deposits it in a box along with the other bottles and then disappears himself, without making a sound.

"Tomorrow I'm having the room painted green." Her father stands in the door opening. "The smell of paint helps."

He is gone before she can ask him what the smell of paint is good for. When he calls for a painter, his voice resounds throughout the house. Charlotte closes the door. She wants to be alone. She wants to ponder whether she's making the right decision. Should she stay or leave? And if she leaves, where should she go? Where can she go? The empty closets stare at her, just like the mirror where she used to see her mother's reflection. *The green dress, where is the green evening dress?* Suddenly she panics, jumps up, runs to the landing, and stops the first servant she sees. "Where are my mother's dresses? I want to see her green evening gown."

The servant hasn't the slightest idea which dress she means, but he nods subserviently and walks on.

"A floor-length green gown. Pale green, with a low neckline."

"I don't think it would be appropriate to go out tonight," says the general, who is standing behind her. "You buried your husband today."

1947 New Delhi ~

"COME ON, PETER, everyone's out in the street." Charlotte gives the conjugal sheet a gentle tug, but Peter rolls himself even more tightly into his fetal position. "It's a celebration! They're all dancing and singing." Peter pulls a pillow over his head and covers his ears. Charlotte sits down on the edge of their bed. Cautiously she puts her hand on his shoulder. She doesn't know whether to caress him or drag him out of the bed where he sometimes takes refuge. "Peter?" She hesitates. Of course, there's no reason why she can't simply leave, without asking him, and join in the festivities on her own. "Is it all right if I go to the club? I'd like to experience this historic day." She can hear the shouting and rejoicing in the street below. A tremor goes through Peter's body. "Do you want me to close the window? Would you rather be alone?" She gets up from the bed, closes the windows, and turns the fan above their bed to the highest setting. The fan rotates, and a cool breeze descends on them. Charlotte strokes her husband's shoulder. "Are you sure you don't want to come along? Just this once? Nothing's going to happen . . . people are happy, everyone's smiling." His whole body tenses. When he looks up, she sees the terror in his eyes. "I would so love to dance with you, just this once," Charlotte whispers.

With a sudden sweep of his arm, Peter throws the pillow to one side. He shoots out of bed. "Can't you see I don't want to! Do I ask you to do things you don't want to do? I don't want to dance, I don't want to see the cheering masses. Before you know it, all those 'happy' people will be murdering and raping each other, burning villages to the ground, just like in Punjab. Don't you realize what's going on? Can't you see? They are going to go on annihilating each other until there are no Indians left. Yesterday the streets were full of bodies, and you want to go dancing? We shouldn't be dancing, we should be running away. Celebrations! How dare you say the word? Whose celebration is it? Yours? Mine? Theirs?" He points to the street, and the exultant crowds. "Haven't you heard about the charred bodies of children? I fought for them. For them and for our fatherland. Our fatherland!" He spreads his arms. "I fought in the goddamned jungle, without rules, without laws. I know what people are like. What they're really like. I know what charred bodies look like, how they smell. I know what a crowd can do. I know why they're singing. I know their songs. I know them better than anyone. And I never want to hear them again. Never. If we don't get out of here, they'll start to think we're parasites. They'll murder us. Here in this room. In this very bed! Go ahead and celebrate, enjoy your gin and tonics at the club, and dance till you drop.

I'm staying put!" He wraps himself in the sheet and curls up.

Charlotte lets the torrent of words rain down on her like a cold shower. And yet the outburst does not produce the effect he intended. Gradually she allows the words to sink in. This is the first time he's ever spoken of his war experiences. His secret terrors. She wants to ask questions, to tell him that he can share his past with her, but the sight of his back, turned so resolutely toward her, tells her that it's better to leave. And yet she doesn't get up. She sits there watching him, his rapid breathing and his bare feet full of scars protruding from under the sheet. "Where do you want to go?" she asks softly. "Do you want to go back to England?"

1947 Grand Palace ~

THOUSANDS OF PEOPLE are standing in front of the palace and the crowd is still growing. The news that the maharaja is distributing food has reached even the most remote villages. Today there is free public transportation across all of India. More and more people are trying to reach the palace. Many of the cheering men are wearing the Ghandhi *topi*. He is their hero, but they also shout the name of the maharaja, and celebrate the independence of India.

From the window of the women's room, Chutki surveys the swarming crowd in the square below. She holds her baby brother in her arms. He's ill again. He's coughing and has a fever. If only Harris sahib were here. He always managed to solve the problem. He wasn't afraid of attacks of fever and coughing fits. He could always come up with a solution. Her sisters and aunts have already gone to the great hall. Today is a red-letter day and everyone is downstairs, except for Auntie Geeta, who's deaf and half blind. As always, she is lying on a couch, asleep. Even the *punkah-wallah* has left. Chutki lays the baby down next to the old woman. He coughs and wheezes, but Auntie Geeta doesn't wake up. Taking a candle, matches, and a stick of incense from a drawer, she goes into the spacious bathroom, which is empty. She takes down a bottle of eau de cologne from the shelf and a bit of cotton, rolling the objects up in a towel. She returns to the hall, walks to the end, and pushes open the heavy door leading to her father's rooms, where it smells of tobacco and coffee. She knocks on the door of his study, but there is no answer, so she gently opens the door and slips inside. On the desk that stands in the middle of the room, she finds a large box of cigars and takes two of them. In his bathroom she finds a sharp knife, which she hides inside the folds of her sari. Quickly she goes back down the long corridor, up the stairs, and into the working quarters. Along the way, she doesn't see any of the *mehtars* or other servants.

Chutki gives a start when she opens the door: the *darzi* is in his customary place at the sewing machine. "Aren't you going to the celebrations? They're for everyone. My father said so."

He looks disconsolately at the richly embroidered jacket in his lap, sticks the needle into the fabric, and heaves a sigh: "This is for the celebrations."

"Have you got a couple of straight pins for me?"

The *darzi* points to a bowl. "Help yourself."

She runs back to the women's quarters and adds the pins to the objects in the towel. In the big room old Geeta is snoring away and the baby is still asleep. Gently she takes him in her arms. The child awakens and starts coughing. "Shush, baby, shush," she comforts him. "I'm going to make you better." Then she goes into the bathroom and lays the baby on the floor. The cool tiles startle him, but his high fever gets the upper hand. She unrolls the towel and lays out all the objects in a row. Then she lights the candle, drips a bit of wax on the floor and positions the candle. Then she lights the stick of incense and places it on the edge of the bathtub. Through the open window, she hears shouts of *"India zindabad!"* — the cry that for weeks has sounded on the roads and in the villages: Long live India! Kneeling down in front of the child, she closes her eyes and folds her hands in front of her chest. She begins to sing softly, in a barely audible voice. A monotone, slightly nasal song. The baby utters faint cries. She places her hands on his stomach and goes on singing. The crying stops. She moistens a cotton ball in eau de cologne and goes over the baby's hands and feet as she sings to him. Then she takes a pin, holds it over the flame, and then very slowly sticks it into the sole of the baby's foot. He immediately begins to howl and kick his legs. She pins the thrashing legs to the floor with one hand. For a moment she stops singing. "Hush now. I'm doing this for you, to get rid of Mama's curse on you. Hush now, baby . . ." The child begins to scream. She takes the knife and holds it over the flame. "You are going to be happy, I promise you. When she dies." Then Chutki picks up the knife and holds it over the candle flame. In the corridor she hears women's voices, and sees that she didn't lock the door. Quickly she blows out the candle, throws a towel over the objects on the floor, pulls the pin out of the baby's foot, and picks him up. The door opens.

"Oh, here you are! Are you coming? It's already started."

"I'm coming. As soon as I change the baby's diaper."

"Can't the ayah take care of that crybaby?"

"The celebrations are for everyone, including her."

"Oh, that's very sweet of you."

1952 Bombay ~

"WHAT'S TAKING YOU so long, you little rat? Put the pants on." Ram Khan looks down at Madan from his rickety lean-to in a side street of the bazaar. Madan doesn't have to be told twice and quickly pulls on the blue pants. "Here." His grumpy boss hands him a shirt. The collar has to be repaired. The boy is astounded but takes the plaid shirt, which is much too big for him, and starts to put it on. "Hey, I don't want your filthy arms in those sleeves," the man barks. "And I don't want blood all over that shirt. You're going to have to work: you bought a pair of pants from me and you're going to pay for them. Did you think I was the mosque or something? I can barely keep my own head above water, and I'm not planning on taking on yours as well!" Madan looks at the shirt. He has no idea what he is supposed to do with it. "Unpick it," Ram Khan snarls impatiently, "there, on the collar. Can't you see there's a false seam that has to be undone? You ought to be able to manage that, even with those runny eyes of yours."

Madan looks at the shirt. He doesn't see anything strange about it, except that the collar is torn. So he sticks his finger into the hole and pulls, making the tear even larger.

"Not like that, nincompoop!" Ram Khan jumps up from behind his sewing machine, smacks the boy, and snatches the shirt from his hands. "I have to repair the hole, dummy, can't you see that?" He takes hold of the collar and shoves it into the boy's face. A calloused finger with a torn nail points to the faulty seam. "I'm talking about that thread. That's the one that has to be pulled out." He shoves the shirt back into Madan's hands. "Here's a straight pin: now unpick the seam. And don't get any blood on it or I'll give you a thrashing."

Holding the shirt away from his body so he doesn't soil it, Madan carefully inserts the pin under the thread and pulls.

Ram Khan watches in fascination as Madan's tiny fingers scrupulously unpick the thread. Suddenly there's a sparkle in Ram's eyes. If his card buddies could have seen him at that moment, they would have been astonished by his ingenuity. In a single fluid movement, the tailor sweeps the pile of garments off the crate and drapes them over his stool. Then he overturns the wooden crate and opens it. It's full of old rags, pieces of lace, shoulder pads, and bags of buttons. From behind the crate he produces a burlap bag, into which he stuffs the sewing materials. He upends the crate, so that the opening is on the side and the lid forms a door. Then he takes the pile of garments from his stool and puts them on top of the crate. Madan, who needs all his powers of concentration to remove the thread neatly, doesn't even look up. Finally, with a sigh, the tailor places the burlap bag on top of the pile of clothes. His ramshackle shelter seems even fuller than before, as if any minute the whole thing might suddenly become detached from the wall.

Peering through his spectacles, Ram examines the collar and sees that the crooked seam has totally disappeared. "Next time give your paws a better wash." He puts the shirt on the sewing machine.

Madan looks up at him hopefully. He is hungry.

"Don't think one piddling chore is enough to pay for your pants. Besides, you still owe me for the tea and the use of the washhouse."

Madan looks at him in alarm.

"It's your choice: either pay me for everything now, or work it off."

Madan opens his mouth; nothing comes out but a shrill throat-clearing sound.

"Oh, no! A mute!"

Madan shakes his head and gives it another try, but all he can produce is the same hoarse sound.

Ram Khan sighs: Why does all his luck have to be bad? The other stall holders in the bazaar have errand boys. When he finally finds someone who'll work for nothing, the kid turns out to be an idiot. Madan pulls at his sleeve. For a second it looks like the tailor is about to give him a clout on the head, but then he sees that the boy is pointing to the pile and smiling up at him.

"So you want to work. And it's a good thing, too, since it doesn't look like you've got any money." Ram Khan, who's never had a servant before, immediately feels more important. He points to the crate. "That's your patch."

Madan peers into the crate: if he pulls up his legs, he can just fit inside.

"When I call, you come. And when I don't need you, you keep the door closed."

Madan, who has spent so many long, sleepless nights alone on the street, cannot imagine a better spot. He immediately crawls into the crate.

Ram Khan watches him in amazement. He had expected resistance, and even thought he might have to give the boy a whack first. "And don't come out until I tell you to," he repeats. Then he closes the door.

Madan immediately pushes the rickety door open again. Before Ram Khan has a chance to explode in anger, he points to the small pan that is still standing on the floor behind the stool.

"Okay, go stuff yourself."

Madan grabs the pan and takes it with him into the crate. Then he shuts the door.

It feels good inside the small, dark space. Vague noises from outside penetrate the walls. He holds the pan between his knees. He can't see what he's eating: the sparse light that comes through the crack in the door isn't enough to distinguish anything. Not that that bothers him. He eats — or rather devours — the entire contents of the pan. It's gone all too quickly. He could polish off another pan, but he knows he'll have to wait until the boss gives him some more. He licks the pan clean. Then he pulls up his knees, puts the pan between his feet, and waits. He doesn't know exactly what he's waiting for, but he's sure the man would be angry if he opened the door. Madan doesn't even want to leave the crate. He's happy to be sitting where it's safe and no one can see him. He hears and feels the sewing machine in action. The plank on which the tiny store rests sways gently to the rhythm of the pedals. He hears someone greet his boss. Peering through the tiny crack, he sees a pair of feet in worn-out sandals. The voices are discussing the cricket game that's due to start that morning in Madras.

Everything has changed so quickly. Not long ago he awakened in the arms of the white woman, who kissed him. He had been in pain and she smiled at him and cuddled him. She put the chain around his neck, the chain that was made of real gold, according to Samar, and then called out that he was bleeding. She smelled like jasmine. His first thought was that he was in a garden full of flowers. The pain wasn't actually part of that. He remembers his sister, in her blue coat, and he still cannot understand why she hadn't stayed with him. Why did she go away? The wound under his chin has started to bleed again. He presses his hand against his neck and listens to the monotone voice of his boss. Slowly he falls asleep.

"Hey, *mukka*!" The door is yanked open and the boss pulls him out of the crate. "I don't pay you to sleep all day!" He thrusts a broom into his hands and says, "Sweep!"

Madan, still in the middle of a dream, squeezes his eyes shut against the sunlight. "My whole store," Ram Khan says, and he grabs his stool and disappears around the corner.

"I've taken him on," Ram Khan says to the other card players, with something like pride in his voice.

"Who?" grunted the man who'd warned him never to give a rat sugar, and who was now trying to keep his mind on the game.

"That kid."

"Oh."

"He's got good eyes and skinny fingers."

"Gotcha." The man throws down his cards and triumphantly rakes in the pile.

Ram Khan looks at his cards in dismay.

"That'll teach you to cut the crap," says the winner.

"Another round?" asks Ram.

When Ram Khan returns to his shop he sees Madan sitting on the edge of the plank. He cannot believe his eyes. The tiny construction wedged between the kitchenware shop and the coppersmith seems to have undergone a transformation. Not only is the floor clean, but the sewing machine gleams. The boy looks up at him, his face beaming.

"Finally got yourself a boy?" the coppersmith asks.

"Only if he works hard, otherwise he's out of here," replies Ram Khan, hiding his surprise.

"I'll take him off your hands," says the coppersmith.

"He belongs to me." Ram Khan picks up the bottle that Madan has been carrying around with him for days. "Here, go fill it up."

Madan takes his bottle over to the bucket, by then almost empty, and carefully pours the last bit of dirty water into the bottle.

When he returns, the boss lets down a kind of metal shutter in front of the store. Holding up the lower part, he says, "Make it snappy, I haven't got all day. Inside with you, and don't forget your bottle."

Madan crawls between his boss's feet and back into the shop. Ram Khan slams down the shutter. In the crate it's pitch black. He hears the boss attach two padlocks on the outside before walking away without a word.

1995 Rampur ~

"WHAT I DON'T understand," said the wife of Nikhil Nair as she bit into her biscuit, "is why she never remarried. She was still attractive when she became a widow."

"She's still attractive now," said the wife of Ajay Karapiet, adding a dash of milk to her tea.

"Yes, but not as pretty as she was when she was young.

Shall I turn the air conditioner up a notch?"

"No, turn it down. I'm cold."

The wife of Nikhil Nair got up and turned the knob next to the door. "She used to be quite desirable, when she was young."

"I don't agree with you there. She's still quite attractive."

"Because she's white."

"I don't consider all white women good-looking, but there's something about Charlotte Bridgwater. . . . She has a kind of translucence, and she's just as distinguished as her father." The wife of Ajay Karapiet took a sip of her tea, and then added some more milk.

"You shouldn't put so much milk in your tea. It's not good for you."

"What do you mean? Drinking milk makes your teeth white. Just look at Charlotte."

"She drinks her tea boiled with milk, just like her personnel."

"Not the English way, like we do?" said the wife of Nikhil Nair. "How do you know?"

"I heard it from my cook," said the wife of Nikhil Nair.

"But that means that she takes milk in her tea, too."

"That's what I'm telling you . . . boiled! That way it doesn't have any effect on your teeth."

"Well, if you ask me, it doesn't make any difference whether it's boiled or not. Drinking milk strengthens your teeth. That's what my father always said, and he heard it from the general. They were on the tennis committee together."

"You don't have to drag General Bridgwater into it."

"I wonder how things are working out with the new *darzi* in the house?"

"Isn't the man a bit strange?"

"Well, there is something about him . . ."

"What's the matter with you today? All of a sudden you think everyone is attractive and special. Are you in love or something?"

The wife of Ajay Karapiet blushed. "No, of course not."

"That's all right then. I don't like women who hang their dirty laundry out in public."

"I have a washing machine."

"That's not what I mean."

"Well, what do you mean?"

"I'm just saying that I want nothing to do with women who . . . well, you know what I mean. Like Brinda."

The wife of Ajay Karapiet put her hands over her mouth. "I would never do anything like that."

"No, I know you wouldn't." She held out the plate of biscuits, but her friend shook her head. As always, she took a second one herself.

"And what if Priya Singh had a lover? She's also been a widow for fifteen years."

"Priya Singh?" The wife of Nikhil Nair almost choked on her biscuit and began to cough. "Good gracious, she's asleep most of the time. How could she have a lover?"

"Charlotte Bridgwater was twenty-three when she lost her husband," remarked the wife of Ajay Karapiet, in a melancholy voice.

"Yes, that's what I mean: it's strange that she never remarried."

"There are no more Englishmen around."

"She could marry one of us."

"One of us?"

"Well, why not? Don't give me that anti-colonial stuff.

Your great-great-grandfather was an Englishman married to a Bengalese woman, and the grandfather of Alok Nath the goldsmith was Scottish and his wife was from Orissa."

"Yes, but they were men."

~

CHARLOTTE TURNED ON the radio to catch the news.

> This morning a courier with Sheppard's Stockbrokers was held up by a man waving a knife in Nicholas Lane in London. The attacker, who was wearing a dark tweed overcoat and cap, grabbed the briefcase, and escaped on foot. The attack is the biggest street robbery ever carried out. The briefcase contained close to three hundred bearer cheques, with a total value of 292 million pounds.

Charlotte heaved a sigh. With that much money she could install air conditioning in the entire house. "A seismographic team from Japan," the BBC newsreader continued, "has announced at a congress in São Paulo that they have developed a device which makes it possible to —"

She switched off the radio and tried to concentrate on the book she was reading. Every time she got to the end of a page, she realized that she hadn't actually been reading. She blamed the suffocating heat, which became more intense with each passing day. The wind and the grey clouds that usually announced the monsoon were nowhere to be seen, and even the crows were sluggish. Only the cuckoo and the tailor seemed oblivious to the heat. She anchored her reading glasses more firmly on her nose, slid closer to the light, and started over again at the top of the page. *If Peter were still alive,* it suddenly occurred to her, *where would we be living now? Would we have gone to England?* Cold, grey England, where the sun never shone, suddenly seemed like a paradise on earth. *Then everything would have been different. Everything!* She shook her head, in an effort to banish such thoughts. *The ruby has to go to the jeweller's, I shouldn't keep it here in the house much longer, it has to be appraised by several different jewellers, and I have to pay Sita.* She tried to go back to her book, but her thoughts kept interfering. *The money I gave Hema this morning to pay the shop-keeper . . . wasn't it on the high side? Maybe he's trying to pocket the extra money when he does the shopping, like the cook used to do?* She turned the radio back on, in an effort to calm her thoughts before they ran away with her again. That would mean another sleepless night. Her favourite classical music programme had come on. She put her hands in her lap and listened. *I should never have sold the grand piano. How could I have been so stupid? It was the only thing that made life here bearable. Can I buy a piano with the money I get for the ruby? A really old one, maybe?* Unconsciously she began to move her fingers in her lap.

She had played that same piece so often. The lamp over her head sputtered briefly and then everything went out. The heat, which had been held at bay by the ceiling fan, descended on her like thick jelly. She found the matches she always had at the ready and lit a candle. *Is Hema back already or should I go and throw the switch myself?* The fact that the switch was in the kitchen made her hesitate, but then she remembered last month. She jumped to her feet and headed for the kitchen.

He was sitting at the sewing machine, by the light of a candle. The gold brocade glittered between his fingers. A pale pink gown hung from the ceiling, swaying gently on its cord. Charlotte shone her flashlight into the meter closet while she looked, watching the figure bent over the table. *There's something about him. Something I've never seen before. His face, the way he stands. Or is it his scent?* She sniffed gently. Shocked at her own thoughts, she quickly bent over the fuse box. She saw at a glance that the problem had nothing to do with the fuse, and guessed that there was a power failure in the neighbourhood. That meant they would have to wait until the local government official came and threw the switch at the bottom of the hill. In this heat, it could take hours. And yet she didn't move from the spot in front of the fuse box. Her eyes returned to the man in the adjoining room. She saw how he held the length of cloth up to the candlelight and examined the intricate floral pattern woven into the material. He gave the fabric a gentle shake and spread it out on the table in front of him. Then he ran the tip of his index finger over the fabric. *What is he looking for?* she asked herself.

Suddenly he looked up.

Charlotte felt as if she'd been caught out and tried to strike a pose. "The power is out. You'll have to manage without it for a while."

He shrugged his shoulders. He smiled and then bent over the table again.

"When the butler gets back, I'll ask him to fix supper for you."

He looked up again. His eyes sparkled.

It must be awful not to be able to speak, she thought.

I understand you without your saying anything, he thought.

"Do you like okra? There's some on hand in the kitchen."

He nodded.

"I hope he gets back soon."

Again he shrugged slightly. *I'm not hungry yet.*

"I don't know why he's so late. He should have been back by now."

Please don't worry. I have hours of work ahead of me. I'm not in any hurry.

"I won't keep you from your work any longer. You have a lot to do. If you need anything, let me know."

You haven't given me the fabric for your dress yet.

"It just occurred to me that I still have to buy the material for my dress. I'll do it this week."

Don't buy any material. Look for something you already love.

"But apparently there's no great hurry. You have so many lengths of cloth on hand. I'll wait my turn." She looked at the pile on top of the cabinet against the wall. "I still don't know exactly what I want."

But I know. Give me a piece of material that's dear to your heart and I'll make something just for you. It will be unlike anything you've worn before.

"I was going to give you a piece of cloth I'd saved, but it had already disintegrated," she said softly.

Keep looking. You'll find it.

There was a slight grating noise, then a thud, and the light came back on. Suddenly their faces were brightly illuminated. Startled, they stared at each other. Both had felt it, the sudden atmosphere of intimacy. Nervously, Charlotte ran her fingers through her hair, said a hurried goodbye, and walked quickly back to the big house. She looked up at the sky, in search of clouds — *Please rain!* — and went into the house.

He blew out the candle. By lamplight the material was less magical. He placed the final mark on the fabric and picked up the scissors.

As he cut the out the various pieces of fabric, he heard the general dogsbody come in. There was no exchange of greetings, and Hema immediately started preparations for the evening meal: blowing on the coals, filling a pan with water, putting it on the burner, chopping the garlic and coriander. The smells reached Madan in the music room, followed by the clatter of plates and bowls. And then there was silence in the kitchen. Madan knew that the manservant was walking over to the big house with the dinner tray. In a half-hour or so, when the leftovers were collected, he would be given a share.

Everyone was asleep. By the light of the stars Madan slipped out of the kitchen. Without making a sound, he took a zinc bucket from the drain board and walked over to the *mali*'s shed, where he filled it with water from the outside faucet. He'd never gotten out of the habit of drinking from a bucket, but now he wasn't thirsty. Carrying the sloshing bucket, he walked around the shed. He had already seen that the tree was parched and its leaves withered. Carefully, he emptied the bucket over the foot of the apple tree. The water disappeared immediately, absorbed by the thirsty earth. He refilled the pail, and now he walked back to the house and the bedraggled borders that lined the path. With great precision he poured water onto the roots of a row of dead sticks. The next bucketful was destined for a shrub at the back of the garden, and after that he watered the overgrowth outside the servants' quarters. When the moon rose, he quietly put the bucket back on the drain board and retired to his room.

1936 On board the King of Scotland ~

THE DECK IS empty except for a ball that rolls back and forth, with the movements of the ship. The passengers have assembled in the dining room. The captain is holding a champagne cooler containing the cards for a game called "The Assassin." All eyes focus expectantly on a colonel from Leeds, who is the first to draw a card. The others try to discern from the expression on his face whether or not he is to play the part of the assassin. He glances briefly at his card and then looks up, an innocent expression on his face. Giggles are heard. Charlotte hates it when the woman she has to call Aunt Ilse suddenly starts to laugh. Now she says in a loud voice that she's "terribly nervous." Charlotte hates the game. Her parents played it once at home: The vicar hid under the cabinet in the nursery. He told her to pretend he wasn't there, and to get into bed and go to sleep. But he spent the whole time staring at Sita, until Charlotte finally climbed into bed with her. No one dared to say so, but they knew for sure that he was the murderer.

In a corner near the door stands Ganesh. There are plasters on his face. She hasn't seen him since that time they'd played the wind game, which was lots more fun than what they're doing now. When Auntie Ilse sees him, she calls out, "What on earth is he doing here?" Ganesh bows his head and quietly leaves the dining room. All eyes are on him. When the door closes behind him, the colonel's wife draws her card and then begins to giggle loudly. Auntie Ilse joins in.

Charlotte slides off her stool and slips out of the room. She wishes that Sita were there. She would never have left her alone, sitting on a barstool. If no one was looking, she would have run all over the deck with her, taken her into the kitchen to sample delicious tidbits, braided her hair, or conjured ginger sweets out of the folds of her sari.

She finds Ganesh on the aft deck. He's looking out over the sea, and he doesn't seem to see or hear anything around him. She walks over to him and takes hold of his hand. "Don't worry. I want to play with you."

1946 Grand Palace

HER FOOTSTEPS SOUND hollow in the large marble hall. Every ten metres there are gigantic crystal chandeliers hanging from the ceiling, and paintings of the forefathers on the walls. They are holding sabres, and their turbans are adorned with precious gems. Charlotte pauses in front of a painting of a young boy. He is holding a sabre almost as big as he is, but his turban makes him look slightly taller.

"That's my father . . ."

She starts: the maharaja is standing behind her. She didn't hear him coming.

". . . on his wedding day."

"His wedding day? But he's only a child!"

"He was ten and my mother was five when they married."

Charlotte does her best to conceal her horror.

"I was twelve when my parents decided that I was old

enough to marry," the maharaja continues. "I swore that none of my children would marry before they turned sixteen."

Charlotte nods. She herself is sixteen and newly married.

"My plan was to have my last and youngest daughter marry next year, but . . . eh . . ." He hesitates.

"Chutki? What's the problem? Doesn't she want to get married?"

"It's not a question of wanting to or not wanting to. The man I had in mind for her suddenly married someone else."

"Just like that? Without any warning?"

The maharaja nods.

"But that's terrible. Is Chutki awfully upset?"

"She didn't know."

"She didn't know?"

"I was still making the arrangements. The man himself didn't know either."

"Really?"

"For years I was so convinced that he was . . . well, the right one. And he was making no effort to look for a wife . . . until suddenly . . ."

For an instant Charlotte and the maharaja look each other in the eye. Then the maharaja turns away and looks back at the painting of his father. They stand side by side in silence. Neither of them moves. It's as if they are holding their breath.

"Are you angry with me?" Charlotte asks suddenly.

"No."

"Or with Peter?"

"No."

1953 Bombay ~

THE BOSS ARRIVES with a bunch of clanging keys, puts down the pan, and unlocks the door just as he has done every morning for the last few months. This is the moment when Madan's world becomes the world of his boss. With his customary sigh, Ram Khan pulls aside the wooden hatch. Madan jumps out of the crate and helps him lean the hatch against the wall. Then he makes a beeline to the end of the alley, takes a deep breath, and enters the pitch-black space that his boss once referred to as the "washroom." He holds his breath, doing his best not to slip and fall. Madan squats over the hole in the floor. Sometimes, but not often, he succeeds in relieving himself without taking a breath. The washroom, which is used by all the shopkeepers on the block, has never been cleaned, but none of the men appear to mind. Nor does Madan. Like the others, he washes his feet at the bucket outside. Back in the street, he sees that his boss and the coppersmith are in discussion. The coppersmith has a device in his hand that Madan has never seen before. He places it against Madan's crate and turns it on. Scraps of wood fall to the ground and minutes later there is a hole in the crate. He then drills four more holes in the side of the crate. "That's enough," Ram Khan growls. Madan looks up at him inquiringly. "For light. Otherwise you'll ruin your eyes and then you won't be of any use to me."

It is much easier to work inside the crate now, because he can see what he's supposed to do. He sits on the floor, bent over, with his knees pulled up; on his lap is the pair of pants with a seam that needs to be unpicked. Using a straight pin, he wiggles the stitches back and forth. Suddenly he can see what's going on outside. The man farther down the street who writes letters for people walks past with his little suitcase, which contains a typewriter. An old woman who comes from outside the city spreads out a cloth and then deposits a gigantic pile of coriander onto it. She won't leave until she's sold every last bunch, even if it takes her days. The coppersmith's errand boy comes back with a purchase. Everyone is on the go. Carts drive past. Dogs sniff at everything and each other.

"Mukka! Thread!"

Madan crawls out of his crate. Bending over the sewing machine, he takes the end of the broken thread, gives it a gentle tug, and then pulls it through the eye of the needle without a hitch.

"Are those pants done?" the boss grunts.

Madan shakes his head.

"You were probably looking outside the whole time. Do I have to block the holes?"

Penitently, Madan looks down at his feet.

"I've got another pair of pants for you, so make it snappy."

Madan dashes back into the crate and gets to work.

~

"Is it better now?" Charlotte lays a hand on Peter's arm and feels that he's trembling again. "We'll just have to wait."

"I'm tired of waiting. I want to leave."

"Just one more day. You can manage one day, can't you?"

Peter begins to tremble even more.

"Shall we go for a walk?"

He looks up with a start. She can tell by the look in his

eyes that the terror is mounting inside of him. She's afraid that one day it will be unleashed, with violence.

"Maybe just a stroll?"

He curls up like a child, with his arms around his head. Charlotte strokes him gently, but the trembling only gets worse. The house they moved into six months ago is far more luxurious than the one in New Delhi. When he accepted an appointment to the staff of the academic hospital in Bombay, she still had some hope that things would improve. But from the moment they unpacked their suitcases, the situation has only deteriorated.

"They said that walking is good for you. Let's give it a try. It'll also make the time pass more quickly."

Peter looks at her imploringly. Charlotte puts his hand on hers and gets up from the bed. She doesn't exert any pressure. She just waits. Very slowly Peter stands up, his back bent, his eyes fixed on the floor. In the six years they've been together, he has changed from a handsome captain into an old man. His hair has started to fall out, his eyelids tremble constantly, and they haven't slept in the same bed for a long time. She often thinks back to that one night of love, when it all started. If her father hadn't caught them, she probably wouldn't have married him. It would have ended that same night, and they would have gone their separate ways.

The servants look surprised to see their memsahib leading the doctor outside. Charlotte puts her arm through Peter's and, one step at a time, they venture onto the sidewalk. Peter is breathing heavily, and from time to time he moans softly. The sun has almost set, and a cool sea wind begins to blow toward the city. A tram passes.

"I should never have married you," Peter says suddenly.

They continue walking. The remark hurts her more

than she expected. It's a thought that has occurred to her on innumerable occasions, but she's never dared to speak the words.

"I've made you unhappy. I know it. I can tell."

The street seems endless, and she finds the dark trees overhead oppressive. She wants to see light from the last bit of afternoon sun. Without either of them directing their steps, they turn into a side street. The houses are lower, and here and there laundry is hanging from an open window. The pressure on her arm becomes lighter, as if Peter's confession has brought him a kind of relief. There are tradesmen sitting in front of their stores, smoking or chatting with their neighbours. The first gas lanterns are being lit. At a leisurely pace, they walk down one street and then turn onto another. They continue in silence.

"Do we have coriander on hand?"

Charlotte is momentarily taken aback, then she shakes her head no. Peter walks over to an old woman sitting behind an enormous pile of fresh coriander. Charlotte can scarcely believe her eyes. He picks up a bunch from the pile and smells it. He exchanges a few words with the woman. Then he searches his pants pocket for a coin and pays her. The woman wraps the bunch in a piece of newspaper and hands it to him.

"Shall we go home now?" His voice suddenly sounds tired. He takes hold of his wife's arm and pulls her along.

"Did you see that?"

"What?" he asks. His voice has lost all its colour.

"Oh, never mind." Charlotte realizes that the improvement was short-lived and that he would probably not have been shocked by what she had just seen: a young child at work inside a tiny crate at the feet of a fat tailor.

1995 Rampur ~

SOMEWHERE IN THE house there must be a length of cloth. She was sure of it. It was no use asking Hema. He'd only say that everything was gone and that it was a waste of time searching the house. She stood in the middle of the large hall and looked up. There was nothing in the attic. She'd already carried out a thorough search there, and also in her bedroom, the music room, the dining room, and the drawing room. The study, which had been her father's, was empty except for a spring mattress. The blue room, for years reserved for guests, was empty. Then she turned to the door of the only remaining room, the nursery. But she couldn't search there until the monsoon came, when she would be forced to empty the room due to the leaking roof. That is, if the monsoon ever arrived. Where were the clouds and the wind? Everyone was longing for relief from the heat: the plants, the birds, the whole city.

Suddenly the door flew open and Hema stormed into the hall. She didn't know he could move that fast.

"What's the matter?"

"He . . . that man . . . he's . . ." He was gasping for breath.

"He's what?"

"Memsahib, terrible, dreadful, he . . ."

"What's happened? Tell me!"

Hema spread his arms wide and looked upward with a dramatic expression on his face. Charlotte followed his gaze.

"No, memsahib, in the kitchen . . ."

"Is he injured?"

"No, no. It's worse than that."

"He isn't . . . ?"

"He's putting sugar on a dress!"

"He's doing what?"

"The *darzi* is putting sugar on a dress. Sugar is expensive. And the sugar's almost gone. The sugar is only for tea and for the sahib's yogurt. Not for a dress. Sugar belongs in the kitchen! The sugar —"

"Calm, calm . . ." The last time she'd seen Hema so distraught was when he caught a thief red-handed in the shed.

"There!" Hema pointed furiously at the door. In the opening stood the tailor. A faintly sweet odour accompanied him.

"What's the problem?" she asked Madan.

"He put sugar on a dress!" Hema repeated his accusation.

"Is that true? Did you sprinkle sugar on a dress?"

Madan nodded.

"Do you hear that, memsahib? I wasn't lying, I never lie," Hema cried.

"Why did you do that?" Charlotte continued her interrogation.

It's important for the person who's going to wear it.

"Do you use sugar as a kind of starch?" she continued.

No. Just the opposite: it makes the material soft.

"You see, he uses it to stiffen the material. So that it doesn't wrinkle as easily," she said to Hema, in an attempt to smooth things over.

"But, memsahib, our sugar . . ."

Madan shook his head. *I bought my own sugar.* He went to the kitchen and came back with a small bag of sugar.

"Is that the sugar from the kitchen?" Charlotte asked Hema.

He looked at the bag and shook his head. "But it's the same colour."

"This sugar belongs to the *darzi*. I appreciate the fact that you were concerned, but now you can see that there isn't really a problem. So you can go back to the kitchen without any cause for worry."

"Sugar on a dress. Sugar is for tea," Hema grumbled. Then he disappeared in the direction of the kitchen, still muttering to himself.

On the landing above, the clock struck one. Then everything was quiet again. So quiet that Charlotte could still hear Hema complaining under his breath. Madan was standing in the middle of the hall holding his bag of sugar. He made no move to leave.

"Is there anything else?" she asked.

You haven't found the fabric yet.

"I looked for material for my dress today. I was positive that somewhere in the house there are really beautiful lengths of cloth lying around, but I can't find them."

You would look lovely in red silk.

"I seem to remember a piece of Italian silk that belonged to my mother. But it's probably just disappeared after all these years . . ." Charlotte wanted him to stay, but she found it terribly awkward trying to carry on a conversation with someone who can't speak.

You understand me. Don't be afraid. You hear everything I say.

Then, like a bolt from the blue, a booming voice sounded from upstairs: "Discipline and order!"

Charlotte looked straight into the eyes of her father, who was leaning over the balustrade on the landing. "Rules! They weren't made for nothing!"

She raced up the stairs. "Father! Father! Why aren't you in your room?"

"Rules! We have to abide by the rules, even if it means death. Straighten your backbone."

Charlotte grasped the handles of his wheelchair and tried to manoeuvre it back to the open nursery door. But he grabbed hold of the balustrade and pulled himself back to the edge. "You were standing there flirting with a darky," he grinned. "I saw you. Brown women — bring 'em on! I'm ready and willing!"

"Father! Calm down! That's the tailor."

"They're no slouches, those darkies. Especially if you keep them on short rations. Then they'll do anything for you."

"Father! Please . . . stop!"

Charlotte pulled at the wheelchair with all her strength, but the general had a tight hold on the railing. She was afraid to pull any harder, for fear he'd fall out of the wheelchair.

"Go get the butler!" she shouted to Madan.

"I don't want any more yogurt! I want a woman! A woman!"

"Calm down, Father. You can have whatever you need. Just calm down and I'll take you back to your room . . ."

Victor began to cry. "I want a cup of tea, he promised to bring me tea with extra sugar . . ."

"Yes, yes. The tea is on its way. Are you coming? Then I'll wheel you to your room."

"Don't lie. You always lie. You're a little sneak."

"Are you coming, Father?"

Victor let go of the balustrade. "I'm thirsty. All day I've been so thirsty," he sobbed, only to raise his voice again and shout, "You're trying to starve me to death, you want to see me lying in my coffin, and then you'll run off with my money . . ."

She heard Hema storming up the stairs. He stood still when he reached the wheelchair, saluted, and gasped, "General sahib, do you feel like a cup of tea?"

A broad grin appeared on her father's face. "Ha, *swaddy*, the brew! Fill up my mug."

1943 Bengal

THE JEEP IN front of him suddenly slows and then stops. He looks at his watch — they're already an hour behind schedule. He gave clear orders not to make any more stops. A young officer gets out and goes to inspect the front of the vehicle. He shouts something that Victor can't quite hear. Now the others are also getting out. One of them, a young soldier from Kerala, comes over to Victor's car.

"Major Bridgwater, we have a flat tire."

"Then get the hell back there and change it!" Victor snaps. "We can't afford to stop here for a single minute!"

The words are barely out of his mouth when an emaciated man steps out from behind the bushes nearby. He grabs hold of the soldier, who tries to walk away, but the man won't let go of him.

"Get out," Victor barks at the men in his car. "Scare him off."

The soldiers get out of the jeep and go up to the man, with their weapons at the ready. He glances anxiously at their guns. But then he falls to his knees, reaches up, and tugs at the uniform jacket of one of the soldiers. From his car, Victor watches his subordinates' attempt to deal with the man. The situation arose after a devastating hurricane passed over this part of the country, destroying all the rice and grain. But Victor doesn't see that as the major cause of the famine. He is convinced that it's the fault of the Japanese, who are now launching attacks from Burma. In this time of war, the British-Indian army simply doesn't have the money or the manpower to deal with all the problems arising from the famine, no matter how pressing they are. In Victor's view, it's an example of the survival of the fittest in its purest form, and he finds some reassurance in the fact that only the strongest will survive. Which is ultimately a good thing, considering the extreme overpopulation in the area. The man is on his knees now, clutching one officer's leg so tightly that he can't move. The soldier attempts to extricate himself from the man's grasp, while the others go about changing the tire, a process that is progressing much more slowly than it should. *If we were at the front, this delay could have cost us dearly,* Victor reflects as he toys with his swagger stick. The thought has barely taken shape when more men, women, and children emerge from the undergrowth. Most of them are skin and bones, and they fall upon the soldiers, all of whom are around twenty years old and have never missed a meal in their lives. He grasps his swagger stick. As their superior he ought to get out of the car, but then it occurs to him that it would be good for his men to solve this problem themselves. Later, when they come face to face with the Japs, they'll look back on this incident as a piece of cake. The door he's leaning against is suddenly opened from outside. He almost falls out of the car and only just succeeds in grabbing the back of the seat as his swagger stick falls to the floor. He is about to unleash a volley of oaths when he sees the girl who opened the car door. Although she's emaciated and her eyes are sunken in their sockets, the promise of beauty is not entirely gone. She puts her hand to her mouth, gesturing to him that she is hungry. Victor knows that the crate behind him is filled with cans of meat, beans, flour, and even chocolate and coffee. But opening that crate would be an invitation for her fellow villagers to seize the vehicle and in the end there would be very little left of him and the jeep. He knows that he should push the girl away and close the car door, but there is something in her eyes that prevents him from doing so. She sees his hesitation and gives him a shy smile. He notices that her teeth are still flawless. Again she brings her hand to her mouth. Unobtrusively, Victor's hand steals to his jacket pocket, where he finds a few coins, a box of matches, and a piece of candy. He wants to give the candy to the girl but has second thoughts. That would be just as dangerous as opening the crate. His hand closes around the piece of candy. The girl holds out her hand, with the palm up, and looks at him imploringly. He clutches the piece of candy. Her begging hand enters the car. He smells the girl: there is a faintly sour odour coming from her mouth. Her skin is dry and the area around her lips scaly. Slowly the girl's hand drops, in the direction of his crotch. He flushes. I must close the car door! She must leave! She places her hand on his fly. He breaks out in a sweat. He wants to take his hand out of his pocket, give her the piece of candy, and then close the car door, but he can feel that the candy is stuck to his hand and he cannot let go. He feels the faint pressure of her hand on his member. He starts to breathe faster. Outside there is shouting, followed by a shot, and another, and another. People disperse.

There is panicked shouting: "Get the hell out of here."

Victor takes his hand out of his pocket and pushes the girl away. She sees the piece of candy sticking to his hand and tries to grab it. One of the young officers hits her on the jaw with the butt of his rifle, knocking her to the ground. Victor wants to toss the piece of candy in her direction, so that it's within her reach, but the car door is slammed shut with a bang. The men jump into the car and take off at high speed. Victor looks at the sticky sweet in his hand. The girl must have been around the same age as Charlotte, whom he hasn't seen in over six years. He shakes his head in annoyance. These are not the kind of thoughts he wants going through his head right now.

"Two dead, Major Bridgwater," the young officer calls out. "Two dead, but it was self-defence. You saw for yourself that it was self-defence. You did, didn't you?"

Victor puts the sweet in his mouth, nods, and bends down to pick up his swagger stick.

1968 Rampur

Dear Donald,

On behalf of Father, I want to thank you for the wheelchair you sent. We could never have found one like that here. You've probably heard that we've come to a decision. Father didn't find it difficult, but I did. In his view, it's clear that we're going to remain here in Rampur. In the end, I made the same decision, which means that both of us are now officially Indian citizens. At least we won't have to make the long train journey every time we need a passport. I used to have to go all the way to the embassy in New Delhi. Actually, I've never really felt English. You do, though, don't you? I guess that's because you stayed in England after you finished school. And now that you and Patricia are married, you probably won't ever come here to live. I really enjoyed the party. And what a big family she has! Patricia's wedding gown was unforgettable . . . with the tiny roses along the neckline, so lovely. It's a shame Father couldn't be there. It would have been his first visit to England. But who knows, once he gets used to this wheelchair, he may come over by plane, now that travel has become so much easier. That must make me sound like an old lady, but it was really fantastic to get to another country in such a short time, and the stewardesses were so very sweet. How was your honeymoon? They say Portugal is a beautiful country. Could you send me some photos? Everything's fine here. But we did have a lot of trouble with red ants in the drawing room. You remember, the big room next to the front door. Did I tell you that Father bought a new couch? It's just as red as the red ants, which is why I didn't see them at first. There's a really nasty kind of poison that a special man comes and sprays all over the room. We weren't allowed to go in there for a whole week, but since then we haven't seen a single ant. We also have a new cook, since the old bobajee regularly suffered from bad attacks of malaria. He says he contracted it during the war, but I think it actually comes from here. There are so many people who suffer from it, because almost no one sleeps under a mosquito net. We're very careful about that. Do you remember that apple tree we planted when you were here? It just produced its first apples. The new cook uses them to make apple pie, since they're too sour to eat raw. I'll stop now. It's almost time to take Father to the club, and I have to drive because the chauffeur is visiting his relatives.

Love — to Patricia too,
Your sister Charlotte

1953 Bombay ~

MADAN PULLS HIS legs back into the crate for the tenth time that morning. He is finding it more and more difficult to work inside the narrow confines of the crate, not only because the heat makes it almost unbearable, but because he's growing. A few weeks ago he tried to make this clear to his boss, but all Ram Khan said was that he still hadn't paid off his debt and that his bill would keep going up as long as he polished off a pan of food every day. Now Madan is unpicking the seam of a pair of brown pants, but they keep getting caught on the inside of the crate and it requires a real effort to work at all. Without his noticing, his legs have slid forward and out of the crate. Ram Khan, who has noticed, picks up the stone that always lies next to him and drops it on Madan's bare foot. With a hoarse cry, he pulls his foot back into the crate. Madan hears Ram Khan say, "Next time I'll chop your foot off." Then he hears a strange voice say, "The Lord has said: if your leg is a burden to you, chop it off. However, this child isn't the one who's bothered by the leg, but you. God has never given anyone the right to chop off someone else's foot." Slowly the white man in a long white robe walks over to Ram Khan. There is a crucifix hanging from his belt. The tailor, who is not often at a loss for words, stares in amazement at the young monk, who continues, "It is written, 'Let the children play.' Tell me why you lock this child in a crate?"

"I can do whatever I want with my own child. Or would you argue with that?"

"Your child?" The man reaches into the crate and gently pulls Madan out.

Ram Khan jumps to his feet. The plank creaks under the sudden movement. "Keep your hands off my son."

"Your son," the man repeats. "Then tell me how he got that scar on his throat."

Madan, who is now sitting half in and half out of the crate, makes himself small. His foot, on which the rock had just landed, is bleeding slightly, but in comparison with the old pain, it is nothing.

"He had a fall once," Ram Khan snaps.

"This is not your child," the man says.

"And just who do you think you are?" Out of the corner of his eye, Ram Khan checks to see whether there are any policemen coming down the street.

"I'm Brother Francis of the Congregation of St. Thomas. I walked past twice last week, and I saw how you treat this child. I know your name: you're Ram Khan, you come from Punjab, and you don't have any children. You've never even been married."

Ram Khan's mouth falls open.

"So I am taking this boy with me, and if you try to prevent me from doing so, I will call the police."

The tailor searches for words, for curses, for a solution. The only thing he can think of is: "My eyes are bad."

"Then buy a pair of glasses."

"I don't have any money."

"That's not the child's fault." Brother Francis of the Congregation of St. Thomas takes Madan by the shoulder. He hasn't been able to get a good look at the boy, who was always scrunched up inside the crate. Now he sees that the child is quite good-looking: the set of his eyes, the broad mouth, the straight nose and curly hair. Only the angry wound under his chin is repulsive. The brother smiles at him, but Madan still doesn't dare take the white hand extended in his direction.

"You see? He doesn't want to leave."

The brother goes down on one knee and looks Madan in the eye. "There's nothing to be afraid of. There are a lot of boys like you in our house, some of them older and some younger. Every boy has a bed of his own, and we have a school where you can learn to read and write."

"He's dumb," says Ram Khan in a final attempt to hang on to the boy.

With an encouraging nod in the boy's direction, he turns back to the tailor. "We're leaving." He takes hold of Madan's hand and pulls him gently to his feet.

"He still owes me money," Ram Khan sputters.

"What for?"

"For his clothes, for his food, and for his room."

The brother takes a bill from his pocket and gives it to the tailor. "Thanks be to God," he says, and pulls Madan along, down the street.

Several streets away, where the bazaar ends, the brother

stops. Nervously he takes a comb from his pocket, bends down, and combs Madan's hair.

Madan is suddenly reminded of his sister. He smiles.

THEY WALK THROUGH an archway and into a square surrounded by a building with three storeys. Madan, his hair now neatly parted, doesn't know where to look. Everywhere there are boys in short white pants and white shirts. Some are playing cricket; others are standing around chatting or shouting from open windows. One of them is lying asleep in the shade of a tree. Among the children, he notices men dressed like Brother Francis.

The brother hasn't spoken to Madan during their trip by rickshaw, but by means of gestures he tried to make it clear that he gave Madan's boss money, so that Madan needn't be afraid that Ram Khan might come after him, and also that he — Brother Francis — would take good care of him.

Hand in hand, they walk into a hall with long tables. Brother Francis motions to Madan to sit down. Then he goes into the kitchen and comes back with a plate of food, which he sets in front of the boy. The young missionary watches in fascination as the boy wolfs down the cold rice with dal, as if he is afraid someone will snatch the plate away before he is finished.

After taking the last bite, Madan sees that they've been joined by another brother, this one with a beard. He hears Brother Francis explain to the other brother that he found him in the bazaar, with a tailor who had locked him up in a crate. "The poor child is deaf and dumb!" he explains in a dramatic voice.

The brother with the beard sits down opposite Madan. He points to his chest and says in a loud voice, "I'M BROTHER

JOHN. I'M WITH THE SCHOOL." Then he turns to Brother Francis and sighs. "How would you explain 'school' in sign language?"

"He probably doesn't have any idea what a school is, so don't bother. First I'll have to take him to see Brother Augustine. The last thing we need right now is more disease among the boys." He reaches out and Madan puts his small hand in his.

That large, warm hand leads him into another part of the building, past big rooms furnished with tables and chairs, shelves full of books, and wall charts with pictures of animals. Behind a large door sits Brother Augustine. He's wearing spectacles with thick lenses. Behind him, there is a shelf with glass jars filled with skulls and dead animals.

"Ah, a new boy," he says cheerfully.

"He's deaf and dumb," volunteers Brother Francis.

Brother Augustine's eyes sparkle. Every new boy who enters the school represents a task awaiting him: not only a physical and intellectual task, but above all a spiritual one. If within a year this little boy has come to see God as his shepherd, then his future will be a lot rosier. That's one thing the brother is sure of. He raises his hand and says, "Hello!"

The skull just behind the brother's head has large hollow eyes and a hole where the nose ought to be. It looks a bit like the brother. Madan hesitates but then he raises his hand. The brother gestures for him to come closer. One tiny step at a time, he approaches the table. When he is standing directly in front of him, the brother picks up a wooden cross that hangs from his belt and holds it against Madan's forehead. He can feel his heart thumping in his throat. The brother closes his eyes and begins to murmur softly.

Brother Francis surveys the situation with a pang of envy. How could he have forgotten what Father Prior had told him so often: receive each new boy with an Our Father.

After the "Amen," Brother Augustine makes the sign of the cross, then takes hold of Madan's hand and helps him cross himself. Then, without any warning, Brother Augustine opens his mouth as wide as he can. The ravaged teeth, brown from years of smoking cigars, encircle a wet tongue. Then he snaps his jaws shut, and points to Madan's tightly closed jaw. Not until he has exposed his wasted teeth for the third time does Madan cautiously open his mouth, revealing a mix of milk teeth and permanent teeth. The brother, who has a spoon in his hand, turns it around, places the back of the cold metal on Madan's tongue, and presses down. The boy begins to gag and a terrified squeak escapes from his throat. The brother quickly removes the spoon, remembering another recent spatula test when a new boy couldn't keep down the meal he had just been given. Continuing his examination, the brother casts a practised eye over the scar on Madan's neck, his eyes, and his ears. Then he runs his hand through the boy's hair, listens to his heart and lungs, and taps each knee with a small hammer.

"A healthy little boy, but I still can't figure out what in the name of heaven they've done to him. It's as if someone has deliberately made him dumb. The way they sometimes gouge people's eyes out or break their arms and legs, in order to make them lucrative beggars." Meanwhile he walks over to Brother Francis and whispers in his ear: "If you ask me, there's nothing wrong with his hearing." Then, raising his voice, he announces that the boy needs a bath and clean clothes.

Madan walks down the long corridors holding Brother Francis's clammy hand. They stop at a large statue of a man hanging from two wooden planks. Brother Francis kneels down and gestures to Madan to do the same. He folds his hands and fixes his eyes on the crucified man, and then mumbles just like Brother Augustine. A shiver runs down Madan's spine when he sees that there are nails hammered through the hands and feet of the statue. The man looks down at him beseechingly. The mouth is open and it is obvious that he is thirsty. Ram Khan's crate was cramped and uncomfortable, but the thought of being nailed to a cross like this man terrifies him.

"Amen," says Brother Francis. He looks at Madan and smiles. "I'll bet they call you Mukka, don't they?"

Madan has no idea how the man suddenly knows that he can hear. Did the other man, the one who looked into his head, tell him so? He wonders if they also know what he is thinking.

"We have a much better name for you: we're going to call you Joseph, just like the father of the man on the cross." With a broad smile, he points to the statue of the man with the nails through his feet. "Come along, Joseph, it's time for you to wash."

The brother leads him into a grubby shower room. There are rusty pipes with showerheads running across the ceiling and taps on the wall.

"Take off your clothes, Joseph," Brother Francis says in a friendly tone.

Madan stands still, without moving a muscle. Brother Francis is no longer sure if Brother Augustine was right about the boy's hearing, so he gestures to Madan to take off his clothes and shows him that water will come down from the ceiling and that he's to wash himself. He hands him a wet piece of soap. In the distance a church bell begins to chime. Brother Francis crosses himself and turns his back to Madan. Drops of water are coming out of the showerheads. Madan takes off his pants and shirt and turns on one of the big taps. There's a rumbling sound and then water comes gushing out. Never in his life has he felt so much water streaming over his body. It's deliciously warm, as if he's walking through the rain. Madan forgets about the brother, the man with the nails, and Ram Khan. He even forgets about his sister. He closes his eyes and spreads his arms wide. He opens his mouth and lets the water stream in.

He can't see that Brother Francis is watching him in the mirror. Looking at the hair that clings to his neck, the water that runs out of his mouth, the hairless armpits and the fragile rib cage, the small penis that hangs between his legs. Brother Francis cannot take his eyes off the small member. He feels his own penis getting harder. He knows he ought to leave the shower room or turn off the water or close his eyes, but he doesn't want to. His skin is tingling, and his tongue is dry.

Madan feels the water streaming over him. It takes all of his thoughts with it, into the hole in the floor. It tickles his hair, cools his back, and slakes his thirst. It washes away all the dust and all his worries.

Suddenly Brother Francis calls out "Stop!" and then turns off the water with a jerk. Madan opens his eyes. With a radiant expression on his face, he looks at the brother, who comes over to him with a towel in his hand, kneels down, and starts to dry him off.

1995 Rampur ~

His mouth opened effortlessly and Charlotte spooned in the yogurt, deftly scraping up the drips and depositing them in his mouth. There was classical music coming from a small tape recorder. By the light of the single fluorescent tube, her father looked old, and the imposing dignity he had radiated all his life had disappeared. For Charlotte, watching the way he sucked on the spoon brought home to her that she had never spoon-fed a child of her own. As usual, Hema had disappeared after fastening the leather straps. Her father had escaped from his room that morning because he had fallen into a deep sleep after his bath and Hema had been unable to properly anchor the slack body in the wheelchair. It remained a mystery how the sly old fox had managed to work the brake loose, but seeing that he had escaped from the Burmese jungle, he wouldn't have had too much trouble undoing a strap. What Charlotte failed to understand was how Hema could have forgotten to lock the door. Nor did she buy the story that he had been too busy because the electricity went off just as his tea water came to a boil. There had indeed been a period of an hour or so when there was no electricity, but it still seemed like a lame excuse. Father could have wheeled himself out to the top of the stairwell, and he would certainly not have survived a fall from that height. She had rigorously erased from her memory the fact that she herself once left the door open in the hope that that would happen. Humming along with the Schubert, she put the next spoonful into the old man's mouth. Her gaze drifted to the large linen closet.

The general followed her gaze. He spat out the yogurt and shouted, "Just what are you planning to do?"

"Nothing, Father. I just thought I'd take a look inside the linen closet."

"It's my linen closet!" he yelled. "You stay out of there!"

"Do you happen to remember if Mother's silk fabrics are still in the chest?"

"They're mine! Not yours!" he thundered. His eyes started to roll and his shoulders shook.

"Calm down, Father. There's nothing to get upset about."

"I'll have you shot, if I catch you at it. And I see everything. Everything!" he shouted.

She removed the bib, wiped his chin, moved the tape recorder out of his reach, double-checked to see that the tires and the brake were properly anchored, and left the room with the leftover yogurt. She locked the door and, with a sigh, put the key back on the nail.

IN THE DISTANCE a dog howled, the crickets chirped in reply, and the moon was a wafer-thin sickle. Madan took the bucket from the drainboard and soundlessly went out through the open kitchen door. The heat of the day had made way for nocturnal scents, and he noticed that there were new ones since he had started watering the plants. The shrivelled jasmine had regained some of its old vigour, and the withered petals of the mimosa weren't quite as limp as the day before. The roses, which had appeared to be dead, now displayed tiny pink dots that signalled new life, and the leaves of the caper plant no longer crackled.

As he poured the water onto the flower beds that bordered the house, he sensed that someone was watching him. His eyes immediately went to Charlotte's bedroom window, but there was no one there. He glanced from window to window, but saw only curtains, shutters, and the reflection of the sickle moon in the glass. Turning around, he found himself looking straight into the eyes of Hema, who was standing in the open kitchen doorway. Madan wondered if he'd awakened him. Or perhaps the general dogsbody had had another exciting dream — something that was always audible in the adjoining room. He emptied the bucket and the earth thirstily drank in the few remaining centimetres of water. Without seeking eye contact with the other man, he walked back to the shed, filled the bucket, and returned to the border. Hema had disappeared, and the door was closed. He smiled and went on watering the parched plants. When the fifteenth bucket had been emptied, he returned to the kitchen building, carefully put the bucket down next to the door, and went into the old shed. It was pitch black inside, and he felt his way to the *mali*'s old bed, put the bundle of extension cords on the floor, lay down, and fell asleep.

When Hema returned from the big house carrying the morning tea tray, Madan was at his sewing machine. Hema picked up the bucket and slammed it down on the drainboard. Madan didn't look up. Last night, it had become overly clear that the *darzi* was trying to get rid of him. The week the *mali* died, Charlotte asked Hema to take over some of the dead man's chores, saying that she didn't expect a profusion of flowers, as before, but only wanted him to see that the borders were neat. As for the grass, she said she would find someone. Hema had nodded politely, as he was expected to do. But he was of the opinion that now that she no longer employed a *dhobi*, there were no coolies in her employ, and the *mehtarani* and even the cook had departed, his memsahib could not expect him to do the gardening, alongside the laundry, the sweeping, the cooking, and all the heavy work, while also caring for her father. Refusing to water the garden was his silent protest; now he'd been made to look a fool by the hateful *darzi*. He poured new water into the pan. Or was it perhaps to his advantage? he asked himself. Hema was not someone who thought things through. Something either was or was not. But wherever possible he avoided dilemmas, argumentation, and other complicated things. Suddenly it occurred to him that his antipathy toward the *darzi* might backfire. So he called out in the direction of the other room, "Coffee or tea?" forgetting that the tailor couldn't speak. Madan looked around the corner, and with a smile pointed to the pan for tea. He bowed his head slightly, a gesture that Hema interpreted as "thank you," and returned to his work.

But I'm not putting any sugar in it, Hema resolved.

1966 Rampur ~

SHE IS AWAKENED by an unfamiliar sound. From her window Charlotte sees five deeply tanned men, stripped to the waist, digging a hole at the bottom of the driveway. They thrust their shovels into the ground, throwing the gravel and dirt behind them. The sun isn't up yet and she hasn't heard her father's heavy footsteps.

After a wait of six and a half years, during which they filled in an endless number of forms and sent letters to the municipality, the state, and even the minister, all of which remained unanswered, the men have started work on a sewer system — something which her father refers to as "becoming part of modern India."

She didn't tell him that she paid the contractor under the table. Charlotte has had her fill of lugging buckets of water to the big house, not to mention the pumps that stall and the leaking vats up in the attic.

She hears heavy footsteps in the hall, and her door flies open.

"They've started!" Victor announces. He is standing at the door with his pyjama top open, his muscular chest revealed. He is well rested and brimming with energy.

Charlotte herself, by contrast, has not slept well. At supper the previous evening he informed her that he has had enough of retirement and that after the monsoon, when the land is green again and the flower beds are in bloom, he will be leaving. When she asked him where he was planning to settle, he replied, "England." "You're going to England!" She was astonished. He has always said that he didn't intend to breathe his last in that dank land of bacon and grey peas. "No," he thundered. "I'm going to stretch my legs! Walk from Rampur to London and back." And then, pointing out the window, he said, "But I'm not leaving until the sewer system is finished."

"I'll make sure everything's up and running by the time you get back," Charlotte says with a smile.

He laughs so hard that the workmen at the bottom of the hill hear him and look up, trying to identify the sound.

"Out of the question. That trench will be finished by next week."

He stalks off, taking huge strides. She always knows where her father is in the enormous house, since everything he does makes noise. In the past she didn't really notice, but as he got older, she guesses, he felt a greater need to make his presence known. Through his footsteps, his voice, his opinions, his ideas. Charlotte looks at him. His gait is clearly that of a military man. *He'll make it to London*, she thinks to herself, *and without a hitch, too.* And then a sudden wave of frustration comes over her; she thinks about all the years in Rampur. Year after year her desire to go to college, get a job, and start a new life has been dismissed by her father. But there might yet be hope for her, now that Father has travel plans of his own.

Nine years before, Charlotte met a charming German engineer, but Victor made the man's life impossible by criticizing every single thing he did. After a year of daily fault-finding and nitpicking, even Charlotte could find no redeeming feature in the man and finally broke off their engagement. Several years later, an Irish teacher whose idealism had brought him to India met the same fate as the German engineer. After that, the possibility of romance was banished to the furthest corners of her mind. She concluded that the man for her simply did not exist, and that she would probably never have children. That was something she found very hard to accept, and only the piano was capable of mitigating her disappointment. Now she watches as her father walks down the driveway, head held high and back ramrod straight. She gets up, straightening her own back, and in that split second, she makes her decision: *I'm leaving, too!*

The sky begins to turn orange, her father greets the men at the gate, and the new butler with the unpronounceable name appears from nowhere bearing a tray with cups of tea. The men talk, drink, and gesture. Her father's voice can be heard above all the others. One man, presumably the foreman, listens with a doubtful expression on his face, and then shakes his head. Victor points to the hole at his feet and then to the great house. Suddenly all the men are looking at her. She feels naked in her lace nightdress, and quickly steps away from the open window.

"A month! The man claims it'll take them a month to dig the trench! And then they'll still have to lay the pipes! We won't be able to reach the front door by car for months, and all that time the weeds will be choking the driveway. I could have finished the job in a morning with a couple of men from my battalion! A month! Do you know what that costs? A month! And he calls himself a contractor! An unprofessional tinkerer, that's what he is. A month for a simple trench! The ground's too hard, he says. Why not rent a machine? They're in use all over the civilized world these days! Not him . . . says he'll make do with his men, a bunch of weaklings and pansies in bare feet. How do you drive a shovel into the ground with your bare feet? Will you tell me that?"

Charlotte is familiar with his tirades: if she doesn't stop him, he'll go on for hours. She says, "Maybe you ought to tell them that it would be easier if they were wearing shoes."

"Don't think I'm planning to furnish his men with shoes: I'm not the army."

"No, I only meant that you could mention it to him. . . . Who knows, he might see something in the idea."

"Well, I'm certainly not planning to pay a bunch of barefoot diggers for a whole month!"

The general puts on his favourite boots. He feels more affection for them, the boots, than for any human being. They know where he has been, where he says he's been but hasn't, the people he's obeyed and those he's humiliated, together with all those he has seduced, embraced, kicked, and trampled. Those are the boots he'll be wearing on his grand hiking tour. The boots he regards as his best friends.

At the bottom of the hill the men are working in their bare feet, shovelling the earth to one side of the driveway. They scrape and root around in the ground until the dirt is loose enough to remove. The retired soldier watches the men. He is seething inwardly, but he knows he has to contain himself. If he flies into a temper in the driveway of his own house, he won't get off as easily as he did before his retirement from the army. He slows his pace, takes a deep breath, and holds it in. Silently he counts to ten, very slowly, before exhaling. Again he holds his breath, and repeats the exercise. On the count of ten he reaches the end of the driveway, close to the hole in the ground. The workmen, who were served tea that morning, sense the tension and do not look up. They continue to dig. Their callused feet, with broken toenails, rest on the sharp gravel. One of them, a young man with a cloth wound around his head, hasn't noticed the arrival of the general and goes on singing. He gives a rendition of a popular film song in a high-pitched voice while rooting in the soil with his shovel. The general grabs the shovel from his hands, pushes him to one side, and takes his place in the row. He then inserts the shovel into the ground and bears down on it as hard as he can. He realizes at once that it's almost impossible to get the shovel into the ground in one go. He takes a deep breath, the sole of his foot poised. When he exhales, he generates power. The shovel plunges into the ground. Triumphantly, he tosses the shovelful of earth onto the pile. Again he stamps the shovel into the ground, this time deeper and more fiercely. And again and again. Beads of perspiration form on his forehead, and his arms begin to tremble slightly. His body creaks and strains: he's no longer used to physical labour. He refuses to acknowledge these sensations: all he wants to do is to dig his shovel into the earth, and to show those weaklings what real work is like. Gradually the men stop working. They stand there, watching the tall, elderly Englishman who that morning had seemed so distinguished and who was now carrying on like a madman. Again and again, he plunges the shovel into the ground, digging deeper and faster.

Then, as they wait for the next thrust of the shovel, he suddenly stops. "This is work," he pants. "I'm an old geezer and long retired, so don't tell me you can't do it. You just don't feel like it. Why do you think this country isn't developing? Because there are too many gutless bastards like you around. Do you think we could have won the war in our bare feet?" He stamps his foot on the ground and continues his tirade.

Then a large truck appears at the bottom of the driveway and comes to a halt. It's full of pipes: long iron sewage pipes. There are four men seated on top of the pile. The driver honks his horn, and from his cabin he waves to the men in the driveway. During this interruption the general has temporarily lost the thread of the conversation, and now he glares at the driver. When he sees the men sitting on top of the pipes, he orders them to climb down. "Another truckload of layabouts! Don't you people understand that you're expected to work for the wages I'm paying you?"

One by one, the men jump down from the truck.

"And now I suppose you're going to tell me that it'll take a week to unload those pipes." He was still holding the shovel. Then, before anyone sees what he is doing, he starts to cut through the ropes holding the iron pipes together. The driver shouts and everyone jumps backwards. As the general slices through the last rope, there's a creaking sound, but that is all. The general is disappointed. He was hoping that all the iron pipes would glide from the truck at the same time. It would have been a magnificent apotheosis to his bout of digging. He gives the pile a final whack and turns away. The labourers are dumbstruck. The pile begins to creak, and one of the pipes works itself free and starts to slide. The man with the cloth wound around his head does his best to pull Victor away from the truck, but Victor doesn't want to be pulled away. He wants to stride away from the truck in his combat boots.

But Victor is too slow. The blow knocks him to the ground, face down, as though a grenade has just exploded behind him. The first pipe hits his calves. It is as if all the power in his legs has been obliterated. His knees hit the ground and he feels them break. The next pipe falls on the one before, breaking his shins. With a thundering roar, the entire load begins to slide off the truck bed. One by one, the pipes land on the general's legs. He feels his feet and ankles shatter. Inside his boots, all his bones are reduced to splinters. Only the leather holds the flesh together. Now the pipes fall onto his back. The men are screaming. They throw their shovels in front of the pipes, trying to stop the onslaught. But the iron pipes continue to come crashing down, like the finale of a breathtaking piece of music.

In the midst of the music, Victor hears the sound of Japanese bullets all around him. They don't hit him: he knows he's invulnerable. The war is over and he's made it out of the jungle alive. On foot. Wearing his boots. He is walking along the river, and his feet feel wet. Blood gushes over the top at every step. He founders in the mud. The sumpy bottom makes it impossible for him to take another step. He lies there, face down. Then he realizes that he's lying on the ground, with his face on the rocks. The drum roll ceases; one final high tone echoes. Then everything goes dark and still.

The driver mutters, "The pipes weren't for here."

1953 Bombay ~

THE BELT COMES down again and again, leaving red welts on his back. In the chapel the boys' choir is singing, their voices high and fragile. Together with the brothers of the St. Thomas congregation, the churchgoers are celebrating Easter. Most of them are descendants of the bastard offspring of English soldiers who, after getting an Indian beauty pregnant, left the mother-to-be behind. Brother Francis hopes no one misses him. He's standing in the shower room, stripped to the waist, and he is chastising himself with his belt. His dream, and the reason he learned Hindi, was to do good work ministering to the poorest of the poor, as a respectable missionary brother. That dream has collapsed. A week ago Joseph, the boy he rescued from the clutches of the tyrannical tailor, disappeared, and it is his fault. He's sure of that.

This morning, when it was his turn to go forward in prayer, he lost his place. Father Prior looked at him questioningly. He desperately searched his missal for the right words, but the sentence was gone. The letters kept spinning around, and the abbot finally had to assign the reading to his neighbour. Later that same day, when they all walked in procession to the chapel, he chose a spot at the end of a row of brothers kneeling at the communion rail. His thoughts turned to Joseph, as they did every second that he was not distracted by more edifying thoughts. Where could he be? The boy hadn't returned to the tailor, that much was clear, since Francis had gone by that morning. Had he run away with the non-believer Abbas? Abbas who wasn't afraid of anything or anyone; he had become the prior's special conversion project. *Please, God, let them keep their hands off him*, he prayed. He felt his member swelling and through his habit he saw a bulge appear next to the wooden cross. He stole away from the altar rail and went to the shower room. There he had untied the rope around his waist, hung the wooden cross on a nail, let his habit slip from his shoulders, and begun to lash himself.

"RUN, MUKKA!" yells Abbas. "Run!"

They duck into an alley and then make a right through a small gateway. They can hear the policeman panting behind them. They shoot down another alleyway, where a woman is on her knees doing the wash. They slip between two houses, and suddenly Abbas pulls Madan behind a wall. A rat streaks past. Abbas puts his finger to his lips. Madan holds his breath and presses his arms tight against his body. They hear the sound of the policeman's boots as he goes clumping past and disappears into the distance. Abbas smiles and holds up his hand. Madan takes the apple from his pocket and hands it to Abbas.

"Way to go, Dummy." Abbas gives him a slap on the shoulder. Not a hard slap, but one that expressed appreciation.

It is a very large, bright red apple. They retreat farther behind the wall, where no one can see them. In the corner, the rat reappears and looks at the two boys. Abbas bites into the apple hungrily and then gives it to Madan. They take turns until even the core disappears into their stomachs. The stem is the only thing they throw away.

"Another one?" he asks.

Madan nods enthusiastically.

From their hiding place, they peer into the alleyway. Halfway down, there's a woman with a bucket on her head, and at the far end a man is busy loading a cart. They crawl out of their hiding place and walk cautiously back in the direction they came from. When they turn onto the main street, Abbas starts to limp.

On the corner there's a fruit stall where a woman is making her purchases.

"*Baksheesh, baksheesh,*" entreats Abbas as he limps along. He is also extremely cross-eyed.

The woman continues her negotiations as if oblivious to the child beggar standing at her elbow.

With longing in his eyes, Madan also looks up at the woman, as he slides his hand underneath her bag in the direction of the crate of apples.

"Out of here, you two!" shouts the man in the stall.

Holding up their hands, they work their way along the row of stalls. Then they dash into the first alleyway they see and dissolve into laughter. Again, Madan pulls a large apple out of his pocket, this time a green one. Abbas is just about to take a bite when he feels a hand on his shoulder. He freezes. A dirty claw appears at the level of his nose. Reluctantly he places the apple in the hand.

"If I ever find you working my street again," says a boy with a large scar above one eye, "I'll break your legs."

1970 Rampur ~

Dear Donald,

Just a line this time. You know all about the idiotic decision taken by the English government. We don't understand any of it. We've written several letters to various authorities, but when we finally get an answer it's always the same. There's nothing they can do for us! They should have told us that when we chose to give up our British citizenship. It's absurd that we have to hear about it this way. My widow's pension is small, but sufficient for the time being. Father's pension from the army is still good, since the cost of living is much lower here than in England, but you can imagine what the future consequences are for us. We argue sometimes, because we're so worried. Don't let on to Father that I've written to you about this, but his legs are not good right now. They're infected again. But every time I hire a live-in nurse for him, he sends her packing within a couple of days. He spends all his time writing to authorities here in India, but they don't even answer his letters. Sometimes it's as if he does nothing but write letters, just as I'm writing to you now, because I know that you are acquainted with Sir Whethamstede. If it's not too much trouble, would you ask him if he can inquire at the Department of Army Pensions about the regulations for inhabitants of the former colonies, and find out if there isn't something that can be done about the freeze on pensions? Is everything all right with you and Patricia? I sincerely hope so.

Love from your sister Charlotte

P.S.: The apples are just as sour as last year.

1995 Rampur ~

The crows pecked the soil listlessly. They wouldn't find any worms until the rains came, and they were already two weeks later than normal. Anyone who could summon the energy to talk was discussing the only topic of interest: the water shortage in the Rampur reservoir.

Charlotte wiped the sweat from her forehead and looked around inquiringly. Something was different, but she didn't know what. Then her nose told her. She sniffed the air. It wasn't the grass, which at this time of year was odourless, but the jasmine bush next to the shed that gave off a faint scent. There weren't any flowers yet — they wouldn't appear until after the rain — but there was a subtle aroma coming from the bush itself, and the branches and leaves. It put her in a good mood. No doubt it was an omen, a sign that the monsoon was not far off. She looked up at the sky, but it was cloudless.

Rays of sunlight shone through the roof of the shed. She noticed immediately that someone had slept in the old *mali*'s bed. She'd have to have a serious talk with Hema about this. Had he again offered one of a hoard of distant second cousins a roof over his head? Like every head servant, Hema wanted to reign supreme in his own kingdom, but because his empire had shrunk to one man, he was sometimes moody, and that annoyed her. He'd "forget" to empty the wastebaskets, iron her blouses, unclog the sewer pipes every week, and water the borders, although he had perhaps taken care of the last chore. His relationship with the tailor was also a concern. It might be better if she arranged for the *darzi* to work in the music room. She felt herself blush and shook her head in an effort to banish the colour from her cheeks. Her bicycle was standing next to the *mali*'s bed, and she saw at once that one of the tires was flat. Her blush intensified, but this time it was one of annoyance. The man who repaired tire punctures could come by only after closing his shop, and she had relieved Hema of that task after several unsuccessful attempts. But this was an emergency. She couldn't afford to miss the Tuesday-morning get-together, since that would mean that all the inquisitive club members would have to come by, one by one, not only to check on the progress of their dresses, but also to peek and pry, and to establish whether her house was really as empty as the gossip would have them believe. So she adjusted her straw hat and pretended that the heat didn't bother her. At the bottom of the path, on the very spot where her father had stood for the last time, she would hail a rickshaw. After all, she still had a good portion of the money from her Wedgwood service, although it was going faster than she had hoped. Worrying about unpaid bills was one of the things that Charlotte was very good at postponing. She had urged her father to find a smaller house, but he refused to sign on the dotted line. Her latest attempt had given rise to such an unholy row that she had finally given up hope.

The sun burned straight through her hat, and perspiration poured from her face. The street at the bottom of the hill, normally full of traffic, was deserted except for a cow grazing absently and a truck full of bananas. No one wanted to spend a minute longer than necessary outdoors in this heat, and she was wondering whether many of the club ladies might not show up when she heard a familiar car horn. The shiny vehicle stopped and the door flung open.

"Come on, jump in," called the wife of Nikhil Nair.

Charlotte was only too happy to comply. "I've got a flat tire," she said as she flopped down next to the portly woman in the shocking pink blouse.

"You shouldn't be cycling at all in this weather. Don't you have the Vauxhall anymore?"

Charlotte smiled. "Cycling keeps me fit."

The air conditioning was on high. Charlotte shivered slightly.

"Is he making progress?" inquired the wife of Nikhil Nair. "I simply cannot wait to see my American dress."

"He's hard at work," Charlotte replied. She had a clear recollection of the pink dress that hung from the ceiling, dancing gently above the bent figure of the tailor.

"I do hope it turns out well. What if I had to take my silk to a third *darzi*? It doesn't bear thinking about! And run the risk of someone cutting off another half a metre."

"According to the butler, he's making great strides."

"The man doesn't do his sewing in the kitchen, does he? I don't want my dress smelling like masala and roast chicken."

"No, of course not."

"Fabrics absorb odours, you know. The *darzi* who made my wedding outfit worked on it next door to the room where my uncle kept a secret stash of liquor, and the whole day I smelled like a brewery. We tried to get rid of the odour by hanging it outside for a night, but I was afraid someone might steal it. My mother sprinkled it with eau de cologne. Not that

that helped . . ." Everyone knew that her tailor back then was a notorious alcoholic, and that by the time the celebrations began, her uncle was already short twelve bottles of whisky.

"He only uses a bit of sugar to stiffen the collars."

"Sugar!"

"That's what he said."

"You mean you can converse with him?"

"No, but the butler saw him doing something with sugar and assumed that it was our sugar he was using. I had to intervene."

"I hear he's a bit strange."

"How do you mean, strange?

"My chauffeur saw him buying flower seeds at the market. What on earth does he need flower seeds for? You can't eat them and there's no use sending them home, since it's the wrong season, so I thought maybe . . . You haven't asked him to do the gardening as well, have you? You still don't have a new gardener?"

There was a touch of disdain in her voice; Charlotte pretended not to notice it.

"He probably saw something he fancied."

"Well, it's still strange. Keep an eye on him. I certainly don't want to end up with a row of sunflowers embroidered on my collar."

When they arrived at the club, all the ladies were anxious to hear how the tailor was progressing with their festive outfits, and Charlotte had to move heaven and earth to convince them to leave the tailor — and more particularly, herself — in peace. "When he's finished," she said, "he'll come straight to each of you. I'll see to that."

~

"HAVE YOU HEARD anything?" sighed the wife of Ajay Karapiet over the phone. She hadn't attended the Tuesday-morning gathering because she was in bed and running a high fever. She was still too ill to listen to the commentary from her friend with the penchant for pink.

"It's really too pathetic for words. I'm almost afraid to tell you, but she was *on foot*, in this weather. Imagine! There was no one on the street, of course, and I noticed a strange odour in the car, so I gave her one of those modern eau-de-cologne tissues, that was the least I could do." The wife of Nikhil Nair rattled on.

"Who?" groaned the wife of Ajay Karapiet, throwing off the blanket she had just pulled up over her shoulders.

"Charlotte Bridgwater, of course! Apparently not a single outfit is finished, and he sprinkles sugar on our fabrics. And the butler, who's actually more of a general dogsbody — although she always calls him the butler — was also against it and they ended up fighting, he and the *darzi*, and she had to get between them, she told me herself. Just imagine him walking into your servants' quarters, you certainly wouldn't have had the courage . . . although I sometimes wonder whether it was such a good idea, that man in her house . . ."

The wife of Ajay Karapiet knew that her friend was waiting for her to say "How do you mean?" or "What are you suggesting?" but her head was pounding and her ears were ringing. She was longing for a glass of cold water and wanted to go back to sleep, so she just groaned faintly, which was interpreted as a question.

"I have a suspicion — but this mustn't go any further — that she's using him as a gardener as well!"

Even with a head full of mucous and a temperature of 39.4, the wife of Ajay Karapiet pricked up her ears. "The tailor! A gardener?" she panted.

"My cook saw him buying a crate of flower seeds at the market. You don't use flower seeds to make clothes, do you? She hasn't had a gardener since her *mali* returned to his cycle of reincarnation, and I know that her handyman hates gardening. I heard that from my chauffeur's brother. And . . ." Her voice dropped, building up the suspense. ". . . someone has seen her cutting the grass before it gets light. Imagine! Cutting the grass herself! The mistress of the great house!"

That news was enough to make the wife of Ajay Karapiet sit straight up in bed. "She mows her own grass?" she asked in a hoarse voice.

"Of course, she doesn't want anyone to know, that's why she goes out before dawn. But if you put those three things together, then the conclusion is clear. Plus the fact that he hasn't produced a single dress. I'm absolutely positive that the tailor — who is supposed to make sure that in a couple of weeks all of us look absolutely fabulous — does the gardening!"

There was a plaintive sigh at the other end of the line. The patient fell back onto the pillows.

"I'm glad you agree with me and, just between the two of us . . . isn't this an example of old-fashioned colonial behaviour?"

The wife of Ajay Karapiet let out a faint croak. She had never really understood what colonial behaviour was. In her eyes, the English were the people who brought both the railroad and the postal service. Both of these institutions were still doing incredibly well, and she and her children, who had decided to continue their studies in faraway cities, were enthusiastic users.

"We have to do something. We can't let this happen. We have to go and see for ourselves."

The wife of Ajay Karapiet groaned.

"Are you really that sick?"

"Come and fetch me," said the wife of Ajay Karapiet. She knew that her friend would go on badgering her until she got up.

~

CHARLOTTE HEARD A car coming up the path, which hadn't been called the "driveway" for years. The hole her father dug had remained open for two years. After the ambulance drove off, the sewer workers had grudgingly helped to load the pipes back onto the truck before leaving. The ground was too hard, they said. Her father was moved to a rehabilitation clinic, where he learned to move about with his useless limbs, and after the monsoon she had hired a new contractor, who reviewed the situation and came to the conclusion that it was much faster and easier to lay the pipes from the other side of the hill. And the contractor was right. His men had no trouble digging a deep trench through the garden. The first time Charlotte positioned herself on the modern flush toilet, it was one hundred and eight years to the day since Queen Victoria had tried out her new toilet. When Charlotte asked the men to fill the hole at the bottom of the driveway, the foreman laughed and said, "You call this rut a driveway?" From then on, everyone referred to it as "the path," and when her father came home for the first time in two years, the garden and the house had deteriorated to such an extent that the term stuck.

The wife of Nikhil Nair got out of the car wearing her bright pink blouse, accompanied by the wife of Ajay Karapiet, who had put on a cardigan. Hema ran out of the kitchen, across the grass, through the servants' entrance, and into the hall, just managing to get to the front door in time to open it when the doorbell rang. He left the ladies in the bare hall and went into the drawing room. Memsahib, who was already aware of the visitors, was kneeling on the floor. Without saying a word, Charlotte and Hema rolled out the carpet and shoved the chairs around so that the room appeared slightly fuller. Charlotte smoothed her skirt, wiped her forehead, and nodded to Hema that he could usher the ladies in. Hands were shaken and courtesies exchanged. The wife of Ajay Karapiet had bright red cheeks and perspiration was pouring down her face. Charlotte didn't know that she was running a temperature of close to 40 degrees, and considered it inappropriate to inquire, now that everyone was suffering from excess perspiration.

"We were in the neighbourhood and decided to drop in. I hope it's not an inconvenient time?"

"No, of course not." Charlotte surreptitiously flattened an upturned corner of the rug with the toe of her shoe.

"We'd like to go by and see the *darzi*. Would that be all right?"

Hema, who was hanging about, waiting for orders to make tea or coffee, was sent to fetch the tailor. Charlotte knew that if they saw the tailor at work in the room next to the kitchen, the complaints about odours would start up again. The fan was going at full speed, and an uncomfortable silence fell. Charlotte had been caught unexpectedly by the two busybodies. The wife of Ajay Karapiet could think of nothing but her bed. The wife of Nikhil Nair had difficulty disguising her curiosity: she looked around the room, which appeared much less shabby than she had expected. She was most surprised to see that the costly Persian rug was still there. But she didn't know that the bank owned the oriental, as well as the chair she was sitting in, the side table where her purse lay, and the dresser (which did seem a trifle bare), together with the rest of the furniture in the room. The door opened and the *darzi* walked in, his head slightly bowed in deference. He was carrying two dresses over his arm, one pink and the other gold brocade. The wife of Nikhil Nair jumped up with a squeal and raced across the room to take possession of her new outfit. She began to crow with delight, snatched the dress from his hands, and danced around the room. The wife of Ajay Karapiet also beamed with delight when she was given her gold dress.

They are truly beautiful, thought Charlotte.

Yours is going to be even more beautiful. If I can find the right material.

You'll find it.

Charlotte looked at Madan, who was looking at the two women. She felt uncomfortable: it was as if he was answering her thoughts.

"I simply must try it on," the wife of Nikhil Nair cooed.

Oh, God, no! Charlotte thought. *Then they'll see that all the rooms are empty.*

They can try the dresses on at home and then bring them back. They're almost finished.

They can take them home?

baksheesh, but only a raw, animal noise comes from his mouth. The man is startled out of his culinary musings by the terrifying sound. Filled with repugnance, he pushes Madan away and without looking at him, shoves a coin into the proffered hand. In a fraction of a second, the coin disappears into the belt around Madan's waist.

Abbas has pointed out that the sounds he utters when he tries to speak work wonderfully well when he's begging. Almost better than walking with a limp and looking cross-eyed. It is a simple fact that people give more money to a maimed bag of bones than to an ordinary child. So all day Madan utters his horrific cries. He discovers that women give more when he uses high tones, which resemble a baby goat that's lost its mother. Men tend to be more generous when he makes use of lower tones, which are reminiscent of a movie hero whose throat is being cut. Madan has also learned that he gets more money from older women when his cries are uttered slowly, while younger women prefer faster and softer sounds. He also knows that men give him money almost immediately when he approaches them from behind, and that the opposite is true in the case of women. Since he cannot explain all these techniques to Abbas, he simply makes use of them while experimenting with new ruses to bring in more money.

His stomach rumbles. Yesterday none of his tricks worked, and the boys made almost nothing. He doesn't think about the man who in a half-hour will be coming out of the restaurant with a full stomach. His eyes search the street for their next victim. Then he hears screams, and a woman with a bucket on her head comes running out of an alleyway. "Help," she shouts. "Help!" Abbas looks at Madan and Madan at

Abbas. Yesterday the proprietor of the vegetable stall shouted just like that when they stole a carrot, but this time they're innocent. The woman is still shouting, as she heads in their direction. "Help!" The boys try to figure out who she's running after, but they both know for sure that no one has come racing past them with an apple or a pear. "Help!" The pail of water falls to the ground, but the woman keeps running.

Then a small dog comes racing out of the alley. By then the woman has disappeared into one of the houses. The dog is a thin, nervous animal and it's running in their direction, panting heavily. Abbas, who has often told him that his only memory is of his beloved dog Bala, who was run over by a police car, now forgets all about his crippled hip and goes down on his knees. The dog is running straight at him.

He's foaming at the mouth! Madan tries to scream, but his friend interprets his cry of panic as encouragement. *Don't touch him. Get away!* Madan jumps behind a tree. His friend opens his arms wide. The dog jumps up and bites him. In disbelief, Abbas pushes the mangy animal away. His ear begins to bleed profusely. It is then that he sees the terrified eyes, the crooked head, and the foam around the dog's mouth. He grabs the umbrella handle, which Madan had dropped amidst all the turmoil, and hits the dog. The animal cowers in fear. He brings down the handle again. Madan wants to shout that he must stop, but it is as if the wordless cries only encourage his friend, who is two years older and much stronger. With the strength of an adult, which Madan has never witnessed before, Abbas continues to beat the whimpering dog.

His father jumps up from the table where he's been sitting motionless all day. Not once has he stood up or even moved a muscle. His mother, who left for the fields early in the morning, comes in with a pitcher of milk and a few vegetables. His father picks up the poker next to the fireplace and strikes. The dog howls. *His mother falls to her knees, and the milk spreads across the floor. And again the poker comes down on her head.* The dog whines. *His mother opens her eyes wide and looks at the iron poker, which again comes down hard.* Something cracks inside the dog. A bone breaks. *Her face is lying in the milk, which turns pink. Mercilessly the poker comes down on his mother's head. Otherwise there is not a sound. The iron poker lands on the scrawny body.* The dog whines. *His father appears to hesitate an instant. A sigh escapes from his mother's mouth. And again the poker comes down at lightning speed.* The dog groans. *His mother lies dead on the floor. His father is crying.* The dog whines: a soft, beseeching whine. Saliva drips from its muzzle, like the blood from his mother's mouth. *His mother . . . Abbas turns his back on his father and goes to the door.* Abbas turns around. The dog lies there, bleeding. *He closes the door behind him.* He does not look back.

Madan doesn't know what to do. Farther up the street people are standing around staring at them. Through the window of the restaurant, he sees the man enjoying his dinner. He didn't see what happened outside.

Abbas walks away. His ear is bleeding. He forgets to limp.

Madan looks at the dog lying motionless in the pool of blood. He isn't afraid of blood. He's afraid of eyes that watch but don't see anything. He is afraid for his friend, who is walking away with blood all over him, holding the umbrella handle. He is afraid of the man who's sitting at the window, having his dinner. Afraid of the bucket lying in the middle of the street, afraid of the people standing around watching. A police car turns into the street. He runs after his friend and pulls him into an alleyway.

Don't leave me alone!

~

In the harbour, between two dilapidated sheds, Madan has discovered a dark crevice; if he holds his breath, it's possible to squeeze in sideways. This brings him to a narrow space between two tall wooden houses that gets even narrower toward the end. There is a gentle but constant sea wind from faraway lands where there are no dogs that attack people and no children who have lost their parents or left them behind. Madan is busy cleaning their hiding place, where he found the remains of rats long since dead. He shoves the bones and skulls farther into the narrow passageway. Using old newspapers, he tries to make a bed of sorts for his sick friend. The patient isn't hungry, and Madan tries not to think about eating. He wants to stay with him, especially after Abbas told him that he hurts all over and his whole body itches.

He finds a crate full of empty bottles outside a shop at the end of the quay. Just before it gets light, he picks up the crate without a qualm and fills the bottles in one of the sheds. He takes them back to their new hiding place. The crate is too big, so he takes all the bottles out and puts them next to his friend.

The boys lie alongside each other. Abbas pants and moans; his eyes are closed. Madan looks up at the narrow strip of blue sky that dissects the darkness: a radiant path leading to a new place, a new land. He wishes that Abbas wasn't ill. Ever since he beat the dog to death, he's been angry and short with him.

Everything Madan did was wrong, until they crawled into the passageway. Since then he's been calmer and he's stopped swearing. But his breathing is irregular, he twitches, and once in a while he suddenly begins to pant. Then Madan strokes his arm and thinks about tomorrow or the day after, when they'll be walking through the city again, stealing apples and maybe a coin from a woman doing her daily shopping.

"My mother is dead . . . ," Abbas says in a hoarse voice. "Just like that . . . one day . . . dead." He is panting, and now and then he moans softly. "No one knows why." He opens his eyes. Fresh saliva dribbles from the corners of his mouth. "For no reason . . ." He moans and gasps for air. "She was a good . . . a good cook." His eyes sparkle. "Every morning . . . she washed . . . her hair . . . and rubbed it with . . ." His eyes roll, and he sniffs as if he's looking for her. ". . . with coconut oil . . ." Panting, he falls back onto his bed of newspapers. His breathing becomes more rapid and irregular. Madan stretches out his hand, but before he can calm his friend, Abbas continues: "She combed . . . carefully . . . so very carefully . . ." Abbas's hair is damp and tangled. Madan resolves to look for a comb the next day. "She had . . . she had a braid . . . hanging down her back." His voice becomes fainter and fainter, and it is only with great difficulty that he is able to continue. He closes his eyes. "In the sun . . . the sun . . . her head was like . . . a shining ball . . ." Then he begins to scratch his ear. Gently Madan pulls his hand away. He doesn't want the wound to reopen. "It stings," his friend groans. "My cheek stings . . . cold . . . my face . . . everything stings, Mukka . . ." He stretches his neck and makes a sudden motion with his arm, as if he's lashing out, but Madan can tell by the look on Abbas's face that he's equally as surprised. "I'm . . . thirsty . . ." Madan hands him one of the bottles. The boy groans as he raises himself slightly and tries to drink. Most of the water runs down his neck, and only a few drops reach his mouth. He begins to gag, and pushes the bottle away from him with such force that it falls to the floor and breaks. Madan takes a new bottle and brings it to his friend's lips. With great care, he pours the water into his mouth. At once Abbas begins to retch, gasping and shaking. His head lolls around. Madan only just manages to grab the bottle before it, too, crashes to the ground. Panting, Abbas says that he doesn't want any water, that he's choking, and then he falls back onto the old newspapers. But a few seconds later he groans that he's thirsty again. This time, when Madan picks up the bottle and brings it to his friend's lips, Abbas panics. His whole body shudders and shakes. He stretches his neck and his eyes roll. Madan lays a hand on his arm and strokes him. The boy becomes quieter. He closes his eyes and groans softly. His lips are parched and the dried saliva around his mouth has formed yellow scabs. The wound on his ear is inflamed. His hair is damp with sweat. Again Madan looks up at the long strip of blue. He doesn't know what to do.

"Mukka?" Abbas opens his eyes slightly. He licks his lips and tries to say something. "Will you . . . will you tell . . . me the story . . . ?"

Madan doesn't know what he's talking about. Abbas knows he cannot speak. He's never told a story in his life. The only story he knows is about the day his sister in her blue coat disappeared into a group of cheering men. Everything that happened before that has gone clean out of his head, as if he'd been born in the midst of those shouting legs. All he remembers is worrying about how to satisfy his hunger and how to find a safe place to sleep. And, of course, there's also the story of his friend Abbas, who's not afraid of anyone or anything, except the police. Outside of those, he doesn't know any stories.

"Tell me," Abbas whispers.

I don't know any stories. A series of hoarse sounds come out of his mouth.

"Yes . . . tell me . . ." Abbas gasps.

"I'm telling you: I don't know any stories," Madan barks shrilly.

A blissful expression appears on Abbas's face when he hears his friend say: ONCE UPON A TIME THERE WAS A BOY . . .

Madan sees that Abbas expects him to go on, although he still doesn't know what he wants him to do. His stomach is growling and he's thirsty. He picks up the bottle, but there is panic in Abbas's eyes. Again he starts to shake and tremble. Madan quickly puts the bottle down. He wishes that Brother Augustine with his glasses with thick lenses was here, so he could put his upside-down spoon in Abbas's mouth and give him a pill that would make him better. Then they could go off together again. They'd compete to see which one of them was the best "limper." But Brother Augustine is much too fat. He'd never be able to squeeze through the narrow slit. Even his head is too big. Then Madan sees the skulls he swept into the corner. They look a bit like the skulls on Brother Augustine's shelf. Their noses are pointing at each other. They look like two friends. He picks them up.

I'm a rat, he has one rat say. *And I'm another rat,* the other skull replies.

Abbas begins to beam; he knows exactly what his voiceless friend is saying. What his hoarse, shrill noises mean: THE BOY LIVED WITH HIS FATHER AND MOTHER IN A LOVELY LITTLE VILLAGE.

Madan plays with the rats as if they were two puppets in a puppet theatre and has them walk alongside each other as he continues his story. *They were very strong little rats, and they weren't afraid of anyone.*

THE FATHER WAS A FARMER AND HE HAD A COW AND A GOAT, Abbas translates his words.

They had promised each other that they would stay together forever.

THE MOTHER MADE THE BEST CHAPATIS FOR MILES AROUND.

Because they were both all alone.

THEY WERE HAPPY AND THEY WORKED HARD ON THE LAND.

They always took care of each other, and they shared all the food they found.

THEN ONE DAY THE WELL IN THE MIDDLE OF THE VILLAGE DRIED UP.

Sometimes an apple just happened to be lying on top of a crate.

THEN THE POSTMAN DELIVERED AN OFFICIAL LETTER.

Or there was a big pear that no one wanted to buy.

THE SCHOOLMASTER READ THE LETTER ALOUD.

One warm day they stole a mango.

WHERE THEIR VILLAGE WAS, A DAM WAS PLANNED.

It was deliciously sweet.

EVERYONE HAD TO MOVE.

Sweeter than the sweetest sugar.

BUT NO ONE GAVE THEM A NEW HOUSE.

They would start a mango farm.

THE BOY'S FATHER STOPPED TALKING.

Together they would have one huge tree.

ALL HE COULD DO WAS THINK, ALL DAY LONG.

Full of luscious mangoes.

THEN HE REALIZED WHAT THE SOLUTION WAS!

A hundred million mangoes.

Madan licks his lips at the thought of their big tree full of mangoes: the two of them would sleep under the tree, so that the mangoes would fall straight into their mouths. Abbas also licks his dry lips. He shivers. A jolt of icy cold shoots through his body, slashing his muscles into useless pieces of string. He gasps for water, but the mere thought of water makes his throat contract. His lips fight for air, but the opening is closed for good. His throat, which had allowed him to shout and sing, is blocked. A shock goes through his body and he stretches his head and neck, as if searching for space, fighting for air, for breath.

With a start, Madan drops his rat heroes. He pushes his friend back onto his bed, but Abbas shakes and lashes out with his arms. Every sinew, every tendon, every muscle in his scrawny body convulses. He begins to drool, a foaming, colourless saliva. "What . . . what . . . ," he moans.

Madan shouts for help, someone has to come, he can't leave his friend alone. Why doesn't someone come? Can't they hear him?

Abbas throws his head back, desperately gasping for air. His arms point toward the sky. The strip of blue above does not move. Only Abbas moves. One last time.

MADAN HAS CLEARED away all the shards and laid his friend down as best he can, stretching his arms and legs out. He's closed his eyes and mouth. He's taken off his own shirt and rolled it into a kind of pillow, and he's spread the cloth from around his waist over the body of his friend, which is getting colder and colder. He's decided to go to Brother Francis and ask him to help get Abbas out of here.

One last time, he looks at his friend. Then he takes a deep breath and squeezes through the slit to the world outside.

No one takes any notice of the boy, grimy and barefoot and wearing only a pair of torn pants. He doesn't look to the right or the left. His legs move mechanically. He doesn't hear the angry clang of the tram when he dashes across the tracks, he doesn't see the handcart that almost knocks him down, he doesn't smell the aroma of freshly baked bread coming from the open doorway. He feels only the cold inside of him.

He can't remember where Brother Francis lives. He doesn't know where Ram Khan lives either. He's even forgotten where the harbour is, where he left Abbas behind. He keeps walking, on and on. He can't stop walking, even though his legs are tired and his feet hurt. It's nothing compared to the pain that Abbas suffered. He walks down unfamiliar streets, but he doesn't see them. He passes houses that keep getting bigger and then smaller. He doesn't notice that the trams have disappeared and the buildings are now farther and farther apart. He doesn't hear the call of the raven or the bleating of a goat. He goes on walking.

He keeps going, on and on. The houses along the road are now huts and hovels. Everywhere he looks, children are playing and animals are rooting around in the piles of garbage. He keeps walking. His legs won't stop. No one can stop him. The sun has long since set. The cool that evening brings has also descended on the outskirts of the city. Small fires are burning, and mothers are fixing the evening meal. He keeps on walking. No one asks him if he's hungry. He's forgotten about food. He wishes he could crawl into the tiny crate and hear Ram Khan lock him in. He wishes he could duck under the covers of his bed in the brothers' dormitory. He wishes he could hide in the passageway under the station. He wishes that Abbas were there. Next to him, like he was every day. He wishes the two of them were limping along now, and earning money. He wishes he could curl up alongside Abbas, as he's done every night, and then fall asleep. He wants to share an apple with his friend.

Beneath the light of a gas lantern he sees a stall full of fruit and vegetables. The pile of apples is huge. He grabs the prettiest apple and walks on. It's a large red apple. Its scent is soft and sweet. The salivary glands in his dry mouth spurt into action, but he doesn't bite into the juicy fruit.

"That's him!" a voice says. He feels someone grab him from behind and push him into a car. He doesn't see the agitated stall owner. He doesn't feel the policeman shove him into the car. He doesn't hear the car door slam shut. He clutches the apple. The apple for Abbas.

1995 Rampur ~

"MA'AM, THE GENERAL says you must come." Hema was standing in the doorway of the drawing room, with a bowl half full of yogurt in his hand. He knew that for some time now memsahib preferred not to be left alone with her father, but in the kitchen supper was simmering, and it would burn if he didn't go back to check on it. If memsahib didn't go straight upstairs, then the general would start to stamp, and the dust would sift through the cracks in the floor and the ceiling. Tomorrow he'd have to dust everything again, and since that *darzi* had moved into the house he'd had almost no time to dust, which is why he repeated the general's request, in a more beseeching tone.

Going to see her father alone was one of the things she had come to dread during the course of the past year. As long as there was a man in the room — regardless of whether it was a plumber or an electrician or Hema — he kept himself more or less under control. But when she was alone with him, he became downright vicious. Sometimes he was so filled with rage that she feared he might tear the leather straps to pieces.

She made her way up the stairs. It was unusual for him to ask for her these days. In the beginning it was a daily occurrence. She'd have to race up the stairs — sometimes as often as thirty times a day — to keep him from smashing things to smithereens. But this past year he had become more manageable. On occasion he was even quite sweet, revealing sides of himself she hadn't seen before.

Charlotte opened the nursery door. He was sitting in his wheelchair in the middle of the room, with the fan whirring directly over his head. He wore only an undershirt and his pyjama pants. Hema had forgotten to remove his bib. His slender, useless feet were encased in old sandals, which were screwed to the footrest. This was a contrivance devised by Hema after the general had tried to stand up and took a nasty fall. His eyes were closed and he appeared to be asleep. His breathing was regular and his hands lay motionless in his lap. She was about to turn around and leave when she caught sight of the large wardrobe. If he caught her looking inside the wardrobe, he would be so furious that he might do himself harm: although he had long been confined by the leather straps, he often forgot they were there. She knew that she needed no more than a few seconds. A quick look would suffice. All she wanted to know was whether or not the lengths of fabric that had been transferred from her mother's bedroom, which was now her room, to the nursery were still there. During the early years when she shared the house with her father, Charlotte had displayed little interest in the objects that were stored all over the house. But recently they had both become more and more aware of the fact that their pension had not increased in twenty-five years. She had recently taken stock of the contents of the house, and now she saw to it that no new pieces were purchased as long as the old ones were still serviceable. Slowly she walked over to the wardrobe.

The wooden floor creaked. She was surprised that her father didn't awaken with a start and make a scene. He continued to breathe calmly as she walked across the room.

"I need to pee," said a voice behind her. It would have been pure luck if her first attempt to look inside the wardrobe had been successful. She turned around.

"The chamber pot is underneath your chair, Father."

"I don't want you in the room when I pee."

"You had me called."

"I did not have you called. I have to pee and I don't want you here."

"Then I'll go, Father."

"You were planning something. I could tell by the way you were walking."

"I didn't want to wake you."

"I wasn't asleep."

"I thought you were. That's why I was being so quiet."

"You weren't being quiet, you were being furtive. You were going to steal something from my wardrobe."

"No, Father, I was simply afraid of waking you up."

"Why did you come here in the first place?"

"You called for me."

"I did not call for you."

"Then I'll leave."

"No, stay. I didn't tell you you could leave."

"I thought you wanted to pee."

"Well, I do."

"That means you want me to go."

"Tell me, have you ever seen a man pee?"

"Father!"

"That husband of yours, did he ever mount you after that one night?"

Charlotte stared at her father in dismay. "He . . . he was a fantastic husband, and you know it. And a very good doctor. It's a shame that he's no longer alive. I know he would have taken good care of you."

"Him? That schlemiel! Who couldn't even operate properly, who lay there shaking like a reed when someone said the word "war," and who cried himself to death! You mean him?"

"I'm going downstairs now. Do you need anything?"

"Right, you go back downstairs, go back to playing lady of the manor."

"Goodbye, Father." Charlotte closed the door with a bang and then locked it. She felt like throwing the key away, so that no one would ever find it again.

1976 Rampur ~

Dear Patricia and Donald,

What wonderful news you just told us on the telephone — at last! We were expecting to hear days ago, and began to wonder if it was really going to happen. A girl, and one with such a lovely name: Isabella! Did you hear that name in Portugal? Here's a little cape I knitted especially for your baby. It's made of angora wool from the Himalayas. I hope that you like it and that Isabella will wear it for a long time. A kiss for my dearest, dearest niece, from her proud Aunt Charlotte.

P.S. Please send a photo!

1952 Bombay ~

THE SUN CASTS its morning rays and a tram bell tinkles. Peter doesn't know if it's the sun, the sound of the tram, their new house, or the new clothes Charlotte bought for him yesterday, but he feels calm. And he isn't plagued by his usual urge to rush off to the hospital. The coffee he ordered is delicious and the view of the harbour reminds him of the first time he saw his wife. It was a good idea to move house. Here in the city on the peninsula, with the sea on all sides, the soothing sound of the waves, and the cool evening breeze, he senses that some of the vigour he enjoyed before the war has returned. On the quay a little girl is jumping rope. Her braid jumps with her, and her striped socks keep falling down. She smiles in his direction when she sees him. For years, his old desire to have children has lain dormant, but as he watches this little girl at play, he doesn't understand why he was so fearful of becoming a father. The fact that Charlotte hasn't raised the subject recently doesn't mean that she no longer wants children. He knows that it is one of her most fervent wishes. He's seen how her gaze is drawn to mothers pushing baby carriages or women placing their hands protectively around their swollen bellies. For the first time, he considers the possibility that a child could change everything. His agitation, his melancholy moods, and his sleepless nights. A sensation of warmth fills his underbelly. He wonders what it's like to be a father. A child — his and Charlotte's — suddenly becomes an ardent and overpowering longing. He smiles back at the little girl jumping rope, and feels a blush coming to his face. Then he feels the blush on his cheeks spreading to the rest of his body. His heart begins to pound frantically and he starts to sweat. The smile on his face freezes into a terrified grimace. He is no longer aware of the girl smiling at him. The insidious plague that led to their decision to leave New Delhi has tracked him down. For an instant he thinks it's the ground that's shaking, a heavy truck passing by, perhaps, or even an earthquake. The smile on his face becomes an expression of panic. Then the cup slips out of his hand and falls to pieces on the marble floor.

~

He doesn't remember how he got to the hospital or who helped him into his white coat. He's standing at the operating table with a scalpel in his hand, and a patient is lying in front of him. The man groans. He hears the sighs of the jungle: the dripping trees and the rustle of the leaves. He sees wisps of mist that obscure his view until well into the afternoon. He is conscious of eyes that are spying on him from their invisible hiding places. He puts the instrument back on the stainless steel tray alongside the others and, without a word, walks away in the direction of the large swinging door.

~

CHARLOTTE IS SITTING in her chair near the door, keeping watch. On her lap she has a book, which she reads after Peter has fallen into a restless sleep. During the hours that he lies there trembling, with his eyes wide open, she continues to watch him, trying to understand what has happened. The dental surgeon, a Scotsman who has a permanent smile on his face and whose office is next door, has left behind a bottle of whisky. All Peter has to do is drink a large glass of single malt before going into the operating room. That was his advice. "We all shake once in a while." Charlotte knew that one glass wouldn't help. Not even a whole bottle helped. She has tried everything.

Peter groans. His gaze is focused on the ceiling and the rotating fan. He's afraid to close his eyes. Afraid of being drawn into the daydreams that transport him to places he never wants to see again.

1944 Burma ~

HE HEARS THE echo of the bullets reverberating inside his skull. He wants to yell that they can shoot his brains out, too, and that he's not afraid anymore, but now everything is still. The bullet he hoped for does not come. Slowly he raises his head. He can taste the blood in his mouth. The piercing sound in his head ebbs away. Why is nothing happening? Where are the Japanese? Why is he still alive? He can still move his legs. He pushes himself into a sitting position. He feels the heavy weight of the rucksack on his back. He tries to shake it off, but that doesn't work. When he holds up his hand, he sees that there's blood pouring out. Through the flow of blood he sees his mates lying nearby, each with a small hole in his forehead. Suddenly there's a resounding clap, and the trees around him shake. He starts to crawl away in a panic. Another explosion. Burning fragments come raining down. A sharp pain in his lower leg. He registers the pain but continues to crawl, until the trees stand closer together and the scent of the jungle overwhelms him. Again he hears that skimming noise. A bullet barely misses his head. He's happy that it's over, that they've seen him, that the torture of fleeing is over. He doesn't want to think about what is coming next. Now it's his turn, he knows that. A corpse in the jungle is less trouble than a wounded prisoner of war in a camp. He wants to stand up and raise his hands, but his legs refuse to co-operate. He hears no orders, no shouts. Nothing is happening.

He lies there for several minutes. Why don't they come? Surely that bullet was meant for him? A powerful boom, the ground shakes. The point of impact is far away. Where are they? Why don't they come and shoot him?

Peter senses that he has to get away, that he can't wait any longer, that they haven't seen him. He starts to crawl again. Away from the spot where he lost more than his little finger. Over tree stumps and between the thick trunks of centuries-old trees. Under bushes with thorns and through muddy trenches. If he doesn't treat his wounds, he might as well stay where he is.

He sits with his back against a tree, panting. The treetops disappear into the dense, leafy canopy. With trembling fingers he works the thread into the eye of the needle, stuffs a wad of cloth into his mouth, and sticks the needle into the flesh of his hand, where his little finger used to be. The little finger that did not save the lives of his mates. That did not save him from madness, from cruelty and injustice. He doesn't want to think about the faces. The panic he saw in their eyes. The cry of the older man. With a jerk, he pulls the thread through his flesh. He bites so hard on the wad of cloth that he can hear his jaw crack. He does not give in to the haze before his eyes. He sticks the needle into the flesh of his hand and pulls on the thread, again and again, until the wound is closed. Then he bites off the thread, pulls the cloth out of his mouth, and tears it in two. He binds one half around his hand and the other half around the gaping wound under his knee.

IT IS DARK. The explosions have stopped, and after an hour of crawling, he gets to his feet as best he can. Pain no longer fazes him. The word has lost its meaning. He hasn't seen or heard anyone. The path he is clearing for himself leads through the woods. By the light of the stars he can see that the woods are becoming thinner. He wants to get back under the protective cover of the trees before it gets light. He has no idea whether he's heading in the right direction, if he's leaving the enemy behind or limping straight into their arms.

He cannot get the smell of rotting meat out of his nostrils, any more than he can banish the memory of the row of men who were shot, one by one. The rucksack he's carrying is heavy, his wounds are throbbing and smarting, he is hungry and thirsty — but those sensations don't even register. He stumbles along haphazardly. Branches lash his face. Sometimes his clothing catches on something, sometimes his hands or feet sink deep down into a muddy hole in the ground. Mosquitoes in their thousands have launched an attack on him: ears, eyes, neck, arms, and ankles, every bit of flesh that is not covered by army khaki is endangered territory. After falling for the umpteenth time, he doesn't get up. He worms himself out of the rucksack and unbuttons the flap. Until now, he's been afraid to stop, but here in the dark of night, he thinks he's safe. He reaches into the bag. The contents consist of something damp and smooth. He pulls it out. The smell is unmistakable.

He awakens with no recollection of having fallen asleep. Next to him lies a large hunk of meat. The mosquitoes are gone, but the flies have found him, and in even greater numbers. They are swarming over the bloody hunk. The sickly sensation of hunger that has been tormenting him for weeks is gone, making way for an unfamiliar feeling that is more like a punch in the belly than an empty stomach. His eyes are swollen from all the mosquito bites. The slightly sweet smell of rotting flesh is all-encompassing. He remembers how one of the Japanese hung the rucksack on his back. He had assumed it was his own. He doesn't want to know what kind of meat it is. He hopes that it's the thigh of a cow, a holy beast that the Japanese do not eat. It doesn't even occur to him to leave it behind. He has no idea how long he'll have to walk and when he might find food again. This piece of rotten meat is his salvation. With a small penknife, which he finds in the flap of the rucksack, he cuts off a small piece. The flies buzz angrily, barely begrudging him a single bite. He wipes the insects off and puts the meat in his mouth. He doesn't try to taste it. There's no point. The smell is stronger. He attempts to get rid of the flies, and when that doesn't work, he just pushes the meat back into the rucksack, flies and all.

~

THE MAN IS younger than he is, actually still a boy. His blond hair contrasts sharply with his dark skin, which has been scorched by the sun. He is naked and he's carrying a Pekinese in his arms. The dog's tongue is hanging out of its mouth. Its protector looks at Peter imploringly. From his rucksack he pulls out the meat that's left. It has turned grey and the smell is so revolting that even the flies have left. He cuts off a small piece and gives it to the boy. His eyes begin to shine. He bites and then chews. For an instant he seems about to throw up, but then he takes a small piece of meat out of his mouth and gives it to his dog. Peter doesn't ask him where he comes from or where he's headed. Even without words, they know that they will move on together. How the boy lost all of his possessions except for his Pekinese is probably the same story as that of the woman who died in his arms yesterday, or the man whose body lay in the ditch in an advanced state of decomposition, or the child who went to sleep and never woke up again. None of the people who lived here were able to take their possessions with them.

He finds more and more people along the way. The first time he saw another man, he hid among the trees and watched him until he recognized the same fear in the man's eyes. They shared the meat. That night the man died. Peter buried him under a few stones, without ever learning his name. He continued his trek down the mountain, and gradually more people appeared. Not military men like himself, but civilians, missionaries, and civil servants who had been dispatched there, whose past had been lost, stolen, plundered, murdered, beheaded, burned. The future of those who survived was uncertain, but they found strength in that uncertainty. It could mean that this very evening they would be out of danger, or perhaps tomorrow. No one thought about two days from now, a week, a month, a year, or never.

The fear that plagued Peter in the jungle — that without a compass he would never find his way back — was unfounded. The meat is almost gone, and there are dozens of people on the path, all going in the same direction. They are all fleeing the jungle. They have brown or white skin and they are hoping that they will not again run into the enemy, who, in this jungle, has yellow skin.

The boy holds out his hand. Peter slices off another strip of meat. He crams it into his mouth greedily, and later pulls out a small piece and gives it to his dog.

"His name is Bear," the boy says, and he licks his lips.

"PETER! WAKE UP! Look at me! Peter!" The boy with the Pekinese shouts and pulls at his hand, shakes his shoulder, and slaps him in the face. The dull light that heralds the beginning of night has blotted out the contours of the mountains.

He can't take any more. He's had enough. This is where his journey ends. An hour ago, things went wrong when they had to cross the river. Peter has led the group for weeks, keeping everyone's spirits up: when someone was ill, he kept them going with encouraging words and stopgap measures. When they got to the bridge, he mounted the rickety wooden construction with the old Frenchwoman whom he had carried on his back for five days. The woman was frightened. Peter told her to look at the sky or the trees in flower on the other side of the river. He would see to it that she made it safely to the other side, he said. He took it step by step. The woman's legs dangled gently alongside his knees. Her legs protruded from holes he had made in the rucksack. She weighed less than the hunk of meat on the first day he found it in the rucksack. Then, without any notice or warning noise, the bridge broke in two. They fell into the fast-flowing water and were dragged down by the powerful hand that lived in the water and pulled unwelcome guests deep into the caverns below. He fought with the burden bound to his back. He didn't want to die. Not here. Not now, when he was almost there. Each time he felt that they were near the surface, they were sucked down again. He kicked, lashed, and swam. Until he felt the backpack slipping from his shoulders. It was as if she was pushing herself away, freeing herself from him. He grabbed her, but the spindly legs slipped away before he could get a grip on them. He came to the surface, gasped for air, and dived down again. She was gone. He came up for air once more and went down again, but she had disappeared.

He doesn't know how he reached the shore. All he can hear is the panic in the boy's voice.

"Peter! Look at me! You can't leave me alone!" The Pekinese barks as he opens his eyes.

1954 Bombay ~

IT'S DARK. SUDDENLY a man emerges from nowhere. He snatches the apple from Madan's hand and crams it into his mouth. Madan has no idea where he is. He wants to protest: the apple is for Abbas. But when he sees the sardonic look on the man's face, he holds his tongue. The lightning fingers glide over his entire body, just as the fingers of Brother Francis did, but they fail to find what they are searching for — Madan is wearing only a torn pair of shorts. He left everything behind, next to the body of his friend.

Slowly he becomes aware of the long, narrow space. There are men sitting all along the walls, staring at him. Madan stands there motionless with his eyes closed.

I have to go back. I have to get help. I can't leave him there alone.

The iron door behind him opens. He turns around and sees an old man being shoved inside, and when the door slams shut, he hears the key being turned in the lock. When he was working for Ram Khan, he was always happy when the shutters were closed and he was locked in for the night. But this is different . . . he misses the sense of security that locks used to represent.

"Let me out . . . ," the old man pleads, beating his fists against the heavy door. "I haven't done anything . . . Let me go . . ."

Suddenly Madan knows where he is, even though he doesn't know he got here. He was on his way to get help for Abbas, who is lying on the ground between the high walls along the quay, waiting for him.

The door opens again and four policemen carrying sticks walk in. The old man takes a step backwards and Madan also moves farther away from the menacing figures. One of them points his stick at a great hulk of a man, who curses as he gets up and is then roughly dragged off. The door slams shut and the old man goes back to banging on the door.

AT REGULAR INTERVALS the heavy door swings open and someone is thrown into the room or dragged out. Many of the new men shout that they haven't done anything. The old man was taken out hours ago. First they beat him into silence with sticks and then they hauled him away.

Madan sits on the floor, like all the others. He's worried. Although it's not terribly hot in the dark basement, he knows it's sweltering outside. He doesn't know a great deal about death, but the year he lived on the street, with Abbas, taught him that when a rat or a goat or a dog dies, the body begins to smell after just one day, and that people start complaining. He can't stay away too long. He has to go back. The next time he hears the turn of the lock, he gets up and walks over to the door. A drunken man walks into the room, and before the door closes again, he worms his way outside. Immediately someone grabs him by the shoulder.

"Back inside, you!" the policeman says, raising his stick.

"He goes to the commissioner."

"Oh, yeah? The commissioner himself?" The man holds onto Madan tightly, keeping his stick at the ready. "Is the commissioner going to do this one himself?"

"No, he's already left, you can take care of him."

"Me?"

"Why not? You've got to start somewhere, and the commissioner was furious when he brought in this little rat. It shouldn't be too hard. Put him in room three."

THE INTERROGATION IN room three takes only a few minutes. The young policeman soon realizes that unlike most of the beggars, Madan is not faking a handicap. Confidently, he starts filling out the papers. It's something he's used to doing, and he's good at it. His account is long and detailed. Madan tries to explain that Abbas is dead, and that he has to get help and then go back to his friend as fast as he can. But the policeman barks that he'd better keep his mouth shut, so Madan sits there and watches the pen in the policeman's hand. He wishes he could write. If he could write, he'd be able to tell him what happened.

With a deep sigh, the policeman finally puts down his pen and proceeds to place six different seals on each sheet; then he painstakingly signs the documents. It was only two days ago that he was given authority to sign documents, and he's very proud of himself. He pushes a buzzer, the door opens, and his colleague walks in.

"How are you doing? Are you done?"

The young policeman sighs and puts on a serious face as he hands over the pile of papers. The other man reads the first line and, surprised, glances at Madan before continuing. "So, so," he remarks. "So, so . . ." When he's finished reading the whole document, he puts it back on the table. "Good work. This is what we call good work."

The young policeman beams.

Without another word, the other policeman drags Madan from his stool, pushes him out the door, through the hall, and into a bus — where the old man is sitting, crying noiselessly.

~

I HAVE TO GET OUT OF HERE! Madan screams.

"Can't you get him to stop that caterwauling?" the fat guard says to his colleague as he opens his lunchbox.

I haven't done anything. Someone has to go to Abbas! He's still lying there, and pretty soon the dogs or the rats will find him!

"Smack him," says the guard who's eating his lunch.

"I'm not about to touch him with my bare hands. He's liable to bite, the beast." The man is convinced that the wild little boy standing in front of him not only is dumb, but also lacks a brain.

I don't bite. And I haven't done anything.

"Then go get your stick. You'll have to keep an eye out. Rats have nasty diseases."

I'm not sick, Abbas was sick, he was bitten, someone has to go to him.

"Where do we put him?"

I have to get away.

"Somewhere where I can't hear him. You'd think they were slaughtering a pig."

"I thought you were a vegetarian?"

"I am, but I heard a pig shriek once, and that's just what he sounds like."

Let me out of here.

"Do your people eat pigs?"

"No, of course not, and take that animal away, before he spoils my appetite."

~

THE ONLY TIME the others cannot see him is when he is sitting on the bucket. A grimy rag separates the corner from the rest of the cell. It wasn't there until a couple of weeks ago, when the old man, whose name is Mister Patel, found a piece of cloth left behind by one of the men who were released. He fastened it to the bars in a corner of the cell, creating a small enclosure where he said his prayers. But one morning the WC bucket appeared in the corner and no one dared to move it because they all knew that Ibrahim had put it there. So Mister Patel has gone back to praying with his back to the other prisoners, and Ibrahim spends most of the day behind the curtain, and not only to poop.

Madan thinks about Abbas day and night. Even when he doesn't want to think about him, he sees his friend's body. He wakes with a start as a dog is devouring the eyes and refuses to stop, even though Madan is beating him with a stick. Or a rat suddenly jumps out of Abbas's mouth, while he dreams that Abbas is only asleep. He still doesn't know why he's in jail, but everyone seems to be convinced that he is guilty of a terrible crime. Everyone except Mister Patel.

"Here you are, son," whispers Mister Patel; he is the only one who doesn't call him Mukka or rat. He slides his bowl in Madan's direction: there are at least four spoonfuls of rice left. "You're still growing. And I'm not."

Madan looks at him gratefully and quickly polishes off the rice. Even Mister Patel can have second thoughts.

"When we get out of here, son, you must come and have dinner with me sometime. I'm a good cook, if I do say so myself."

There's nothing Madan would like better. He's accustomed to eating irregularly — bad food and very little of it — but even Ram Khan gave him more to eat than he gets in the prison. Some of the others think that Mister Patel is his grandfather. Even Ibrahim, who is violent and abusive to everyone, has thus far left the old man in peace.

"That time will come, my son. I know it will. And then I'll make dal for you, with as much rice as you can eat." Mister Patel turns over and closes his eyes. Madan listens to his incomprehensible prayer. Sometimes Mister Patel prays for an hour at a stretch. And when he's finished there's always a serene expression in his eyes, something that none of the other men seem to have, not even after their prayers.

"Do you ever pray?" Mister Patel asks as he tries to pick the dirt from under his fingernails.

Madan shakes his head.

"Have you never learned to pray? Or aren't you a believer?"

With an effort, Madan can dredge up a few vague memories: once he was taken to a temple where bells were ringing and incense was burning, and he remembers the holy pictures where Ram Khan did his *pudja* every day, and Brother Francis, who knelt down next to him and took hold of his hand to point to the man on the cross. He shrugged.

"Do you want to learn how to pray?"

The serenity that Mister Patel radiates after finishing his prayers appeals to Madan, but he's afraid that if he prays, Mister Patel's god will get into his head and reproach him for forgetting Abbas. Even though he hasn't. But that's hard to explain.

Mister Patel sees the hesitation in Madan's eyes. "You don't have to do it the way I do, using real words. You can pray in your head. Did you know that?"

Again, Madan nods his head. Praying inside his head is something he does all day long. He doesn't call it praying, of course, but talking.

"It's not just talking inside your head," Mister Patel says. "When you pray, you start by emptying yourself and concentrating. Then you can start your prayers."

Madan's mind reels: *emptying yourself* and *concentrating*. He doesn't have the faintest idea what Mister Patel is referring to. But he nods earnestly, and Mister Patel continues.

"We are all part of Cosmic Awareness. You don't have to understand everything, but it's good for you to know that. The aim of prayer is to show respect, to make a request, or to guide your own thoughts and emotions. I pray to Brahma, Vishnu, and Shiva. But if you aren't yet acquainted with those gods, then as long as you're here you can also talk to the god inside you. Do you understand a bit of what I'm saying?"

The god inside him? He hasn't the faintest idea.

"Your god is part of you."

Abbas! Suddenly he understands what Mister Patel means. So that's what Mister Patel does: he talks to someone he loves very much. Abbas is always with him, every minute, every hour he thinks of him, and yet he's never dared to talk to him.

"I can see that you understand," says Mister Patel with relief. *This is really something*, he thinks to himself: an innocent prisoner in a filthy prison, trying to teach a deaf boy to pray.

1995 Rampur ~

THE DOORBELL RANG for the fifth time that day. Hema had brightened visibly in his active role as butler, but Charlotte retired to her bedroom; she was annoyed with the women from the club, who had not kept their part of the bargain. The last time they had this many visitors was four years ago, when her father turned ninety. She hadn't planned to celebrate his birthday, but a steady stream of servants and former personnel had come to congratulate the general, in the hope of receiving a gift. It was a tradition that he had initiated on his seventieth birthday, when he gave generously to all and sundry, and one that he had attempted to equal on his eightieth. Charlotte had run up to the attic dozens of times that day, in search of items that could serve as gifts. She had cursed her father for initiating a tradition that they could no longer afford. Looking at the empty sideboard, it suddenly occurred to her that her father might very well live to be a hundred. She heard Hema open the front door and ask someone to wait. He knocked on her door.

"Come in."

"Mrs. Nath is here to see you."

"Ask her in."

The wife of the goldsmith, Alok Nath, had never been inside the large house on the hill, so she looked around with interest. Charlotte had always had a problem with the goldsmith's wife, since she had the ridiculous idea that speaking very softly was the hallmark of chic. She also ate very little, because she regarded being fat as bourgeois.

"W . . . t," she whispered.

Charlotte couldn't make out what she said but welcomed her amiably and asked if she'd like a cup of tea. That was another problem. Her normal supply of tea lasted one month, but now it was almost gone after just three days. The same was true of the sugar and milk. She'd also had to buy extra biscuits, since tea can't be served without a biscuit.

Hema, who was waiting by the door, was of the same mind, except that he was delighted that at long last there was shopping to do. He'd visited five different shops before he found the right biscuits, and he enjoyed the rare luxury.

Charlotte sent him off to make tea and to let the tailor know that the wife of Alok Nath was there. As she uttered the word "tailor" a blush came over her cheeks. The wife of Alok Nath didn't notice, since white people always colour in such stifling heat. She'd seen people who had blisters on their sunburned skin or who developed a sty. Such extreme temperatures always gave her a headache, which was exacerbated by the interminable cries of the cuckoo and the barking of wild dogs. As those sounds were not audible inside the great house, she happily sank back into her chair and asked Charlotte how her father was doing. Charlotte was under the impression that her guest had commented on the weather, so she lamented the fact that the monsoon was so long in coming and the level of water in the reservoir was exceptionally low. This was interpreted by the wife of Alok Nath as an indication that her father wasn't doing well and that she shouldn't pursue the subject. Suddenly the room went dark.

"Oh, no, not the electricity again!"

"B . . . l."

Charlotte felt her way to the window, drew the curtain aside, and opened the shutter a fraction of an inch. A light shot into the room through the narrow slit, together with the searing heat that inundated the room like some kind of oily liquid. She heard the back door open and then close. Her heart began to beat faster. She wiped the perspiration from her forehead and ran a hand through her hair. There was a knock at the door.

"Come in."

Madan entered with a length of cloth that belonged to the

wife of Alok Nath. The heat, until then almost unbearable, became even fiercer. Charlotte felt the blush on her cheeks spreading all over her body.

Madan bowed his head slightly and held up the length of cloth. *It's not finished yet.*

"It's not finished yet," said Charlotte, who had vowed the evening before not to listen to the voice.

"M . . . g," whispered the wife of Alok Nath.

What did she say?

You can't understand her either? Charlotte felt the beginning of a smile.

"A . . . . l," the wife of Alok Nath continued.

I've never heard anyone speak so indistinctly!

That's the way she always talks, Charlotte replied, without looking at him. *I answer her and just hope that I got it right.*

But you can understand me. He didn't look at her either.

Charlotte's blush deepened and the tingling sensation in her belly intensified. She didn't want to think, but the thoughts came anyway. She wasn't sure if he was actually answering her or if his replies were a figment of her imagination. The sentences she heard in her head were so unashamedly direct that they couldn't possibly come from him.

You're not sure.

Charlotte nodded.

The wife of Alok Nath was under the impression that Charlotte had just agreed with her: the choice of fabric was wrong and she ought to buy new material. Charlotte looked on in surprise as the woman took the cloth from Madan's hands and stuffed it into her bag. She nodded to Madan in a friendly manner.

"H . . . . . . f."

Well, I'll be going.

Stay. The thought came faster than the self-control she'd always thought she possessed. Startled, she looked at Madan. *No, just go. I don't know what's going on anymore. I don't understand this. It's never happened to me before.* She covered her face with her hands.

The wife of Alok Nath concluded that Charlotte had suddenly been overcome by the heat, and for the second time in her life Charlotte heard what she said: "Call the butler!"

Mechanically, Charlotte rang the bell.

"Don't . . . well?" The gaunt woman walked over to her.

"I'm fine," said Charlotte. She heard the door open and then close, and she knew that Madan was gone. A bullet made up of long-concealed emotions shot through her body with such power that she gasped. She was immediately filled with fear. Her body was shaking.

The wife of Alok Nath looked at her anxiously and breathed a sigh of relief when the fan over her head began to rotate again and the lamp came back on. "G . . . . . . s," she said as she closed the shutter and drew the curtain.

Hema arrived with the tea tray and began to pour. The wife of Alok Nath declined the biscuit, and Charlotte decided then and there that she'd have to find another workplace for the tailor — and that she'd be wearing an old dress to the party.

WALKING BACK TO the kitchen, Hema caught sight of Madan sitting in the shadow of one of the big acacia trees. While he was pouring the tea, he'd overheard that memsahib Nath had taken back the material for her dress. It annoyed Hema that at the very first setback the man had gone into the garden to sulk. But what irked him most was the fact that he couldn't order the tailor around as he'd done with the other servants. For the fourth time that day he wished that memsahib had never taken the man into the house, and for the fourth time he took back his wish: if it hadn't been for the *darzi*, he would never have been able to do so much shopping.

Madan leaned against the tree and closed his eyes. *I don't see how she can hear my thoughts. Up to now, you were the only person who understood me. Other people never understand me — you know that. How is it possible that she does?* He opened his eyes and looked at the house with the closed shutters. *She hears all my thoughts, even the ones that last only a second. It's as if she can look into my mind.* He closed his eyes again, took a deep breath, and slowly exhaled through his lips. *It's because of her that I suddenly say whatever comes into my head. You're not supposed to say what you're thinking, but inside your head you don't have to be polite. How can she hear my thoughts?* He opened his eyes and looked at the house. *She thinks I'm cheeky. And that I don't respect her.* He closed his eyes again. *But I do respect her, in my head as well, really and truly. But I can't think in a servile way, and if I have to talk in my head the way other people talk with their voice, where can I do my real thinking?* He heaved another sigh. *I'll have to stop talking to her. If only I hadn't taught myself that I can say anything in my prayers. I'm going to do my best not to think about her, even when she's not there.* A deep frown line appeared on his forehead above his closed eyes. In the distance a peacock screamed. *But when I look at her hands, the way she walks and moves, and smell her scent . . . I feel that I'm safe. Please, tell me how I can stop all this, I don't know how. I think about her the whole day, even when I don't want to. Tell me. I don't want to be sent away, I want to stay here. I'm afraid. It's as if I have to protect her.* Madan opened his eyes and shook his head. He got up and walked back to the kitchen, head bowed. Only then did he hear the scream of the peacock. He hoped it was dancing: that meant that the monsoon was coming.

He went to the faucet to fill up a bucket, but only a thin trickle of water came out. All the windows of the big house were thrown wide open. There were no lights on, and perfect calm reigned, even in the kitchen. The sound of the water trickling into the bucket was drowned out only by the sound of thousands of crickets, taking advantage of the cool of the night to serenade their lady loves. Madan stared at the open window on the first floor and tried not to think, because he was afraid that his voice, like a real voice, could be heard in the bedroom. He picked up the bucket, which was half full, and walked away from the house as fast as he could. When he got to the apple tree, he stopped. He sniffed the bare trunk. The scent of apple wood was returning, and that reassured him.

1955 Bombay

At the end of the long corridor there is another barred gate. This time it's opened by a guard with rotten teeth.

"So, sonny, did you come to pick up your grandpa?" he sniggers. The smell from his mouth is even more nauseating than the odour that came from behind the curtain after Ibrahim had relieved himself.

Mister Patel takes Madan's hand; they bow their heads, stare at their toes, and say nothing. They have learned that silence sometimes minimizes the number of blows, although it was no guarantee where Ibrahim was concerned — if he lost something, he'd give everyone in the cell a good thrashing. The guards also beat them when they didn't return the metal bowls fast enough after meals, or the toilet bucket overflowed. The fact that they are being set free together comes as a total surprise. Since the interrogation at the police station, neither of them has seen anyone except their fellow prisoners. At one point Madan heard from one of the guards that he was charged with raiding a shopkeeper who was a second cousin of the commissioner. Mister Patel told him that he had a shifty landlord who was also a distant relative of the commissioner. Several of their fellow prisoners had also fallen foul of one of the man's relatives. But not Ibrahim: he'd murdered three men who he was certain had looked at his wife. And he was proud of what he'd done.

"Has the little guy come to pick up his grandpa?" says the guard as he breathes into their faces. Then he turns the key and the gate opens with a creaking sound. "These days people do what they damn well please. It was different during the Raj. Back then you could tell the good guys from the bad guys, but now . . ." The stench from the man's mouth is revolting.

Madan wants to hold his nose, but he doesn't take his hand out of Mister Patel's. Slowly they walk toward the next door. He feels the urge to run.

The guard opens the large wooden door.

On the other side, they see cars on the street, and a bus honks its horn.

"Don't I get my money back?" Mister Patel holds up his hand.

The guard gives him a stony look, accompanied by a blast of foul breath. "Did you fill out the form when you came in?"

"No, I wasn't given a form. They took away all my money."

"Write a letter to the director. It's not my department."

Madan, who arrived and is leaving clad in nothing but a pair of torn shorts, tugs gently at Mister Patel's hand. Mister Patel continues to protest, but when the guard pushes the heavy gate shut, they have to jump back in order to avoid being hit.

THEY WALK SIDE by side, still holding each other's hand. After all that time in a small, dark space, they are alarmed by the hustle and bustle of traffic and the people walking in all directions. They turn a corner and enter a quieter neighbourhood, with the occasional small shop displaying its merchandise out front. On the sidewalk, next to a chair under an umbrella, stands a cart overflowing with apples. Madan sees it from a distance, but Mister Patel does not notice until they are quite close. Mister Patel's hand tightens around Madan's, as if he is reading his thoughts, and he doesn't relax his grip until they've turned the corner.

The streets are broader now and there is more traffic. Madan recognizes the neighbourhood. It's an area where he and Abbas often begged. And suddenly he misses his friend more than he did during all those months in the cell. Unconsciously he begins to limp. "Does it hurt, my boy?" Mister Patel points to Madan's leg. Madan shakes his head and quickly adjusts his pace. He knows he must go back to the harbour to see if the body is still there. He owes it to his friend. But not today. Mister Patel walks into a narrow alleyway and stops in front of a low gate. All around them there are dark stairways. He lets go of Madan's hand for the first time.

They walk to the end of the alleyway and climb a narrow flight of stairs. Some of the steps are missing, and the handrail has also disappeared. Madan is glad that it's dark here. The bright sunlight hurt his eyes and burned his bare torso. They walk along a rickety gallery, and beneath them Madan sees that there are courtyards in between the housing blocks, where craftsmen have their workplaces. The smell of paint rises from below. Mister Patel knocks at a door with a carpet out front. They hear thumping noises coming from inside, like objects being shifted, and then a heavy-set man opens the door.

"Good day," says Mister Patel.

"Yes. What is it?" the man says. His voice is raspy from smoking.

"This is my house."

"Your house? No it isn't. It's my house."

"But it was my house."

"Maybe it was, but now I live here. I pay rent and I have a lease."

"Then perhaps you know where my furniture is?"

"Furniture? The place was empty when we moved in." Behind him, they hear a shrill female voice. The woman wants to know who's at the door.

"No one!" the man calls back.

"Then maybe you know what they did with my things? My books?"

"I don't read. Ask the neighbours." And before Mister Patel can open his mouth again, the door is slammed in his face.

Mister Patel doesn't ask the neighbours. He walks slowly back to the stairs. Madan knows that he's crying, just as he often cried in the prison, when he thought no one was looking. They cross the courtyard, go out the gate and back through the alleyway. Madan senses that Mister Patel doesn't know what to do next. They have no money, and the crevice where Abbas is lying is too narrow for Mister Patel to squeeze through. When they reach the street, Mister Patel takes hold of the boy's hand again and starts walking. Madan realizes that there is a big difference between being a beggar and walking hand in hand with an old man. People are much friendlier and some even say hello. Mister Patel stops in front of a greengrocery. Madan sees the huge pile of apples and mangoes. Would Mister Patel mind if he quickly grabbed an apple?

"Uncle!" cries a surprised voice from behind the counter. "It's been a long time! Where have you been?"

Mister Patel pulls Madan into the shop. The smell of fresh fruit and vegetables makes his mouth water. With a deep sigh, the old man sits down on a rickety stool. Madan can't take his eyes off the apples. "Go ahead and take one," the nephew says.

Madan gazes at the apples. He can already taste the sweetness in his mouth. Never before has he been able to look around before making a choice: he always grabbed the first one he could get hold of. His hand hovers over the crate. Then he picks up the biggest, reddest apple he's ever seen. He holds it in his hands, turning it over and over. Suddenly he takes a bite. The sweet juice runs over his lips, and the cool, firm flesh dissolves between his teeth. At each chew, the juice spouts against the inside of his mouth. As if he's in paradise.

"No house?" There is surprise in the nephew's voice. Mister Patel explains what happened and where he's been. His nephew looks at him in disbelief, occasionally uttering a cry of disgust, especially when Mister Patel tells him about the bucket behind the curtain and the quirks and moods of Ibrahim the murderer.

Madan doesn't hear any of it. He is aware only of the taste and smell of the apple, more heavenly than the most delicious fruit he has ever tasted or even dreamt of.

Mister Patel drops his hands into his lap, heaves another sigh, and asks if his nephew has a place for them to sleep.

"Here?"

"You're my only relative in Bombay."

The nephew looks askance at Madan, who is smacking his lips. "But not for him."

"Just for one night? Tomorrow I'll see if I can find something for him."

"Does he have lice?"

"I'm afraid we both have lice."

The nephew tries to disguise his aversion, and Mister Patel looks away in shame.

"If you can lend me a little money, we'll go to a barbershop and have our heads shaved."

"And have your nails cut, too," says the nephew, glancing at their hands.

THE SHIRT IS too big and the pants too long, but Madan feels like a prince. He and Mister Patel both have a cloth wound around their head. Madan smells of soap and isn't hungry. People greet them as they walk down the street, even more than yesterday. Mister Patel seems to know everyone, and when they pass a fruit stand where Madan and Abbas more than once stole fruit, the owner proves to be an old friend.

"Your face looks familiar," the owner says to Madan.

"Impossible," says Mister Patel. "He's not from around here."

"I could swear . . ."

Although he's not hungry — he had a real breakfast for the first time in ages — Madan cannot keep his eyes off the shiny apples.

"How's your back these days?" Mister Patel inquires. "Still lugging those crates around?"

The man mutters something under his breath.

"He's a very bright kid," Mister Patel says, "even if he can't talk."

Blandly, the fruit seller studies the small, thin boy. "You mean he's . . ." The man pointed to his own mouth.

"Can he have an apple?" Mister Patel sees the longing in Madan's eyes.

"Sure, go ahead," the owner says affably, in the hope that an apple will enable him to say no to his friend's request.

Madan is impressed by the prosperity of Mister Patel's friends. They all have stands full of vegetables and fruit, which they simply give away!

"He's strong," Mister Patel adds.

The owner has no intention of taking on a boy who can't talk. He doesn't understand why his friend is going to so much trouble for the child. He isn't even a relative of Patel's.

"Ramdas. He's looking for someone," the fruit seller says. He is visibly relieved.

"But they only hire adults. You know that."

Madan is eating his apple and getting used to the idea that he's arrived in paradise.

The men sit there, side by side, in silence.

"Chandan Chandran!" the man suddenly calls out.

"Who?"

"Chandan Chandran, the man with the ponytail who comes by here every morning."

"Him?"

THE BUILDING NEXT to the bookstore has dingy grey walls. The windows are narrow and the door opening is so low that Mister Patel has to bend down to enter. It's a building that everyone walks straight past. It does not inspire pride, but there is nothing repugnant about it: people simply don't notice it. Mister Patel and Madan walk by it four times before finally asking for directions to Chandan Chandran's workshop. They enter a low, narrow hallway filled with the heavy odour of oil and iron. It's hard to tell where the smell is coming from, since there are no workplaces to be seen, but they are also aware of a barely perceptible vibration throughout the building.

At the end of the long, dark hall, they come to a flight of stairs. A bare bulb hangs under the wooden staircase, and a man with a ponytail is seated at an old, broken-down wooden loom. Madan is already on his way up the stairs, but Mister Patel just manages to grab him by his shirttail. He points to the man sitting at the loom. Madan shakes his head. Mister Patel, who also regards Chandan Chandran as somewhat eccentric, gives Madan a smile and whispers that the man is a master craftsman. He hopes that Madan doesn't realize how little he actually knows about the man.

Chandan Chandran pulls the set-up comb toward him, to anchor the new thread. Of course, he's aware of the man standing next to him, who is fidgeting nervously, and the boy on the stairs, who's stubbornly shaking his head no. Chandran doesn't like visitors breathing down his neck. He prefers to be alone with his loom, in the security of the small, dark space underneath the stairs.

A portly woman with her arms full of umbrellas appears at the top of the stairs. Madan has to press himself against the wall to let her pass.

"Good morning, Mr. Chandran."

"Good morning , Mrs. Gutta." He glances up at the woman as she goes by, but immediately returns to his work.

"Good morning, Mr. Chandran," says Mister Patel in turn, although his voice is somewhat uncertain.

Chandan Chandran looks up as if he has just noticed him. "Good morning" is his reply.

"My name is Patel."

Chandan Chandran calmly continues his weaving. Mister Patel is conscious of the vibration of the floor, and he notices how the bulb under the stairs swings gently back and forth. The weaver's shadow is like some ghostly apparition that is about to pounce on the man with the ponytail but doesn't quite dare.

His nephew's words that morning echo through his head: "You can come back, but only if you come alone." Mister Patel understands his nephew's position. The space inside the shop — where the three of them spent the night surrounded by crates of vegetables and fruit — is indeed limited. They'd had more space per person in prison. His nephew slept in his regular spot, against the door, Madan lay down with his feet on a bunch of turnips and his head on a pile of radishes, while Mister Patel spent the night sitting on a crate of eggplants. Around eleven o'clock the crates in front of the store were brought inside and piled on top of each other. The stool and the moneybox found a place on top of the potatoes. The narrow plank that served as a counter during the day became a bed for his nephew, and also ensured that the door could not be opened.

Mister Patel clears his throat diffidently, hoping to catch the attention of the man under the stairs. "I'm working on a dissertation about the cross-fertilization of native urban plants," he says. "I studied biology." Mister Patel cannot understand why he doesn't simply ask the weaver if he has a job for Madan, but the right words refuse to come. "Even as a child I was fascinated by plants, indoor and outdoor, and I knew I didn't want to live in Bombay. But it was clear that that was the best place for my studies."

Again Chandan Chandran pulls the set-up comb toward him, adding another thread to the fabric.

"One day I'll go back to Hyderabad, where I was born, but there aren't nearly as many native urban plants there as there are here. I used to have boxes full of books with specimens, but they've all been lost."

Madan doesn't understand why Mister Patel is telling the weaver all this. He can't wait to go upstairs and find out where the humming sound is coming from. Surreptitiously, he moves up to the next step.

"Some of my books were quite rare specimens. Not that anyone would pay a penny for them . . . far too specialized. But irreplaceable, especially my own book, *Genetic Metamorphosis in Single-Celled Organisms.*"

Another step. Madan taps Mister Patel on the shoulder and beckons him to come. The story peters out. Chandan Chandran looks up.

"Is that the boy?"

Mister Patel nods.

"He can start by unpicking that piece of cloth." He points to a tightly folded length of red and white cotton lying behind the loom. Mister Patel smiles in relief. Then he picks up the piece of cloth and shoves it into Madan's hands.

The little boy believes that Mister Patel is his friend, and he is astounded when the old man raises his hand, wishes him good luck, and walks down the corridor to the door. Why is he leaving him? He doesn't want to be alone again. Mister Patel has to go down to the harbour with him. He's afraid to go alone. And he doesn't want to work for this weaver with strange hair, underneath the dark stairs. *Mister Patel!* he tries to shout. *Mister Patel!* Madan watches as Mister Patel walks down the long corridor, wishes them all the best, and, with a wave of his hand, disappears from sight. *He's leaving me behind!*

OUTSIDE, THE OLD man hears the boy's bestial, high-pitched screech. He stops in his tracks. He cannot leave him behind, all on his own. He must find something else, something for the two of them. He turns on his heels and is about to call out when he notices the display in the window of the bookstore: there, alongside several other books, lies *Genetic Metamorphosis in Single-Celled Organisms*. He sees the brown binding and the illustration of the egg-shaped planctomycetes, and the cell wall made of glycoprotein. Mister Patel's skin begins to tingle and suddenly his mouth goes dry. The brown book, dry as dust, seems to reach out to him. It's as if Madan never existed. As if he never spent months in prison unjustly or went to see the weaver under the staircase. As if he has never had a landlord who cheated him, or an unsympathetic nephew. He forgets everything and pushes open the door to the bookshop.

1966 Rampur ~

THE MEN WATCH in silence as the hospital brothers place the unconscious man on the stretcher. The ambulance drives off with the siren at full tilt. Charlotte runs to her father's car, but just as she is about to get in, she remembers that he keeps the car keys in his pants pocket, and that they are probably in the same sorry state as he is. She jumps out of the car and hails a rickshaw. The men start to load the pipes back onto the truck. On some of them there are spots of blood, which are already drying in the heat of the sun and will soon be unnoticeable on the rusty iron.

"Faster!" Charlotte urges the rickshaw driver on. The two-tone siren has stopped, and with it the hope that her father is still alive. She sees her world collapsing around her. The houses along the road crumble as they race by. The paving bricks sink into deep craters and the water seller drops dead as soon as she has passed him. The sound of clanging steel and the shouting that gradually died away are repeated over and over in her head. The silence that followed the deafening roar swells and swells. She no longer hears the cars that pass them, the milkman's shout, the barking of a dog: everything fades away in the face of the deathly silence within which she searches for that one liberating word, the watchword that tells her it's over, that it isn't true, that it never happened.

The hospital, a colonial edifice built more than two centuries ago, has the original entrance gate. She's been here once before, when she arrived in Sita's arms. She was five years old, and she'd fallen down the stairs. Her teeth went through her lip, and there was so much blood that her dress was completely red. Mother had tried to dry her tears, but Sita was the only one who could comfort her. It was also the one time that — with her father's permission — the nursemaid was allowed to ride in the car. Just that once. Sita cuddled and kissed her. The scent of coconut and ginger that surrounded her had a calming effect. Mother remained standing in front of the house, since Sita had taken her place in the car and was holding the bleeding child in her arms. The chauffeur sped down the hill. Sita began to sing softly — in a warm, slightly nasal voice — and through her tears Charlotte could see how her nostrils vibrated and her lips strained to form the strange words. Listening to the dreamy tones that filled the car, Charlotte forgot about the wound and the blood. By the time they reached the hospital, the pain had disappeared.

Charlotte touches her upper lip: the scar has faded, but the pain recurs more fiercely than she remembered it.

THE SMELL OF disinfectant is overwhelming. "Nothing left," she hears the duty nurse whisper to a colleague. The operating theatre is located behind olive-drab doors: the colour hasn't changed in two hundred years. She once read that olive green is a soothing colour. But her heart is thumping, her ears are ringing, and there's a pounding in her throat. She can't sit down. She paces back and forth from one end of the corridor to the other. She intended to tell him at dinner that night that she was going to look for a place of her own. That plan now hangs over her head like an evil omen. He must never know. Not now. He must live. Get back on his feet . . . and back to his daily walks. He must not die. The large door opens and a nurse comes hurrying out. She has a worried look on her face. She avoids Charlotte's pleading gaze and ducks into a room. Shortly afterwards she re-emerges carrying a fat book and disappears back into the operating room. Doesn't the doctor know how to operate? They have assured her that he is the best surgeon in the area. She wonders how inexperienced the other doctors are. Peter's last operation went wrong, too. His trembling hands could no longer do the work, no matter how hard he tried. He didn't need a book. He knew exactly what to do, but the uncontrollable tremors made it impossible. Had this doctor also served in Burma? The olive-drab doors have a forbidding quality. Is this the gate of death, the inconceivable world known as the hereafter, where Peter and Mother are supposed to be together, along with all those other dead soldiers and civilians? Have they found each other? It was a thought she has always shrugged off as absurd, but now, in this damp corridor, it besieges her. Is Father with them now, or is he still alive? If only the doctor can find what he's looking for in that book. If only he doesn't die. She doesn't want to be left alone. *Papa, don't leave me alone.* At the end of the corridor the doors fly open, and a nurse with a wheeled cart runs down the corridor. The steel instruments make a loud clanking noise. Without so much as a glance in Charlotte's direction, she pushes open the olive-drab doors and heads for the operating room. The door at the other end of the corridor also flies open and a doctor with one arm in the sleeve of his white coat races into the operating room. He's still alive, she thinks with a sense of relief. He must be. Otherwise they wouldn't be running.

The door opens and a doctor comes toward to her. She can tell he is exhausted by the expression on his face. After a perfunctory introduction, he informs her that the chances that her father will live are slim. Charlotte is about to faint, but she refuses to listen to her body. She wants to see him. Although it takes all her powers of persuasion, the man agrees to let her have just one minute with her father. He mutters that the last thing he needs now is foreign bacteria.

All she can see of him is his undamaged face. The rest of his body is concealed within a white tunnel. He seems to be asleep.

"He doesn't look that bad," she says in surprise.

"Well, not his face. But the rest! Nothing's in its normal place," the doctor says. "As if he's been through a meat grinder."

Speechless, Charlotte looks at the man. Only then does the doctor realize that the woman next to him is a relative.

"In a manner of speaking," he hastens to add, in an attempt to play down his words. Gently, he ushers her out of the room.

"Thank you, doctor," she whispers. Then she walks back down the long corridor, out of the hospital, and into the warm tropical night.

1995 Rampur ~

"Did you call, ma'am?"

Charlotte was standing in the music room. "I'd like you to move the table from the *darzi*'s workplace into this room." She pointed to the middle of the room, directly under the revolving fan.

"But the *darzi* is working, ma'am."

"This is going to be the *darzi*'s workroom."

"Here?"

"Yes, here."

Hema looked at his employer despairingly.

"But, ma'am, he is a *darzi*."

"Yes?"

"An ordinary *darzi*."

"I remember quite clearly that when my husband was still alive we often visited Maharaja Man Singh. The property of the maharaja was gigantic. There were stables with Arabian horses, English and Italian gardens, fountains, four large gates, and a driveway ten kilometres long, which he once had covered with oriental carpets. The maharaja had the largest continuous hunting grounds in India, and all over his palace there were tigers and elephants on the wall. He also had a ballroom and a large library, and he was very well read. And in the middle of his palace the maharaja had a special room where the *darzi* worked."

"In the palace?" Hema looked at her in disbelief.

"Yes, in the palace."

Hema wanted to protest. His prediction that the *darzi* would ultimately seize power had come true. Memsahib, who after the disaster with the tenants had never again allowed strangers into the house, was now determined to give the *darzi* the music room, so that the awful man could pull a cord, and a bell in the kitchen would ring: MUSIC ROOM. No matter what happened, he resolved that he would not respond to any summons that came from the music room.

"The floor needs cleaning, and the walls have to be washed down. I'll take care of Father today."

There isn't enough time to mop the floor, thought Hema to himself. *Who would do the shopping and the laundry? And who's going to cook, make tea, and all the rest?* He had always accepted his lot in life and performed his duties to the satisfaction of everyone, himself included. He was shocked by his own defiant reaction and immediately feared that he had contracted the same malady as the general. He placed a finger on the tip of his nose. He had seen how the doctor asked the general to perform that manoeuvre, and that he was never able to do so. His finger went straight to his nose, landing on the very tip. He heaved a sigh of relief.

"Is there something wrong?"

"No, memsahib. I'll do the floor tomorrow."

"I'd rather you did it today."

And again a wave of anger boiled up inside him. He was struggling to contain himself when suddenly the electricity went off again. This was immediately followed by a loud thud above their heads. He turned and raced up the stairs.

She didn't understand it herself. She had been standing in the middle of the music room when she noticed that there was a loose wire hanging from the lamp. It occurred to her that it might have something to do with the fact that the electricity regularly conked out. Hema had knocked and walked into the room, and when she opened her mouth she'd said things that she was positive she never intended to say. No matter what she did, the words continued to pour out. She had waged a battle with herself, inside her head, but the sentences paid absolutely no attention to her. They brushed her aside politely as the words tumbled out of her mouth at full speed. It had been years since she had last thought of the maharaja, and the tailor who had made her first evening gown had never crossed her mind again. But suddenly there they were, like a swarm of homicidal starlings scouring her lawn for unsuspecting victims. She heard Hema enter the nursery, and soon everything was quiet again. What must he think of her? She knew he was very sensitive about his status, and she had no desire to anger him. He had served them faithfully for so many years that she had gradually come to regard him as a member of their little family — except for the fact that he was a servant and slept in the kitchen, while they were the people he served. But it was true that the tailor's room had been centrally located inside the palace of Maharaja Man Singh, and that people were constantly coming in and going out. There was always someone who needed him, and the tailor's servant and his errand boy were constantly at work. Maybe it wasn't such a bad idea to have the *darzi* work in the music room. It was much cleaner than the area next to the kitchen, and the wife of Nikhil Nair was right when she said that fabric was quick to take on food odours. It had become clear to her that he had to go, and yet here she came up with one reason after another to keep him. The power wasn't back on yet. She heard Hema lock the door upstairs. She would tell him that she'd been mistaken and that the *darzi* would be leaving soon. She'd ask him if he knew of a house where there was an extra workplace, since she was aware that the personnel liked nothing better than exchanging the latest gossip. She was standing in the dark doorway of the music room, and she saw Hema coming down the steps. He had a slight limp and he paused at every other step, heaving a small sigh.

"Ma'am!" He started when he saw her standing there.

"I want you to mop this room now."

MADAN STARED OUT the window. There were no shutters in the servants' quarters, and it was incredibly hot, but the heat had never bothered him. He glanced at the jasmine bush under his window and saw that his nocturnal watering was beginning to bear fruit. The leaves, which not long ago were dry and withered, had regained some of their former vitality. He reached out and broke off a twig. He scratched the surface of the bark and then smelled it. The scent had returned.

1955 Bombay ~

MADAN IS ABOUT to jump up and run after Mister Patel when he sees a boy with a shiny black face coming down the stairs.

"Hello," the boy says.

Madan stares in amazement at the boy, who is covered in oil. He's the same height as Madan. There's oil running down his face, which he keeps wiping with the back of his hand. Madan offers the boy the piece of cloth that Mister Patel has just thrust into his hand, but the boy waves it away. He says admiringly, "Mister Chandran made it himself. It's beautiful, isn't it?" The boy points to the fabric with a grubby forefinger. "Do you get to unpick it?" There's a touch of envy in his voice.

Madan doesn't see why the boy should be envious of someone who's allowed to unpick a piece of cloth. He shrugs.

"The white threads are the warp and the red ones are called the weft. You have do it very carefully, you know."

Do you work here, too? Madan croaks unintelligibly.

The boy gives him a long look, wrinkling his brow. Then he leans forward and says to the weaver underneath the stairs, "He can't talk."

The man mutters something and Madan looks at the cloth in his hand. It's nothing special. Just an ordinary piece of cloth, in a red and white diamond pattern.

"Are you coming?" The boy turns and heads back up the stairs, leaving an oily footprint on each step.

Madan casts one last longing glance down the hall in the direction of the gate, but Mister Patel is well and truly gone. So he follows the boy up the stairs. Gradually the smell of oil and iron becomes sharper and the sound of whirring machines grows louder.

DISAPPOINTED, MISTER PATEL walks out of the bookstore. He held *Genetic Metamorphosis in Single-Celled Organisms* in his hands, and he knew immediately that it was his book. But the man at the counter refused to give it back to him, even after he recounted in detail all he had been through. The man had even retorted that it was the best story he'd heard but he wasn't a philanthropist. If Mister Patel really wanted the book, he could buy it, just like anyone else.

As he passes the small gate leading to the weaving mill, disappointment gives way to guilt. He should never have deserted Madan. As he walks down the long, dark corridor, his footsteps sound hollow on the cement floor. Chandan Chandran is still sitting at his loom, but the little boy Patel took under his wing during those long months is nowhere to be seen. If it weren't for the disappointment at not getting his book back, the pressure put on him by his nephew, his sleepless nights, in addition to the worry about the house that has been stolen from him and the money that was not returned after the five months he spent in prison unjustly, he would no doubt have gone back and inquired about young Madan. But now, for the first time in his life, Mister Patel is overcome by a sense of rage, because Madan has disappeared. He leaves the building in indignation and resolves on the spot to return to his birthplace, Hyderabad.

THE ENTIRE TOP floor is filled with looms. They are made not of wood, like those in the studios and workplaces along the street, but of iron, and they are powered by small motors. The exhaust fumes disappear through pipes in the ceiling.

"I'm the oiler," the boy says with pride.

Madan gazes in fascination at the rumbling, chugging semi-automatic machines with their taut threads, where men are throwing the shuttles back and forth, and at the roll of fabric that emerges at the other end. Never in his whole life has he seen so many machines in action. On one of them he sees the red and white fabric. He points to it and the boy nods enthusiastically. His words are lost in the loud clanging produced by the machines. Overwhelmed by the sounds and movements of all those iron rods and bars, he follows the boy. They pass a wall containing hundreds of spools of thread, in more colours than he thought possible.

In a corner next to a ladder, they stop, and the boy motions to Madan to follow him to the floor above. Upstairs he pushes open a hatch. Madan climbs into the opening. He is aware of a pungent, spicy odour. The small, poorly lit room has no doors or windows, and the rattle and clang of the machines is muted. Along the walls there are shelves with tin cans and boxes, small wooden crates, and bags and bottles filled with various unidentifiable substances. The smell of oil and iron has disappeared, replaced by an aroma he has never smelled before and cannot identify. The room is so permeated with odours that he's suddenly dizzy and has to sit down. Cautiously, he takes a breath. The air stings the sensitive lining of his nose. In prison he often tried not to breathe, especially when he was behind the curtain, but now he does the opposite. He cannot get enough of the intoxicating sensation in his head and the tingling in his nose. "Hey!" he hears the boy call. "Come down!" Madan could have spent hours sitting there, sniffing those smells, but the boy slams his hand down on the ladder, urging Madan to hurry. As he comes down the steps, Madan is so overwhelmed by the multitude of scents that he has to hang on to the railing.

"And don't let on to the boss that I showed you his room, okay?" the boy says.

Madan shakes his head, wondering how he was presumed to convey his thoughts to the boss.

1995 Rampur

HEMA SWORE TO himself as he mopped the music room, and when the bucket tipped over, he almost burst into tears.

Charlotte knew she ought to go downstairs to reassure him, and to cancel her plan while it was still possible to do so. But her legs refused to move, and when she tried to lift her right leg with both hands and put it down next to the bed, it was so heavy it wouldn't budge. She fell back onto the pillows and, without thinking, picked up the wooden box, took out a cigarette, and lit it. She realized after she had inhaled and began to cough that the cigarette was actually lit. The ritual of "smoking" a cigarette from the little box enabled her to think more clearly, but that had suddenly been destroyed.

Her thoughts shot off in all directions, and her normally relaxed contemplation became impossible. Even gazing at the statue of Ganesh could not calm her nerves. She took another draw on the cigarette. It was so very long ago since she'd last smoked . . .

She was not disturbed by the fact that the cigarette tasted good to her. It seemed to be part of all the strange things that were happening. While everyone around her was waiting and longing for the monsoon, she said things she never meant to say, did things she didn't mean to do, and read thoughts she didn't want to read. And she knew for certain that all that had nothing to do with the extreme heat.

MADAN PROTESTED WHEN Hema informed him that from then on he would be working in the music room. When it came to blocking his thoughts, he had no faith in the thickness of the ceiling and floor between him and Charlotte. The more he protested, the more adamant Hema became. Again and again he stressed that those were memsahib's wishes, and that she knew a maharaja whose tailor lived in the middle of the palace. He added haughtily that he was glad he wasn't the butler there.

Madan placed his sewing machine on the table, which Hema had positioned in the middle of the room. He didn't know where to begin. He looked around the room, then reluctantly sat down and started fiddling with the wheel. The needle shot up and then down again. In front of him lay a pile of fabric, and beside him his scissors and the tiny bottle of lubricant. He picked up the bottle and absently started oiling his machine. Suddenly, he heard footsteps above his head. He stopped and cast a worried glance in the direction of the ceiling. He listened to the sound of footsteps that went in the direction of the window and then back to the middle of the room. His glance shifted toward the dark spots on the wall where paintings must have hung. He went on oiling his machine. Above, he heard a door open and close. The hand holding the bottle shot out and a small puddle of oil formed around the presser foot. Startled, he looked around for a cloth to mop up the mess, but he saw nothing but the costly fabrics belonging to the members of the Rampur Ladies Club. He opened the cabinet, but the shelves were empty except for several photo albums wrapped in plastic. Someone was coming down the stairs, and that made him even more nervous. He raised his leg and used the inside seam of his trousers to wipe away the oil. Then he quickly sat down at the machine, and, taking the topmost length of fabric from the pile, he began sewing at the spot where the needle came down. When the sound of footsteps grew faint, he stopped, looked at the fabric, heaved a sigh, and began unpicking the useless seam.

1966 Rampur ~

There are no rickshaws or taxis waiting in front of the hospital. She doesn't realize that it's already well past midnight and that her father's operation lasted more than twelve hours. She waits for a while and then decides to walk. Guided by the light of the stars and the odd street lantern, she walks away from the city centre of Rampur. Their house is on the other side of town. She's not used to walking alone. She always has a coolie with her to carry the groceries, or the *bobajee*, who's better at bargaining at the market.

Except for a snoring dog and a sleeping goat, there's not another living soul on the street. The unrest of the day has made way for a serene hush.

She pauses in front of St. Stephen's Chapel. It's too dark to distinguish the cemetery behind the church. *Let Papa live,* she prays, directing her words to the steeple. Charlotte never prays. Not since her last year at boarding school, where she had to go to church every Sunday, year in, year out, and always said her daily prayers. None of her pleas for help were ever answered. After Peter died, she renounced prayer for good. *Let him live, please.*

Perhaps it's the nocturnal calm, or the dark of the night, but the nauseating anxiety that gripped her at the hospital seems to be ebbing away. It's as if she has entered a kind of vacuum. The concern for her father's life fades away, and her feet seem to leave the ground. The fact that she is on her way home is of no importance. She is no longer walking, but dancing, her arms spread slightly, like elfin wings.

Only then does she hear the music, so gentle and rarified that it seems part of the starry sky, millions of light years away. She turns into an unfamiliar alley and sees a house whose doors are wide open and welcoming. She steps inside a room filled with cigarette smoke. There are people sitting on the floor. The music that enticed her here is just as fragile and ethereal as it was a moment ago, when she first became aware of it, but now the sounds are richer and fuller. In the middle of the room, on a small, raised platform surrounded by lighted candles, there are three Indian musicians: one is playing the tabla drum, one is seated behind a kind of xylophone, and in the middle there's a zither player. No one in the audience seems to be surprised by her entrance, and despite the fact that her blond hair and fair skin contrast starkly with the outward appearance of the other people in the room, she senses that she is welcome. She sits down on a cushion that someone has shoved in her direction and closes her eyes. The celestial tones take possession of her, and all the events of the day are forgotten.

The zither player starts to sing. Charlotte opens her eyes, and by the light of the candles she sees the man's face. The song has a nasal tone, and it is full of unintelligible words. She cannot take her eyes off the singer. She watches his long fingers as they glide over the strings, his black-rimmed eyes, his mouth, singing about a world she's never experienced before.

SHE HASN'T SEEN anyone get up or heard anyone leave, but when the musicians stop playing, only a handful of people are left in the room, which was packed when she first arrived. The final notes fade away. People begin to talk quietly. The musicians get up and put away their instruments. The panic that had faded away begins to force itself upon her from all four corners of the room. Closing her eyes doesn't help: where a moment ago there was light, there is now darkness. Her breathing accelerates. She wipes away the traces of tears on her cheeks, tears that brought some relief. She gets up and walks over to the singer. He looks at her and she looks back. Each step in his direction is a step away from the world she comes from. She knows that if she keeps walking, everything will change. She does not hesitate.

The room is empty except for Charlotte and the zither player; they are sitting next to each other in silence. One last candle is still burning. He offers her a cigarette. She hasn't smoked in years, but she takes it. He gives her a light. The brief touch of his hand goes through her like an electric shock. She shudders. He lights a cigarette himself. She inhales the pungent tobacco smoke. A wave of dizziness sweeps over her, and when it fades away, she takes another drag. There are no memories, only longing.

They sit perfectly still. Outside, an owl hoots. It's calling them. She blows the cigarette smoke toward the open window: a cloud that is free to rise up to heaven. The tobacco is hot on her tongue. Soon the last candle will go out. She listens to the sounds of the night. He takes her hand . . . or perhaps she takes his.

NOT A WORD is spoken. She doesn't know his name, but she can still taste him on her lips and smell his skin. The sky was turning pink when he slipped out of her. They got up, put on their clothes, and walked outside. They went in separate directions. The owl hooted one last time as she turned onto the road leading home.

~

Dear Donald,

There's a lot I have to tell you and I don't know where to begin. If you were here, it would be so much easier. I called the telephone number you gave me, but there was no answer. I do hope that nothing's happened, and that this letter will reach you. Father has had a very bad accident. For four days he was at death's door, but last night he opened his eyes and looked at me. At first I thought he was angry with me, but later I realized that he was in a great deal of pain. It's hard to describe what happened. A load of heavy iron pipes fell on him. The worst part is that it was his fault. He'll probably never walk again, but he doesn't know that yet. He also doesn't know that they had to cut his boots to pieces. I sometimes think that's going to be the worst blow of all. I'm not looking forward to telling him all this. That's why I wish you were here now, so that we could do it together. He's in a plaster harness from his toes to his neck. The doctors said that it was ridiculous to put a cast on his shattered legs, but I'm positive that Father wouldn't have survived if his legs had been amputated. If he still has his legs — even if he can't walk — he will probably find the courage to fight for his life. No one can say how long he'll have to stay in hospital, but it's certain to be a matter of months. Will you call me as soon as you get this letter? I'd really like to talk to you. I'll send this by special delivery, so it'll get to you quickly.

Regards from your sister Charlotte

1955 Bombay

MADAN UNPICKS THE material very carefully, without breaking the thread. He's amazed that a thread can be so long: as if it'll never end. He's sitting on the ladder leading up to the scent attic, as he calls it, and working on the red and white cloth. Subhash, the oiler, asked Mr. Chandran if it would be all right for Madan to work upstairs, and he gave his permission with a curt nod.

Madan is still very angry with Mister Patel. Now he won't be able to filch an apple if he wakes up in the middle of the night. He feels his stomach rumbling, and he has no idea whether he'll be given some scraps at the end of the day, like when he was working for Ram Khan, or maybe nothing at all. He can't ask Subhash, who's just crawled into one of the machines clutching his can of lubricating oil, and the weavers are all just as busy. He continues to pull on the thread — but this time he pulls too hard, and it breaks. Subhash told him he was supposed to unpick the entire length of cloth without breaking the thread, so he ties the two ends together, which is pretty tricky because it's so fine.

"DID YOU LEAVE him behind with Chandan Chandran?" Mister Patel's nephew asks, with a hint of concern in his voice.

"You were the one who said he might find work there."

"I never thought he'd say yes."

"Well, he didn't." Mister Patel has decided to go straight back to Hyderabad, and he's only stopped by his nephew's shop to pick up the kit bag containing what remains of his possessions.

"But you left him behind there?"

"I came back half an hour later and he was already gone."

"Oh, that's all right then," says the nephew in relief.

"What do you mean, all right! I do my best to find something for the boy and he just walks away."

"Chandan Chandran . . . ," a customer mutters, but loud enough for the others to hear. "I'd have my doubts."

"Doubts about what?" Mister Patel asks, looking in surprise at the man with the three bananas in his hand.

"Oh, nothing, really," says his nephew.

"What do you mean, nothing?" Mister Patel asks. "You're the one who said I should send the boy to him."

"Did you really say that?" the customer asks the nephew in alarm.

The nephew raises both arms in a gesture intended to absolve himself of all blame. "It was one of the possibilities."

"What's wrong with this Chandran?"

Mister Patel wishes he hadn't come back to pick up his kit bag. There's nothing of value in it, since Ibrahim the murderer took everything he was attached to and the rest is in the police commissioner's pocket.

"They say he's rather . . ." The customer searches for the right words. "Rather peculiar."

"He wanted the boy to unpick a length of cotton!" confirmed Mister Patel, who also found the weaver a bit strange.

"Is that what he wanted him to do?" said the customer with relish. "And what else did he want him to do?"

"Nothing. He just wanted the boy to unpick the piece of cotton."

"Did he say anything else?"

Mister Patel is not planning to tell the customer that he was reluctant to ask the man at the loom if he had work for the boy because he sensed that Madan didn't want to stay there. Just as he had been able to do in prison, he could always tell when the boy was afraid. That's why he rambled on about the dissertation he's been working on for ten years and the fact that he'll probably never be able to finish it because all his books are gone. He does recall that the weaver suddenly asked, "Is it that kid?" Now, how did the man know that that was his question?

The nephew sighs and weighs the bananas. "What's all the fuss about, anyway? The kid is smart enough, and there are more important things in life. Did you hear we're playing Pakistan again?"

"When?" asks the customer.

Mister Patel picks up his kit bag, takes an apple from the crate without his nephew noticing, and drops it into his kit bag. "I've got to be going, otherwise I'll miss my train."

MADAN UNDERSTANDS HOW the threads criss-cross each other: a lot of short ones and one long one. Every time the colour changes, a new thread is used, tied to the one before, just as he has done. He's figured out that the easiest way to pull out the long thread is to lay the cloth with the short threads flat on the floor, so they don't get tangled. He's kneeling on the floor. He's forgotten about his rumbling stomach, and he's no longer angry with Mister Patel. He's fascinated by the thread, which is getting longer and longer. Things become more difficult the closer he gets to the end: the long thread keeps getting tangled up with the short ones.

He's rolled up the entire thread and holds the spool proudly in his hand. It's only then that he smells the lubricant again and becomes aware of the machines. He sees the man with the ponytail coming toward him. The man holds up his hand, and Madan places the spool in his palm. Chandan Chandran beckons him to follow.

They walk back to the stairs and go up to the next floor. On the flat roof there's a kind of lean-to made of wood and long grass, with several grass mats and a chair.

"Are you deaf, too?" asks Chandan Chandran.

Madan shakes his head.

"If you want a job, you can sleep here and you'll get breakfast and your evening meal." He gives Madan a penetrating look.

I'm hungry. Madan nods and points to his mouth.

The man with the long hair goes down the stairs and Madan follows him past the mechanical looms to a small room in the corner. Subhash and the weavers are sitting on the floor eating.

Madan fills up a plate with rice and dal, and sits down on the floor next to them. He is nine years old, but he feels like an adult.

1995 Rampur ~

CHARLOTTE TIED THE bib around her father's neck. It was a large bib, made at her request by Sanat, the previous *darzi*. She remembered the first time she had to feed her father, and how awful it was. She couldn't get a spoonful of lukewarm cereal into his mouth without showering everyone and everything in the vicinity. Nowadays she had no trouble, and the bib wasn't even necessary. But the closer she kept to the daily routine, the calmer he was. She stirred the yogurt and gave him a spoonful. Her father smacked his lips contentedly. She'd ask Hema to change his diaper: it attracted flies, and that would interfere with his afternoon nap.

"Does it taste good?" she asked.

"Delicious."

Charlotte was surprised that he had actually answered her question. It had been some time since she'd been able to carry on a normal conversation with him. He did have some lucid moments, but they were becoming more and more rare. "Is there enough sugar in it?"

"I already told you it was delicious."

"I'm glad to hear it."

She put a heaping spoonful into his mouth and he slurped it up with evident relish.

"Are you going to the party?" he asked as he licked the yogurt from his lips.

"What party?"

"The party at the club, of course. It's coming up to the two hundredth anniversary."

"Yes, I'm planning to go." She had no idea how he had found out about the party. She hadn't mentioned it to him, Hema never concerned himself with such events, and none of the ladies who had visited her the last few days had gone upstairs. She couldn't imagine that the thought had simply come to him out of the blue.

"I want to wear my uniform."

"You mean you want to go to the party?"

"Of course. I'm the oldest member. I was a member long before the Indians were allowed to join." He pointed to a plaque on the wall that he'd won at a tournament held at the club, long before his accident. "Get my uniform out of the wardrobe."

"First one more spoonful," she replied, holding the full spoon to his mouth. He kept his lips tightly closed.

"Come now, Father. We're almost there."

"I don't want any more. I want my uniform," he peeped through his tightly closed lips.

"Just two more bites."

The general began to cry softly. The spoon was suspended

in front of his mouth. "Come now. The bowl is almost empty."

"I don't want any more."

"You can have your uniform when the bowl is empty."

With one stroke he knocked the spoon out of her hand. "I want my uniform!" The globs of yogurt hit the wall.

"Now why did you do that?" she asked as she picked up the spoon. "You were almost finished. You know it's important to eat well."

"Finish it yourself. You're thin as a rail."

It was true that Charlotte had got into the habit of economizing on her own food, in order to buy biscuits and sugar to serve with tea when she had guests. A few days before, Hema had suggested, in his typically vague and discreet manner, that she ought to eat more. She told him that the extreme heat took away her appetite, so that no one would know that for days she'd gone to bed with her stomach rumbling with hunger.

"I WANT MY UN-I-FORM!" her father screamed, now in tears.

The only way to put an end to his whinging was to give in. Otherwise it would end in a flood of abuse. As a rule, Charlotte stood her ground — many of his requests were simply so ridiculous that it would be impossible to give him his way. But this plea gave her an opportunity to look in the big old wardrobe. She put down the spoon and bowl, and before he could renew his tirade, she opened the huge doors. There hung the uniform in all its glory, enclosed in a transparent plastic garment bag. As Charlotte took the garment out of the wardrobe she saw the enormous piles of fabric. They were enclosed in yellowed plastic, so that it was impossible to distinguish the colour of the fabrics inside.

"Father?" She unzipped the garment bag and took out the uniform. "Would it be all right if I used one of these fabrics to make a dress for the party?"

The general didn't hear his daughter's question, but he brightened at the sight of the shiny medals and insignia. Charlotte laid the uniform in his lap. The odour of a recent bowel movement was noticeable. With the tip of his forefinger, the old man — known to all as "the general" though it was now clear that the highest rank he ever attained was that of lieutenant colonel — stroked the embroidered cords, insignia, and medals, and then the Order of Distinguished Service, his highest military decoration, awarded for heroism while he was stationed in Burma.

Charlotte took a cloth and wiped the remains of the yogurt from the wall. She wondered what was going through her father's head. Did he think he was back in Burma, at the Officer's Club, perhaps, or had his fantasy already transported him to the party at the club? He was so obsessed with the threadbare uniform that he didn't see Charlotte transferring the piles of cloth, all neatly wrapped in plastic, from the wardrobe to the landing. The shelf, which had been overfull, now looked almost empty. She closed the door quickly, forgot to take the bowl and spoon with her, locked the door, and heaved a sigh.

1944 Burma ~

USING A SPOON with a bent handle and a bowl worn thin from years of scraping out the contents of his mess kit, he manages to swallow the sticky substance concocted from some kind of bitter fruit. It's the first food he's tasted in days. The odour is revolting and the first spoonful makes his stomach churn, but he continues to chew, trying not to think about what it had been in its former life. They finally have something to eat, and that's what matters.

Victor and two other men are lost. The day after he gave his seconds-in-command orders to spread his men along the front line, he has lost contact with them. His liaison officer stepped on a land mine and took the sole radio to his grave. His batman, who carried the maps, was suddenly felled by some rare form of malaria and died that same night. The maps have been reduced to pulp by the rain and can't even be used to start a fire. He has suppressed the memory of how the other men had come to their end. No use dwelling on the past. They have to go on.

Victor's brain is beginning to function again now that he has something in his stomach, even though it's an effort to keep it down. Their hunger is so great that the soldier across from him is eating his own vomit.

The major looks at what remains of his men. Two young soldiers. No danger of anyone deserting — where would they escape to? Each step they take in the impenetrable jungle is dangerous, and it is a miracle that they haven't fallen into an enemy trap. Are the Japs in front, behind, to the left, or to the right of them? There's no way of knowing.

Now that he is able to think more clearly, the fear returns. He has despised cowardice his entire life, but it has dogged his footsteps ever since they lost their way. Here, in this green hell, he doesn't fear the bloodsuckers, the snakes, or the black scorpions. They're a necessary evil, like the tigers. But he is terrified of the enemy, ever since he saw and smelled what they did with the men of the fourth battalion. No one talks about it: he has declared the subject taboo since the day it happened. When they're not sleeping or resting, they crawl as close as possible to the ground, invisible. The sun has reached its zenith and now it penetrates the canopy and hits the foot of the trees. Amid its flickering rays, the men scrape their mess kits clean.

Victor is hot. He lost his tie and shirt a long time ago, and he has nothing but his tunic. Their uniforms are made of indestructible canvas that is useless in this heat. If he gets out alive, he resolves to write to the general staff in London, to those idiots who never stopped to think before they sent them into the jungle. They sweat themselves silly, and after that the rough fabric scrapes their clammy skin until it bleeds. He sees the two soldiers nodding off. He has to tell them that it's important to remain alert. But a full stomach produces a longing for sleep, real sleep, such as they've not enjoyed for weeks. He takes off his tunic and rolls it up. Then he places it behind his head and leans back against the tree he's sitting under. He doesn't know when his eyes fall shut, but suddenly he hears the ringing voice of Vera Lynn.

The voice is very close. For an instant he thinks that the singing is part of a dream within his forbidden sleep, but then he realizes that it really is the voice of the "Sweetheart of the Forces" that echoes through the jungle. The two other men also jump to their feet. That voice can mean only one thing: there's another British unit nearby. Briefly it occurs to him how odd it is that the silence of weeks should be broken so suddenly, but the joyful prospect of finding fellow countrymen here in the jungle prevails over all doubts. They stumble as fast as they can in the direction of the voice, which is calling to them like a temptress.

They run into a clearing. Emerging from the shade of ancient trees, they are almost blinded by the sun. In the middle of the field stands a wind-up gramophone.

There is no one in sight, just the lone gramophone. They look at each other. Their doubt and astonishment, which lasts only a few seconds, seems endless. Victor watches the black vinyl revolve, sees the shine of the grooves, the reflection of the sun, the oscillating needle swaying to the rhythm of the 78 r.p.m. gramophone record. Vera Lynn's familiar voice crackles through the jungle. He recalls watching the woman in the white suit up on the stage, so far away that she was only a tiny dot. Everyone sang along with her. And here, not ten metres away, her voice reaches him from the horn. Where are the others? Sleeping under the trees? Where there's music, there must be tents, food, ammunition, medicine, a map . . .

He is just about to raise his hand, signalling that there's something wrong here, when a bullet whizzes through the air. The young man next to him, a second lieutenant from Gloucester and a newcomer to India, is struck and falls down dead. Without a flinch, without a sigh. Between his eyes there is a small hole, and a trickle of blood as Vera holds the last note and the piano completes its last run. Out of the corner of his eye he sees the other man, a private first class, raise his hands. The needle gets stuck in the last groove, like a sluggish metronome.

Where are they? Why don't they show themselves? The fear that has constantly plagued him re-emerges. He wants to raise his hands. He wants to cut their throats, he wants to take revenge on them for what they've done. Why don't they come out of the woods? Who pulled the trigger? Perhaps it wasn't the Japs but some desperate Brit who's suffering from hallucinations and has taken them for the enemy. The needle continues to tick in its groove. He knows that the Japs consider surrender a sign of cowardice, and that cowards are often summarily shot, but he decides to risk it. Slowly he raises his arms . . . until he remembers what they did to that major in the fifth battalion. Then his mind begins to spin in a wild panic. He remembers that his uniform jacket and his helmet are still lying under the tree. In his stained khaki undershirt and trousers, he looks exactly like the soldier next to him. There is nothing to distinguish him from the cannon fodder, except perhaps his age. But his face is just as dirty and unshaven, his hair just as long and grimy: even at close quarters, a Jap wouldn't see the difference. He raises his hands still higher.

Two Japs emerge from the trees and bushes, guns at the ready. Their uniforms are just as ragged as his, their cheeks just as hollow, and even the hatred in their eyes is the same. Until they stop next to the gramophone and one of them lifts the needle lovingly, removes the record, and replaces it carefully in the sleeve. Victor wonders how many others have fallen for this trick, devised by the yellow vermin, who probably don't appreciate anything but the twang of an untuned lute.

Now that the ticking has ceased, the sounds of the jungle are doubly prominent. One Jap places the record in a box, together with the gramophone and the horn, while the other keeps his gun trained on Victor and the young soldier, who are standing next to each other. One of the Japs disappears into the undergrowth. Victor prays that he doesn't find his jacket: he wants to go into captivity anonymously.

"Major," the young soldier whispers.

"Shut up," Victor hisses.

"But, Major . . . ," the frightened boy begins again.

"Do you want to get me killed?" he growls in a voice that only the boy can hear.

The boy is silent. Their enemy returns with three rifles. He says something to the other Jap, and the entire group sets off. They walk into the jungle, leaving the uncovered body of the second lieutenant from Gloucester behind. It could be five kilometres or ten or two. Victor and the boy walk slowly with their arms above their heads. It's no use trying to escape: the jungle is more dangerous than the enemy, and it might just be possible to talk to them.

They walk into a camp just as the sun starts to set. There are a few shabby huts, and in front of one of them stands a chair. During the march, Victor has considered all the possible scenarios, and in each case he came to the same conclusion: the best thing is to just wait and see. They are led to a fenced-off area, where they collapse onto the ground. The Japs shout something in the direction of the huts, but there is no answer. The enemy is just as exhausted as they are, especially the man who led the group, carrying the gramophone and the rifles on his back. Again they call out, exchanging worried looks. Victor senses that a chance for escape may present itself sooner than he expected. One of the men enters a hut and quickly reappears. He calls to his mate, who suddenly readies his rifle and aims it at the prisoners. Victor withstands it all in silence, happy for a chance to drop his arms. He sees the other man go into the tent, and feels the first mosquitoes of the evening launch their attack on his bare arms and neck.

"Major . . . ," the young solder whispers.

"Don't call me that, for Christ's sake," snaps Victor.

"What am I supposed to call you, Major?"

"Anything except that."

"What do you mean?"

"Call me Jack, for all I care."

The Jap aims his weapon at them and shouts something, presumably that they're not allowed to talk. They fall silent and look straight ahead.

Victor slaps a mosquito just as it's about to stick its dart into his arm. Suddenly he is reminded of his daughter. His children mean little more than their faraway addresses to which he sends a letter at Christmastime. He didn't see them grow up. Would he even recognize them? Will he ever see them again? It's been a long time since he felt like a father. He's a soldier. He's been a commandant for many years, but now that he's pretending to be an ordinary soldier, something inside him has changed. He feels a maudlin sensation coming over him, something he had always loathed and detested when he saw it in his young recruits. He does his best to shake it off.

Suddenly the camp is swarming with Japs. Victor has no idea where they came from. The enclosure that holds Victor and the soldier is opened and a small group of British and Indian soldiers are brought in. They appear more dead than alive. The private first class jumps to his feet to welcome the men. The Japs don't even allow him to finish his sentence: a bullet bores its way into his forehead, and he falls down dead. No one dares utter a word.

By the light of the half moon, the men gaze at the dead body lying in their midst. No one has touched it, after an attempt to cover it was swiftly punished. No one sleeps, not because of the mosquitoes, but because they are all convinced that closing their eyes could mean the end of their lives.

The mosquitoes have been replaced by flies: at first light they found the body of the young soldier. It has also been discovered by ants, which are now visiting it in huge numbers. A representation of the order Hymenoptera marches past Victor's foot in the direction of the dead man. He has no idea what these scavengers find on the body. It appears to be intact, with the exception of the face. The bullet fired at dusk was less accurate than the one that struck the second lieutenant from Gloucester in the forehead, and the eye is missing.

The sun rises and the guards are changed. Now Victor can distinguish the faces of the new prisoners. The four new men are even more dishevelled than his men were. They have long beards and none of them are wearing boots. Their feet are covered with wounds and there is little left of their uniforms.

A crow hops into the enclosure as if it's perfectly at home there. When one of the men adjusts his position, the bird flutters up and then lands next to the body of the young soldier. It pecks a few ants from the long column heading toward the body and then hops onto the face, where it pokes its beak into the coagulated blood next to the eye socket. The soldiers watch in silence as the jet-black bird proceeds to make a meal out of the boy.

As the sun rises, decomposition sets in. The crows have descended on the body, which is slowly turning green. The slightly sweet cadaverous smell mingles with the heavy odour of decomposition emanating from the tropical jungle surrounding them. Victor cannot think about anything except food: the heavily laden tables at the club, a wild boar grilled over an open fire, clear chicken broth, plum pudding with currants and raisins, fresh trout, rack of lamb with mint jelly and a generous shot of Tabasco, pork stew with apples, salmon with cucumber sauce, Lancaster hotpot, sausages with onion gravy, garlic soup, country pie, pears with whipped cream, poached eggs, Christmas pudding, brandy butter, beef Wellington, turkey casserole with beer . . .

A crow pulls the last piece of the eyeball out of its socket. The muscle doesn't give easily, and the bird has to tug sharply. The longer Victor stares at the body, the less he sees of it: millions of insects are crawling over the boy's remains. All he knows about the soldier is his rank and surname.

It is Victor's own fault that he is here. Nineteen days ago he called a meeting of his seconds-in-command in a large tent not far from the Indian border. Unrolling the map, he explained his plan. All the men nodded their assent, except for a dour Scot who called it madness. Victor put the man in his place with a brusque remark, but in the end he was proved right. On the way back to the command post, things went wrong, and that's why he is here, thinking about butterscotch truffles instead of eating them.

It's not the odour of the body itself that drives the men up the wall, but the lack of shade and the fact that they are constantly besieged by dung flies. The sole exception is a young captain who, unlike the others, remains calm and goes about what he sees as his task: dressing the wounds of his fellow prisoners. The first day that the soldier's body lay there, no one dared to move a muscle until the sun went down. By the last bit of daylight, the captain went over to the body and carefully untied the man's boots. Everyone looked on in silence, and when this did not elicit a rifle shot or a volley of curses from the Japanese, he also removed the man's trousers.

He then adjusted the position of the body, placed the arms along the sides, and even succeeded in folding the hands over the chest, before crawling back to his own spot with the trousers and the boots. Victor is mildly surprised that none of the men protested when the captain took the boots. But he is the highest-ranking soldier, and Victor himself had often enough taken advantage of his rank.

AT SUNRISE IT becomes clear that there is a lot going on inside as well as outside the body. Small white worms come crawling out of the mouth and nose and are devoured with relish by the crows. And there still is no food or water for the prisoners. The men shelter under their shirts, except for the captain, who spends the whole day tearing open the seams of the trousers with the aid of a small stone. To Victor's surprise, it is his neighbour who now wears the boots. At the end of the day, the captain has a small pile of cloth squares and the dead soldier has turned into a balloon. Everyone hopes fervently that he will not explode.

IT IS LATE in the afternoon on the third day — during which time not a word has been spoken — when one of the Japs shoves a battered iron pan full of dingy water under the fence. The men make a mad dash for the pan. A fight almost breaks out over who gets to drink first, but the captain shouts that they'll all get their chance. Victor Bridgwater is happy that no one knows he's a major. He waits his turn in line and drinks.

1995 Rampur ~

SHE FAIRLY DANCED down the stairs. There was enough fabric for thirty gowns! She would ask him to make her a new blouse and a skirt. And somewhere she had a piece of lace and red buttons. Or would he find them a bit old-fashioned? She would ask him to make the back of the gown a little longer than the front. She'd always wanted an evening dress with a small train. Or were they no longer in fashion? She'd borrow a few of the fashion magazines from the club's library, and they could look at them together. He would know what suited her best. And now she had a choice of material. She would ask him . . . She started. Madan was standing at the bottom of the stairs. How long had he been standing there? What was he doing there? Why wasn't he at work?

"Are you checking up on me?" The question sounded brusque.

No. I heard you coming.

"That's still no reason to leave the music room."

That's not why I came out.

"Oh, no? Then why did you?"

Because you asked me to.

"No, I didn't."

Then I apologize. I must have been mistaken. Madan turned around and walked back to the music room.

Don't leave, Charlotte begged silently.

Madan stopped short. *Do you want me to stay?*

She looked at the back of the man who had thrown her into confusion from the very first time she laid eyes upon him. *Yes, stay. No, go away.*

He didn't move. *What do you want?*

"Nothing," her voice said, while her thoughts cried, *You.*

Very quietly Madan walked back to the music room and carefully shut the door.

Charlotte wanted to run after him. Hadn't he heard her? Hadn't she thought the word "you"? He could hear her thoughts, couldn't he? By this time, he must know that she feels something for him. She walked away from the closed door. She had gone too far. She had thought the one thing she had told herself she must never think, and he had not replied. He had simply closed the door.

She hadn't heard him because he had managed to close the door just in time. *I understood you!* he had thought. *I heard everything. I know how you feel.* He hunched down at the table, as far as possible away from the door. He was afraid that his thoughts were too strong, and that she might have heard them because the heavy wooden door didn't provide enough resistance. He pulled the lengths of cloth from the table and began to wind them around his head wildly. She mustn't hear his thoughts! With one hand, he reached for the finished gown that was hanging from the table, shook it from the hanger, and pulled that over his head as well. Then he curled up and threw his arms around the fabrics.

Disappointed, she went back upstairs. His rejection had upset her more than she wanted to admit. She undressed and turned on the shower. As she stepped into the bathtub, she looked into the flaking mirror on the back of the door, where she saw a scrawny old woman getting into the bath. A failed woman. An unhappy woman. She picked up the porcelain water jug. It was a family heirloom. It had belonged to her mother, who had used it during her much-too-short life. It was the jug Sita had used to wash them, the one in which she had arranged flowers when she was feeling sad, the one no junk dealer was interested in. Then she threw it at the mirror as hard as she could. It was as if her mirror image veered to one side in order to avoid the projectile. The pitcher smashed to pieces against the wall. She didn't look at the fragments but stood with her back to the mirror and let the water stream over her body. Why had she destroyed something that meant so much to her? Why couldn't she get a grip on herself, as she usually did? She was the one who never lost control, never shocked people, always did what was expected of her, played according to the rules no matter how unfair they were, had never rebelled. . . . What in the name of God had got into her? She was angrily working the shampoo into her hair when the water stopped running. She turned the faucet. But no matter how far she opened it, no water came out. There was only a rumbling sound that seemed to come through kilometres of empty pipes. The soap made her eyes smart. How could she have forgotten? Hema had told her when she sent another meal back to the kitchen untouched. The wife of Alok Nath the goldsmith had reminded her when she called to inquire whether the new fabrics had arrived. Even the man from the bank had mentioned it that morning when he brought her a letter, which she had placed in the drawer along with all the others. The reservoir in the hill was empty and she had failed to take the necessary precautions.

1944 Burma ~

THERE ARE SOUNDS of shouting, and suddenly the sleeping men are surrounded by a group of angry Japanese soldiers with guns, dressed in ragged uniforms. Their eyes are hollow and their expressions grim. Peter Harris is more surprised than shocked. He was convinced that they were nowhere near the front lines. He even thought they were getting close to civilization, after weeks of wandering through the jungle.

They're told to kneel down with their hands behind their heads. Could this be the end? Were they about to die? Would he get a bullet in the back of the head? Would he feel it, or would it be too quick for that? The last few days he'd begun to think they'd made it, that they wouldn't all die. Although they found nothing edible except for some roots and berries, they laughed a lot, and every evening one of them would tell a story. Sometimes it felt a bit like a summer camp for boys, where a small group was sent on a night orientation march that turned out to be too long and too arduous. But their long beards, the growing hunger, and the accompanying lethargy destroyed that illusion.

THE SHOUTING HAS stopped. His knees hurt and he'd give

anything to drop his arms. But the sight of enemy soldiers watching them from a distance with their weapons at the ready discourages such thoughts, and they all keep their hands in the air. He hopes that Felix, the deputy battalion commander who told him all about his unhappy childhood, also makes it. Every evening, while they exchange stories, Peter dresses the wound on Felix's knee. What began as a small cut became infected, turned into a throbbing abscess and later an open wound. Peter knows that the knee and everything below it doesn't stand a chance if he isn't able to give Felix real medication. The officer, who has great respect for Peter's medical skills, moans softly. An order is shouted. Peter feels a hard blow to his back and he falls forward onto the ground.

"We're supposed to stand up," he hears Felix say. "Hurry up!"

He scrambles to his feet. He can tell by looking at the sky that it will be dark within an hour or so. One of the Japs, a small man wearing slippers, points to Felix's boots and growls. It is clear that he's expected to remove the boots. Felix unties the long laces. Now the man points to Peter, who, as a doctor, was promoted to captain soon after he was sent to the front. Peter also begins to take off his boots. Then the man screams at the three other men. They all untie their laces. It's been weeks since they've taken off their boots. Peter puts his on the ground in front of him. The Jap gestures that he wants Peter to throw them to him. The penetrating odour of sweat doesn't overcomes him; rather, he is overwhelmed by a sense of vulnerability, standing there in his stocking feet. His characteristic optimism disappeared after he took off his boots. The others also throw their boots in the direction of the little

Jap, who is still gesturing wildly. At his feet is a growing pile of boots. He sits down on the ground and starts trying on the boots. All the men know that none of them will fit him.

Peter feels a twig sticking through his sock. He hopes the man doesn't choose his boots. This is immediately followed by the fervent wish that Felix will not have to give up his. Without them, his wound will only get worse.

The Jap takes his time trying on the boots. Once in a while he shouts something to his subordinates, who are standing close by with loaded rifles. After trying on the fifth pair of boots, he gestures that he wants their socks as well. The men hesitate at first: surely one pair of socks is enough? But the man insists that they all have to take off their socks. The men are even more uncomfortable, and are overcome by a childish sensation of modesty. The Jap stuffs a pair of socks into the toe of each boot and then tries them on. Satisfied, he stands up. When he sees the soldiers of the British-Indian Army looking expectantly at the pile of boots, he starts shouting. The men have no idea what he is shouting, and Felix makes a move as if he is about to pull his boots from the pile. This almost gets him shot, and he quickly retreats. The little Jap picks up a sock and holds a lighted match to it. When the sock catches fire, he throws it onto the pile of socks, setting it alight. Then someone shouts that they're to form a line, and they begin marching. They go straight past their own piled-up shoes, which refuse to burn, and march into the jungle. It is almost dark.

THE GROUND CUTS, pricks, stings, lacerates, chafes, sucks, slides, slashes, hampers, scratches, itches, slices, slithers, bumps, scrapes, catches, and torments. He cannot see what is left of his feet, but he is aware of a gash filled with dirt under his left foot and he suspects that the nail on his big toe is hanging by a thread. The soles of both feet are pierced by thousands of the tiny spines that lie on the path. Or maybe there is no path. They're constantly warding off low-hanging branches and tripping over tree stumps, and anyone who slows the pace can expect a blow from a rifle butt. Peter can't fathom why they started walking just as it was getting dark. No one has a lamp, not even the Japs. They stumble on, in total darkness.

The sounds of the jungle are drowned out by the groans of the men. He feels like crying himself. He knows from experience that tears help to ease the pain, but they won't come. Felix, who's walking behind him, is silent. For the first hour he moaned softly at every step. Peter surmises that, like the others, he has exceeded his own pain threshold.

Branches lash Peter's face. He is conscious of a creature slithering away beneath his feet. What was it? Perhaps a tiny viper that was equally startled, or a leech that wasn't fast enough, or maybe one of those giant slugs that make their home among the thorny roots.

As it begins to get light, Peter looks over his shoulder to see how Felix is holding up. The young officer has disappeared. Behind him is a stumbling Jap with a rifle. Did he whack Felix because he couldn't keep up the pace? Why didn't he call out? Peter blames himself for not seeing to it that Felix was in front of him when the row of men set off. The Jap looks at him dispassionately. Did he simply step aside when Felix collapsed, leaving him behind? There is nothing to be gained by speculating on what happened, since no one has an answer. Dead or alive, Felix has been left behind in the jungle. They will never meet again.

The evening that Felix told his story was special. It was a full moon and they had found a decent place to shelter for the night. They lay in a circle, sucking on the small sour berries that grew there. Felix had looked up at the moon and asked them if they had ever heard the story of the moon-woman. The unanimous answer was no. So Felix sat up and, in an unexpectedly gentle voice, told them about a woman with a long braid who was always dressed in white. With every word he spoke, Peter was more convinced that Felix was describing the woman he loved, and that he had never told her of his love. They lived in the same village, and from his window he could see how the moon rose behind her house. And when that heavenly body was round and full, there was always a snow-white sheet on the wash line. That square of cloth, flapping in the wind, had cast a spell over him. But he had never lain under that sheet alongside his beloved. The war had called him and taken him away. And now no one would ever know where he died, not even Peter, who for weeks had tended to his wound.

There are no stops, not for a minute. It's the thirst that plagues them. It intensifies from sunrise on, slowing the tempo. Their feet are red and black with blood. The procession continues on its way, occasionally moving faster when they come to what resembles a path. The pace is excruciatingly slow. The men fall and scramble to their feet as quickly as they can. These falls, and their frequent cries of pain, enable them to pass messages to one another without the knowledge of the Japanese. Now they all know that Felix has disappeared, and that the little Jap has put the boots in his rucksack and is barefoot again, apparently unbothered.

They stumble along, and are now entering their second night. No one can figure out why the Japs don't stop to rest. The Japs must be just as exhausted as they are, although not as thirsty, since they each have a water bottle.

The prisoners' falls and their efforts to get to their feet again also provide them with the opportunity to devise a plan and pass it on. When it gets dark, they'll take the last Jap by surprise and then get rid of the two armed soldiers in the middle. In possession of three rifles, they will then be able to eliminate the others. It's Peter's job to disarm the Jap who brings up the rear.

Although it was originally his plan, Peter never expected the others to take it seriously. It was something he had thought up because it might boost the general morale. He looks over his shoulder at the man walking behind him, whom he can hear but cannot see. Maybe he never noticed that Felix had fallen? Maybe the boy simply allowed himself to fall to the ground because he didn't want to be a burden?

Peter drops to the ground. The Jap doesn't stumble, as he had hoped, but kicks him hard. Peter climbs to his feet and groans, this time without a message for any of the others. He could kick himself for coming up with such a stupid plan.

The soldier in front of him moans: "Is anything happening?"

Just as Peter is about to tell him that the plan didn't work, they stumble into a deserted village. By the light of the stars, he can distinguish a few empty huts with a chair in front of them. Even before he can hope that they are going to rest, a gate made of branches is shoved open and they are led into an enclosure where two British soldiers are sitting on the ground. The younger of the two jumps to his feet. Peter recognizes him immediately. It's Benjamin Parker from Hull, with whom he made the long trip to the border by train. The boy opens his arms wide in welcome and in that same instant a shot rings out. The young soldier — who confided to Peter that he was crazy about chocolate cake and had never kissed a girl — falls dead at their feet. Peter bends down, wants to pick the boy up, is unable to believe that he's dead, just like that. Then the barefoot Jap growls, "Go sit I shoot you!" Peter realizes that the Jap understood all their groans, and that he is lucky to be alive.

The dead soldier Benjamin stares glassily at Peter with his remaining eye. Peter wonders if the soldier shot Benjamin as revenge for their escape attempt, which he had dreamt up in order to keep up their morale. Opposite them, on the other side of the enclosure, sits a British soldier, apparently older than the others, who, like his dead comrade, is no longer wearing a jacket and is constantly scratching his arms and neck. Peter wants to tell him to stop scratching, since it increases the chance of developing boils and infections, but no one, including Peter, dares speak. "Now you're a captain," the major in New Delhi had said. He'd been handed an envelope containing three stars, which he had to sew onto his jacket. He found it more difficult than suturing a surgical wound. He looks around at the handful of men and concludes that he is the highest in rank. The responsibility that this entails takes him by surprise, and he resolves not to give up. He will see to it that the men recover their faith in themselves.

A crow announces its arrival with hoarse cries. The pitch-black bird lands next to the body, which is now decaying more quickly as a result of the heat. Peter tosses a stone at the bird.

It flutters up momentarily, but then attacks the open wound that until recently contained the eye. The sooner the rotting flesh is done away with, the better it will be for the health of the men. Peter suspects that the Japs have left the body there deliberately, as part of their strategy. In the extreme heat, the process will be accelerated, but even a week is too long — the exhausted men seated around the body are weak, and they are getting weaker. In the end, the flies, which number in the thousands, will have taken possession of the body. If he can manage to remove the trousers from the body, the process of rotting will be accelerated.

After fifty hours without sleep or water, he sees the little Jap and his rifle through a kind of haze that hangs in front of his eyes. And yet he knows that the man is looking at him. He bows his head, pulls his foot toward him, and begins to work the dirt out of his wounds. He feels his way, since the glazed mist shrouds his vision. When he thinks he is finished, he rubs his tongue over the roof of his mouth to produce a bit of saliva, which he spits onto his hand and then works into the wound, by way of disinfectant. The soldier next to him is momentarily surprised when, without a word, he picks up his foot and does the same thing. He forgets that he is hungry and thirsty. He is only aware of the large, hairy foot covered with cuts and scratches.

One of the Japs watches with interest as he treats the feet of the other soldiers, one by one, without saying a word. Except for the feet of the older Englishman, who is still wearing his boots. After treating the last pair of wounded feet, the captain crawls over to the body of the soldier. The guard's finger glides toward the trigger. Peter picks up the arms and legs of the dead soldier and lays the body straight. In such extreme heat, rigor mortis disappears more quickly than usual, and without exerting too much force, Peter manages to pull the body out of the grisly posture it assumed after falling to the ground. The flies buzz around him. He can tell by the feel of the greenish body that it is becoming pulpy, and that the process of decomposition will proceed much faster than he had expected.

The dead soldier had not eaten for a long time, like all of them, and the trousers are far too big, which makes it easy to strip them off. Then it occurs to him that he can use the material to bandage his comrades' feet. Among the angry flies on the soldier's chest, he sees the glint of a small silver cross on a chain. Peter picks up the emaciated hands and folds them, one over the other, on the chest. This is the only ritual he is able to perform. With the boots and the trousers in his hand, he crawls back to his place. Clad only in stained khaki underwear, the body appears quite chaste and boyish. Only the flies and the missing eye take away from the dignity of the green soldier lying in state.

For the first time in days, he has slept, leaning against one of the stakes of the enclosure. It is still dark when he wakes up. He is aware that the slightly sweet odour of the cadaver has been transformed into the bitter smell that ushers in the second phase. In the coming hours the body will swell up like a balloon. His hunger has completely disappeared, but not his thirst. His lips are cracked and his tongue searches desperately for moisture in the hidden recesses of his mouth. As dawn comes, he is aware that the haze before his eyes has disappeared. He picks up a small stone from the sand, pulls the trousers onto his lap, and begins to cut open the seams.

He resolves that as long as he remains alive, he will get his men out of this situation.

1955 Bombay ~

MADAN RUNS DOWN the street, carrying a length of cloth wrapped in paper. Now that he is an apprentice in the weaving mill, he seldom goes out on the street. He sleeps under the lean-to on the roof, alongside Subhash. He eats with the weavers in the tiny room next to their looms, and during the day he carries out the tasks assigned to him by Chandan Chandran. After spending several days unpicking cloth, he has figured out how the fabric is woven. In the following weeks he helps to regulate the thread tension and wind up the spools. Chandran, his boss, has taught him how to hem a piece of cloth, using a coarse or a fine stitch, depending on the material. He wouldn't have been sent to deliver the fabric wrapped in brown paper if things hadn't been so busy and the coolie had already returned with the bicycle. Chandran stressed that it was a rush job, so Madan runs as fast as he can to the villa behind the temple with the tall tower. In the past when he ran through the streets, he was always with Abbas and they were always on the run. Now, as he passes the same buildings and the same alleyways, he's on a mission.

He knows where the temple with the tall tower is. Sometimes they were given a plate of food, if they'd had no luck begging and the priest was in a good mood. Now he runs down the alley, hugging the wall that surrounds the villa. There's a guard at the gate. He's wearing a uniform with shiny buttons and a cap with piping. He stops Madan. "Who are you looking for?"

Madan shows him the package.

"Who's it for?"

"For Madame," he squeaks, but his message is unintelligible.

The man looks at him in horror and snatches the package out of his hands, as if he's afraid Madan has contaminated it.

Madan would have liked to duck under his arms and run to the front door in order to deliver the package himself. That would almost certainly have earned him a tip, as the coolie told him. But the guard looked at him with such suspicion that he is afraid to go any farther.

IF HE'D OPTED for the shortest route back to the weaving mill, he would have gone back down the same alleyway, past the temple. But the harbour, which is a bit farther away, draws him like a magnet. He doesn't want to go there — but he has to.

He is shocked at the sight of the two dilapidated sheds. There is something threatening about them. It's as if they've gotten tired of waiting for him. His feet, which had been propelled forward, suddenly come to a halt. Confused, he stares at the spot where the two sheds join. The crevice they used to creep through has largely disappeared. It's as if the sheds have subsided, bringing them closer together. Not even a scrawny dog or a fat rat could get through. With some hesitation, Madan places his hand over the opening and feels the current of air racing through it. Cautiously, he sticks his nose into the crack and takes a deep breath. *Where are you, Abbas? Where are you?* He smells old wood and tar instead of decay and rot. Madan takes a step backwards. He looks around, wondering if this is the right spot. Maybe the opening is farther on. But none of the buildings look even vaguely like the sheds the two of them used to squeeze past. Except for the two in front of him. He presses his face into the narrow chink and peers into the space. *Where are you*? It's pitch black and he can't see a thing. In frustration, he slams his hand against the narrow opening. *I haven't forgotten you.* Isn't there some maxim or watchword he can pronounce to make the walls give way? *I didn't mean to desert you. You have to believe me.* Calmer now, he runs his hand over the narrow opening. *I wanted to come back, but I didn't dare.* His fingers curve into the opening. *I was scared. Afraid that you would look like that dog. Remember . . . at the station. I was afraid that you would smell like that dog and the rats would have eaten part of you. I didn't want to see that, because you're my friend. My only real friend.*

1995 Rampur

THE WINDOWS WERE wide open, and her fingers danced over the keys. Playing the piano blocked out all the thoughts, the worries, the brooding. Listening to romantic music, she was transported away from her bedroom . . . she was dancing off, out the door and into a celestial space filled with heavenly tones. On the edge of the night table her fingers played Mozart's love sonata, Schubert's *Moments Musicaux*, Debussy's *Clair de Lune*, and Liszt's *Liebesträume*, one after the other. She could play them all from memory, and never once did she think about the day she sold her piano.

Sita had fallen to her knees, grasped the hem of Charlotte's skirt, and beseeched her. Parvat, who was much younger than Sita's other children, was suffering from a mysterious illness. Every evening for months, he had run a high fever, vomited all the food that Sita had prepared for him, and then become delirious until sunrise. At the break of dawn the fever would subside and he would be hungry again. During the day, the child was perfectly normal. He went to school and played with his friends. Until evening, when the sun set. Within five minutes his fever would shoot up, to a dangerous level. Sita sat up with him all night, positive that he wouldn't live until morning. There was no money for another doctor, and she had come to the big house on the hill to ask for help. Charlotte knew that her bank account was empty, but she also knew the value of her grand piano. She did not hesitate for a moment. That was the first time she called a dealer.

By sunset the piano had disappeared from the house and a medicine man from Calcutta was at the boy's bedside. Various herbs were immediately ordered and all objects made of copper were banished from the house. Charlotte never understood exactly what he had done, but two weeks later the boy had returned to normal, and life went on as if there had never been a problem. Except perhaps for Charlotte, who wouldn't admit how much she missed her piano.

Suddenly she was jolted out of her reverie. She became aware of a shrill, piercing sound. A fire engine sped by, its heart-rending siren going full tilt. The sound seemed to fill the night. She peered out the window to see if there was any sign of a fire on the horizon. All she saw by the yellow light of a street lamp was a line of people, all of them carrying buckets on their heads. These people were not on their way to the fire: like everyone else, they had no more water and were going in search of wells where they might find some. *If the monsoon doesn't come pretty soon, we're all going to die,* thought Charlotte.

Hema knew his mistress better than she knew herself. He had filled the tub in the nursery with water, as well as the one in the guestroom and the barrel outside the kitchen door. Charlotte had told him she would fill her own bath, since she would be busy in her bedroom all morning, but she had forgotten to do so. Hema had initially expressed his concern over the amount of water the tailor used, but it appeared that he succeeded in washing himself from top to bottom with a single bucket, a feat that had always been beyond Hema.

There seemed to be no end to the procession of people carrying buckets. Not only the reservoirs were empty, but also the river. The only water available was thirty kilometres away, where there was a small lake. The local landowner was selling the water at exorbitant prices, so they wouldn't be going there. All they could do was dig pits in the river bedding until they hit groundwater.

The siren faded into the distance. Charlotte forgot about the music and crept down the stairs as quietly as she could. She heard the whirr of the sewing machine coming from the music room.

She didn't take the path down to the road but went in the opposite direction, into the garden and past the apple tree. Outside it was just as hot as indoors. She noticed that it was much less arid than a few weeks before. It even occurred to her that there might be a new natural source on their property, but her father had explored that possibility on several occasions. The only well that had ever been dug had produced water that stank to high heaven. After two years, even the *mali* refused to use it, claiming that it "made the flowers sad." The only good thing about the drought was that without rain, the lawn didn't have to be mowed and the Lloyds didn't have to be repaired.

She walked past the shed where the old *mali* had lived and down a gentle slope, until she came to a small, arid woodland at the bottom of the garden. When the rains came, these trees would be in flower within a week. Their honey-sweet scent would attract birds whose song would keep her awake for weeks. She made her way through the shrubbery. There was a path there that no one else ever used. She had to push away a branch, which was so dry that it snapped in her hand.

Anyone watching her would have noticed that she moved quite differently than she did during the day, when she went about her chores or visited the club dressed in a presentable outfit. Then she carried herself with a refined reserve that she had unconsciously developed over the years. She held her head ever so slightly to one side, and at each step she put her feet down so carefully that one might think she was afraid of falling into a hole. Now her gait was different, lighter, and there was eagerness in her step.

She arrived at the wall surrounding the garden, a wall that was as tall as a man. She always had to search for it, but then she placed her foot in a small hole in the wall. There were also hand holes in the wall that she'd made use of in the past. There was no longer any trace of her usual respectable gentility, and, puffing slightly, she climbed over the wall. It was clear that not only the heat but also her age had begun to take its toll: she didn't have the litheness she'd had in her younger years, yet she made it over the wall. Out of breath but determined, she turned onto a narrow alleyway that became a small road leading up a hill and away from town. Fifteen minutes later she arrived at a clump of trees that looked much less healthy than her own apple tree. Beyond the trees the road led down to an intersection, where a small house stood. She opened the door without knocking.

"Oh, it's you!" The tiny Indian woman rose from her chair to embrace Charlotte. "I thought you'd forgotten me."

"Sita, I could never forget you."

"It's been three weeks since I last saw you."

"I've been terribly busy."

"Oh, really? Have you eaten?" Sita put her hands around Charlotte's waist. "You're way too thin. Way too thin."

"Ah, it's the heat . . ."

The former ayah opened the refrigerator and pulled out a whole battery of stainless-steel containers. "I have some shrimp curry and a piece of fried fish." She removed the lid from another container and looked inside. "Oh, and these tomatoes are delicious!" She dipped one finger in the sauce and gave Charlotte a taste. She closed her eyes and smiled. "The chickpeas are too spicy for you, but you'll like the *aloo gobi* and the dal." She had already filled a plate when she turned and asked, "You do feel like something to eat, don't you?"

Charlotte's mouth was watering. It was only then that she realized she was hungry. With her mouth half full, she gave Sita a rundown on the coming gala evening at the club, and recounted contritely how she'd forgotten to fill her bathtub. She also talked about Hema, who had been upset with her, about her father, who ate nothing but yogurt and yet was making plans to attend the gala at the club, about the puncture she still hadn't repaired, about the minister and the devotional books he tried to interest her in, about the coming renovation of the library, about the wife of Alok Nath the goldsmith, whom she could never understand, about the water jug that had been reduced to smithereens, about the old tailor who had died and the fact that the electricity regularly conked out while the thermometer registered forty-four degrees, about the special homemade cookies produced by the wife of Nikhil Nair, about the lengths of fabric that had belonged to her mother and that she had rediscovered in the wardrobe in the nursery, about the delicious tea that Hema made, and about the apple tree, the jasmine bush, and the roses that hadn't wilted, about . . .

"You're in love," said Sita.

1966 Rampur

THE *DHOBI* HAS left four freshly laundered and ironed pairs of pyjamas on the hall table; she'll take them up to her father later on. And the *mali* has left behind a bouquet of flowers. Charlotte knows that her father doesn't want flowers in his hospital room, so she puts them in a vase near the radio, which she has just turned on and then off again for the fifth time. She's still completely off balance, as are all the servants. Since the day of the accident, all the rituals and habits have been at sixes and sevens. The *mehtarani*, who normally works inside the house before moving on to his chores outside, absent-mindedly sweeps all the dust into the house; the *punkah-wallah*, who for years has followed her father around like a shadow, now dogs her footsteps because there's no one else around who needs the cooling breezes he creates. The cook has burned the evening meal for the third time, and the old chauffeur is smoking so much that the *mali* has asked permission to buy an ashtray, since all the cigarette butts are ruining his borders. The only exception is the new butler with the long name, whom for convenience's sake she has christened Hema. He is always on time, and the entire day he races up and down the stairs making sure everything is in order, which sets everyone else's nerves on edge. As if that wasn't enough, Charlotte doesn't feel well. This morning she's already thrown up three times, and if she's not in the bathroom because she has to throw up, then she is there because she has to pee.

"Charlotte?" She hears Sita's voice. Sita hasn't been employed by the family for many years, but she always drops by at the most impossible times.

"I'm coming!" Charlotte wouldn't shout a reply from the toilet to anyone but Sita. Although they may not see each other for weeks, their bond is very special. When she threw herself onto Peter's grave in total despair, Sita was there to comfort her, just as she had done throughout Charlotte's childhood. Sita was well acquainted with her father's dictatorial behaviour, her brother's indifference, the heartache of Peter's war trauma, and her unfulfilled yearning for a child. Although Charlotte often shared her longings and doubts with her, Sita never judged or condemned her. She listened and prayed that one day everything would be different.

Sita knocked on the bathroom door. "Is anything wrong?"

She wanted to reply, but a wave of nausea interfered.

"Open the door." Sita, who's used to dealing with dirty diapers, wet sheets, and bibs full of puke, pulls open the unlocked door. She is startled to see Charlotte hanging over the toilet seat, deathly pale. She manages to cajole her out of the bathroom with pet words from her childhood. In the bedroom, she moistens a towel and pats Charlotte's face, which is bathed in perspiration. Then she unbuttons her soiled blouse, revealing two large, dark nipples which stare proudly back at her. Sita, who will be forty-six next month, has two married daughters who live with their in-laws, and a husband who three months ago paid her his annual visit. He's still paying off the dowry of the youngest daughter, so he has moved to New Delhi, where he has a day job as a rickshaw driver and at night works as a shoemaker in a factory. Sita looks her straight in the face and says, "You're pregnant."

A deathly silence fills the room, but Charlotte is aware of a thunderous din in her head as she realizes what Sita has just said. In the midst of this deafening cacophony, there falls a brief moment of icy silence in which she says to herself that it's not true, that it cannot be true. But this is only because of her conviction that she would never bear a child. Slowly she lays both hands on her slightly bulging belly.

Sita looks at her with her usual humble expression. Charlotte knows she's now expected to tell her who the father is. The scent of tobacco smoke burns in her nostrils, a sweet taste returns to her lips, and she remembers the calluses on his fingertips, the passionate embrace, the candle that went out by itself, the call of an owl. As the sun rose she had walked home and in the garden she had picked a huge bouquet of flowers. There was no vase large enough to hold them, so she had put them in the water jug. She had had her morning tea and written a letter to her brother with an urgent request to call her. It was not until six weeks later that he had telephoned, by which time their father's condition was no longer critical and the nurses in the hospital were being driven out of their minds by her father's tirades. She hadn't even noticed that her period hadn't come, and she'd blamed her nausea on the fact that the cook was so upset.

All she said was, "I don't even know his name."

~

Dear Donald,

Father is improving. He was operated on again two weeks ago. According to the surgeon, it's a miracle that he survived it all. His kidneys are still working, and that's one of the things they were very concerned about. He'll never be able to walk again, of course, but I haven't told him yet. I'm afraid that once he knows, he'll lose the will to get better. Peter used to say that a patient who believes he'll get better recovers faster. The sisters take very good care of him. I couldn't do any more for him myself. He's still on a drip, and now they've got him in a full-body cast, which doesn't make things any easier. What bothers him the most is that he has to drink from a bottle with a nipple that the sister puts in his mouth. I make sure I'm out of the room before the bottle arrives. He gets so angry and then he starts cursing and everything. I'm also writing you to let you know that I'm leaving Rampur for a while. The last few weeks have taken their toll, and now that I know Father's being well cared for, I can get away for a while. Of course, I've discussed this with the doctor, and he agrees. All my life, I've wanted to see the Himalayas. Tomorrow I'm taking the train to

New Delhi, then on to Kalka, where I catch a taxi that will take me to Simla. At first Father said I should wait until he was better, because he wanted to go along. But I promised him that after he gets out of the hospital, we'll go again. I've given the staff some time off, except for the *mali*, of course, and the butler. They'll make sure that everything is kept clean and in good condition. I've taken the car to a garage, and I can leave it there as long as I like. If you suddenly decide to vacation in India, then you're welcome to stay at the house. Hema has all the keys, except the one to the safe, which I've already taken to the bank. But I assume that you're too busy with the new job. Is everything going well? I hope so. I'll write to you when I get to the mountains.

Greetings from your sister Charlotte

1951 Grand Palace

PETER IS SO pleased that he is about to see the maharaja again that he takes giant steps, fairly dragging her up the stairs. Charlotte is excited. The moment he sees his old friend, the constant trembling of his hands and the sombre, withdrawn look disappear as if by magic. He strides toward the large door, where the maharaja greets him like he is a brother and they have been reunited after years of separation.

"You are more lovely each time I see you," the maharaja says to Charlotte. She blushes and replies that in a month she will turn twenty-one. "Twenty-one," the maharaja exclaims. "The most beautiful time of our lives! I wish I were still twenty!" He throws a friendly arm around Peter's shoulders and leads him away. Charlotte follows them to a large hall where all the women, attired in magnificent saris, await their arrival.

"Doctor sahib," they coo and call, as they bow in greeting. Among the female voices directed mainly at Peter, she also hears "Charlotte memsahib, welcome." She sees Chutki, the youngest daughter of the maharaja, with a little boy at her side, among the group of women attired in colourful saris. They wave to each other enthusiastically. Drinks are passed around, and dishes filled with delectable hors d'oeuvres are brought in by servants in magnificent uniforms.

"To the hunt!" the maharaja toasts.

Peter smiles and raises his glass. Charlotte, who didn't know that there was to be a hunt, turns to Peter in surprise. He admits with a smile that it's news to him as well but that he is delighted at the prospect of a day in the saddle together with the maharaja.

"And how about me?" Charlotte asks. "Can I come along?"

"No, of course not. It's only for men," Peter whispers.

CHARLOTTE AND CHUTKI are lying in a large double bed in the women's quarters, eating cookies, with Chutki's baby brother, who is whimpering. The girl points to Charlotte's belly.

"And?" she asks.

"Not yet," Charlotte says. "Not yet."

"But you're very pretty."

"Peter is always so busy."

"Doctor sahib better not wait too long," Chutki giggles and covers her mouth with her hand.

"Why?" Charlotte asks.

Chutki rolls her eyes. She pats her little brother, but he continues to whimper.

Charlotte is shocked. "Oh, no. I only want Peter's baby."

"Why is doctor sahib so busy?"

"There's so much work for him at the hospital."

"He's going to cure my little brother."

"Does he have the same thing as you and your father?"

Chutki nods and pulls the toddler onto her lap. "I'm going to get married and pretty soon I'll have a baby of my own." She gives the boy something to drink and he quiets down. Then she looks at Charlotte roguishly and says in a low voice, "Is doctor sahib affectionate?"

"Yes, he's affectionate."

"Really affectionate?" And her hand goes from the child to her breasts, which she fondles. "Is he affectionate?" she asks again.

Charlotte cannot lie, and the expression on her face speaks volumes.

"Oh!" Chutki cries. "So he's not affectionate?"

The occupant of the bed beside them, an older aunt, is listening in and echoes her cry: "Oh, oh, doctor sahib is not affectionate . . ."

Within seconds the other women have climbed onto the double bed and it is so full that Charlotte cannot even move her legs. The shocking cry is repeated: "Doctor sahib is not affectionate!" This is followed by a disapproving hiss.

"You should try this perfume," says a woman with an armful of jangling bracelets, pressing a tiny bottle into her hand.

"Do you always make sure you've brushed your teeth?" says a woman with long earrings, as she pulls up Charlotte's lip.

The women nod in agreement.

"And he should eat a raw egg," giggles a woman with dark circles around her eyes.

"Serve dinner early, otherwise he'll be too tired. And he should eat the eggs during the day, then they're sure to work," stresses a woman in pyjamas.

"Wear a dress with a deep décolletage," advises another woman, and she presses her breasts together, forming a provocative cleavage.

"Is there another woman?" The question comes from the adjacent bed.

All the women break into laughter. Charlotte is aghast: she's never considered that possibility. He always comes home late and goes straight to bed.

"Don't worry," Chutki reassures her. "Doctor sahib loves you. But there are things he has to learn."

The women are howling with laughter. "Doctor Sahib can operate but he can't make babies."

The child begins to wail again, in reaction to the exuberant laughter.

"When is the doctor going to perform the operation?" sighs the woman in pyjamas. "He's always crying."

"Isn't that the little boy I saw just after he was born?" Charlotte asks, pointing to the toddler in Chutki's arms.

Suddenly, all of the women fall silent. Some get up from the bed, looking embarrassed, and some turn away and begin new conversations. And when Charlotte turns to Chutki, expecting an explanation, the girl avoids her eyes. The little boy on her lap is only a crying baby with red-rimmed eyes and a glob of snot hanging from his nose.

"Peter's going to operate on him. He told me so himself,"

Charlotte says, even though Peter has never mentioned the maharaja's son to her. "And if he should happen to forget, I'll remind him."

"Really?" Chutki asks.

Charlotte nods.

PETER BRIEFLY PRESSES his cheek — unshaven for days — against Charlotte's: it isn't exactly a kiss. Chutki gives her a wink. Charlotte feels like Ava Gardner in the new dress the *darzi* has made for her. With her arms she presses her breasts together and gives her husband a sultry look. "Can you smell my new perfume?" she asks in a low voice.

"We're leaving. Have you packed your things?"

"You mean right now?"

"Yes, the train leaves in an hour."

"But . . ." Charlotte has gone to great pains to make contact with the women, and she doesn't want to leave. She's finally enjoying herself.

"You must take a look at this sweet little boy," she says. "He has the same ailment as Chutki and the maharaja."

Peter, who normally displays the utmost dedication to all his patients, picks up the little boy, tells him to open his mouth, and takes a quick look at his throat. Then he nods and hands him back to Chutki. "Next time I'll bring my instruments with me. Charlotte, would you pack your suitcase now? We can still make the train."

A COOLIE AND one of the palace chauffeurs are the only other people on the platform. They left so quickly that there was no time to organize an official farewell at the railroad station. The sombre mood that has taken possession of Peter is even more impenetrable than usual. Charlotte can smell the perfume she applied when she heard that the men were on their way back from the hunt. Now she wraps her shawl tightly around her shoulders, to hide the décolletage she had been so proud of. The makeup that one of Chutki's sisters applied now seems overdone.

"What happened?" she asks, after Peter had sat in the train compartment for an hour without moving a muscle.

"I shot an animal dead," he whispers. "A living animal."

1985 Rampur ~

"CAN'T YOU SLOW down a bit? When you go so fast, I feel as if I have to pee."

Charlotte pushes her father across the parking lot behind the club. With a dexterity that makes it clear that they're not doing it for the first time, she and the chauffeur help the old man out of the wheelchair and into the car. The chauffeur then folds up the wheelchair he detests and places it in the boot. Charlotte waves to Priya Singh, who has just arrived in her shiny 1957 Ambassador, and gets into the old Vauxhall next to her father.

"When did you last wash this car?" thunders the general.

"This morning, sahib."

"Then why doesn't it shine?"

"It's old, sahib."

"That Ambassador is even older."

"Yes, sahib."

"Yes, sahib, no, sahib . . . Why can't you get this car to shine?"

"Yes, sahib."

Charlotte gives her father a nudge.

He gives her an angry look. "Well, would you call this car clean?"

"I hear a fire engine."

The general rolls his window down. "You're right. I must be going deaf." He turns to the chauffeur, and says, "If he comes by, follow him!"

The chauffeur laughs.

"Father, you said you wanted to go home."

"You don't think I'm going to miss a chance to watch a fire. A really good blaze is headier than a beautiful woman."

The sound of the sirens is getting closer. "Don't let him get away!" he says to the chauffeur, who is all set to take off.

The bright red Ashok Leyland truck races past. The chauffeur hits the gas pedal. The general is laughing, and so is the chauffeur. But Charlotte is petrified that they're going to go off the road.

"Women don't belong in cars," the general mutters to his chauffeur.

The heavy emission of smoke is visible from some distance. By the time they draw to a stop behind the fire engine, flames are shooting from the roof. The general throws open the door. For an instant Charlotte thinks he's forgotten that he can't walk, but he waits impatiently as the chauffeur hurries to unfold the wheelchair.

"Father, you mustn't do this. You're going to get in the way of the firefighters."

"How could I get in anyone's way?"

Next to their car, the hoses are being unrolled. The senior fire officer, who has a row of medals on his chest, comes over to the general and they shake hands. "Everything in order, General?"

"Ah, Commandant, you wouldn't know anything about getting old. My memory is failing and the lower half isn't getting any better. But outside of that, I can't complain."

The hoses are connected to the water tank and the pump is soon going at full power. The chauffeur helps the general into his wheelchair. The fire officer excuses himself: he has a fire to fight. Charlotte is still in the car. She feels the heat of the fire, even with the window closed. She takes no pleasure in watching a fire, and fails to understand her father's fascination. Once, when she was little, he took her to see a huge warehouse blaze, and he was angry when she kept her hands over her eyes the whole time. Not because she didn't want to watch the fire, but because he mustn't see that she was crying.

Then her heart skips a beat when a young fireman carrying an axe walks past the car. He hasn't seen her, but she recognizes him immediately. He nods in the direction of the general, goes up to the front of the burning house, and buries his axe in the door.

She wants to jump out of the car, tell him not do it, tell him that it's a dangerous situation and he mustn't go in there, that he can become disoriented by the heat and the smoke and might not be able find the exit. That he can suffocate or the smoke can be poisonous, that his lungs can burn up and his suit can catch fire, even though it's a real fireman's suit. That he doesn't have to rescue anyone, that that's the work of the senior fire officer with all the medals, who has more experience. Why did he have to become a fireman in the first place, the most dangerous job there is? Why him?

The young man doesn't hear her prayers. He hacks a hole in the door, pulls his mask over his face, and, without hesitation, steps inside. She wants to close her eyes, but instead she stares without blinking at the hole in the wrecked door. Now flames are also shooting out of the windows, and the inside of the car is becoming stiflingly hot. She implores all the gods she knows. She curses herself for her cowardice, her sneakiness. She wants to turn all the clocks back in time, especially the large grandfather clock on the landing. Why doesn't anyone else go in, why is he the only one? Someone has to help him. Maybe he's lost his way, or is unable to breathe. Can't anyone hear him shouting? He's on fire. Charlotte can't stand it any longer, and opens the car door. The heat drives her back into the car. She can barely stand on her own two feet. She is about to shout at the commandant when she sees a pair of gloved hands holding a little girl appear in the hole in the door. The fire chief grabs the child and the young man climbs out of the opening. No one is looking at him. All eyes are on the little girl.

THE AMBULANCE DOORS are closed and one of the orderlies jumps behind the wheel and drives off.

"That was close," says the general.

"Yes, we're lucky it didn't take any longer," says the fire officer. "I hope all this doesn't give her nightmares."

The fire officer looks at the man in the wheelchair. He cannot fathom why the old English soldier always turns up to watch fires.

"Parvat is a real asset," says the general.

"Indeed he is . . . and he has great courage." The fire officer nods to the boy, who has just picked up a heavy rubber hose and is aiming it at the house. "He looks a bit like you."

The general beams, thinking back with contentment on his medals.

AS THEY HEAD up the driveway and the general sees the great house, he turns to Charlotte. "That fire officer said that the ayah's son resembles me. That was nice of him, wasn't it: to say something like that to an old, handicapped bloke like me."

"Yes, he looks like you."

1995 Rampur

IT BEGAN AS a gentle ticking, then it gradually became a hammering sound, and it ended up as a thumping noise that did not stop. He wondered how Charlotte and the general dogsbody could sleep through all the racket. Madan put down the dress he was working on, took the candle from the table, and went up the stairs. The electricity was off again, and the oppressive heat clung to his body like a sticky blanket, even with the windows open. Madan had never been upstairs before, and for the first time he got a good look at the gigantic chandelier that hung in the stairwell, with its countless drippings like candle-wax stalactites, and at the large standing clock whose hourly chimes he could hear from the music room. He had no trouble determining the source of the racket. Next to the door there was a large, old-fashioned key hanging on a nail on the wall. The door of what he knew was Charlotte's bedroom was ajar. Surely she couldn't help but hear the din emanating from the other room, unless she wasn't there. It was quite possible that Madan hadn't heard her leave the house. He had been completely absorbed in the gala outfit for the wife of the president of the club, who had impressed on him that she wanted to be the most beautiful woman at the party. He took down the key and inserted it in the lock. What he had originally taken for frenzied shouting turned out to be a male voice belting out "Oh, my darling, oh, my darling, oh, my da-arling Clementine!"

In the middle of the room sat the old man with snow-white hair whom he had previously glimpsed at the top of the stairs. His wheelchair was anchored to the floor by an iron rod. His legs were also strapped down, and there was a bib around his neck. His upper body was naked and he was wearing a worn pair of pyjama bottoms. In one hand he held a metal bowl, which he was banging against the tray of his wheelchair, and in the other a spoon. All around him there were globs and spatters of yogurt on the floor, and there was a puddle underneath his chair. On the walls behind him hung a huge set of antlers, a tiger head with long tusks, the head of a cheetah, a brown bear with his tongue hanging out, and various smaller specimens of billy goats, deer, and wildcats. Madan felt as if he had just entered some distant past.

"You are lost and gone forever! Dreadful sorry, Clementine," sang the man with evident pleasure, slamming the dented bowl down with extra vigour at the word "sorry." When he caught sight of Madan, he switched effortlessly to a different repertoire and sang even louder: "Ye'll take the high road and I'll take the low road, and I'll be in Scotland afore ye. But me and my true love will never meet again. On the bonnie, bonnie banks of Loch Lomond . . ." The bowl resounded against the metal side panel of his wheelchair. "Come on, buddy, sing along!" he called out to Madan, who was also wearing nothing but a pair of thin pants.

Madan put the candle down beside him and tried to clap to the rhythm of the unfamiliar song. The general raised his spoon, by way of baton, and kept time. "It's three-quarter time, buddy, can't you hear that?" He kept time by banging the bowl on his wheelchair as he again broke into song. Then, in the middle of a sentence, he suddenly began to shout: "Take cover! Take cover!" He threw his arms over his head, holding the bowl in front of his face, like a kind of shield.

Madan did not react. Not because the word "cover" was unfamiliar, but because he had no idea what was going on.

The general peaked through his arms at Madan, who was still standing near the door. A smile appeared on his face. "You don't know the meaning of the word 'fear,' chappie. Right?" There was admiration in his voice. The general beckoned him to come closer, pointing to the chair that was just beyond his reach. "Sit down."

Madan did as he was told.

"Do I know you?" the general asked.

Madan shook his head.

"Did they hire you to keep an eye on me?" He gestured with contempt toward the floor below.

Madan shook his head.

"Oh, you're the new cook," said the general, relieved. "It's about time. The food they give me here is foul. We ate better during the war. Maybe they think I'm some kind of swine, someone who'll be satisfied with leftovers, but all the swine get from me is a bullet. One bullet. Right here," he said, pointing to the spot between his eyes. "This is where you aim. Then the lights go out quickly: no mess, no moaning, just a shot and then . . . dead."

Madan shook his head again.

"Hey, buddy, open your trap, will you? I don't hold with all those mysterious goings-on. Name, rank, and regiment."

Madan shook his head again.

"Playing dumb with an old geezer, is that how you get your kicks?"

"I'm the tailor." It had been years since Madan had tried to use his vocal cords. He was startled by the shrill, unintelligible squeaking sound that came out of his mouth.

The general stared at him in amazement and then began to laugh uproariously.

Madan was used to being cursed, rejected, ignored, and even manhandled when he tried to use his voice, but never before had someone laughed irrepressibly at his handicap. The general's laugh was so contagious that Madan began to laugh himself. It started as a cautious smile, but turned into a real laugh. Soon he was shaking with laughter, hiccupping, and clapping his hands.

The general waved the bowl in the air, sprinkling the remaining yogurt all over the room. The general's laughter made way for song and he began belting out "My Bonnie lies over the ocean, My Bonnie lies over the sea. My Bonnie lies over the ocean. Oh, bring back my Bonnie to me, to meee . . . Bring back, bring back . . ." He banged the bowl as hard as he could against the side panel of the chair, which was already full of dents as a result of previous excesses. "Bring back my Bonnie to me, to me. Bring back, bring back. Bring back my Bonnie to me . . ."

Neither one of them knew how long they'd been singing and laughing, but after a while the general's voice was hoarse and Madan's hands hurt from all the clapping. Panting, they sat across from each other, enjoying the afterglow.

"We should do this more often," the general croaked.

Madan nodded, got to his feet, and picked up the candle, which was almost burned down. He shook hands with the general, who saluted in return, and walked back to the landing. He locked the door, hung the key on the nail, and went down the steps. He saw that the door to Charlotte's room was still half open. He wondered where she could be. Until now he'd had the impression that she retired early or in any case shut herself up in her bedroom. He was about to go outside to see where she was when he heard her come in the front door. He blew out the candle quickly and went straight into the music room and closed the door. Then he grabbed a pile of fabrics and crept under the table. He had to make sure she couldn't read his thoughts.

1966 Simla ~

Dear Donald,

Thank you for your letter, which I have received. Three weeks ago I arrived in the "former British summer residence," as Father always refers to Simla. It's a magnificent city, full of English houses built on the hills. It's so steep that if it starts to rain here, I'm afraid all the buildings will simply slide down the hill! Driving is a bit scary, since the roads are really narrow and full of hairpin curves that my chauffeur usually can't make in one go. Sometimes I think I'm back in England, especially when I walk past the half-timbered houses or go down the big shopping streets.

The best thing is that it's nowhere near as hot. In the evening I sometimes have to wear a cardigan. I eat a lot, too. It's probably the fresh air that gives me an appetite. In two days' time I'll be moving on. I want to see the real mountains, I can only catch a glimpse of them from here. I understand that Father is doing well — I call Hema every Friday morning — I hope the same goes for you. I'll write again when I'm actually in the Himalayas.

Greetings from your sister,
Charlotte

~

"ARE YOU READY to go? The car is waiting downstairs," says Sita.

"Already?" Charlotte buttons her coat so that her belly disappears. No one in Rampur knows that Sita is travelling with her. The lodging-house keeper in Simla thinks that Sita is her personal servant. And in a sense, she is. Every morning, after Charlotte takes her bath, Sita massages her belly with a vegetable extract to reduce the chances of developing stretch marks. In the beginning it tickled, and Charlotte couldn't stop giggling. But now that she's used to it, she is content to entrust her physical well-being to a woman who apparently knows everything there is to know about being pregnant. The nosebleed she had last night is apparently part of it, as are her swollen feet and ankles, her unpredictable mood swings, crying bouts, headaches, and back pain. There is also the sensation in her belly when the tiny creature that is growing inside her begins stirring, which often happens just when she's trying to get some sleep.

"You wanted to get there before dark." She closes the large suitcase and puts it down next to the bed.

"Sita?"

"Are you starting to worry again?"

Charlotte unbuttons her coat and loosens her blouse. Her swollen breasts protrude from her bra, now much too small. "Look . . ." She points to the wet spots in the cotton fabric.

"That's drip milk," Sita says. "There's nothing wrong. A lot of milk means a big baby. Big babies are healthy. You have to eat well. And that means eating a lot." Sita smiles. "Otherwise there won't be enough milk for the baby."

"Sita?" Charlotte has already asked a thousand questions, but not the one that's been going round and round in her head and keeping her awake at night, the question that plagues her whenever she momentarily forgets that she is pregnant, the question that makes her feel insecure and ultimately sends her into a panic.

"It's going to be all right," Sita says. "Everything's going to be all right. Don't be afraid."

Charlotte buttons her blouse and coat. She's not worried about travelling into the mountains, and she isn't afraid of the cold or the delivery or the pain. She's afraid of what comes afterwards. Not a word has been said about what happens afterwards. It is as if the world will cease to turn when the child is born. While actually that will be the beginning of everything.

"I'll help you," Sita says softly. "You know that."

1967 Manali ~

Dear Donald,

It's almost impossible to describe just how beautiful it is here. The mountains look exactly like the paintings in Father's study, except that they're much more beautiful, higher and more imposing. I've never seen anything as enchanting as these mountains. Sometimes I spend the whole day out on the terrace, watching the clouds that seem to bump right into the side of the mountain, and the waterfall that comes splashing down all day and all night, and the eagle that circles high in the sky, the sun that shines on the peaks, and the monks in their red habits who pass by so silently, and the donkeys with the huge crates on their backs making their way along the narrow paths, and the village children playing on the grass. Now, of course, you're thinking how very lazy I am because I just sit there the whole day, but actually I do go for walks as well. But not too long, since my feet have been giving me a lot of trouble. But the doctor here says they'll get better. All I have to do is rest a bit more, and take alternating hot and cold baths at night. That's why I've taken up knitting again, something I haven't done since boarding school. My first attempt was a scarf. It didn't turn out as well as I'd hoped, since I'm a bit rusty, but if the next one turns out better, I'll send it to you. Father doesn't need it in Rampur. I can always wear the first one myself, since it's nice and warm. The room I've rented here is simple but adequate. My window overlooks a valley, with a river running through it. Apparently the river becomes quite wild in spring, but I won't be staying here that long. There are lots of apple trees, planted by the British. The other day I was walking toward the old part of town and as I was crossing the bridge, a young Englishman spoke to me. He asked me if I wanted to be happy. A rather odd question to ask a perfect stranger! I told him that I was very happy, and then I walked on. It wasn't until later that I heard who the boy was. There's a plant that grows here, and people use it to make something that's supposed to "expand your consciousness." That's what he wanted to sell me. There aren't many Europeans here, but apparently all of them come for that stuff, and not for a vacation, like me. It is so beautiful here. I'm eating well and getting plenty of sleep, and if my second scarf turns out better, I'll send it to you.

Regards from your sister,
Charlotte

~

CHARLOTTE IS SITTING in the big chair next to the window; she's wearing the red socks she knitted herself, which are tight around her swollen ankles. Sita is on her knees in a corner of the room, doing her *pudja*. Charlotte, who is not a regular churchgoer, would love to look inside her head, to see whether her prayers really give her strength. Charlotte herself is increasingly fearful of what lies ahead.

In the last few weeks her belly has become as big and round as the globe in her father's study. Every time she feels the stamp of a tiny foot, she thinks of him. Fortunately, the tiny creature inside her is not wearing boots, she muses as she inserts the needle: *insert, yarn forward, pull through, slip off.* What if it's not a child that's growing inside me, but a monster? *Insert, yarn forward, pull through, slip off.* A freak with one eye and no nose? A head with only a few large, hairy feet that immediately step into a pair of boots? *Insert, yarn forward, pull through, slip off.* And again she feels a sharp stab in her lower abdomen. Sita, who is still sitting on the floor with her back bent and murmuring softly, told her an hour ago that those were "practice contractions." They will prepare her for another stab of pain in her belly, this one harder and more piercing. She groans.

Sita raises her hands, makes another deep bow, stands up, and inquires cheerily, "Has it started?"

"It hurts," Charlotte says, as she tries to pick up the stitch she's just dropped.

Sita puts a hand on her belly. "It won't be long now. Today, maybe tomorrow."

"Tomorrow!"

"Or the day after tomorrow. The baby is the boss, not the mother. The stars have to be in the right position."

"Ah!" Charlotte winces, as the pain shoots through her body. "Call the sister, it's starting!"

"No, you haven't even dropped your knitting. The really big pain hasn't started yet."

"Sita, please?"

"No. The sister won't come until you're ready."

Charlotte looks at the yellow baby cape on the needles in

her hand. After the four scarves, the last of which she sent to her brother in England, she's also knitted spencers for Sita and herself and a pair of socks for each of them. After that, she concentrated on the cape, which provided more distraction because she had opted for a complicated pattern. Sita bought the pale yellow angora wool from a spinner in the old town. Charlotte decided against pink or blue, since she doesn't know whether it's a boy or a girl. *Insert, yarn forward, pull through, slip off.* Another stab; this time it lasts a long time. Then she feels something in her belly snap, and the fluid flows from between her legs, over the seat of the chair, onto the floor. She pulls herself up by the window sill and stares at the puddle. No matter how hard she tries, she cannot stem the flow of water.

Sita looks at the liquid on the floor and says that everything is fine.

"What do you mean, fine? Sita, everything's coming out! What's happening? Go and call the sister!"

"Not yet. Patience. Everything's going to be fine, just be patient for a while. Go put on a clean pair of underpants."

"I've waited long enough. I want it to start."

Sita, who throughout Charlotte's pregnancy has become accustomed to her violent mood swings, mops the floor and grabs the cape, which just misses falling into the puddle of amniotic fluid.

"You see: it's started. I dropped my knitting."

Sita smiles: "You're a smart girl."

AGAIN THE TIDAL wave of pain sweeps over her. It begins slowly and gradually takes possession of her. Impossible to stem, to staunch, to avoid. She groans and cries out. The nun, who an hour ago accompanied her to the delivery room, puts a hot-water bottle on her belly and tells her to breathe in and out calmly. The wave of pain reaches its high point and slowly subsides.

THE NUN IS wearing a white apron over her habit, which in Charlotte's view makes her look like a butcher. She opens Charlotte's knees and inserts her fingers. There's no room. She must feel that there's no room. Something is in the way, but the woman pushes her fingers farther inside. Charlotte feels like screaming. She wants to kick the hand aside, grab her suitcases, and leave. It doesn't matter that it has just started to snow. She has plenty of scarves and warm socks. Sita pushes her gently back into the pillows and massages her neck. Charlotte wants to crawl into that gentle hand, wants to disappear inside it, wants it to be over. She hears the music of the zither. And again she feels the fingers that caressed the strings and her skin, the mouth that sang and that kissed her, his legs that opened her knees, easily, unopposed. She inhales his smell, savours his taste, but no matter how hard she tries, she cannot recall his face.

"You're not there yet. Not even close," says the nun, as she removes her fingers.

"Not yet?" Charlotte moans.

Sita pats her perspiring forehead with a damp cloth. "It'll come when the stars are in the right position."

"What stars? The sun hasn't even set!" She wants to make jokes and forget about what is happening, then the next wave comes. "Stop!" Charlotte pushes the nun's hand away. Again she says that there's not enough dilation. "I've had it. I've had enough. I want to go home. I don't want to be here. Why am

I here? Why?" Tears roll down Charlotte's cheeks. She takes deep breaths, and sobs as the next wave engulfs her.

"Through your nose. Let the air go down into your stomach." Sita is standing behind her, with her hands on Charlotte's sweaty shoulders. "Hold your breath. Tense your stomach muscles. Just a little longer. Breathe out through your mouth."

She tries to follow these instructions, but the powerful paw of pain drags her along. She utters curses she didn't even realize she knew. Her ears are ringing. Her mouth is dry. She is unaware of the heavy snowstorm blowing outside. The clatter of shutters and the howl of the wind have become part of her battle to bring this human being that has been swimming and stamping around in her belly for months into the world.

The latest contraction fades, and Charlotte falls back into Sita's arms. She closes her eyes, longing for sleep. Why didn't they tell her that giving birth is an unfair battle, in which you're trying to protect, rather than kill, the enemy, in which your body goes its own way and refuses to listen to its master, in which the pain is bigger and stronger than the peaks of the Himalayas? She walks, she sits, she stands, she squats, and she hangs. She vomits, craps, and pees in Sita's arms. She's soaking wet and half naked. Outside, the storm is gaining in force and the stars have disappeared. The contractions that descend upon her banish all sense of shame, dragging her down into a deep, black chasm in which nothing exists except breathing and pain. She screams, she feels how the lump in her pelvis descends. Her legs are open wide. "Come!" she calls. "Come!" All of her muscles are tensed. And then the contraction disappears as quickly as it came, and the pain subsides. She pants. Then, in a flash, a thought streaks through her mind: *This is like the war. This is like the pain that Peter felt.* The man who had not given her a child because his suffering did not ebb away like her contractions. His pain never went away: with every breath it entrapped him still further. All at once, she knows that the humiliation and injuries that he suffered were a thousand times worse than the fight that she was engaged in now. Sita and the nun have no idea what is happening. Charlotte straightens her back, breathes in through her nose, and smiles. The contraction takes her by force, and she welcomes it like a long-lost friend. The stabs and wounds that had been unbearable before now give her strength. She hears the sound of bullets whizzing by and people screaming. She sees the blood flowing. Her legs shake and quiver. It is impossible to keep them under control. She shrieks when the muscles in her calves tense up. She trembles, her teeth chatter, and she perspires profusely. She feels hot one minute and cold the next. She cries and screams. The tanks continue to roll forward. Her vagina is on fire, and a dagger pierces her lower back.

"Push," the nun urges. "Now you can push!"

I'm supposed to push, she says to the stranger awaiting his entrance cue. *Are you ready for this? Are you ready?* She's panting like a galloping horse that has suddenly come to a standstill. She clenches her fists, braces herself with her feet against the foot of the bed, and pushes. She hears jungle noises that merge with the sound of exploding grenades. It's as if she's being torn in half. She lets out one loud, long-drawn-out scream. The plug that has been jammed between her legs for so many hours suddenly wrings itself loose and slithers out.

Everything is quiet.

Sita looks over Charlotte's head at the baby lying between

her legs. There is a tremulous cry, like that of a baby mountain goat that's lost its mother.

"Do you want to know what it is?" the nun asks.

1995 Rampur ~

THE JET-BLACK HORSE galloped over the hill. The dry ground crumbled under its hooves and flew into the air. On its back was a man with a turban and a long velvet coat that completely covered his legs. He did not appear to be bothered by the terrible heat. Charlotte was on her knees in the grass. She was trying to dig a hole in the ground because she was convinced that there must be water somewhere. She recognized Maharaja Man Singh immediately.

He came to a standstill next to her. The dust that he had raised slowly settled. She saw the horse's black legs through the veil of dust covering the wilted and drooping plants in her garden. She was immediately aware that the shabby pyjamas she was wearing were not the appropriate garb in which to welcome the maharaja. She should have quickly disappeared before the cloud of dust settled, but he had already recognized her.

"Madame Harris!" he called out.

It was only in New Delhi and Bombay that people had called her "Madame Harris." She had gone back to using her maiden name, Bridgwater, the moment she had returned to Rampur. She didn't know herself whether she did so because it would make her more attractive to potential suitors or to help her to forget her unhappy marriage, or perhaps she did it to please her father. But when the maharaja called her

"Madame Harris," her gaze went straight to the window of the music room. She became worried when she saw that all the windows in the house were wide open.

"What brings you here?" She only pretended to be surprised. The news of his impending arrival had travelled faster than the hooves of his horse. Charlotte saw the traditional embroidery on his collar and sleeves, which contrasted sharply with the gleaming Ray-Ban sunglasses he was wearing.

"Why didn't you attend the wedding of my daughter Chutki? We sent you an invitation."

It was several seconds before Charlotte could remember receiving the invitation. It was engraved on magnificent gold paper, which smelled of roses. The maharaja's hand went to his coat pocket, withdrew an identical envelope, and handed it to her.

"My son has found a wife." He didn't wait for her to open the envelope, but trotted off, leaving her behind in a cloud of dust.

She had always wanted to attend a princely wedding. The maharaja would spare neither effort nor expense for his son. The palace would be decorated with millions of flowers, the men forming the guard would be mounted on elephants, the driveway would be covered in hundreds of Persian carpets, the fountains would spout rosewater, and everything else would be covered in gold leaf. The new princess would be attired in fairy-tale robes and laden with centuries-old family jewels, and those living within a wide radius would be given free food. The festivities would last more than a week, and people would talk about the event for years to come.

The snorting and stamping of the maharaja's horse had died away, and she heard the whirring sound of the sewing machine coming from inside the house. She opened the envelope and took out the invitation. The gold paper, which was blank, gleamed in the sun. There was no writing on it. She turned it over. At first she thought there was nothing on the other side either, but then she noticed the tiny letters at the bottom of the page. They read: DON'T DO IT.

DUE TO THE heat, even simply sitting on the sofa was a tribulation. The dream from which she awakened would not be banished from her mind. Images of the maharaja on his horse continued to pass in front of her. It was years since she had thought about his daughter Chutki. On the day they took leave of one another everything had gone wrong, so she never received an invitation to the wedding, due to take place several months later. At the time, she was very worried about Peter, who had not spoken since the operation on Chutki's little brother. Even if she had received an invitation, she would have been unable to attend the wedding.

She heard Hema's shuffling footsteps, followed by a knock on the door.

Hema entered carrying a tray with a cup of tea and a plate of cookies.

"You can take back the cookies."

"But they're very good cookies, memsahib."

"I don't care for any cookies."

Hema knew that she used to be very fond of cookies with her tea, and that the general used to joke that her sweet tooth was the only thing Charlotte had inherited from her mother. Hema had never met the general's wife, but he had heard from an old chauffeur who worked for a high-ranking civil servant in Rampur that she was just as beautiful as Charlotte. Hema thought his mistress was much too thin, so he pretended not to hear her and put the plate of cookies on the table. "Did the man on the radio say anything about rain?" he asked, for Hema had a lot more worries than the poor appetite of his mistress. He had to cook for four people and wash for three, and since there was no more water coming out of the faucet and the level in the bathtubs was going down, he would soon be forced to buy water from the door-to-door pedlars. In his view, the fact that they would be dependent on crafty hucksters for the necessities of life was the fault of the civil servants, who hadn't seen the problem coming and had not arranged for extra supplies of water.

"The BBC says the monsoon is on the way, but Radio Rampur is convinced that it'll be another couple of days yet and the temperature will go up."

"How much water do we have left?"

"General sahib's bath is almost empty, the bath in the guest bedroom is half full, and the one in the kitchen is empty."

"How long will that last us?"

"The *darzi* ought to pay more, with so many ladies coming for a fitting." Although he knew very well that the ladies also came to get a glimpse of the half-empty house, Hema was convinced that it was the tailor's fault that the water was running out so fast. But he conveniently forgot that the general was bathed from head to toe twice a day, with a washcloth and soft soap.

"What's the current price of drinking water?" asked Charlotte, who was already doing the calculations in her head. She had also decided that the time had come to convince her father to sign the papers so that she could sell the house, the outbuildings, and the hill.

Before Hema could answer Charlotte's question, for which he had no answer, the doorbell rang. He was also thinking about prices, rates, and haggling as he shuffled to the front door.

Outside in the blazing sunlight stood a young man with slicked-back hair wearing shiny sunglasses and a wristwatch with stones that looked like diamonds. "Good morning," he said in a lilting voice. "I've come for Mrs. Bridgwater."

"Who can I say is calling?"

"Sylvester Ferrao, son of Professor Dr. Bernardo Ferrao of Goa."

Hema had never seen the man before, but he was most impressed by the titles and the shiny sunglasses. The prediction in the newspaper suddenly made sense. He showed the stranger in and then went into the salon, where he rolled out the large carpet so that this important man could enter the room.

The music room door was ajar, to catch what little draft there was. Madan had heard the bell and was expecting to see one of the nosey club ladies appear at any moment. When he didn't hear a shrill voice, he looked through the crack of the door and saw a slick-haired, fashionably dressed man wearing dark sunglasses. He was rocking back and forth on his heels. Madan could tell that the man was a charlatan from a distance of a hundred metres away. He'd met so many thieves and swindlers throughout his life that he had ultimately developed a kind of sixth sense for crooks. Madan grabbed the ochre-coloured silk cape he had made for the wife of Alok Nath, the goldsmith, threw it around his shoulders, and opened the door. The man had visited the oldest illegal gambling joint in Rampur, where he had heard that the big house on the hill was the home of a ruined English lady and her demented father, and that she was in dire need of money. He was expecting something quite different. The Indian nobleman standing opposite him radiated authority, and judging by his attire, he was extremely wealthy.

"I, er . . . I . . . ," the man stuttered. He had originally planned to sell tickets for an imaginary lottery with a story about winning a million at the end of the month, but he sensed that it was no use trying that story on this man. He started to panic. The first thing that came to his mind was to say that he was selling tickets for an animal protection society, until he realized that this man had probably hunted his entire life. Then he thought about pretending that the lottery was for Mother Teresa's Missionaries of Charity, something he'd done before and with some success, but he began to have misgivings — this man had such an air of power. And because he doubted that the lotto would work, he suddenly didn't know what to say. He had nothing on him aside from the book of lotto tickets and a false identity card. He didn't want to pretend that he was looking for work, as he'd done in his younger years, since there was a good chance he'd have to do something he didn't fancy. So he asked a question that, as a child, had gotten him into houses where he was able to nick the odd bauble: "Would you happen to have a glass of water?"

Madan turned around, causing the cape to swirl elegantly, and picked up the pitcher he'd filled that morning in the kitchen under the watchful eye of Hema. He poured a glass and gave it to the man, who was becoming more and more nervous in the presence of this handsome but uncommunicative gentleman. Sylvester Ferrao, which was not his real name, emptied the glass at one draught, thanked Madan, and said that it was about time for him to leave. Madan accompanied him to the front door and let him out. He slid the cape from his shoulders and was back in the music room by the time the door to the drawing room opened.

Hema and Charlotte had unrolled the Persian rug at breakneck speed, and they were both perspiring: laying out the carpet was becoming an increasingly arduous chore in this heat. The faithful butler looked around the hall in consternation. He couldn't figure out where the professor had got to. He had made it clear to the memsahib that this was an important man who — and here he had to search for the right words — would no doubt be able to help relieve their current situation. He was certain that this gentleman with the unusual sunglasses would bring her luck. The horoscope, which the neighbours' butler had read out loud to him, said that "riches were waiting at the door." He had asked for permission to tear it out of the paper so he could give it to Charlotte memsahib to read, but the butler told him that his employer hadn't seen it yet, and that he was expected to leave the newspaper behind intact.

Madan was about to close the door of the music room when Hema called out, "Where did the professor go?" Madan pointed to the front door.

"Gone?" After inhaling the dust, Hema had fervently hoped that this was the last time he would have to unroll the carpet. Suddenly he knew for certain that the tailor had chased the rich professor away. He ran to the door and saw the man striding down the path to the road. He wanted to call him back, tell him that memsahib wanted to receive him, and that she needed his riches, that the extra expenses for water were a real problem, and that, as the butler, he had to solve all these problems without help from anyone. But the man jumped into a rickshaw and disappeared.

Charlotte saw the smile on Madan's face and found him even more handsome than she had a few hours before. She thought back to the letter from the maharaja — DON'T DO IT — as she closed the drawing-room door and began to roll up the carpet by herself.

By the light of a candle, Madan was busy rubbing a piece of rosewood across a gleaming red ribbon. All around him, the house creaked and moaned. Not only were the trees and the plants suffering under the extreme heat, but so was the house itself. He could hear the mice everywhere, and the insects were gnawing away at the interior, while in the garden the crickets were screeching so loudly that the rain clouds that preceded the monsoon would be arriving pretty soon. Charlotte still hadn't given him the fabric for her dress, but he hoped that he would be able to work the red ribbon into her gown. Red suited the colour of her hair, and the lustre of the silk would illuminate her delicate skin, like an angel.

What are you doing? Her voice echoed in his head. He immediately stopped rubbing the rosewood. He looked in the direction of the door. It was closed. He jumped up and peered through the open window. The crescent moon illuminated the skeletons of the wilted trees, the dark outlines of the kitchen building, and the rocks that gleamed white along the path to the road. There was no sign of the woman who floated through his thoughts all day. Madan didn't understand how he could have heard her voice so clearly when she wasn't there. Had the distance over which they were able to hear each other's thoughts suddenly been extended? Did the walls of the house no longer provide him with protection?

Had she heard the things he was thinking about her eyes and skin, her slender build, and her curly hair? He went back to the table and picked up the red ribbon.

Do you want me to bring my fabric?

Madan looked up again, startled. She must have hidden somewhere. He peered at the pile of fabrics under the table, in which he had buried his head when it was overflowing with thoughts. He looked behind the folding screen, where several dresses hung awaiting a fitting. He even looked under the chest, where only a small child could have hidden. Cautiously, he opened the door, slowly enough to allow her to sneak away and avoid being caught. But the hallway was empty, and he heard no footsteps. *Where are you?* he wondered, but there was no response from the deserted hall. Madan walked back to the table, pushed aside the empty plate, and was just about to unroll a new piece of fabric when he heard her voice — *You finished everything!* Madan looked at the empty plate. He was no longer obsessed with food. He ate if food was available, and otherwise he did without. He had never cooked for himself, and was satisfied with a bit of rice and dal from a sidewalk vendor. He found it strange that the women always exchanged recipes while waiting for a hem to be finished or a dart to be unpicked. Food was food. He didn't enjoy an empty stomach, but he had no trouble cycling for hours with his heavy sewing machine on the luggage carrier without having had breakfast. He was starting to get used to the idea that he could hear her thoughts and she could hear his, but the fact that her voice could creep into his head while he was alone in the room was something he found disturbing. If it was a romantic reverie, then he could have taken it for an expression of his own longing. But after hearing her voice, which seemed to delight in the fact that he had finished what was on his plate, he was hopelessly confused. He wanted to pray to Abbas for an explanation, but he didn't know whether she could hear his prayers as well. So he did his best to think about nothing but the gown for the judge's wife. He cleared away the ribbon, reached for the blue organza, and started cutting.

THE CORK HAD become smoother over the years and it had taken her a while to find it. The mouse that had made the original hole — the one she had fulminated against because the rodent had gnawed at her sheet music — was the recipient of her retroactive gratitude. She knelt down and started fiddling with the stopper, using the contents of her manicure kit as tools. She didn't actually remember stuffing shredded newspapers and pieces of sisal rope into the hole. But now, using a pair of tweezers, she plucked out the remains, bit by bit, as she thought about the maharaja's letter. Her curiosity and longing were greater, and she continued to fiddle with the bits of paper. The very last wad of newspaper popped out. She blew out the candle, knelt down, and looked through the hole. Between the planks that formed the ceiling of the music room she saw narrow chinks illuminated by candlelight. To get a better look, she lay down on the floor, so that her eye was directly above the hole. There was no more than half a millimetre between the planks, but suddenly she saw part of his hand, which held a piece of red ribbon. *This will go around her neck.* His hand drew back with a jerk. Now only the ribbon was lying on the table. Charlotte adjusted her position, in the hope of getting another glimpse of him. She couldn't hear his thoughts anymore, now that he was out of her field of vision. Would he pick up the ribbon again? Had he sensed that she was spying on him? Had she gone too far? She was even worse than the wife of Nikhil Nair: at least *she* didn't collect her gossip by lying on her stomach and peering through a hole, like a thief in the night. Charlotte was just about to get up when she saw him pick up the ribbon. And again she sensed that he was thinking of her and that the ribbon was intended for her. *Do you want me to bring the material?* It was an idea that popped into her head before she realized it. She drew back with a jerk, as if he'd caught her doing something. She quickly put her hand over the hole. He mustn't know that she's lying here in her bedroom, spying on him. She wanted to grab the cork that she'd pulled out, but in the dark all she could find was a pile of newspaper clippings and pieces of string. Her hand went on searching in the dark. The cork had to be there somewhere. And she had to cover the hole before more of her thoughts could escape. She had one hand over the hole and the other feeling around her when she heard him open the door and then close it again. Had he finished his work, and was he going back to the room next to the kitchen to sleep? Charlotte found the cork. She couldn't help herself: with the cork in one hand, she bent over one more time and peered into the hole. The light was still on. Suddenly she saw him move the empty dinner plate with his right hand. *He's finished everything*, she thought, and immediately she heard his confused thoughts shooting upward. He wanted to know where she was. She quickly put the cork back into the hole and pushed it down so that it wouldn't be easy to pry it out again. She crawled away from the hole, to a corner of the room. She didn't hear him, and she wondered if that meant that he couldn't hear her. Weren't his antennae far more developed, because he could not speak? Her stomach rumbled. She had had the food intended for her sent to the tailor, with her usual excuse: "I'm not hungry." Her hand slid down to her belly. She could feel her ribs. *Tomorrow I've got to eat something.* She pulled the small wooden box toward her. She had forgotten that it was empty.

1959 Bombay ~

CHANDAN CHANDRAN IS sitting cross-legged on the ground, surrounded by a variety of bottles, boxes, and tiny bags. Madan is sitting opposite him, inhaling an intoxicating aroma. This is the first time his boss has taken him up to the tiny attic room. Since the day two years ago when he was assigned a rug of his own in a corner of the weaving mill, where he hems scarves and lengths of cloth, Madan has been happy. He doesn't know that he is thirteen years old, and numbers and dates mean very little to him. He considers himself a man after he discovered black hairs growing around his willy. And his shoulders are just as broad as those of the men at the machines, who all call him Mukka, like his friend Subhash, with whom he shares the lean-to on the roof. Mister Chandran has never addressed him by name.

Sometimes, in the morning or afternoon, or just before they finish work, boss Chandran sits down next to him, picks up the piece of cloth where Madan keeps his needles, and inspects them. If a needle is blunt or rusty, he pulls it out, muttering that only good tools produce good work. Then he takes one of the good needles, threads it with red thread, and sticks it into a piece of cloth. This is how he teaches Madan the various stitches: the open hemstitch, the invisible hemstitch, the scallop stitch, the three-cornered stitch, and the blanket stitch. Madan also learns that each fabric requires a different stitch. Without a word, Chandran hands the cloth back to Madan and watches to see whether he can duplicate the stitch. If he's successful, Chandran tells him what it's called. If not, Madan has to unpick both his own work and that of the weaver and wait until the next time Chandan Chandran sits down beside him to demonstrate the stitch again.

It's quite an honour that he has been allowed to enter the attic room. He had only been there once before, with Subhash. One day he did climb up the ladder just to enjoy the scent, and noticed that there was a lock on the door. No one ever told him who had the key.

"This scent promotes perseverance," Chandan Chandran says in his pleasantly low voice, as he takes a handful of small, dried orange flowers from a bottle. Madan holds out his hand and Chandan Chandran places a few in his palm. Madan presses his nose into the flowers, but the scent is not as strong as he expected.

"First they have to be crushed and soaked. Then you immerse the fabric in the water." He crumbles a few of the flowers and holds them up to Madan's nose. "Calendula. The farmers call them marigolds." Then he takes a large bottle with a stopper from the shelf behind him, and opens it. "*Jasminum*, or jasmine, stands for purity. The leaves have to be boiled with the fabric. Purity is a powerful force, one that's often undervalued. Exercise great caution."

Madan doesn't understand why he should exercise caution with a handful of sweet-smelling flowers. After each monsoon the entire neighbourhood is filled with the scent of jasmine, and everyone is happy. Men who were grumpy during the hot months start smiling again and bring bowls full of petals to the temple. Children who were cranky because it was too hot to sleep race around as if reborn, and women who accepted without complaint the conduct of their unpredictable spouses and unruly children are regenerated by the first drops of rain, like flowering sprigs.

Chandan Chandran empties a small bag of short brown needles into his hand. "These are from a cactus. They promote wealth."

For Madan, money is just as foreign a concept as dates. The word "wealth" calls up visions of apples, pears, or bananas. When Chandan Chandran says that these small spines have to do with riches, he simply nods. In jail, he only got to eat after Ibrahim had given him a wallop, or after he was ordered to sit on the shit bucket so that the murderer could eat without being inconvenienced by the stench.

His boss pulled a lemon out of his jacket pocket. "The *Citrus limonia* promotes chastity."

"Chastity" is another word that means nothing to Madan, but the sour taste of a lemon and the expression on the face of the weaver makes it clear. He remembers Brother Francis praying in front of the wooden man on the cross, and the vinegary smell of the washhouse where the brother dropped to his knees.

The man with the ponytail gets up and searches among the bottles and bags until he finds what he's looking for. "These are from the *Passiflora*, or passionflower," he says in a calm voice. His open palm holds white and bluish purple stamens. "These can evoke silence."

Silence is something that Madan can relate to. Not the

silence in his head — there he's always talking a mile a minute — but he has a desire to pronounce words, to construct a sentence, to tell a story. One night, when Subhash and the moon were asleep and the city around him had descended into such repose that even the rats had gone to ground, he got up and walked over to the very edge of the roof. Using the air he managed to squeeze out of his lungs, he opened his mouth and tried to form a sound that resembled the attractive low timbre of Mister Chandran's voice. What came out was a shrill, piercing scream, so blood-curdling that any living creature that heard it awoke with a start — the birds in the trees, the dogs on the street, the rats, the mice, and even the ants and the beetles. Subhash, who had also been startled out of his sleep, told Madan to come and lie down because he'd heard the shriek of an evil spook. Madan returned to his mat and resolved that he would never again utter a sound.

"The *Rosa*, or rose," Chandan Chandran says softly, nodding toward the red flower in his hand, "calls up love."

Madan sees a smile appear on the weaver's face. The serious, earnest expression has disappeared. Madan puts out a hand, and the rose falls into his palm. He doesn't know whether it's the scent or the colour of the soft, velvety petals, but he's aware of something happening inside his heart. He closes his eyes and remembers his sister in her blue jacket; he feels the hands of the blond woman caressing him and the kiss she gave him; he hears loving words and smells sweet scents. He thinks of Abbas taking a bite out of a big apple. Could that be what the weaver meant by love? He knows that the men who work at the weaving mill sometimes talk about love, but Madan has never seen those women, and he doesn't know whether they're real or exist only in the imaginations of the men. When he opens his eyes again, Chandan Chandran has exchanged the rose for a tiny bunch of blue flowers, without his noticing.

"The *Myosotis*, or forget-me-not, is a token of lasting remembrance."

The flower in his hand is tiny, insignificant. And yet the sight of it is accompanied by an unexpected wave of sadness that takes possession of his adolescent body. Most of his memories are painful, and yet the rose awakened thoughts of the past that did not make him feel lonely. But now, with the tiny flowers in his hand, all those feelings have been turned upside down, and he remembers how he wandered barefoot among the legs of a whooping, ecstatic mob of men. The fear and the loneliness. The pain and the blood. The hunger and the thirst. He sniffs the flowers, which seem to be saying, "We haven't forgotten." He doesn't know whether it's the scents that overpower him or the memories, but Madan feels the strength draining from his body. He hears Mister Chandran's words fade away, as the carousel of scents impose themselves and he can no longer distinguish between them. He sees Mister Chandran's hand coming in his direction, and then everything begins to revolve before his eyes.

Then he is lying alone on his mat. He hears the hum of the looms, and the forget-me-nots are lying next to his head.

1967 Himalayan Queen Express ~

THEY ARE SITTING opposite each other, but not a word has been spoken since the train left the station. Charlotte stares at the landscape racing by without seeing the farmers bringing in the harvest, the women doing the laundry, or the mountains that rise in the distance. Sita stares at the marbled wall of their carriage, where she keeps discovering new shapes: a face without eyes, a groping hand, a woman with long, flowing hair . . .

Everything has gone differently from what had been agreed. During Charlotte's first conversation in the hospital, the nun told her that the baby would be taken away immediately after birth, as there were enough young parents who wanted to adopt a child. Charlotte did not look at the baby because she was afraid she might want to keep it.

While Charlotte lay on the bed with her legs wide apart and her eyes shut tightly, Sita took the dark-skinned baby from the arms of the nun. The former ayah didn't understand how the fair-skinned woman whom she had more or less raised could have given birth to such a dark child. After the umbilical cord was cut, Sita left the room, carrying the damp little creature in her arms. She was followed by the nun, who told her to take the baby to Ward 4. In the corridor the baby began to cry and Sita felt her breasts contract violently in a frantic attempt to produce milk. She walked past the door with the number four on it, straight to the simple room that Charlotte had rented for her. The nun asked where she was going, and Sita replied that she and she alone was going to adopt the boy. She went into the bathroom, washed the baby with warm water from a flask, and laid him in her own bed. She used the spencer and the scarf that Charlotte had knitted for her as blankets. Then she returned to Ward 4 and announced that she had come to sign the adoption papers. Twice the nun asked her whether the mother had given her consent, and twice Sita nodded her head. She didn't understand what the form in front of her said, and it was only after the nun pointed to the line where she was supposed to put her signature that she wrote her name, in an unsteady hand. These were the only words she knew how to write. When the nun asked her what the boy's name was, she replied "Parvat," or "mountain." She asked for a bottle of milk and then returned to her room.

Not until two weeks later, when the taxi arrived to take them back to Simla, did Charlotte discover that Sita had the baby with her. The tiny Indian woman, who had been her confidante for as long as she could remember, did not reply to her questions. The baby was tightly wrapped in a cloth, barely visible within the folds of her clothes. If it hadn't cried for a few minutes as they were getting into the car, Charlotte would probably not have discovered the child until much later. Her attempts to catch a glimpse of the infant were unsuccessful, as Sita had covered the child with a cloth.

The train gently rocks and sways. The baby is still asleep, hidden among the folds of Sita's clothes. The two women avoid each other's eyes. Charlotte is angry and Sita is afraid. Then the baby starts to cry. Sita conjures up a bottle of milk, which she has warmed up between her thighs, from under the folds of her clothes. The hungry baby lets out a protracted howl, and Charlotte, whose breasts are still tightly bound, feels a rush of milk that she has not experienced before, not even when she heard the cries of one of the babies in Ward 4, waiting for their future parents.

There is no trace of accusation or reproach in Charlotte's voice, rather something akin to surprise. "It's my child," she says.

Sita looks nervously at the woman across from her. She sees that her previous anger has given way to curiosity, evoking a faint smile. She nods timorously. The earrings that Sita has worn since her wedding night sway slightly. Then, without further hesitation, she brings the baby out from under her shawl.

Charlotte stares in amazement at the dark-skinned child. "Is that my child?"

"Yes, a boy."

Charlotte watches breathlessly as the woman who was her surrogate mother for so long routinely pushes the pacifier into the mouth of the baby, who immediately begins to suck. His black eyelashes, his black hair, his dark eyes, his brown skin: nowhere does she recognize herself. Until she looks at his tiny hands, which aimlessly clench and unclench to the rhythm of his feeding. The hands are just like her own, with the overly long thumb and the short middle finger. She studies the face: the chubby cheeks, the sucking lips, the swallowing motion, the sighs, the tiny hairs on the forehead, the skin so unmarked and flawless . . . And to think she carried this child inside her all those months! Although she knows that the baby's father is Indian, she never stopped to think during all those long months that the child might be dark-skinned. He looks nothing like the Eurasians she knows who — depending on their background — either loathe or love their fair skin, their eyes, their nose, their hair, and their name. What will Father say when he hears? And her brother? And the members of the New Rampur Club? Her personnel? Reverend Das? The tennis ladies? The man she buys her apples from? People are reluctant to deal with someone of mixed blood. Like the timid woman at the library who bears the name Johnson, after the soldier who impregnated her mother. And the owner of the garage, who pretends he's British but is ridiculed because he's only a half-caste. The headmistress of the domestic science school, who wants her children to study in England, which she regards as their native country, but cannot get a visa for them. The pedicurist who spent years trying to change her name and now suddenly wants her own name back. The tears that have waited for this moment are waved aside. What will happen to this child when she is no longer able to protect him, when he is old enough to make his way in the world? Will they taunt him because he's a bastard, dark instead of blond, fatherless, and without rights? Will people at cocktail parties call her a whore, like the railroad director's daughter, who had a relationship with a man from Kerala? Will she be disinherited, like the woman who ran away with a famous poet from Calcutta? Or poisoned, like the girl who planned to marry a teacher from Orissa? Should she move to England? To America? To Africa? Where could they be happy, without having every move they make censured?

The suitcase she packed that morning to take back to the big house on the hill is lying next to her. If the journey goes as planned, they will be back in Rampur in two days' time. She breaks out in a sweat. She wants to snatch the child from Sita's arms, tear the bindings from her breasts, and suckle him. She wants to comfort him, tuck him in, protect him, and never let him go. She'd like to put him back inside her, to undo everything that had happened, to go back in time, to obliterate her shame. No one must ever know that he is her child. It's as if she has forgotten that she gave her baby up for adoption two weeks ago. Suddenly she realizes that her son can be happy only if she is not his mother.

"When did you and your husband last make love?"

Sita looked up, shocked by such a direct question.

"Did you and Deepak make love the last time he was home on leave?" Charlotte persisted.

Sita remembers how dry she was when he climbed on top of her. She had forgotten his smell, and his hands had become rough. Not until he lay beside her, snoring, did she feel his sperm streaming out of her. She hadn't told him that she'd had no periods that entire year. What little intimacy they used to share had completely disappeared after he went to work in New Delhi. She was even surprised when he entered her. Although she had never shared the thought with anyone, she was convinced that he had found a replacement for her, and that it was out of a sense of duty that he returned to Rampur one week per year.

Charlotte can tell by the confusion on Sita's face that she had indeed been intimate with her husband. "From now on, this is your child."

Sita, who has the adoption papers in her purse, nods her head.

"Don't ever tell anyone that you've adopted the child. Introduce him to your daughters as their little brother. And call Deepak to tell him that at long last he has a son. He will be proud and learn to love you again. As long as I live, I will support you financially. This boy must go to college, have a chance to become a doctor or an engineer if he wants to, but you must never tell him that I'm his mother. Never! Will you promise me that?" Charlotte was panting.

Sita doesn't understand why Charlotte is making a fuss all of a sudden. It is clear for all to see that he's her child. She nods, bends over him, and begins to sing softly: the nasal sound full of unintelligible words, which Charlotte knows so well. The baby falls asleep with his mouth open.

1967 Rampur ~

THE TEARS HAD dried by the time the heat in Rampur took them by surprise. The chauffeur was waiting for her near the station. He had looked confused when not only the daughter of the house got into the car, but also the former ayah, carrying a baby. And he was further taken aback when the general's daughter told him to take the ayah and the baby home first, and to drive to the big house after they had been dropped off.

The fan is revolving above her head, and the windows are open. She longs for the cool of the mountains as she opens the suitcase, which Hema has placed on the bed. On top of her own things lies the little angora baby cape she knitted. Her fingers stroke the soft wool. She feels like jumping into the car and driving straight to Sita's house, but she knows that she has to control herself, that he is no longer her child, that she will never be a mother, and that the cape is much too warm for Rampur. She wraps the scarf in plastic, along with the angora cape, and shoves it onto the top shelf of the cabinet, so that it is out of sight. No one will ever wear them. Outside she hears the hum of the Lloyds and the panting of the *mali* as he pushes the machine forward across the lawn. She must ask him to pick some flowers for the dining room. The house is too quiet, too empty. She takes her pen and a sheet of paper and begins a letter to her brother.

Dear Donald,

I'm back home. I'll never forget the months I spent in the Himalayas. I have one of Father's paintings hanging over my bed, the one with Mount Everest. That way I'll never forget the beautiful mountains. The green grass in the pastures, the cool wind, and the snow. The power the mountain radiates is overwhelming. There is nothing in the world as beautiful, or exceptional, or gigantic. When I think about them, I almost feel like crying. Do you remember how Father never allowed us to cry? Not even when we were really young. Thinking back, I realize just how strange that was. All babies cry, because they're hungry or have cramps in their tummy. You probably don't remember when we were little and he put us outside in the baby carriage, in the pouring rain. One time when you were out there, it started to thunder and you kept on crying. Sita wasn't allowed to stay with you. I hid behind a bush so I could get as close as possible to you, without Father seeing me. Did you hear that she has a son? I would like to give her a present. In a magazine I saw at the station in New Delhi there was an article about a new kind of baby carriage that someone in England has designed. It's called a "buggy." Do you think you could order one for me in London? It's made of lightweight aluminium tubing, and you can fold it up until it's quite small. The patent number is 1.154.362. I think Sita will be very pleased with it. If possible, would you try to have it sent by airmail, since the boat takes such a long time, and I want her to have it as soon as possible? Do you think you can find the time? Is everything all right with you? Father is happy that I'm back. I think his nurses are happy, too. He's able to do a lot more than he could before I left. His left hip joint bends now, and he can almost sit up by himself. He won't ever be able to walk again, but you knew that, didn't you? I thought he might be angry because I stayed away longer than I had planned, but he hasn't said anything about that. He's been in the hospital for a year, and he says that now that I'm back, he wants to come home. Are you planning to come to Rampur? I can't very well leave here for the time being, and I'd really like to see you again.

Regards from your sister,
Charlotte

P.S. You won't forget the baby carriage?

1995 Rampur ~

THE CHANDELIER HADN'T been taken down in years, but now it lay in the middle of the hall like a phantom ship, stranded and draped in cobwebs. Hema was on his knees, prying the hundreds of candle stumps out of their holders, one by one, with a small knife. He had closed the door to the music room because he didn't want the tailor to see him doing the work of an errand boy. With the tip of the knife, he carefully loosened each candle, trying to lift it out of its holder in one piece. Some of the candles were long enough to give a few more hours of light, while others would have to be melted down. Although he considered it menial work, he was happy to be sitting down for a while. Beads of sweat dripped from his eyebrows, and his shirt clung to his back. There was still some water left in the bath adjoining the guestroom, and he had managed to get a good price on drinking water, so he had lugged twelve full buckets up the hill. Tomorrow he'd ask memsahib if the tailor couldn't give him a hand. The man paid rent, but when the price was agreed, no account was taken of the possibility that they would run out of water.

The river that ran through Rampur had fallen dry. Only that morning Hema had seen dozens of women digging holes. They hoped to find water to wash themselves and their clothes, since the water that was sold at the roadside was too expensive for that purpose. The newsreader on Radio Rampur, unlike the BBC, was now saying that the monsoon was about to break, although the cloudless sky told a different story.

THE ELECTRICITY HAD gone off for the fifth time that day and Charlotte was trying to generate a bit of cool air with a fan. In the suffocating heat of midday, the mere movement of her arm was more of an effort than was warranted by the faint breeze that it produced. One shutter was slightly ajar, but she was too listless to get up to close it. A narrow strip of sunlight bored itself into her bedroom and shone on the pile of fabrics. Her father had not mentioned the fabrics again. Since it was too hot to move about, he had been quite subdued the last few days, even when his yogurt and his tea didn't arrive precisely on time. She had yet to choose a piece of fabric for her own dress, and she did not look forward to taking it to the music room. She had pushed the cork back into the hole so firmly that she could only remove it with a corkscrew. She mustn't allow herself to think of him, for fear those same thoughts would come into her mind when he was nearby. She tried to shake her head in order to dislodge her worries, but the heat had taken such total possession of her that she was even incapable of moving her neck.

In the background she heard the zoom of the sewing machine. Apparently *he* was impervious to the heat.

The topmost piece of fabric was a gleaming length of pale pink silk: just the colour she would have chosen for a dress when she was a girl. But back then it had been decided that it would be nonsense for her to wear anything but her homely grey school uniform during those few weeks a year when there was no school. Now that colour — as well as the deep pink fabric underneath — weren't options, because the wife of Nikhil Nair always wore pink. Next came the purple, the colour of the cloth on the pulpit during funeral services, followed by yellow, which she immediately associated with the sun, heat, fear, sweat, and suffocation. She wondered how he managed to work in temperatures like this. The gold fabric was too shiny and the one with the silver embroidery was old-fashioned; the blue was ordinary and the white too virginal. She didn't consider black appropriate for a party, she already wore a lot of green, beige was uninteresting, red was common, and brown was dull.

The brilliance of the colours faded with the setting of the sun. Getting up from her bed, she walked over to the window and pushed open the shutters, in the hope of finding some relief from the heat. The moon had not yet appeared. Below, the sewing machine whirred busily. It took no effort to conjure up his profile: the straight forehead, the aristocratic nose, his lips and his chin . . . He had a noble quality, something quite patrician, she mused. Her thoughts turned to Parvat. She wondered if there were those who looked at him and had doubts about his origins. She picked up a pile of fabrics and walked out to the landing. The clock struck eight o'clock. If it weren't for the fact that her father refused to go to sleep before the stroke of ten, she would have sold the thing long ago. She put the other piles of fabric down on the landing. Since she couldn't come to a decision, it might be better if he made the choice for her. She paused at the door of the nursery, as she always did. She was about to turn away when she thought she heard something. Pressing her ear to the door, she listened. It was a muffled sound, one she couldn't bring home. She took the key down from the nail and opened the door. Her father was sitting in his wheelchair in the middle of the room. He was wearing nothing but his white underpants and his diaper, and his scars were clearly visible. There were wads of cotton wool under the bands on his arms and legs. His body was drenched in sweat. His face was also wet. Not with sweat, but with tears.

"Father! What's wrong?" she asked.

The pent-up sobs that had alarmed her turned into long wails. He opened his almost toothless mouth, sucked in air, and then launched a tearful moan into the air. She took the towel that lay next to him and dried his shoulders, his neck, his chest, and his back. The tears were streaming down his cheeks. She knelt next to him and very gently patted his forehead and his cheeks as he went on crying. Never before had she stroked him, not in the hospital when he was at death's door, not when he had an attack of malaria and lay in bed, delirious and with a temperature of forty-one degrees, not a while back when the doctor had come to tell her that he was very ill and would never get better. She didn't even know whether he had ever caressed her. When she was a baby, or later, when she was a toddler? She couldn't recall a single moment when he had displayed tenderness toward her. She put the towel in his lap and warily raised her hand. She didn't want him to sense that this was something she found scary, something that was strange. She brought her hand to his hair and brushed a lock off his forehead. Her hand went farther, over the crown of his head. His thin grey hair was sticky with sweat, but she did not find it distasteful. The sobs ceased and the tears ran from his eyes.

"Would you like something to drink?"

He nodded.

Charlotte picked up the bottle with the nipple and put it in his mouth.

Gasping, he sucked up the water.

"Is that better?"

"I'm evil," he said, and began to sob again.

"Hush now, Father . . ." She tried to caress him again, but he pushed her hand away.

"I was in Burma." His voice was unsteady.

Charlotte, like everyone else, knew that he had been in Burma. There was even an article about him in *The Times of India*, celebrating his acts of heroism.

"Did you know that?" he croaked.

"Yes, Father, I know. You were there during the war."

"Yes, the war," he repeated, twice murmuring the word "war" softly to himself.

He looked straight ahead. Silently Charlotte stood up and opened the windows and shutters. That modicum of cool that accompanied the evening drifted over the windowsill and into the room. She hoped that the electricity would soon go back on and the fan above his head would start working again, but the municipal officials who had to deal with the problem probably weren't suffering as much as they were. No doubt they were sound asleep beneath a gently humming fan, in an area where the electricity was still on.

"I lied."

"Hush now. That was all so long ago."

"It's not long ago! He still calls me that."

"Who?"

"That butler. He calls me general." He straightened his back. "I'm not a general."

"I know."

"You know?" He looked at her in surprise, as if he was seeing her for the first time. "Who are you? What are you doing here?"

"I brought you some water." She picked up the bottle and pushed the nipple into his mouth.

He began to suck with relish.

She looked out the window, hoping fervently that it would begin to rain soon.

1967 Rampur

SHE GETS INTO the car and tells the chauffeur to drive to Sita's house. But halfway there she orders him to stop at a pharmacy. She's forgotten to bring something for the baby and doesn't want to arrive empty-handed. She's already given him a blue sleeping bag, a polka-dot rattle, a stack of diapers from one of the most expensive stores in town, a teddy bear specially ordered from New Delhi that was bigger than Parvat himself, and a handmade mug with his name on it, and just yesterday she brought along a special baby cream for nappy rash. She blithely ignores the fact that it's too hot for a sleeping bag, the teddy bear takes up more room in the house than the baby, and Parvat doesn't have nappy rash. She walks into the pharmacy, buys an expensive imported baby shampoo, and has it beautifully gift-wrapped.

The chauffeur doesn't even ask where she wants to go. When he stops in front of the house where Sita lives, Charlotte jumps out and makes a beeline for the open front door.

"Look what I brought you," she says to the sleeping infant, who is startled awake by the unfamiliar voice and begins to cry.

Sita picks up the howling Parvat and rocks him until he falls asleep again.

"I don't know how you do it," Charlotte whispers. "I remember how you always managed to quiet Donald, he cried a lot. . . . Do you remember? Is he a good eater? How often does he wake up at night? Are you managing all right? Just let me know, and I'll jump in the car — an extra pair of hands always comes in handy. This shampoo is supposed to be excellent, it's American, and I thought I saw a scaly spot." Charlotte bends over the baby. There's no sign of a rash. "Donald used to have a rash, did I have one, too, and are his bowel movements better now, are the new diapers nicer, they were the softest they had so if you need any more, just let me know."

Sita walks over to the chest with the baby on her arm. The teddy bear is sitting on the only chair in the house and is listing to one side. Charlotte goes on and on about baby formulas, nappy rash, stomach cramps, the advantages of safety pins, runny noses, earache, the first tooth, burping, coughs, and measles. Sita has just opened a drawer and taken out a sheet of paper covered with official seals and stamps, which she hands to Charlotte.

She reads aloud: "Manali Hospital. Sex: male. Time: 5:35. Date: 16 October 1967. First name: Parvat." Charlotte stops and then continues reading in silence. After she's read the whole document, she looks at Sita again, who is still standing there, gently rocking the baby in her arms.

The women look at each other. Thousands of thoughts flow back and forth but are never spoken aloud. Desperate thoughts, hesitant thoughts, heart-rending thoughts, encouraging thoughts, despairing thoughts, comforting thoughts, yearning thoughts, loving thoughts.

Charlotte gets up, walks over to the mother holding her child, kisses the little boy's forehead, and walks to the door.

"Shall I come only on Monday from now on?"

"Yes, Monday is a good day."

1963 Bombay ~

THE HOUSE WHERE Chandan Chandran lives is on the other side of the block. Subhash occasionally goes there to do repairs, but in all the eight years that Madan has worked for the man with the ponytail, he's never been there. The men in the weaving mill say that his wife has shorter hair than her husband, and that they have four children who never go upstairs to the weaving mill but who occasionally bring their father his lunch in that dark workplace beneath the stairs.

Madan turns into a narrow alley, under a large sign depicting a photo camera, and keeps on walking until he comes to a blue door. Mister Chandran asked him to go to his house to fetch a piece of rosewood he forgot that morning. Madan is one of the few employees who have mastered the art of treating fabrics and threads with herbs and flowers. He knows that if he dries the flowers of the basil plant and works them into the seam of a blouse, the wearer will develop more discipline. And if he soaks cotton for a day in a bath with white chrysanthemums, the person wearing the garment will have more life-force energy. Rose petals awaken love, *rhodiola* can release feelings that lie hidden deep inside. The tiny flowers of the sweet William encourage obedience, while the anemone promotes honesty. Madan rings the bell next to the blue door. The sound is much louder than he expected, but no one inside seems to have heard it. After several minutes, he is still standing in front of the closed door. For the fourth time he rings the bell, and this time he presses harder and longer. The clapper strikes the riveted metal, and the reverberation echoes throughout the house.

"Who's there?" asks a soft voice.

Madan looks around in panic. He hadn't expected this. Why didn't Mister Chandran send someone else, someone who can speak? Should he clap his hands or knock on the door? Why isn't there a window in the door, so that she can see him?

"Is someone there?" says the same voice.

He hears a thump and then what sounds like retreating footsteps. Mister Chandran stressed that he should be quick about it, since it was urgent. So once more he pulls the bell as hard as he can.

"Who's there?" And again it's the same voice.

Madan is panting slightly and rolling his eyes. Why doesn't she open the door? Why didn't Mister Chandran send

Subhash? Why doesn't she realize that there's someone there, after he's rung the bell five times? Now he knocks on the door, softly, as if he's using a kind of code. His taps are meant to say that he's waiting outside, that there's nothing frightening about him, that he's only there to pick up something that Mister Chandran forgot.

The door opens slightly. Not enough for him to look inside, but enough for whoever is standing behind the door to look out. Suddenly the door is thrown wide open.

"Are you Mukka?" asks a girl in a black and white checked sari.

Madan blinks his eyes. He's never seen such a beautiful girl. Her eyes shine like dew crystals on a white hibiscus, her lips are as red as a poppy, her skin as soft as a budding snapdragon, her hair is black as ebony, and her nose turns up like a butterfly emerging from its cocoon.

The girl is smiling. "What do you want?"

It never occurred to Madan that he would have to explain what he came for. His eyes dart to the corridor behind the girl. There is nothing that resembles rosewood, only a large pile of old slippers.

"Did you come to get something?"

He nods.

"Something for Daddy?"

The notion of someone calling boss Chandran "Daddy" brings a smile to Madan's lips.

The girl smiles, too.

"Is it for the workplace?"

Madan nods.

"Come inside. Maybe you'll see what you're looking for."

Madan follows the girl down the hallway. He can't take

his eyes off her. Her bare feet tread lightly over the tiles, her hair bounces on the back of her black and white checked sari, and as she walks, her fingers move. It's a long corridor, that turns at the end. The girl begins to hum softly, a song he's never heard before. She opens a door.

"This is Daddy's room. Do you see what you came for?"

The room is the opposite of the one that Madan would have designed for his boss Chandran. It is white and empty. Along one wall, there are simple shelves filled with small black boxes, all exactly the same, with lettering in white ink in the same precise handwriting. There is also a small bookshelf with a single book. Under the window, with its net curtains, there is a narrow shelf that holds all sorts of samples and smaller pieces of fabric in neat piles. And in the middle of the room, on a white table, lies a gnarled piece of wood.

"Is this what you're looking for?" The girl picks up the piece of rosewood. Madan nods and he is now positive that the girl's father wove the black and white fabric for her sari himself.

"What an unusual piece of wood! What does Daddy need it for?"

The girl's hand strokes the bark.

Madan watches the movements of her hand, as she caresses the wood, following the twists; how her slender fingers find each hole, each bend and curve in the wood. She doesn't say anything. She stands there, in a graceful pose, wearing her black and white checked sari and stroking the piece of wood. Madan feels his stomach contract strangely and his heart begins to beat faster. Then suddenly she hands him the piece of wood. He starts, and doesn't dare to take the cherished piece of wood from her hand, fearful that just touching it might have the same effect on him as wearing a garment treated with rose petals. Smiling, the girl presses it into his hand.

1968 Rampur ~

Dear Donald,

We've been lucky — the monsoon began a week early this year. We were all sure we were going to melt, that's how hot it was. Father is home now. According to the doctors, it's a kind of miracle that he's doing so well. It's only his legs that no longer function. They think that in a few weeks he may be able to get into his wheelchair by himself. We've converted his old study into a bedroom. In the beginning he was against the idea. He wanted an elevator like the hotels in London, but there's no one around here who can build one, so we're doing it this way. In the past few months I've often thought back to the summers in England. Sometimes I regret that I didn't go back, and wonder what in heaven's name I'm doing here. I'm alone a lot and I don't know who to talk to about my feelings and worries. You're so far away. The last British family in Rampur has returned to England. The atmosphere at the club is totally different, and the people who go there now are all Indian. Father sits in his wheelchair in the living room — usually in a bad mood — and begins to curse and swear when his tea or coffee doesn't arrive fast enough. A few years ago I met a very nice man, but Father ran him straight into the ground, so that after a while even I didn't like him anymore. So now I read a lot: I've read all the books in the library at least twice. The only time I'm happy is when I'm at the piano. And when I visit Sita, our former ayah. I go there every Monday from five to seven. I play with her son, Parvat, an intelligent and handsome little boy. I asked her if I could play the piano for him, but she'd rather I didn't take the baby to the big house, so I sing children's songs to him in English when I visit.

Yesterday was a really bad day. I was playing the fourth impromptu, a magnificent piece by Schubert, and I'd just got to a difficult passage when Father started banging his cane against the door of the music room, which is next to his bedroom. That meant that I had to stop playing, because he wanted to take a nap. I want to get away. I'm going crazy here. Why can't you come for a while, to give me a breather, just a few weeks, then I wouldn't have the feeling that I have to do everything on my own? After all, he's your father just as much as mine. Surely I wasn't put on this earth to be his nurse until he dies. I just can't do it. And I don't want to . . .

She crumples the letter into a ball and throws it into the wastepaper basket. Then she goes over to the piano, lifts the lid, and begins to play. When she hears the tapping on the wall, she goes on playing, but louder and faster. The tapping turns into banging. Then the door flies open and he hurtles into the music room in his wheelchair.

"Stop!" he shouts.

She goes on playing.

"I order you to stop playing!"

She is not listening.

He pulls at her blouse and tells her he's the boss, that she has to stop when he tells her to, that she shouldn't make such a fuss, that's she hysterical, that she knows nothing about playing the piano, that she mustn't think that he'll put up with such goings-on in his house, and that he's going to sell the piano.

In the middle of the piece, she stops playing. She gets up from the piano stool and looks down at him. Her voice is steely. She barely recognizes it. "If you keep me from playing the piano one more time, I'll leave." Deadly calm, she walks out of the room, up the stairs, and into her bedroom. She opens the drawer next to her bed and takes out the photo of Parvat that she took when no one was looking. She begins to cry softly.

1963 Bombay ~

He can't sleep, he's not hungry, and he keeps confusing the white rosebuds with the white rose petals, and the orange ones with the pink, so that the effect "you're too young for love" gets mixed up with "innocence," and "passionate love" with "first love." He takes advantage of any excuse to leave the weaving mill, and after dinner he wanders around the area, hoping to see the girl again. And he's forever making up excuses to go downstairs, to where Chandan Chandran is busy making extracts in which he soaks the warp threads or weaves dried petals into a piece of fabric, in the hope that Chandran's daughter will come by with her father's lunch.

His nights are spent half awake and half dreaming. In one of those dreams he's dancing with the girl, and when he wakes up, his pants are wet. During his morning bath, which he always takes in the shed behind the weaving mill, he has another erection. There's no time to masturbate, since he can hear Subhash singing as he walks down the stairs. He grabs a bucket of cold water and throws it over his swollen member. The icy water makes him shiver, but his member remains expectantly on high. "Can't you calm down?" Subhash grins when he sees his friend trying to hide his genitals behind the bucket. Madan blushes.

"Okay, I'll leave." Subhash grins. "But not too long, okay? I have to get washed, too."

Madan is grateful that his friend understands. He grabs his penis firmly and as he gets into the rhythm, he fantasizes about the girl whose name he doesn't know and the motions of her slender fingers. He doesn't hear the unloading of the crates of cotton thread, the call of the imam, the honking of an impatient taxi driver, the dog that begins to bark when the postman comes into the courtyard, the mother calling her offspring, the shrieking children, the gong that signals the start of their working day, or the sound of Subhash knocking on the door.

When Subhash opens the door, he sees that his friend is still in ecstasy. "Mukka, we have to start work. Didn't you hear the bell?"

A blush of shame colours Madan's cheeks, but his penis is unperturbed and remains on high, like a drawn sword.

"Put on some clothes and hurry up." Subhash throws Madan his trousers and then watches in amazement as the boy first binds his penis to his belly with a long, narrow piece of cloth before pulling on his pants. "Have you had this problem before?"

Madan's blush deepens now that he realizes that his friend knows his secret. Ever since he first set eyes on the unattainable daughter, he's had an erection almost constantly.

"I have a solution," says Subhash.

Madan gives him a look that is both woeful and relieved.

"Tonight, after work."

HE RECOGNIZES THE place right away. During the period that he and Abbas lived on the street, they sometimes came here. The women stayed up all night, and some of them had beautiful voices.

Subhash is just as nervous as his companion, and from under his eyelids he peers at the various houses. A man with a huge moustache stands in front of a door, and after they've walked past three times, he opens the door and lets them in, without uttering a word. The boys enter the house, panting slightly with excitement and anticipation. They hear the sound of music and don't dare look at each other. Then Subhash opens the lone door at the end of a poorly lit hallway. Madan feels the music flowing toward him, together with the acrid smell of tobacco smoke. When his eyes have adjusted, he sees a large room where men are sitting on benches along all four sides. They're laughing, singing, and drinking beer. In the huge space, which is boarded by a low wall, girls in brightly coloured saris are dancing.

Subhash pulls Madan inside and gestures to him to sit down. Madan chooses a spot close to the door. Next to him there's a man with a fistful of bills. He calls to one of the girls. She turns and walks in his direction, wiggling her hips provocatively.

Madan gasps. The girl is stunning, even more beautiful than the princess in his dreams. She dances in the direction of the man, still moving her hips sinuously. When she's standing in front of him, she gives him a seductive smile. Her teeth gleam and her eyelashes quiver. Suddenly the man throws his entire pile of bills over the girl. They come wafting down, swirling over her shoulders and her breasts. They fall to the floor, where her bare feet with their brightly coloured nails go on dancing, without treading on the bills.

A little man in dark clothes dashes onto the dance floor and, quick as a flash,collects all the bills and stuffs them into the dancer's hands. Now Madan notices that she already has a thick wad in her hand. Rotating her hips, she moves on to the next man who calls out to her. The man sitting next to Madan drains his glass at one draught, gives him a knowing wink, and leaves.

Madan watches the gorgeous creature, who is now dancing for another man. After a while he, too, showers her with bills. Again the little man appears out of nowhere and gathers the bills from the floor, while the dancer moves on to the next benefactor. Madan is conscious of his sole bill, which is burning a hole in his pocket.

Madan notices that Subhash also has his hand in his pocket, but for a different reason. He himself doesn't have an erection, for the first time in weeks. He is intimidated by the abundance displayed by the men, and feels himself shrinking.

A girl in a flowered sari is dancing in the middle of the room. Until now he has seen her only from behind. Compared to the other girls, she is scarcely dancing at all. Her hips do their best, but it's mainly her shoulders that sway and gyrate. She has no money in her hands and she's looking at the floor.

Madan hears Subhash's voice. At first he thinks his friend is calling him, but then he sees that his attention is focused on the beautiful dancer. She doesn't respond but continues to dance in front of a fat man with a large wad of bills in his hand.

~

THE BOYS ARE again standing in front of the dance hall. The doorman with the huge moustache has disappeared. Subhash, who has lost all his money, groans at the thought that it's at least an hour's walk back to the weaving mill. "Or do you still have some money?"

Madan, who has just one bill in his pocket, isn't looking at his friend.

"Do you still have some money?" he repeats.

Then the door opens and the shy girl in the flowered sari darts past them. She's thrown a large shawl over her shoulders and her eyes are fixed on the ground. She hasn't earned anything the whole evening. Madan turns to follow her, but Subhash stops him. There's an inquiring look in his eyes. Madan pulls the bill out of his pocket and gestures that he wants to give the money to the girl. Subhash grins, nods, and then whispers that he'd better make sure he gets back to the weaving mill on time: Mister Chandran doesn't like latecomers.

Madan, who only intended to give the girl his bill and then go back home with his friend, suddenly looks with new interest at the girl's back.

Subhash doesn't understand what his friend is waiting for. "Go on, then," he says encouragingly.

The titillation in his belly, which has been absent the entire evening, suddenly returns. Anxiously, he glances back at Subhash, and then runs after the girl.

She's afraid to look up at the boy who had sat quietly by the door the whole evening. The paving bricks seem to change at every step she takes: everything looks different. The house where she lives is at the end of the street. Again, she is the first to leave. Yesterday, too, she was the only one who came home without earning a penny. The owner of the room she's renting with the other girls has already threatened to throw her out if she doesn't pay up.

HE FOLLOWS HER up the stairs. The tension of a moment ago has disappeared. He hesitates when she opens the door. The room is dark.

She takes his hand. Her hand is clammy, just like his. The tension in his belly returns. She closes the door. He can no longer see her. She leads him to a mat on the floor. She lies down and he lies down next to her. He feels the tingling in his penis. He hears that she is breathing faster. He hears his heart booming in his chest. The skin of her arms is like an amaryllis flower. He bends toward her. She smells like honeysuckle. The tips of her fingers glide over his back. He purses his lips and searches for her face. He gives her a cautious kiss. He feels his member throbbing, in an effort to escape. Her mouth finds his. She tastes like young lathyrus. Her hands glide over his body. She finds his pants, unbuttons them, and pushes them down. He closes his eyes tight and sees how she walks in front of him, how her fingers move as she caresses the rosewood, the way she smiles at him with her poppy-red lips, her ebony hair, her butterfly nose, her eyes as clear as crystal. The urgency he feels is unbearable. Her soft body is beneath his. Her black and white checked sari has disappeared. Her fingers help his search. He moans. She lies still. He is panting. She lets him in. He opens his mouth and lets out a single self-indulgent cry.

The girl freezes when she hears the horrific shriek. In a fraction of a second, all her pores close. She pushes the boy off her with a hard shove. "Who *are* you?" she cries. "*What* are you? A beast, a monster!" In a panic, she starts hitting and kicking him. "Go away! Go away!"

Madan doesn't understand what is happening to him. With his pants still around his ankles, he stumbles outside as she continues to shriek "Go away, go away!"

~

HE IS STANDING under the stairs, and Chandan Chandran is seated at his old loom, like the first time he walked in. It was as if nothing had changed, except for Madan himself and the length of his boss's ponytail. The few possessions he has collected over the years are wrapped in a piece of cloth, which he wove himself. The man who had for so long been his mentor does not ask him why he is leaving. Madan holds up a hand in a farewell gesture. Chandan Chandran nods.

Madan goes down the low, narrow corridor, which still smells of oil and rusty iron. He has almost reached the street when he hears the voice of Mister Chandran. He turns around.

The man is walking in his direction with a piece of paper in his hand. "This is where you should go," he says in a soft, low voice. "I've written down the address. He'll take you on, I'm sure of it."

Madan accepts the piece of paper. He has no idea what is written on it.

"It's a long way away. In Madras," says Chandan Chandran. "You'll have to go by train." He takes some money from his pocket and wants to give it to Madan.

Madan shakes his head, pulls out the single bill that's still in his pocket, and shows it to his boss, as if to let him know that he's perfectly capable of looking after himself.

Chandan Chandran smiles. And for the first time he hears Chandan Chandran laugh. He waves again and leaves.

1963 Circular Express

He had no idea that his country was so huge. For twenty hours Madan has been on a train that stops everywhere and he has watched people fight their way into and out of the compartments along with their household belongings and livestock. He is happy that at long last he has a seat, and he notices that there is a kind of haze hanging over the landscape as they glide past.

He spent the first ten hours standing in the narrow gangway. It was not until a man with a bleating goat and two baskets full of chickens got off that he managed to secure a seat on a wooden bench in the third-class carriage. He tries to take catnaps, since he did not sleep all night. But as soon as the sun shows itself, everyone starts talking and eating. Tempting aromas tickle his nose. Bowls and pans are unpacked, laps serve as dining tables, and someone begins to sing, with the accompaniment of a small drum.

Madan, who for eight years lived in the weaving mill where everyone knew that he couldn't speak, is no longer accustomed to communicating with strangers. When the man directly opposite him asks where he's going, he becomes rattled and doesn't know how to explain that he doesn't know himself, except that he has to get to Madras. Until he remembers the piece of paper. He pulls it out of his pocket and shows it to the man.

The man glances at the piece of paper and announces loud and clear that he can't read.

Before Madan realizes what's happening, his fellow passengers have descended upon him and the paper. Not that the majority of the travellers can read, but they are all curious. Madan watches as the piece of paper is torn in two by a man wearing a turban and a man with a red beard. Their neighbours are also curious, and before long there are four pieces. Madan jumps up and tries to retrieve the pieces of paper, but they go from hand to hand at breakneck speed. He wants to shout that the paper belongs to him, that they have to give the pieces back because that's the only address he has and he has nowhere else to go. But the hands of his fellow passengers are too fast for him, and Madan doesn't dare to use his voice.

At that point, a slightly built, elderly man in a corner of the coupé, who spent the whole night with a cloth over his head, snoring loudly, manages to get hold of one of the pieces. He reads what it says, glances in surprise at Madan, kicks off his shoes, climbs onto the wooden seat, and begins banging his umbrella as hard as he can against the metal luggage rack. The noise is so overwhelming that everyone looks up to see what's happening. The former teacher still knows how to exert his authority, and he demands that all the pieces of paper be turned in.

Some grumpily, others reluctantly, the passengers surrender their snippets of paper, which the old man deposits in a small plastic box. When Madan makes his way over to the man to collect the torn remains of what he thought was his future, the man raises his hand, indicating that he is still busy working out a solution.

Having lost his seat when he got up from the wooden bench, Madan stands somewhat forlornly amidst the legs of the seated passengers and watches as the old man puts the paper back together, one piece at a time and with great precision. To make sure that the draft from the open windows doesn't destroy his work, he licks each snippet of paper and sticks it onto the bottom of the box. Everyone gazes intently at the old man and his puzzle.

Enjoying his unexpected authority and the attention from the other passengers, he straightens his back, polishes his glasses, looks at his audience, and coughs once. "Here before me . . . on this card," he says in a solemn voice, "is a name and an address."

"Whose name and address?" someone calls out.

Again the old man coughs, in order to reinforce his words. And then, very slowly and clearly, as if he's repeating a dictation exercise, he says, "Dr. Krishna Kumar, 45 Angappan Street, Mannady, Madras."

A respectful sigh goes through the audience.

Madan's heart misses a beat. He's going to a doctor in Madras! That's why Chandan Chandran sent him there. At long last, something will be done to solve his one great problem. Before long he'll be able to speak! He no longer cares that someone has taken his seat, or that he's hungry and thirsty, that he couldn't take a bath this morning, that he has no idea how long the journey will take, that he's afraid of catching lice from his fellow passengers. Soon he'll be able to talk, just like everyone else.

The drummer comes up with a drum roll. The singer breaks into a new melody and Madan begins to move his hips, just like the girls at the club. People are clapping and whooping. The drummer steps up the tempo, the singer sings the melody above the instruments. And Madan dances, in the middle of a crowded train between Bombay and Madras.

1995 Rampur ~

BY THE LIGHT of the candle in her hand, Charlotte locked the door of the nursery and hung the key back on its nail. Feeding her father did not awaken in her any maternal feelings, but rather something akin to disappointment. Although he had moments of great clarity, she'd noticed that his intellectual powers were declining. That's why she no longer followed his orders. Today she found it worrying that he had suddenly remembered the war. Often this triggered horrible nightmares, and sometimes his screams were so loud that the people living at the bottom of the hill could hear him.

At the top of the stairs she saw the crate where Hema had deposited all the candle stumps he had removed from the gigantic chandelier. Hema was the only person who faithfully carried out all her father's orders.

Downstairs the sewing machine was humming. Should she go to him? Should she tell him that she has discovered piles of fabric in her father's room? The stair creaked under her foot. Could he hear that she was coming downstairs? Did he hope that she would come into the music room? Did he ever do anything but work? He was so serious.

She put her hand on the doorknob. The candle illuminated the old wood. . . . She saw how the grain swirled across the door like a churning river. She could feel the pressure of the water against her back.

She opened the door.

You're here.

Yes.

I was waiting for you.

Waiting? For me?

I knew you would come.

Five million thoughts and questions shot through her mind, all of them leading her in the wrong direction.

Take it easy. I can't hear you if I can't see you.

"But you're not even looking at me," she said in surprise.

He raised his eyes.

They looked at each other for an instant. A faint gust of wind that came in through the open window set the candle flames in motion. Their shadows danced on the wall.

She took a deep breath. "I've found fabric."

Fabric you like?

No, she thought, and she said, "Yes."

May I see it?

"Yes," she said, but she thought, *No.*

If you don't want to . . .

Charlotte felt awkward and embarrassed. She put her hands in her pockets and took them out again. She clenched her fists and unclenched them again. *I just don't know. I don't know what's wrong with me. I don't know what's happening. Of course, you can see the material. You can have it.* She smoothed her skirt and straightened a button on her blouse. *I don't even know what I feel anymore, what I think. I don't want to think. I don't want to hear all this. Why are we doing this? It's impossible. I'm so much older than you. I'm white. I'm British. Can't you see that this is impossible?*

He got up and reached for the lid of his sewing machine.

No, stay. I want you to stay.

He stopped collecting his things. Once more they looked at each other for a fraction of a second, and then looked down again. The clock up on the landing struck ten. Neither of them moved.... Only their shadows danced in the candle-light, as if conscious of their agitation.

After the last chime, he asked, *Will you show me the fabrics?* He needed all his willpower to simply ask that question, to break the tension. He knew that if he allowed himself to drift into her thoughts, he would want to take her in his arms. He knew he must not do that, because then, at a stroke, he would lose everything he had built up at the cost of so much effort and perseverance.

Slowly she turned around and went back to the stairwell. She strode up the stairs: a dark shape, with only the contour of her body illuminated. The creaking stair and the ticking of the clock accompanied her.

Time. Give me time, she thought.

You have time. All the time you need.

Her footsteps were soundless. The rustle of her clothes was also stilled. There was only the ticking of the clock.

Who are you? Where do you come from?

I don't know. He put his foot on the first step.

At each step, the stairs groaned softly and the fabric of his trousers grazed his leg.

"It's too dark here," she said softly, suddenly realizing that her father might not be asleep yet.

He's asleep.

"Can you hear him, too?" she whispered in surprise.

Can't you hear him?

All her senses were so focused on his tall figure that she hadn't noticed the regular sound of snoring that emanated from the nursery. He knelt down beside the clock. His hand slid across the pile of fabric. He felt raw silk and wild silk, taffeta and silk damask, the soft nap of sumptuous velvet, gossamer-thin cotton, and sturdy linen. His hands glided over embroidery and lace, woven and knitted fabrics, dyed material and prints. He caressed the lengths of cloth that her mother had bought sixty years ago. Given the climate, it was a miracle that they hadn't mouldered away or been devoured by vermin, like everything else in the house. That they were still intact was thanks to the general, who ordered the last of his wife's mementoes to be packed with a load of mothballs in sturdy canvas bags, and then covered in plastic. Charlotte took a candle stump out of the trunk and lit it. Then she carefully placed the burning candle next to him on the floor.

They knelt there are the top of the stairs. Only then did he see the colours. The gleaming rose-coloured silk that lay on top and the deep pink beneath it. The length of purple that had reminded her of funerals now had a royal air, while the yellow cotton that had resembled the murderous sun was now the colour of sunflowers. Underneath there were lengths of turquoise cotton and cobalt blue linen. Madan's hand skimmed over a piece of yellow-green silk and then — as if it was now demanding attention after lying hidden for years — he pulled out an ethereal blue fabric embroidered with bright red roses. He was beaming.

For the dress you should wear on the day the first flowers come into bloom.

"But blue isn't my colour." she whispered.

Blue? Of course it is.

"I thought green was the only colour I looked good in." He cast his eye over the pile and pulled out a piece of azure blue silk, which he held up to her face. He looked at her with a critical eye, frowning slightly.

"You see!" she cried out, forgetting her father.

No, it's not the colour. There's not enough light. I can't see the colour of your eyes.

Shyly, she held the candle up to her face. *He thinks I'm ugly.*

You're so beautiful! He caught the scent of jasmine and saw his own face twice reflected in her greyish-brown eyes.

That same instant they both lowered their eyes. Charlotte began to move around nervously, rushing over to the crate with the candle stubs. She grabbed a handful, put them down on the floor, one by one, and lit them.

Madan, who also understood that he had gone too far, again busied himself with the pile of colourful fabrics. He felt like pulling all of them over his head, but he realized that she was so close that he couldn't hide his thoughts from her.

They sat with their backs to one another.

I don't want to think, and yet I'm thinking, he thought. *I've never been afraid of my thoughts. I'm constantly thinking, praying, hoping, dreaming, finding, fantasizing, reflecting, wandering . . .*

I'm afraid. She closed her eyes.

So am I. He looked at her.

I'm afraid. The thought echoed through her mind.

He pulled a vermilion-red length of silk from the pile, walked over to her, and draped it over her shoulders.

She kept her eyes closed, but her hand stroked its soft folds.

It goes beautifully with your hair.

My hair is grey.

It's not grey . . . there are some grey hairs.

Charlotte opened her eyes and was startled when she saw that it was red. "Red is for girls!"

Stand up. He ignored her reaction, and again looked at her with a professional eye.

Cautiously she rose from the floor. The fabric slid off her shoulder. She suddenly felt naked. He snatched a length of crimson from the pile and draped it over her shoulders. *You look beautiful in red.*

She smiled uncertainly.

If I shape the neck like this. He began draping the material. *Your shoulders like this.* His eyes sparkled. *And your back like this.*

He walked around her, and although he didn't know how to handle the situation and she was silently begging him to stop, he went on. He didn't touch her. He only draped the fabric over her body, but the sensation was the same. He pulled another length of fabric from the pile. This one was marigold orange.

And this can be used for a very narrow border along the hem.

She pulled the material from her shoulder.

Why did you do that?

"Red is common."

No it isn't. Red is the colour of rage, the colour of danger, the colour of blood and revolution, of guilt and martyrs, of despair. Red is power and strife. Red is cherries and tomatoes. Copper and the earth are red. Fire, and the sun when it's about to disappear. The tulip, the gerbera, the rhododendron, the amaryllis, the orchid, the rose. Your lips are red. Red is the colour of . . . love.

Charlotte pulled the red cloth from her shoulders. She blushed and walked away from him. She could hear his thoughts, but she didn't want to hear them. Just as she hoped he wasn't listening to hers.

Madan, who in his enthusiasm to design a dress for her had overturned the entire pile of fabrics, now began to straighten them.

I'll leave. Perhaps it's for the best.

Best for whom? The words shot through his mind. *I'm sorry, I mustn't think that,* he excused himself.

Best for me, Charlotte replied. *I don't know whether it's good for you, too. But it's better for me.*

Then I'll go.

Where will you go?

Somewhere, just move on.

Farther, in which direction?

Farther. Down the road.

And then?

I'll find work.

And the ladies and the party . . .

There must be another tailor.

There isn't.

There's always someone else.

Not here.

Here, too.

You can't just leave.

Why not?

They would blame me.

Who?

The ladies.

I know women. I've always worked for women. They'll understand you.

Do you understand me, too?

Yes.

Why are we talking? What are we doing?

You wanted to show me the fabrics. In his hands he held the gleaming length of red silk.

"Do I really look good in red?" she asked softly.

He nodded. *Do you know what you don't look good in?*

Charlotte slowly came closer.

He drew a length of beige cotton from the pile. *This.* And again his hand delved into the pile, and he came up with a khaki-coloured cloth. *And this.*

She snatched it from his hand, threw it over her shoulders with a flourish, and wrapped it tightly around her body, so it looked like a military greatcoat. Then suddenly the silence of the night was broken by a horrible scream. *Father!* She grabbed the key from the hook, opened the door, and ran over to the bed.

The sudden scream was so deafening that Madan felt like putting his hands over his ears. Still wearing the khaki remnant wrapped around her body, she ducked under the mosquito netting, which hung like a slack tent around the iron bed.

"It's all right now, I'm here," she said to her father.

He looked at her anxiously and tried to break loose from the straps that bound him to the bed. "Go away!" he begged. His lame legs lay still, but his entire upper body fought with a vigour one wouldn't expect from a man of ninety-four. He was sobbing, hawking, and groaning, all the while looking at his daughter with frightened eyes.

"Calm now," she said, trying to soothe him.

"Not me, not me." There was genuine panic in his voice.

"It's all right now, Father."

"Father? I don't have any children. Go away!" he screamed.

Madan ducked under the mosquito netting and reappeared on the other side of the bed. When Victor saw him, he stopped screaming. He was wheezing, exhausted, and his body was still quivering from the aftershocks. Slowly, his breathing returned to normal. But not his eyes.

"Shoot her dead," he suddenly whispered.

Charlotte started.

Madan didn't move a muscle.

"Shoot," her father roared. "They're all over the place. We have to kill them."

Charlotte was about to bend over her father, to reassure him, but he immediately started screaming again.

"Shoot! Shoot, for God's sake!"

Madan walked around to the other side of the bed, so he was standing next to Charlotte.

"She's wearing a disguise. You can see that, can't you?" he shouted. "She's a spy."

Calmly Madan pulled the piece of khaki material from Charlotte's shoulders and handed it to the old man.

He shouted: "You see? Didn't I tell you?" He drew the khaki material over himself and began to laugh.

Charlotte was used to her father's unpredictable onslaughts. She bent over him. "Did you have a bad dream?"

"A dream? I've never dreamt. Never in my whole life."

"Do you want some water?"

"Yes. I'm dying of thirst. Why do they always give me those army blankets?" He pushed the khaki material away. "Much too hot!"

Charlotte gave him the bottle with the nipple.

Charlotte and Madan looked at his hollow cheeks, the greedy look in his eyes. The grey hair, the wiry body, and the thin, fragile legs that had hung there like useless appendages for the past thirty years.

With his tongue, he pushed the nipple out of his mouth. "Is she your lover?" he asked Madan.

Charlotte blushed.

Madan shook his head.

"No?" he asked in surprise.

"Father, this is Madan. He's the tailor."

"Shut up. And don't tell me lies."

"I'm not lying."

"This man is no tailor."

"Father, have some more to drink."

Victor turned to Madan and gave him a long look. "Where do you come from?"

Charlotte was about to say something, but Madan shrugged his shoulders.

"What family do you come from?"

Again, Madan shrugged his shoulders.

"Are you saying that because I'm down and out, without a cent to my name?"

The two men looked each other in the eye, for a long time and without moving. They never blinked.

Charlotte felt uncomfortable and busied herself folding up the khaki material.

"She's a widow," the general muttered. "Has she told you

that? And I've kept her here, supposedly to protect her, but that wasn't the reason. She had to care for me, wipe my bottom, because I didn't want some nurse or other to do it, and cut my toenails and massage my legs with oil, and if a man came anywhere near her, I used every weapon I could find — I couldn't bear the thought that she might leave me. She did once, went off to the Himalayas, and when she came home she did nothing but cry, and I can't abide women who cry, it's enough to make you sick, women in general, I've never understood them, but you have my blessing."

"Father! Stop! He's the new tailor."

Her father glared at her. "I don't know whether you ruined your eyes with all that snivelling, but this nobleman is in love with you, and if you can't see that, you're blind." He closed his mouth with a snap and shut his eyes. As far as he was concerned, the subject was closed.

THE KEY GRATED when she turned it. She was afraid to look at him. The candle in the holder was almost out, and she went over to the crate to get a new one. She lit it and pressed it into the soft, hot wax. The chandelier, which Hema had pulled back up to the ceiling, hung there like a forgotten crown. *Do you suppose they ever burned that many candles in this hall?* She looked over the balustrade, and remembered that as a little girl she used to peek down at her parents. The images of dancing soldiers in gala uniforms and ladies in floor-length gowns returned, like the scent of her mother's perfume and the lively music. Madan, who appropriated portions of her memories, bent down and picked up a handful of candles from the box, lighted them, and placed them, one by one, along the edge of the balustrade, one in a recess in the wall, and another on a narrow shelf against the wall. Charlotte grinned and grabbed a handful of candles. Walking down the stairs, she put a burning candle on each step. Downstairs she placed more candle stubs on the ledges where statues had once stood, and on the windowsills and the marble floor. The darkness in which the house had so long been shrouded gradually disappeared. In the flickering candlelight, the bare landing and the dismantled hall regained something of their old glory. The clock sounded twelve stately strokes. Madan picked up the royal blue velvet fabric, threw it over his shoulders, and strode down the stairs. When he reached the bottom, Charlotte bowed, and then ran up the stairs, pulled two brightly coloured lengths of fabric from the pile, and hung them over the balustrade. She then wrapped herself in pale green lace and, like Madan, strode regally down the stairs.

There was music in her head, which he, too, could hear: the tones of a long-forgotten orchestra enticing everyone onto the dance floor. They stood opposite each other and slowly began to move, circling around to the music that had been forgotten when the British troops departed.

Charlotte closed her eyes, surrendering to the tones in her head. She was floating on air. She felt his presence, how he sometimes took over the music, altered it, and then sent it back to her. The sounds of the past became the present, filling the great marble hall. Time passed without their hearing the clock: they were the music. They whirled and danced. The lace that enveloped her blew over the candles. The flames could not catch the gossamer fabric. She was young again. She was radiant.

Madan also danced with his eyes closed. His movements were much slower, more tentative. Her music was foreign to him but enticing. He was in a large ballroom, where huge crystal chandeliers hung from the ceiling, and the paintings on the walls were metres high. They danced together, surrounded by men in exotic outfits and women in costly saris.

They were one, without ever touching each other. Dong! The clock struck. She opened her eyes and looked up. Dong! The second chime sounded. Dong! And the third, after which it fell silent. She had no idea that they had been dancing for so long. She'd been in a different world. A world she'd forgotten, one that she thought existed only in dreams.

"You haven't chosen the material for my dress yet!" she called out, and then ran up the stairs and tossed the length of sea-green silk over the balustrade.

It fluttered down and, just in time, Madan managed to snatch it away from the flickering candle flame.

She laughed and threw down a piece of lavender silk, which fluttered like a butterfly, and again Madan pulled it away from the flames. One colour after the other descended. A shower of ultramarine, silver, orange, jade, ochre, violet, pink, golden yellow, russet, and sky blue. Laughing, he plucked them out of the air, like a juggler.

When the last one had reached the ground, she ran down the stairs and stood in front of him. "Which one are you going to use?"

He spread the lengths of silk out on the floor. *Red is the colour of passion and longing.*

Charlotte could tell she was blushing.

Orange goes with young fruit and lends vitality and sexual power. Gold, of course, is success and wealth. Just as yellow stands for science, logic, and the intellect. Pale green, a field of grass after the first rain, signifies openness and anticipation. The green of old grass is the colour of nature and mortality. Turquoise is linked to spiritual consciousness, blue to the sky and all that is insubstantial. Indigo represents pure knowledge, and violet creates power and dignity.

"But what looks best on me?

Red.

The blush on her cheeks glowed. "There are so many different shades of red. Does each shade mean something different?"

Blood red signifies drama and cadmium distance; red ochre means warmth and vermillion titillation; magenta stands for dominance, carmine for lust, and scarlet for pure love. He picked up several lengths of red cloth and laid them next to each other on the stairs.

"It's like a red carpet," she giggled, trying to draw him away from the subject. "I'll make a canopy for you." She gathered up some blue remnants from the floor. And each time a piece of fabric fell, she heard his voice: *blue-black, violet, azure, Delft blue, indigo, Prussian blue, lapis lazuli.* She tied the lengths of cloth to the banister, but her canopy was a failure. The remnants just slid away, and her creation collapsed as quickly as his red carpet had taken shape.

Madan began to laugh, noiselessly, but Charlotte heard him in her head. For an instant she felt insulted because he was laughing at her, for his laugh tumbled through her head. But when she looked at him, at his radiant eyes, she understood the unaccustomed laugh, which was full and pure. And she began to laugh herself. First a laugh with sound, as she was used to, but when she heard her laugh reverberating shrilly in the marble hall, she searched for the noiseless laugh in her head. It was a completely different laugh than she was used to.

They didn't hear the personnel door being opened, quickly closed, and then set ajar. Hema's mouth dropped when he saw memsahib and the *darzi* sitting on the staircase, with their mouths open in a laugh. For a split second he thought they were both suffering from stomach colic, but the hundreds of candles and the colourful remnants spread out all around them told him that there was something else going on. He wasn't sure whether he should knock to announce his arrival or just walk in and surprise them. He did neither.

He stole back to the kitchen, fervently wishing that he had never witnessed the scene. This was so terrible that he didn't even dare to tell the neighbours' butler about it. The idiocy that has taken possession of his employer would only degrade his position still further. He wouldn't say anything to anyone, not even the second junior assistant in the barbershop at the bottom of the hill, who told him a new joke every day, or the shopkeepers who let him buy on tick, or anyone else. He wanted to forget the whole thing and persuade himself that it had been a dream. He sank down on his mat and pulled the sheet over himself. What on earth were they doing? He looked at his watch and saw that it was almost four o'clock. The sun would be up soon, and then he'd have to boil the water for the tea. He hoped that nothing of what he had just witnessed would still be there. And that everything would be back to normal. If only that *darzi* would leave. He was the cause of all this misery . . .

THEY WERE SITTING next to each other on the bottom step. All the remnants had been folded up and were in one big pile, with the scarlet red silk on top. For the first time that night, their thoughts were calm. There was no sense of shame. The uncertainties and unasked questions had disappeared. And the fear had gone. What remained was an openness they both experienced as blissful. The clock struck six. The last candle was still burning, and Charlotte blew it out. The sun was already above the horizon and would soon banish the memory of the night. Their eyes radiated joy. She smelled his scent and he hers. They looked at each other without blinking, aware that if they closed their eyes, the moment might simply disappear. They knew they had to say goodbye but tried to prolong the present. It mustn't end yet. She could imagine how his body felt, his face, his skin. He saw the colour of her eyes and her lips. His hand reached out to hers. Her fingers were extended. They wanted to be together forever.

A click. They heard the personnel door open. Their eyes gleamed.

"Hello? Is anyone here?" It was the voice of an Englishwoman.

They looked at each other in surprise. Only Hema, Madan, and Charlotte used the side door. Visitors always came to the front door.

Are you expecting anyone?

Charlotte wanted to answer his question in the negative, but her thoughts were spinning. She had expected Hema to bring the tea, which they would drink together. Then they would take the pile of fabric to the music room, and she would watch as he made her scarlet red dress. She had decided that she would never again be led by the glances of outsiders or by the foreign tongues that had determined her entire life and had brought her nothing but loneliness. She would no longer allow herself to be held back by shame, fear, or principles.

She would hurt no one. She would go away with him, quietly. Leaving cowardice behind on the doorstep.

He heard her thoughts. Her release from fear had carried him along, raised him up, to a sensation that was new to him. His hesitation lay on his wings, ready to shake off, to fly away, to overstep boundaries, to go to places that had walls they could demolish brick by brick. It was the sparkle in her eyes and the laughter of her soul that had given him the courage to stand beside her, and he had done away with his shyness in her presence.

"Hal-lo!" said the voice impatiently.

He sensed that the courage that had seemed invincible was beginning to fade. He heard her thoughts becoming confused; she raised questions and barricades that had not existed a moment before.

Charlotte walked over to the side door and saw a young white woman, still a girl. She had a green fluorescent band over her red hair, which was sticking out in all directions. She was wearing a blue jacket and baggy, bright yellow silk trousers with an embroidered design, and dangling earrings.

"Are you looking for someone?" Charlotte asked.

"Yes, you." the girl said.

"Me?"

"I'm Issy."

"Issy?"

"Didn't you get my letter?" She heaved a sigh. "Nothing works here. I tried to call, but the thing doesn't work."

"Letter?" said Charlotte, who in the past few weeks had received nothing but bills and letters from the bank, and had no idea who the girl was.

"It's awfully hot, isn't it? Do you have anything to drink?"

She kicked off her shoes. "The trains here are fabulous. I travelled first class, I had to promise Daddy, since anything can happen in second and third class. I had a real bed and I slept really well, and at the station they knew exactly where I wanted to go. All I had to say was "Bridgwater House" and the rickshaw brought me here, but I think he took a detour since I've already seen half the city. Everything is so cheap, how do people make a living here? I don't understand why Daddy left, a person can easily live on a pound a day and that includes two hot meals, even though in this heat I'm not allowed to have ice cream, because Daddy said that even he doesn't do that when he's in India, they use dirty water, he says. I've already had diarrhea, the first couple of days, the man at the hotel in New Delhi even called a doctor and he gave me some medicine and it was gone in no time. I've got medicine for malaria as well, Granddad got malaria, too, during the war, it must be a horrible disease since it stays with you all your life."

"Are you Isabella, my niece?"

"I don't answer to that horrid name anymore." The look on her face and the gesture of contempt spoke volumes. "My new name is Issy."

Madan, who until then had been out of her field of vision, had picked up the pile of fabric and was heading for the music room, with his head bowed.

"Hi!" she called out and then, in a lower voice, "Is that the butler?"

Charlotte wanted to say that he was the man she loved, the man she wanted to spend the rest of her life with, the gift that had unexpectedly been thrown into her lap, and that her life had begun last night. But she said nothing. Madan, who was used to looking away when he saw a woman he didn't know, especially a white woman, was blissfully happy until he heard her say, "No, that's Mukka. He's the tailor."

"Oh, he can make something for me, too. Everything is so frumpy here, this is all I could find. In my travel guide it says that you should buy all your clothes in India because everything is so cheap, but they don't tell you that everyone walks around in tent dresses or saris. I've been wearing the same clothes for two days. Can I go to the toilet? The one in the train was filthy and there was no toilet paper anywhere, would you believe it — the first-class carriage has clean sheets but no clean WC. I had to hold my pee all night, at one point we stopped at a station and I was going to go behind a hoarding, but what if the train left without me? Did you know that men and little kids all pee alongside the rails?"

I'm going to get back to work.

I didn't mean to say that you're the tailor.

I know.

I didn't mean it like that.

I know.

It just came out.

I know.

"Well . . . ?" The girl looked at her aunt.

"What?"

"The WC."

Charlotte showed her the door to the guest room. The girl pattered off, now clearly desperate, and shut the door behind her. Charlotte turned toward the music room, but that door had also closed. She wanted to go after him, hear him say out loud that that night had not been a dream, but the closed door told her: DON'T.

Hema came out of the kitchen building. He was carrying a tray with the tea. It was later than usual because he'd had to filter the water, which was full of sand. But he was in no hurry. He hoped that when he entered the house everything would be back to normal. Walking up the path to the side door, he saw a bright yellow rucksack leaning against the house. He hadn't heard or seen anyone. He wondered whether it contained yet another selection of accessories that each of the ladies of Rampur hoped would make her outfit just that bit more attractive or unusual than those of the others. He pushed the door open with his foot, as he always did: the worn spot at the bottom of the door was clearly visible.

Although the lengths of fabric had disappeared, he knew that he hadn't dreamt the whole thing. There were candle stubs all over the place and blobs of melted candle wax on the marble floor and the stairs. He sighed. It had been a short night for him, too. Unable to get back to sleep, he had started to worry about how best to dispose of the remains of the nocturnal festivities.

He was about to go upstairs when he heard memsahib call out to him from the drawing room.

She was holding the photo that had stood on the mantelpiece for years.

"We have a guest!"

"A guest?"

"My niece from England is here!"

"Your niece?"

"My brother's daughter."

"Here?"

She pointed to the little girl in the photo, who had braids and was holding an enormous ice lolly. Hema had looked at it countless times because it was such a sweet, comical photo.

Suddenly he started fussing around. "Where is she?"

"In the guest room, freshening up. She'll be down in a little while."

"I'll go get some more cups," he said, and hurried off. At the back of the kitchen cabinet there was a lovely little cup — he would get it for her.

"Not yet?" he asked when he came back with the teacup, which was decorated with a dancing Mickey Mouse. "Maybe she's fallen asleep."

"You can pour my tea," said Charlotte, she was very thirsty, "and take a cup in to the *darzi*."

Hema did not feel like bringing the *darzi* a cup of tea, and he went on putting the cups and saucers on the table, along with the sugar pot that memsahib never used but that he always brought with him, and then he polished the spoons once more on his apron. He heard unfamiliar footsteps in the hall. He picked up the teapot and turned around respectfully. The white woman who walked in was just as naked as the women in the photos in the magazine he bought once when he was far away from Rampur. Long strands of wet hair hung alongside her neck, and she was wearing a mini shirt and an even tinier pair of knickers. Her shirt was wet due to the water dripping from her hair, and he could see her nipples through the fabric. He saw her navel, too, and her long white legs. The teapot fell to the floor with a crash, and the hot water spread in all directions. Hema called out that they mustn't panic, that he was going to fetch some cloths, that they should be careful not to step on the shards and the spilt tea because they might hurt themselves. His heart was pounding like mad. Was this the little girl with the pigtails?

"Auntie, thanks for running the bath for me, it was just what I needed after such a long trip!"

1963 Madras ~

MADAN IS SEVENTEEN years old when he rings the doorbell at the house of Dr. Krishna Kumar. There is nothing to indicate that there is a doctor living at this address. It's an ordinary house with a bell. As he withdraws his finger, the door flies open.

"So you're Mukka? I'm Dr. Krishna Kumar." A bald man wearing glasses with thick lenses is looking at him with a friendly smile.

Madan begins to beam. From the moment he got off the train, he's been nervous. How is he supposed to explain to the doctor that he wants to be able to talk, that Chandan Chandran sent him, that he's never been to a doctor, and that he has no money?

The man, who had obtained a doctorate with a dissertation on a problem related to the textile industry, holds the door open for him. "From what I hear, you have a feel for it."

Madan has no idea what the man is talking about, but he follows him into a large room, filled with dark antique furniture, where it smells of mothballs and beeswax.

"Is that all you have with you?" the doctor asks.

Madan nods.

Dr. Krishna Kumar takes a small box from one of the overcrowded cabinets. "If it turns out you're really worth it, as my respected colleague has assured me, then I'll pay you well. He knows that I only accept the best of the best. He told me on the telephone that you know all about fabrics and thread, you're a quick learner, and in your whole life you've never once talked nonsense." He laughs heartily at his own joke.

Madan laughs, too, although he has no idea what thread has to do with medical science.

The doctor opens the box and takes out a shiny sewing-machine bobbin. "This is your bobbin. As long as you work for me, I don't want you to use any other bobbin than this one. And I don't want you to use more thread than you need. That means that when you wind up your spool, you'll have to make an exact estimate of the amount of thread you'll need for the entire garment. Is that clear?" The doctor looks at him sternly, and then he starts to laugh again. "I'm not saying this because I'm a penny pincher, but because I demand precision and craftsmanship." He hands the spool to Madan. "I'll take you on for a week on trial, without pay. I know you have a lot to learn, but a week is long enough for me to see if my esteemed colleague was right."

MADAN IS SITTING on a stool in the middle of a room, with a bobbin in his hand. He is dejected. In front of him is a large, black treadle sewing machine, painted with graceful letters, and in a corner of the room there's a sleeping mat. What he would really like to do is simply leave, now that he knows for sure that Dr. Krishna Kumar is not a real doctor. But because boss Chandran gave him the special letter, complete with address, and also telephoned, Madan does not leave. Perhaps another doctor will come by, or maybe Krishna Kumar has a brother who's a doctor? Or a cousin?

On top of the sewing machine lies a length of black silk, along with a spool of white thread and a pair of scissors. No one has entered the room after a quarter of an hour, and his feet unconsciously begin to experiment with the treadle. The machine is very much like the one that Ram Khan had, except that it's newer and looks nicer. The room also reminds him of the crate he was kept in, especially since Dr. Krishna Kumar locked the door on his way out. Madan is disappointed and he doesn't understand why he has to sit here, but he's glad there's no one around to ask him questions or give him orders. He watches the sewing machine needle go up and down, faster and faster, depending on how hard he pushes down on the foot pedal. He picks up the silk cloth and slides it under the presser foot. The material moves forward, driven by the foot. But since there's no thread in the bobbin, this does not produce a line of stitching.

It is the combination of Ram Khan's flood of abuse while he was threading his machine and Subhash's eternal chatter about machines and mechanisms when all he wanted to do was sleep that prompts Madan to wind the white thread onto the bobbin, open the slide plate, and try to work the spool into the hole underneath. He makes several attempts, but it isn't until his foot accidentally comes down on the pedal and the needle shoots upward that the spool drops into its slot. He looks up with a sense of satisfaction, but there's no one there to see his triumph. Again he thinks about the doctor who isn't a doctor at all and he begins to suspect that a real doctor will never come. With a jerk he pulls the fine thread from under the foot, something he often had to do for the far-sighted Ram Khan. Although he has no direct experience, he knows that with this machine it is possible to make something truly beautiful. He unfolds the length of silk. It's not large, but he knows that it is expensive material. He doesn't touch the scissors. He only wants to feel how the machine sews. He wants to see how the needle goes through the material and forms a straight line with the thread. Again he places the material under the presser foot and then lowers it. Using a treadle sewing machine requires a certain amount of skill, that much is clear to him. The thread has formed loops and what a moment ago was a pristine length of silk has become shoddy work by a third-rate tailor. With a dexterity born of practice, Madan carefully unpicks the thread and starts all over. As he slides the piece of silk under the presser foot for the fifth time, he realizes that he must keep up the speed, and that the wheel, which is driven by the movement of his foot, must not be allowed to stutter, but must continue at a constant pace. His first evenly stitched white line appears on the black silk beneath his fingers. And again he looks up from his work with a sense of pride, only to realize that no one is watching. His stomach growls: he's had nothing to eat since the evening before. He sews another line and another. The lines become straighter and his stitches more even. When the spool is empty, he winds it up again and goes on sewing, one line after the other. In the beginning, the lines sometimes wander slightly, but gradually they become straighter and straighter. After a while, he rotates the material a quarter turn and goes on stitching lines. Although he hasn't planned it, he has produced an exact copy of the black and white checkered material that the daughter of Chandan Chandran was wearing.

It must be evening by now, although no daylight enters the room. The growling of his stomach has abated, along with the sense of hunger. Madan strokes the blocked material in his lap. The tingling in his abdomen, which disappeared when he got on the train, has returned. It is as if his fingertips can feel the girl's skin through the fabric, the curve of her throat, the dimple in her neck. He knows that Chandan Chandran has long since arranged a marriage partner for her, and for his other children. And yet he cannot forget her. The girl has awakened something in him that refuses to go back to sleep. He feels how the swelling increases, under the piece of cloth. His breathing accelerates. He's afraid to touch the cloth. He doesn't even want to look at it, for fear the agitation that has taken possession of him will be visible to others. Why won't it go away? Why does his willy refuse to listen to his pleas? Madan is afraid to move, hoping that the unwelcome guest will retreat and disappear into the shadows. But the organ in question has its own rules: it remains erect, and proudly lifts the checkered cloth. He knows that the only solution is to take it in his hands and release its charge. But the thought that any minute Dr. Krishna Kumar could open the door and witness the act leaves him without the will.

You have to help me. You always come up with a solution. Think of something. Something I can do. I can't get her out of my head. I didn't intend to make the cloth like that. It just happened. I wasn't thinking about her. I was watching the needle, which pierced the cloth, over and over. It was as if I was piercing something myself, as if there was something that I was penetrating. I couldn't stop it. I had to penetrate it. Pushing the needle through the cloth. I wanted to make a line. A sharp line, and I wanted it more and more. I wasn't thinking of her. Honest. It wasn't until the pattern was finished that I saw it. It happened without my wanting it to happen. As if she'd cast a spell on me. That's not possible, Abbas, is it? She can't have done something to me that will never go away? Tell me that it'll go away, that I won't always be the way I am now. I want to be ordinary again. I can't stand it that each time I think about her, everything in me changes. If the doctor suddenly walks in, he mustn't see me like this. No one must see me like this. It's bad enough that Subhash caught me. People already think I'm strange. I know they talk about me and point at me. It's only when I'm very, very quiet that I'm allowed to exist. I don't want this feeling in my belly. It scares me. I want to be ordinary, just like everyone else. I wish I could speak.

The piece of cloth on his lap has descended. Madan hears the door open. It would have suited him better if it had remained closed. He hasn't finished his talk with Abbas. His prayers have only just begun.

"He wasn't exaggerating," Dr. Krishna Kumar crows, as he snatches the cloth from Madan's lap. He takes it over to the lamp and pushes his glasses farther up his nose. Carefully he studies the work. "For you, I won't even need a week." He walks out of the room with the material in his hand, leaving the door open.

Madan shuts the door and crawls onto the sleeping mat in the corner. He closes his eyes and tries to continue his prayers, but he doesn't know what to say, except that he wishes the bald man with the glasses were a real doctor.

1968 Madras ~

EVERY MORNING AT six o'clock Dr. Krishna Kumar comes into the atelier and inquires whether Madan has slept well. Every morning for five years. And every morning Madan nods his head, even when he's lain awake for hours, battling his dreams and frustrations. He lives in a tiny room behind the courtyard and works together with fourteen other tailors in Dr. Krishna Kumar's large atelier. He has his own cutting table, which stands in a corner of the room. There are patterns hanging on the wall, everything from a simple *salwar kameez* to a complicated fitted mantle with pockets and a stand-up collar. In the beginning, before the others got there in the morning, the doctor would lay out a length of cloth and indicate with a piece of chalk where Madan was to cut. But now he does that himself. The doctor has taught him how to cut velvet, how to sew a sleeve and attach a facing. From the very first day, the doctor realized that Madan had a special talent when it came to cloth, but it was a surprise that he also had a talent for transforming cloth into clothing. Month after month the doctor devised increasingly difficult assignments, as if he were setting traps for him.

This morning the doctor tossed a length of ash grey cotton onto the table. Madan, who has not been awakened by turbulent dreams and his languishing organ for the last two months, awaits the task that follows with anticipation. The longer he works here, the happier he is. He has never revisited the room where the doctor left him that first day, and he seldom leaves the house. He throws himself into his work and focuses on the fabrics and the patterns, much to the satisfaction of the doctor.

"Today we have a visitor," Dr. Krishna Kumar says, with a big smile on his face. "I want you to make a coat for this man that fits him like a glove."

It is not unusual for the doctor to bring someone in and for Madan to be told to make a garment for them. Most of them are gentlemen from his club or their wives. Madan has also made complicated garments for almost all the neighbours and family members. Madan looks at the door. He hears the sound of shuffling feet in the hall and deep sighs. His breath catches in his throat when he sees the guest. The man's neck is located where other people have their chest, and on the spot where the head is usually located, there rises a pointed, hairy hump, which vibrates slightly at every step. His face is full of pockmarks and his hands, which hang limply alongside his body, almost touch the ground. Because his shoulders are crooked, he has to ball one fist to keep it from dragging along the floor, while the other hangs slack. The man stares at the ground, and the crumbs of the free meal that the doctor probably used to coax him to come are still on his torn shirt.

"I thought this might be a good assignment for today." Dr. Krishna Kumar turns the man around as if he's a tailor's dummy, and the beggar follows him, awkwardly but willingly.

Although Madan has grown into a handsome young man, for the first time in years he again experiences the sense of shame that accompanies a physical handicap. Before he can make a sign, Dr. Krishna Kumar has disappeared and the man, who smells of urine, is standing diffidently next to him. The silence in the atelier is broken by the groaning sighs of the beggar, and Madan has difficulty taking his eyes off the quivering hump. He wants to pick up his tape measure, but it occurs to him that the man probably finds it distasteful to be touched by others and to have his hump, which he didn't ask for, measured. The man stares shyly at the ground as Madan's eyes glide over his misshapen body. Although his head is in the wrong place, he has fine ears and his eyebrows give the impression of strength. Madan discovers the man's arms are long but muscular, and his legs and feet are straight as an arrow. He tosses away the grey material that Dr. Krishna Kumar brought with him and selects instead a piece of ochre-coloured linen that is lying under his table. As the other tailors drift in, one by one, they cast curious glances and then take their places behind the sewing machines. Madan walks around the man and tries to understand the shape of his body. Then he goes over to his table, where he spreads the fabric out and makes a few careful chalk marks. He looks at the man, erases a line, and draws a new one.

The man, who had begun to shuffle nervously with his feet when the other tailors came in, gets a sign from Madan that he can sit down. The beggar sees that the tailor doesn't look at him in the same way as the people on the street. Madan's eyes don't have the same repugnance. Madan studies the man each time he looks up from his cutting or pinning. Then it is as if the tailor has forgotten him: he goes back to the sewing machine, his foot presses down on the pedal, and the material glides faster and faster through the machine. The beggar watches as the tailor sighs, stares hopelessly at the material, turns it around, unpicks a section, and then reattaches it.

"How is it going?" He hears the voice of Dr. Krishna Kumar long before he enters the room. "Is it finished?"

The doctor walks past the machines where the other tailors are working, making the odd remark or suggestion, and then he sees that Madan is sewing a button on an ochre-coloured length of cloth.

"Why didn't you use the cloth I gave you?" the doctor asks.

Madan hands him the coat.

The man with the hump watches with interest as the bald

man holds up the garment at arm's length and examines it closely.

"I thought I made myself clear," the doctor says sternly as he turns the coat inside out and studies it. "I told you to make a coat that fits him like a glove." He points to the beggar, who immediately pulls in his neck and watches anxiously.

Madan nods.

"But this is an ordinary coat, without room for his hump."

Madan nods again.

He takes the coat from the doctor's hands and hands it to the beggar, who isn't sure whether he's supposed to take it or not. Not until the bald man gives him a stern look does he dare to take the garment and put it on. He tries to button the coat, but the hairy hump presses uncomfortably on his neck and towers even farther over his head.

The doctor fusses and fumes. He doesn't understand how his talented pupil has managed to create this horrible garment. He was confident that the young tailor could deal with such a complicated body. Obviously, that was not the case.

Madan, who until now has not touched the man, sees him fumbling with the collar and the buttons and goes over to him. With a single light movement, he pulls the material over the hump and adjusts the collar.

Dr. Krishna Kumar cannot believe his eyes. Over the years he's seen many wondrous things. Once, on an organized trip to Kerala, he saw how a fakir lay on a bed of nails and allowed the nails to penetrate his legs. And once, on a visit to a holy temple, he saw an ascetic meditating, with an enormous rock weighing at least twenty kilograms hanging from his penis. Fire-eating yogis and holy men who could charm snakes . . . all these extraordinary accomplishments evoked his admiration, but they were nothing compared with what he is seeing now. The other tailors are crowding around the man, and Dr. Krishna Kumar sees that the hump, which a moment ago loomed so large, has disappeared. And the head, which previously hung like a strange bulge, is now looking him amiably in the face. Dr. Krishna Kumar notices that the man has good ears and forceful eyebrows, things he always pays extra attention to. The doctor, who is never at a loss for words, is speechless. He sees that the man standing opposite him is smiling. Shyly, he smiles back. He doesn't know whether to sink into the ground or burst into ecstatic jubilation. This beggar, this monstrosity he found at the train station and for whom he ordered a plate of food set down in front of the WC, is now standing before him like one of his friends at the club.

"And he never even took his measurements," stammers one of the other tailors.

1973 Madras

THE FACT THAT everything could change in a single second was not new to Madan. But this time the change worked to his advantage. After he made the coat for the beggar, he was promoted to the main cutting table, and from then on he has allocated the work to the other tailors. Over the years, his colleagues have become accustomed to the way he communicates with others. Madan speaks by means of glances and gestures, indicating what they're to do with the material and the garments. When someone new is taken on, they have to get used to the quiet tailor who heads the atelier. Madan enjoys the prestige that goes with the post that he has attained, and he is seldom plagued by troubled dreams.

Until this morning. The monsoon has just ended and the air is fresh and clear. The windows of the atelier are open and a slight breeze caresses the bodies of the toiling tailors. Suddenly Madan looks straight into the eyes of a girl who was hired two months ago. It is as if he's been struck by a bolt of lightning. The girl goes about her work calmly. She sits on a mat next to the door and her job is to finish the seams of each piece of clothing that leaves the atelier. Except for the elderly ironing lady in the hall, she is the only female employee. Madan has just made a cutting error in a piece of cloth destined to become a *kurta* for the secretary of the tennis club, and he has forgotten to tell the errand boy to get more needles. His eyes keep straying to the corner where the young woman with the long braids carefully picks up every piece of clothing from her pile, turns it inside out, cuts the remaining threads, and tucks the ends into the seam. If he hadn't spoiled the *kurta*, he would have gone over to her sooner. Now he neatly folds the pale grey *kurta* and walks in her direction. He feels as if everyone is looking at him, which they are. Not because he's walking over to her, but because they're hungry. Just before he places the garment on the girl's pile, he remembers that it's lunchtime. He turns around and holds up his hand. The men jump up from their sewing machines and scurry outside, chatting to one another. He puts the *kurta* on the pile next to her. The girl remains seated but does not look up. He shuffles his feet, but the girl continues her work. *It's lunchtime*, he wants to say. *You can go for lunch.* She pulls the needle through the material. *Why doesn't she look up?* Then she bites the thread with her teeth. *She must see that I'm standing here.* She turns the garment right side out and checks her work. *Please look up!* The girl looks up. When she sees that Madan is looking at her, she immediately lowers her eyes. She sits there quietly. *Isn't she hungry?* Then she takes the *kurta* and turns it inside out. *Doesn't she want to have lunch?* Her fingers go over the seams that Madan has just sewn. Near the elbow, at the exact spot where Madan made the cutting error, her finger stands still. *She sees it.* Then her finger glides farther, until she gets to the hem, where she cuts off a loose thread. *She's so beautiful.* Her fingers glide along the hem and then up to the neck. *Has she been married off as well?* As a street orphan, Madan is sometimes envious of his colleagues, who often spend years searching for the most appropriate marriage partners for their children. And with his handicap he doesn't stand much chance of finding a partner, not even as head of Dr. Krishna Kumar's atelier.

The girl looks up. Madan begins to blush, and then turns and goes back to his sewing machine. He isn't hungry. He doesn't feel like taking a break with the others. He doesn't want to hear all the stories about their children and their demanding wives, their bossy mothers-in-law, the houses that are too small, and the high cost of schooling and food. All he wants is to find someone who loves him.

He doesn't hear her coming . . . until suddenly she's standing next to him. Her eyes are averted and she's holding an empty spool in her hand. He points to the cabinet with the thread. The girl doesn't move but fiddles with the wooden spool.

Do you want me to wind it up for you?

He puts out his hand and the girl gives him the spool. He walks over to the large wooden cabinet. In the courtyard outside, under the big banyan tree, he hears the men laughing.

The girl is still standing next to him, and although her head is still bowed, he feels the tension she exudes. Slowly and carefully, he winds the thread onto the spool. Dr. Krishna Kumar's rules — never use too much thread and always use your own spool — don't apply to the girl, since she will never be allowed to sit behind one of the sewing machines. He hands her the spool. She bows her head even lower and returns to her place, where she picks up the next garment. Madan also goes back to his post. He wishes that they were all free, that they didn't have to work until eight o'clock at night, and that he knew where the girl lives. His eyes wander from the silent machines to her. He sees how she quickly lowers her eyes.

~

"MUKKA!" THE VOICE of Dr. Krishna Kumar resounds through the atelier.

The only light burning is at Madan's table.

"Mukka, where are you?"

Madan appears from under his table.

"Problems with the machine?" asks the doctor.

Madan shakes his head.

"Do you know where the new scissors are, the ones I bought last week?"

Madan has also noticed that the scissors are missing. With a worried look, he shrugs his shoulders and raises his eyebrows.

"They must be here somewhere."

Madan knows that the scissors are not there. He's looked everywhere, even under his own table.

"I have a feeling that things have recently begun to disappear from my atelier," Dr. Krishna Kumar says, with a serious expression on his face. I know for certain that I had one long green zipper and a short yellow one, and now they're nowhere to be found."

Madan, who has been in charge of the store cupboard for the last year and a half, is missing even more items: a new box of hat pins, a tracing wheel, a ripper, the package of darning needles, a thimble, a roll of elastic, gold band, and a small bag of red buttons. A lot of snaps have also disappeared from the bin, but even worse, a roll of white cotton is missing.

Krishna Kumar looks him in the eye. Madan feels nervous under the gaze of his boss.

"Take care of it," he says, as he strides out of the workshop. Madan has some idea of where the missing items are, but he's been praying for days that he's mistaken and that no one will notice.

He has trouble getting to sleep that night, and when he finally dozes off, he dreams of two female arms that caress and embrace him until the arms suddenly turn into a boa constrictor that is about to strangle him. Suddenly, he's wide awake and he realizes that he has an enormous erection.

At the end of each day they all have to clear their work tables and sweep the floor. Madan has made it clear to the man who sits next to him that he has to leave early, and asks him to lock the door of the atelier and give the key to Dr. Krishna Kumar.

He, the sly dog, is standing behind the wall, watching the men head for home, one by one, and when the girl comes out, he, the lovelorn, begins to sweat. From the moment their eyes first found each other, they have exchanged glances when no one was looking, or passed each other more slowly than necessary. In his dreams he, the hankerer, is in love with her and they never stop talking. For weeks he, the debased, has thought and thought, searching for a way that he, the blunderer, could approach her. He, the orphan, has no father, uncle, or brother who could go to the family, and he, the serf, does not dare ask Dr. Krishna Kumar to take that role upon himself, for what father would want his daughter to marry a man with no background, no family, and thus no future? She doesn't realize that he, the insignificant, is following her as she regularly disappears into a crowd, and he, the tribeless, sees nothing but the flapping tip of her sari. He, the lovesick, has often dreamt of doing this. He, the casteless, doesn't know where she lives. Dr. Krishna Kumar has never told him, and he, the coward, has never dared ask her. She turns into a street where there's a small market and she buys some vegetables at one of the stands. He, the non-existent, sees that she's haggling, and he, the spy, can tell by the look on the seller's face that she is a regular visitor. With the vegetables under her arm, she turns into an alley that he, the pursuer, has never seen before. The alley leads to a busy street, and he, the fearful, is happy that he, the invisible, can again disappear into the hustle and bustle. She is in no hurry. Does she perhaps sense that he, the spy, is following her? If only he, the remorseful, could simply return to his room in the courtyard. He, the futureless, wishes that he, the tyrant, had never been made boss of the store cupboard. It was the first key that he, the unpropertied, had ever had in his life. If only he, the guard, could throw the key into the sea. The sea where the sun rises rather than sets, as in Bombay. He, the lost, wishes he could sink between the paving stones; he, the infatuated, doesn't want to walk behind her; he, the passionate, longs to walk beside her, take her hand in his, and ask her to marry him, Mukka, the dumb tailor. She goes into a house. She doesn't close the door. There is no greeting, no conversation. All is quiet. Time passes. The street noises fade away. Night falls.

He walks up to the house. A dog barks. He knocks, and he hears her clear voice. He pushes the door open. She is startled. She hadn't expected him. They look at each other. She lowers her eyes. He wants to leave, close the door behind him, disappear, forget everything. He doesn't want to go in, but he realizes that if he doesn't, he won't be able to go back to Dr. Krishna Kumar. He must carry out his mission. He has to know. He has to know that it's not her. In front of her lies the missing pair of scissors. She pulls the flap of her sari over the sewing basket, but the sari is too short. On the mat, where she's working, lies a white blouse, half-finished, alongside a pile of finished blouses, all of them white. The roll of cotton is leaning against the wall. She is breathing fast. So is he. They don't move. They both look at the gleaming pair of scissors. He remembers the shiny apples and the sweet mangoes that disappeared into his pocket with lightning speed. He bends over. His hand reaches for the implement, which in his eyes has suddenly become absurd. Two pieces of metal that glide past one another in order to cut something in two, to divide, irreparably separate the pieces. He doesn't pick up the scissors. His hand floats above them, purposeless and uncertain. He smells her breath. He knows that she's afraid. Does she have a father? A brother? A cousin? Where is the rest of her family? She pulls the elastic out of her hair. Her long hair falls over her shoulders. He picks up the scissors and lays them on the table. He sits down next to her on the floor. He has a thousand questions, all of them the same as his fears. Glistening drops appear on her forehead. She stops breathing. She opens her mouth. She wants to say something, but then she closes it again.

Don't say anything. Please don't say anything. I already know. You don't have to say anything. I won't betray you. Stay with me. Stay with me forever. I'll take you with me. We'll leave this place. Don't be afraid. I love you. I've loved you from the first moment I looked into your eyes. Believe me. Trust me. I'll take care of you. Protect you. For the rest of my life I want to wake up next to you. Come . . . sleep in my arms.

Slowly she takes her hand in his. Her hand is cooler. He shivers. He is becoming aroused. He doesn't want her to see, and pulls up his knees. She strokes his arm. Very slowly. With the tip of her finger she touches the hairs on his skin, one by one. The throbbing in his lower abdomen turns to pounding. The blood races through his veins.

Aren't you afraid of me? Don't you think I'm scary? Where is your father? Where is your brother?

She bends forward. Her breath brushes his cheek. He wants to take her in his arms, kiss her, but his entire body is as stiff as the part of his body that he hates. She begins to laugh and pushes him backwards into the pile of blouses. She shakes her wild hair loose. He can see her teeth. Illuminated only by the faint light of the bulb that hangs next to her, she's like a lioness about to pounce. She dives forward, throwing herself on him. He feels his shirt tear and her nails scrape across his chest, while her tongue flicks his ear, and her laugh rings out as he seeks her mouth, feels her breasts, which are the exact size that he had imagined them, and her hands seek his hands and guide them to her hips, then she wraps her arms around him, bites him, licks him. She exudes a scent that is foreign to him, which doesn't remind him of any flower he has ever smelled. The pain he feels is not pain, and her panting sounds like a song as she becomes entangled in her hair and her laugh rings out. She is naked and he doesn't know how he became naked, her skin glides over his skin, makes him shudder and tingle, stuns him, as if nothing else exists in the world except for the woman he has worshipped for months, the woman he has fantasized about. The reality is much more titillating, more overwhelming than in his dream. When he realizes that she won't break under his weight, he takes the lead, discovers and explores every hollow of her body. Her laugh gives way to a voluptuous groan, and he feels that he's crying but doesn't understand why, since he has never been this happy. She licks away his tears and climbs onto him and tickles him with her long hair, and for the first time in all those months she speaks to him: "It's all right . . ." And that makes him cry even harder. She puts her mouth to his, her tongue searches his wordless cavern, he finds her and they throw their arms around each other, and outside the dog barks again. She starts, and quickly pulls one of the blouses toward her. He doesn't understand why she's suddenly stopped. She ties her sari around her waist and gathers her hair into a knot. Then she gets up and motions to him to get up, too.

He sees the scissors on the table. The sewing basket that stood next to her has overturned on the floor. He sees the snaps, the tracing wheel, the ripper, the thimble, and the gold band. She snatches his clothes from the floor and turns off the light. He understands that he must get dressed as fast as he can, that what happened is over. He hears footsteps, the door opens, and a man's voice asks why the light is out. She doesn't reply but shoves him against the wall, and he senses that the man is entering the house, and then she lets go of him and springs in the direction of the other man, calling out "Peekaboo." Again he hears her laugh, merry and ringing, and then a grumbling voice. He searches for the door, feels that it isn't shut, and dashes out of the house, leaving behind her strident laughter. He hears the man tell her to keep her voice down.

The dog barks.

Madan runs back into the street.

At the end of the street he feels that his bobbin, which he always keeps in his pants pocket, has disappeared. He is twenty-seven years old as he walks in the direction of the station. He will never see Dr. Krishna Kumar again.

1973 Chilakalurupet

HE WALKS DOWN the road that the man said leads to Hyderabad. "If you put on some speed, you can make it three weeks or so," the man joked.

Madan never expected to leave the city just as poor as when he arrived. Even poorer, since after a couple of hours the implacable ticket collector unceremoniously threw him off the train. Embarrassed, he follows the newly paved road while cars pass him at full speed. He hopes one of the trucks will stop and pick him up. The destination makes no difference to him, as long as it's far away from here. One truck passes so close to him that a ricocheting stone hits him in the leg. He is happy that the piercing pain temporarily distracts him from the other pain.

He limps away from the street and drops down on a fallen tree limb. He isn't hungry or thirsty. All he feels is the cold. His leg is bleeding. He tries to clean the wound with his finger and some spit.

Next to his foot he sees two small red beetles. They are gnawing away at the tree trunk he's sitting on. A third beetle crawls out from under the bark, hobbles off slowly in the direction of the other two, and then climbs on top of one of them. The beetle underneath doesn't seem to notice and goes on gnawing on the wood, while the male on her back does his best. She crawls farther in search of a fresh morsel, and discovers a budding shoot. Madan gazes in admiration at the male beetle. He doesn't lose his head but continues what he was doing. Then along comes the other beetle, who until now has not interfered in the activities of his fellow insects. He climbs onto the female's head and continues in the direction of the male on her back. He also joins in the fun. Madan stares in amazement at the lack of interest displayed by the female, who goes on eating while on her back the future of the species is being secured. He wishes he were a beetle.

1995 Rampur ~

"AUNTIE!" ISSY'S VOICE resounded throughout the house. "Auntie Charlotte! There's no toilet paper!"

Charlotte had no idea whether there was any toilet paper in the house, or if there was even anything that could serve as an alternative. She hadn't bought paper in years: like everyone else in India, she used a jug of water. On her way upstairs she noticed that the indefatigable heat had found its way into the house. Her blouse clung to her back. She took the key from the nail and went into the nursery.

Her father sat in his wheelchair, the sweat pouring down his face. He gave her a stern look. "What are you here for?"

"Is there any toilet paper?"

The general began to sigh and groan. Charlotte went into the bathroom and searched the cabinets. Behind her, she heard her father filling his diaper. Why hadn't her brother written that she was coming? Or called? How long would the girl be staying? What was she going to feed her? Was there food on hand, or should she send Hema to the market? If only she didn't ask for white bread, which was frightfully expensive. Charlotte would like nothing better than to crawl into the cabinet under the washbasin, the way she did when she was little and Sita wanted to put her to bed. Then suddenly she saw her father's gold watch lying on the washbasin. Hema must have forgotten to put it back after bathing him, since it always hung on the wall opposite him. How much would it fetch? She picked it up, noting that it was quite heavy, and then slid it into the pocket of her skirt. In the hall, the voice sounded again: "Auntie!"

MADAN TRIED TO concentrate on the bust seam of the dress destined for the wife of the manufacturer of coconut oil, but the girl's voice distracted him. Something about her reminded him of someone, but he couldn't recall who. It wasn't her uncombed locks or wild manners. He'd seen plenty of hippie girls from Europe, and this was something different. He turned the wheel of his sewing machine. The humming sound was soothing. If the girl hadn't appeared, would they have kissed? he asked himself, and for the third time he saw that he'd set the sleeve incorrectly. He pulled the silk garment from under the machine, and for the first time wondered whether deep purple was the right colour for the portly Indian lady. Even after he had treated it with the peel of a ripe mango, it didn't have quite the graceful, elegant effect he had envisioned. And if they had kissed, would he still be sitting here, or would everything have simply collapsed? He drew the thread out of the fabric with the utmost precision, but the tiny holes from the needle were still visible. Or — if they had kissed — would he now be sitting on his bicycle with his sewing machine on the luggage rack? He wound up his spool again, the one he'd bought in Hyderabad with the first money he'd made by begging. Or would she have come over and sat down next to him, and would he now be working on her dress? He put the spool back into the machine and gave the wheel a turn as he tried again to shape the bust line in such a way that the sagging breasts of the wife of the manufacturer of coconut oil would be shown off to advantage.

"Hi." Issy walked into the music room. She was wearing her blue jacket again, clearly with nothing else underneath. "Do you have time to make something for me?" She rummaged around in the pile of fabric Madan had placed on the table. "These colours are pretty hip. Did you buy them here? I should never have shopped in New Delhi, they had absolutely nothing, I don't understand why the travel guide made it sound like there are all kinds of fabulous things for sale." She pulled the scarlet length of silk from the pile. "This is the one I want," she said, looking inquiringly at Madan. He did not look up, as he had already seen which piece she'd picked out. "That's okay, isn't it? You have lots of other reds." She tossed the length of cloth back on the table, walked over to the window, and drew the curtain aside. "Why on earth do all of you keep the rooms so dark? It's really bad for your eyes. You don't want to go blind, do you? If you open the window, at least you get some fresh air." She pulled the window open and shoved the shutters aside. The blinding sunlight poured into the room. She blinked. A stifling wave of heat poured into the room. "Jesus Christ, how can you people stand it here? Now I understand why Dad went to live in England. This can't be real! It's not only bad for your eyes, but for your skin, too." Within seconds, large drops of perspiration had appeared on her face and were running down her cheeks like a dripping candle.

Madan saw that he had again put the bust seam in wrong but didn't want to unpick the thread while the girl was in the room, so he continued to sew slowly.

"I didn't know my aunt was such a slave driver. In England, the Union of Tailors — if there is such a thing — would have forbidden their members to work in this heat. I'd go on strike, if I were you," she panted, as the scorching sun poured into the room. "She can't really expect it of you? Isn't there a pool somewhere around here, so I can go swimming? I haven't had my bikini on since I got here." Issy's eyes slowly became accustomed to the glaring light. Although Madan was roughly the same age as her maths teacher, she saw that he was quite handsome. "Have you ever seen that actor?" she asked, as she moved closer to him. "You know, the one who plays the lead in *The Buddha of Suburbia*? You look a lot like him. Did you know that? His hair is longer, but if I saw you on the street, I would swear that you were him."

Madan, who understood only snatches of what she said, wished fervently that she would go away. He was anxious to take the material out from under the foot and start over.

"Do you take photos of the clothes you make?" She watched as he turned the wheel. "I don't want a dumb thing like this." She pointed to the blue jacket she was wearing. "I want something super, something really special that nobody else has."

That jacket, Madan thought, *it's the same kind of blue jacket . . .*

"Miss Isabella, Charlotte memsahib is looking for you." Hema had appeared out of nowhere, since he had the gift of being able to move noiselessly when he wanted to.

"Please, call me Issy, and where is Auntie slave driver?" Issy smiled at Hema. "I'll ask her to give you the day off, then we can go swimming somewhere."

"Memsahib is in the drawing room."

The girl left the room and Hema's expression changed. The smile disappeared from his face, making way for a furious glance in Madan's direction. Grumbling under his breath, he went over to the open windows, closed the shutters and windows, and drew the curtains. Then he slammed the door of the music room, leaving Madan behind in the sweltering heat.

"Why do you make that man work in such a dark, stuffy room?"

"The monsoon should have started ages ago, and the house stays cooler with the shutters closed."

"You can't force someone to go on working."

"I'm not forcing him."

"But he is working."

"That's his choice."

"I asked him if he would make something for me. Something snazzy. That's all right, isn't it?" Before Charlotte could reply, she continued: "Actually, he's a bit of a hunk.

He looks like the guy who plays the lead in that TV series. I told him so, but I don't think he has a TV. Do you happen to have a wall plug socket?" Issy reached into her bag and pulled out a bunch of electrical cords. "So I can charge my telephone."

"Your what?"

"My mobile phone. Yeah, neat, isn't it? A present from Dad. It's the latest thing and really expensive, but he wanted to be able to reach me. He wasn't keen on my travelling alone, so he bought one for me. But everything's gone really well: I've met nothing but friendly people. Where's the wall socket?"

Charlotte had heard of mobile phones but had never seen one, and she gazed in fascination at the device her niece was holding. "Can you call any number in the world?"

"Not America, but it should work in India and Thailand. I tried to call here, but no luck. I thought maybe your phone was down, but I just checked it and it was working. So it's probably the battery, it's almost empty. Dad took out a special subscription. He said I'd have to pay it back later, but that's ridiculous. After all, it was his idea, wasn't it, and — hey, here's another outlet."

"Are you going to Thailand, too?" Charlotte asked. There was a hint of relief in her voice.

"If I feel like it, but it's fun here, I've never lived in such a big house with a butler, can I just call him if I need something?"

Charlotte, who was already perspiring profusely, felt a tightness in her throat, and a trickle of sweat began to run down between her breasts. She mumbled, "I'll ask him if he can help you with the cords."

"If he knows how it all works, he's so old. And where is Grandpa?"

Charlotte felt the watch burning a hole in her pocket. She had hoped the conversation would not turn to Father. Although she had written that he was becoming very forgetful, she had never told Donald just how much he had deteriorated, and that they now had to secure him to the wheelchair. That had been Hema's idea, after Father had fallen for the second time, fully convinced that he could walk. Now they also tied him down at night, since that same conviction led him to get out of bed if he had to pee or wanted something to drink. He categorically refused to sleep on a mattress on the ground: that's what the inlanders did, but not the general.

When he was fastened to the chair, he often thought it was wartime. In the beginning he had had terrible crying bouts, which always ended in an onslaught of rage, when he'd grab anything that was at hand and throw it at his daughter. One day he picked up a vase, one of the few heirlooms to survive their growing poverty, and threw it at her. The instant the vase grazed her head was the last straw for Charlotte. When it hit the wall and shattered, she had screamed that things could not continue as they were, and that he would have to go. But there was no money to place the old soldier in a house for demented pensioners, and returning to England was not an option. So the wheelchair was fitted with extra straps to anchor his arms, and Charlotte continued to nurse him. She had suspended her search for a cheaper house. Not only did her father refuse to sign the papers, but no one was interested in purchasing the enormous but dilapidated villa.

"He's asleep," Charlotte said to her niece. "It's best not to wake him up."

"Does he still have that huge moustache? We were afraid of his moustache. Dad told us that you both thought it was scary when you were little, and by the way, I never wore the baby cape that you knitted for me when I was born. Mama said it was ugly, but Elsa, my doll, wore it a lot. I can't throw that doll away, even now that I'm grown up." Issy put her feet up on the table and wiped the sweat from her forehead. "You've gotten rid of a lot of stuff, haven't you? In the old photos there are big pieces of furniture all over the place and a grand piano. Can't we open the window, I'm suffocating. How can you stand this heat? Why don't you buy air conditioners? We have air conditioning and it's great, you'd never think that Dad was born in India, he doesn't like the heat, he likes rain."

Charlotte got up and turned the fan over their heads to the highest setting.

"Don't they have rain dances here, like the Indians? Did you know that the pharaohs in Egypt had them, too? I heard that from my mother's brother, he writes travel guides. When he hears about the stupid old guide that I have with me, he'll probably come over next year and write a better one. He's so much fun and he always takes me out to dinner in famous restaurants, did you know that London has great Indian restaurants, they're supposed to be even better than here, I've heard." She waved the panels of her jacket back and forth, but when she saw her aunt's shocked expression, she buttoned up the jacket with a sigh. "Can't we ask the butler to do a rain dance?" She giggled at the thought. "We can't just sit around waiting for that . . . that monsoon. It's really too, too hot."

Charlotte stood up and rang the bell.

"Are you going to ask him?"

"No, he's too busy, but I'll have him bring you something to drink."

"Do you have Coca-Cola? As long as it's not tea again, everyone drinks nothing but tea here, but in this heat it makes me feel even hotter, just like the spicy food, it really makes you sweat."

With a sigh, Hema put the jerry cans down on the kitchen counter. His legs were trembling and his back ached after carrying the heavy load. As he trudged up the hill, he kept asking himself why he wasn't peevish when the girl used the five-day supply of drinking water to take a bath. He told himself that it was because she was Charlotte memsahib's niece. But deep in his heart he knew that it was for quite a different reason that he went around whistling all day, something he hadn't done since his teenage years.

The bell sounded. He picked up the tray and almost danced up to the big house. In the hall he bumped into memsahib, who immediately put a forefinger to her mouth.

"Do you know where they sell Coca-Cola?" Charlotte whispered.

"At the bottom of the hill," he whispered back.

"Will you get me a bottle? My niece drinks Coca-Cola."

Hema hesitated, the tray still in his hands.

"What's wrong?"

"I can't buy on credit there."

Charlotte fished her wallet out of her pocket. She almost dropped the watch, but managed to shove it back in.

"How much does a bottle cost?"

"A large bottle or a small one, memsahib?"

"Large . . . she'll be here for a few days."

Hema beamed. "Not much, memsahib, not much."

"How much?"

"About the same as two packages of fancy cookies."

"What?" She forgot they were whispering. "Two packages!"

Hema nodded with conviction.

"Can't you get the price down any further?"

"Not at the bottom of the hill, memsahib, maybe in the centre."

"Auntie," called a voice from the salon, "ask him if he can bring along a chocolate bar!"

Hema looked at Charlotte, who sighed, nodded, and resolved to sell the watch today.

MADAN SENSED THE unrest that hung in the house, and he knew that this time it wasn't caused by him, but by the girl. After Hema had gone off in search of Coca-Cola for the lowest possible price and a chocolate bar, he had heard Charlotte going up the stairs. He was glad she didn't come into the music room. He wanted to be alone. His thoughts shot off in all directions, and after that sudden recollection of his sister in her blue coat, he'd made one mistake after the other. He unpicked the entire blouse destined for the wife of the manufacturer of coconut oil, and when he made yet another mistake, he put the cap over the machine and went outside.

The rays of the sun pierced his back. Even in the shade of the withered trees, there was no relief from that fiery heavenly body. It was not often that he thought about his sister and wondered whether he had any other brothers and sisters. There were vague memories of a scene long ago in which there were a great many adults and children around him, but it wasn't clear to him whether it was indoors or outdoors. He did remember awakening in the arms of a white woman. She smelled like jasmine and she kissed him. His sister was crying, and when he tried to console her, she got angry. He didn't know what he'd done wrong, but it must have been something serious, since she was so furious that she left him standing there, amidst all those men's legs, and never even turned around.

He walked down the hill, crossed the road, and went down a street with houses. The sun was nowhere near its pinnacle, but already there was almost no shade. The only protection came from a large banner stretched across the road with a picture of the building that housed the New Rampur Club and in giant numerals the number "200."

The gala was two days away and the dresses were almost finished. But all of them still needed the finishing touch: an open seam here, a loose hem there. When he was finished, he would have to move on, but he tried not to think about that.

In the distance he heard the fire engine siren, a sound that had become more and more frequent now that the monsoon was so long in coming. A rickshaw passed him at high speed, with Hema sitting in the back. He was cradling a large bottle of Coca-Cola in his arms as if it were a baby, and gazing at it fondly.

~

THE WIFE OF Nikhil Nair filled her glass with cold lemon water. "That tailor isn't anywhere near finished," she sighed, and fell back into the cushions, panting.

"Oh," said the wife of Ajay Karapiet, as she took a pair of glittering black evening shoes from their box and showed them to her friend. "These are the ones."

"I thought you were going to wear the gold mules."

"I like these better."

"Have you tried them under the dress?"

"No, he still has to do the hem."

"That's just what he told me." There was disbelief in the voice of the wife of Nikhil Nair.

The wife of Ajay Karapiet looked dubiously at her new shoes. "You just might be right. The gold mules are probably better."

"Priya hasn't gotten her dress back either, and Deepa called to say that he was still working on her collar. Isn't that a bit strange?"

"The only thing is . . . the black ones are more comfortable."

"Do you know if Harita already has her dress?"

"Harita's going to wear gold shoes, too, but with a much higher heel. I can't do that, of course, not with my back."

"Does she have her dress already?"

"Well, she's tried it on, and it fits like a glove."

"But could she take it home with her?"

The wife of Ajay Karapiet hesitated and then shrugged her shoulders. "Kalpana doesn't have hers either. I talked to her this morning. She was quite taken with these shoes."

"Kalpana as well!" The wife of Nikhil Nair pushed the cushions out of her way and got to her feet. Despite the air conditioning, she was still warm. "And apparently Mandira's in the same boat. It's only two days until the party, and we still have to choose our accessories."

"Which shoes are you going to wear?"

"Is your glass empty?"

"I wouldn't mind some more."

"Later on."

CHARLOTTE DIALLED THE number. By now she knew it by heart. The raucous voice at the other end did not give his name. She did, although with some hesitation. She knew that if she sold the watch, there would be a great many problems.

"I thought you didn't have anything left?" snapped the man she disliked so intensely. "Only if it's something valuable, otherwise I'm not interested."

He hung up before she could reply.

Her niece was lying on the sofa, panting from the heat. Her father was asleep, and even the sewing machine was silent. Was Madan, too, finally floored by the lethargy that had overcome everyone? She tiptoed to the coat rack, put on her wide-brimmed straw hat, went to the front door, and slipped outside. Just as she pulled the door gently shut, she saw the black car that belonged to the wife of Nikhil Nair turn into the driveway. Her first impulse was to go back into the house and call Hema, to receive the ladies. But whether it was the sleepless night and the dance of love or the fact that she'd had her fill of the club ladies and their eternal gossiping, she ran down the steps and quickly hid under the branches of a withered Christmas rose that stood in the shadow of the house. She saw how the wife of Nikhil Nair alighted from the car, immediately followed by the wife of Ajay Karapiet. She heard one of them whisper that the ancient butler would probably serve those same old cookies that looked expensive but were actually cheap, that it would be a miracle if there were enough chairs to go around, that she couldn't understand why they remained in that enormous house since everyone could see that they were living beyond their means, and that . . . Charlotte did indeed wish that Hema weren't so old and that he could get to the door faster. And she didn't enjoy being told that last night her father's cries of distress could be heard at the bottom of the hill, and that people wondered what else was happening in the enormous house, and that when it came to the Bridgwaters, they never knew what to expect . . .

The door opened, and Isabella sounded surprised as she explained that she had just seen her aunt leave the house, and that they should have passed each other on the path. Then the girl stuck her head out the door and shouted Charlotte's name as loudly as she could. Charlotte ducked farther under the shrub and pulled her hat down over her face. They mustn't find her. Not now, not here. She heard Isabella let the women into the house, saying that she'd go and call the tailor. The door slammed shut with a bang. Charlotte thought to herself, *Hema may be old, but at least he knows how to shut a door properly.*

Charlotte looked at a fat beetle sitting on a twig. The heat didn't seem to bother him, even though he had a very thick coat. She wondered if he was ever afraid. She'd like to be able to hide under a big wing case the way he did, so that no one could see her. The beetle shook his gleaming wings and continued to walk along the twig, taking tiny steps. It was the sudden golden lustre of the beetle's case that made her reach into her pocket for the watch. Would her father already have missed it, would he have had another tantrum, and whom would he accuse this time? She ought to tell Hema, since otherwise he might suspect her niece or "that *darzi*," as he referred to him with unmistakable disdain. It had surprised her that Isabella also found him handsome; the girl was at least thirty years younger than the tailor and ought to be interested in boys her own age. The thought disturbed her as she sat there, half hidden by the shrub. That youthful interest might have evoked certain feelings in Madan, just like the winter rose that blossoms fiercely after each monsoon. The likelihood of rivalry was not merely an illusion, it was fed by the searing torpor of the climate and the loneliness of the house. All things considered, she was no more than an older woman who stole from her father to make a good impression on her niece by buying a drink she herself had never tried. An older woman who hid under a shrub to escape the hungry eyes of two notorious gossips because she was afraid that they could tell by looking at her that she had fallen in love with the dark-skinned tailor who had to pay for a workplace in her father's house and whom she allowed to work in the music room because that way he was closer to her . . . Could anything be more pathetic? What was happening to her? Why didn't she tell her niece that there was no money, that the furniture had been removed not for aesthetic reasons but so that they could continue to eat, and that she, like any woman, wanted to look beautiful at the party, but that there was no money for fabric, and that she had again been forced to rob her father of the last memories of his wife in order to indulge her own desires. Why didn't she tell her niece that she was so ablaze that she feared the bush would catch fire if she were to sit under it too long, and that — although they had never even exchanged a kiss — she was convinced that she had already lost him . . .

The beetle was creeping up the trunk. A bit farther on, Charlotte saw another beetle. Was the second beetle his wife? Or was that her husband? Were they together? Were they relatives? Lovers? Did they have secrets from each other? The beetle climbed higher and higher, and it was as if the other beetle was looking down over the edge of the branch, waiting for it to reach the top. Could beetles kiss? How did beetles make love? Didn't their wing cases get in the way? Charlotte sat stock still. Holding her breath, she watched as, step by step, the tiny creature climbed higher. Defiantly, almost provocatively, it drew closer and closer to the other beetle. Mesmerized, Charlotte forgot about the suffocating heat as she waited to see what would happen. He had almost reached the other beetle. They looked at each other. *Come on! Don't give up now!* The beetle took another step. Charlotte felt an urge to push the tiny insect toward the other beetle. They faced each other. *Love her!* He took another step and their heads were almost touching. Then out of nowhere she heard a rustling sound. Charlotte froze. But before she could think about what it might be, a crow swooped into view among the leaves, picked up one of the beetles from the branch, and flew off. The remaining beetle cowered and closed its case. Charlotte also cowered, with her head between her knees and her arms around her head. She wished she'd never listened to the women at the club, who had convinced her to take him into her house, she wished she had never seen him, had never let him move from the servants' quarters to the music room. She wished she hadn't danced with him, hadn't let him look into her heart. Again she heard a rustling among the leaves and hoped that the crow would devour the other beetle as well, so at least they'd be together.

What's wrong?

Charlotte looked up, startled. Through her tears she saw his face among the withered leaves of the winter rose.

You're crying. What happened?

There was a bird.

Just a bird?

A crow. It ate the beetle.

Was it a special beetle?
No, just a tiny beetle, an insect.
Had you seen the beetle before?
No, it was the first time I saw him.
And he was eaten by the crow?
Yes, just as he was about to kiss his wife.
A broad smile appeared on Madan's face.

"CAN YOU REALLY call anywhere?" The wife of Nikhil Nair and the wife of Ajay Karapiet gazed in admiration at the device in Issy's hand.

"It has to be charged, the battery is low. In the store they said it would last around two hours, but it seems to me it went down much faster. Anyway, once it's recharged, I can call you from the garden."

"From the garden! Did your aunt give you our numbers?" asked the wife of Ajay Karapiet, who loved talking on the phone.

"No, of course not, but it sure would be convenient if Aunt Charlotte had one. Then I could call her and she could answer, even if she was sitting in a taxi."

"In a taxi!"

The two ladies sighed. They were overwhelmed by the unexpected presence of the girl, as well as by her clothes, which left little to the imagination, the unkempt ponytail on the top of her head, and the fact that she was sitting on the sofa and didn't even invite them to sit down. She chattered on about how she had made a phone call while she was sitting in a rickshaw in New Delhi and that the driver was so startled he almost ran into a cow. The wife of Nikhil Nair gestured to her friend to sit down unasked. She was thirsty and tried not to look at the large glass of Coca-Cola in front of the girl. She was annoyed that the old butler had not arrived to offer them a cup of tea, and she regretted not having finished her glass of cold lemon water before hastily getting into the car.

"I have absolutely no idea where she's got to," Issy said. "She was just going out the door when you two arrived, so it's odd that you didn't see her. She left only a couple of minutes before. I couldn't imagine why she'd want to go outside in this heat, I'd probably just melt, and what I'd really like to do is take off all my clothes and lie down under the fan. She didn't say when she'd be back."

"That's quite all right," said the wife of Ajay Karapiet, putting a good face on it. But she was shocked at the very thought of the girl taking off all her clothes.

"Actually, we came to see the tailor."

"Oh, you want him to make clothes for you, too? I don't know where he's got to, I told him he ought to go on strike, it's much too hot to work." Issy laughed when she saw the ladies' shocked faces. "He'll be back, he's so serious. This morning he was working on a purple blouse, a terrific colour but too dark for me, and I asked him if he'd make something for me out of a piece of red silk."

"Oh, are you coming to the gala too?"

"Gala?"

"Yes, the New Rampur Club is celebrating its bicentennial with a huge gala. All the dignitaries from the surrounding districts will be there, and even the state minister for sport and recreation has promised to attend," said the wife of Nikhil Nair, conjuring up a mental picture of how jealous all the other ladies would be when she appeared in her splendid new pink outfit. She'd wear her black shoes, the ones with the really high heels, and a tiara with ten genuine diamonds in her hair.

"Oh," said Issy as she reached for her glass of Coca-Cola.

The two women looked at each other in bewilderment. Although the tickets for the gala had sold out within a week, they would probably have made an exception, since she was Charlotte's niece and the granddaughter of the oldest member. But the girl seemed singularly uninterested.

The wife of Nikhil Nair stood up. "We must be going, otherwise it'll be too late. Would you ask the tailor to deliver the clothes today or tomorrow morning at the latest?" She motioned to her friend, but she was staring at the girl as she downed her Coca-Cola. "Shall we be off then?" she repeated impatiently. Her friend was not listening. The wife of Nikhil Nair gave an angry cough and headed for the door.

It was only then that the wife of Ajay Karapiet realized what was expected of her, and reluctantly rose from the sofa. She didn't want to leave. She wanted to listen to this exotic young girl's stories.

"Shall I give you my phone number?" she asked.

The wife of Nikhil Nair looked at her friend in amazement.

"I'd love to get a call from that special telephone of yours."

Charlotte and Madan heard the ladies come down the front steps. The chauffeur had already started the engine, but it was still clear that the two women were arguing.

They want their dresses, Charlotte giggled.

They're not finished yet.

I thought they were ready to be picked up.

Not quite. I'm waiting.

For what?

Rain.

Rain? But we have water, don't we?

Not enough.

They looked up at the sky through the withered branches. There wasn't a cloud to be seen. It felt good to be sitting next to him, looking up at the sky together. If only she could make time stand still until the first drops began to fall.

It can't be long now.

On the radio they've been predicting rain for two weeks, said Charlotte, as if it was perfectly normal to converse by means of thought rather than speech.

We have to show the rain that it's welcome.

So, you believe in rain dances, too? Charlotte pulled a dry leaf from the Christmas rose; it immediately crumbled under her fingers.

Not a dance—just a sign, a signal.

What kind of sign?

Buckets.

Charlotte began to laugh — as if the monsoon could be seduced by a bunch of buckets!

It works. Really.

"If you say so," she said aloud. But she was actually thinking *no*, and he heard that, too. *I should be going*, she thought.

Are you going to sell it?

Charlotte looked at him in surprise. She felt the watch in her hand, but she was certain that she hadn't been thinking about it. Only the money problems had briefly crossed her mind. How could he know that?

You were thinking about it.

I wasn't thinking about it. We were talking about rain and buckets, not his watch.

You were thinking about it before. When you told me about your niece.

You mean you can understand more than I'm aware of?

I don't know how I could have heard it, but I heard it.

"I must be off." She crept out from under the bush, brushed the dust and the leaves from her dress, adjusted her sun hat, and walked briskly down the hill. She didn't want him to read any more of her thoughts.

Hema was surprised to see his memsahib crawl out from under the Christmas rose. He knew that she secretly mowed the lawn, so she wouldn't have to pay a gardener, but he was unaware that she also pruned the bushes. He took a step backwards, so as not to embarrass her, and watched as she walked quickly down the hill. Seconds later he saw the tailor crawl out from under the same shrub, and it gave him such a fright that he started to choke, even though there was nothing in his mouth. He was overcome by a fit of coughing.

Madan heard him and realized that they'd been caught. He was furious with himself. He should never have gone to her, under the bush. He should have taken himself to hand when he heard her whispered thoughts under the branches. Her thoughts were not intended for him. He would have to leave. He must not stay, for whenever he thought he'd found happiness, it all went wrong.

1973 Hyderabad ~

HIS STOMACH RUMBLES. He's had nothing to eat since the apple he stole yesterday. He knocks, and on hearing a voice, he pushes the door open. An old woman is sitting at a table in the corridor. Her hands are resting on a rusty metal box in front of her. He shows her a piece of paper. For weeks he has shown it to anyone who was willing to read it. She glances at the paper, shakes her head, and clutches the box tightly. He walks back outside and pulls the door shut. Slowly he continues on his way. He knocks on the next door and waits patiently. When no one comes, he walks to the following door. Again he knocks. He hears a thumping noise and the door opens. He sees a man with a long beard before him. Madan hands him the piece of paper. "I can't read. What do you want?"

Madan motions that he can't speak. Before he can make it clear that he's looking for work, the man closes the door in his face. The note flutters to the ground. Madan picks it up and continues on his way. His stomach rumbles.

~

HE'S STANDING IN front of the station. An endless stream of people pass by. No one looks at him. He hasn't shaved in months and his hair has never been this long. His trousers are in tatters, his shoes were stolen while he was asleep, and the shirt — once his showpiece, made from a length of costly silk — is torn and filthy. It's the moment he has always dreaded. He and Abbas managed to escape this fate because there were two of them and they were fast on their feet. And later Ram Khan, Brother Francis, Mister Patel, Chandan Chandran, and Dr. Krishna gave him work and a roof over his head. He doesn't want to, but he has no choice. Very slowly he raises his hand.

He doesn't dare look at the passers-by. He sees nothing but shoes, slippers, and the hems of fluttering saris filing past. No one stops. They're all in a hurry. They're on their way to their work, their house, their family, their wife, their children. They have goals, a destination. In his head, their footsteps sound like music played in the wrong key. He wishes he were deaf and blind as well, so he couldn't see and hear that other people are happy. He wishes he were dead.

A pair of feet in worn brown leather slippers stop in front of him, and he feels a coin being placed in his hand. He looks up. The young man is gone. He wishes he could speak. He would have said "thank you."

1995 Rampur ~

MADAN NEEDED CRUSHED mimosa petals to finish the dress intended for the wife of Nikhil Nair. He had decided to make a dress that would emphasize her fragility. For the wife of the secretary, who rarely attended club functions for fear of somehow interfering with her husband's work, he would add teak tree blossoms, so that her husband would take more notice of her. For the unassuming wife of the commissioner, he had chosen the cinnamon tree, and for the woman who had begun to stoop after losing her only son, he would use a mix of dried forget-me-nots and marigold roots. He had manipulated the bust seam of the dress destined for the wife of the manufacturer of coconut oil. The dress would make a new woman of her, once he had rubbed ground petunia seeds into the fabric on which her well-formed bosom would rest. He was still searching for the stamens of a wild orchid for the dress of the wife of Ajay Karapiet. He needn't worry about what he would add to Charlotte's dress. From the day he arrived at the house on the hill, he had watered the plants he needed, and in some cases, he had carefully dried them. The other things he needed were found during his visits to the market. These included not only the powder made from young rose thorns mixed with the juice of the pomegranate, but also the bark of the apple tree, and the newly opened petals of the jasmine. He'd had to wait for the fabric to which the niece now laid claim. He had concealed his collection in the old *mali*'s shed, one of the few spots never visited by the factotum, who was convinced that it was haunted by the old man's spirit. Madan, who also believed in spirits but had never seen any sign of the old *mali*, turned the collar of the dress of the wife of the goldsmith and used his thumb to flatten the dried freesia petals before sliding the fabric under the needle again. He was almost finished.

She'll understand.

He turned the wheel of the machine and the fabric released a subtle scent.

She knows that it's impossible.

He was turning the wheel faster than was good for the collar. The material shot underneath the needle, and some of the freesia petals were folded double.

It's the only solution.

He pulled the collar out from under the needle and saw that it was slightly puckered. With the palm of his hand he pressed down hard on the fabric in an effort to smooth it out.

Not only for me, but for her as well.

Madan was becoming entangled in his own thoughts and emotions. He again put the collar under the foot of the sewing machine and gave the wheel a firm shove. The needle broke.

Issy had seen her aunt go into the upstairs room once, and the butler had gone in twice. They unlocked the door using the key that hung on the wall. For years she and her father had watched episodes of *Agatha Christie's Poirot* on TV, and now the detective in her began to stir. She wanted to know what was hidden in that room.

When she heard the personnel door close, she stole upstairs on tiptoe and lifted the key from its hook. She felt as if she were in a movie. She was struck by the decor in the gigantic, dilapidated colonial house. There was a huge chandelier draped in cobwebs; above it rays of sunlight forced their way through the skylight, the worn stairs gleamed from years of beeswax, the walls bore the outline of paintings that had hung there, and on the landing stood a huge grandfather clock. She cocked her ears, but outside of the humming of the sewing machine, there were no sounds that suggested the presence of other people. Carefully she turned the key. In Agatha Christie novels such rooms always contained a dead body: someone murdered with an antique letter opener or a razor-sharp ice pick. The door creaked. The room was dim, like the rest of the house, and it smelled like the toilets next to the bicycle shed at school. She pushed the door open a little farther.

"I'm asleep," said a man's voice.

She started. She'd imagined all sorts of things, but she never expected to hear a human voice. For an instant, she thought of her grandpa, but he wouldn't be kept under lock and key, which meant that there was a prisoner in the house.

"Go away and close the door."

Because Poirot never followed orders, she crept inside, closed the door, and remained motionless. She was afraid to breathe. She could hear wheezing sighs and the rotation of the fan overhead.

"I want to sleep," he said again. "Go away."

Issy stood without moving a muscle. She heard the man stir. His breathing was faster now and the gasping was becoming worse. She regretted entering the room — what if the man turned on her? Of course he was dangerous; otherwise, he wouldn't have been locked up. But the noises weren't coming any closer.

"Hands up or I'll shoot."

Her heart stood still. The first thought that went through her mind was: *He's going to kill me.* The second thought — as her heart started to beat again — was: *Don't anyone tell Daddy!* At the airport, he had taken her aside and said in a serious voice that he counted on her not to place herself in dangerous situations. "Go to Rampur," he said. "You'll be safe there." Issy sensed that the prisoner had a gun and night-vision binoculars aimed at her, and that he could see her. She raised her arms in surrender and didn't move a muscle. She heard a click, a sound familiar from films: the cocking of a gun.

"I surrender," she stammered.

"Turn on the light," the man snarled.

Issy had no idea where the light switch was, but ran her hand cautiously across the wall next to the door. She was so scared that she wouldn't have been surprised if she were suddenly bitten by a snake.

"What's taking you so long?"

"I can't find the light switch."

"It's next to the door."

In that same instant she found the switch and turned the light on. She had expected to see the murderer sitting in a leather armchair with a loaded rifle in his lap, but the man she saw was almost naked and had large scars. He was sitting in a wheelchair. There were leather bands around his lower legs and lower arms, and he was holding a bottle with a nipple. The man blinked: the sudden light bothered him. Behind him, on all the walls, hung the heads of dead animals.

"Mathilda?" There was uncertainty in his voice.

"My name is Issy."

"Not Mathilda?" He peered at her.

"No, I'm Issy. Issy Bridgwater."

"Bridgwater! Are you a Bridgwater?"

"Yes."

"Victor Bridgwater, lieutenant colonel, Fourteenth Regiment, Seventh Batallion, reporting!" He straightened his back. She noticed that the leather bands limited his movements but that he was still able to move his hands and lower arms.

"I think I'm your granddaughter." She said it hesitantly, since she couldn't believe that this strange man was really her grandfather.

"All the children are dead."

"Well, I'm not dead."

"You're not a child."

"No, I'm not. I'm nineteen."

The general stared at her in disbelief.

"I turned nineteen four weeks ago," she said emphatically.

"What are you doing here?"

"I'm on vacation."

"Vacations are for losers."

"I've finished school and this trip is my graduation present from my parents before I go to college."

"Girls can't go to college. Where's my bedpan?"

Issy picked up the bedpan that was under the table and handed it to her grandfather.

"This one?"

He nodded but did not take it. "I'm hungry."

"The butler said he's serving lunch at two o'clock."

"He can't cook."

"Oh."

"Everything's nasty and revolting. Pure poison. No one can live on trash like that. I want meat. A big piece of meat. Venison, swine, or even beef. I haven't eaten in days. They're starving me, that's what they're doing: starving me until I tell them who I am." Then his voice dropped. He spoke softly, looking around as if he was afraid someone was eavesdropping on him. "But I'm not going to tell them, not even if I have to bite off my little finger, I won't tell them, they'll never force me to give in. Not me. Never. I'm no coward!" He was panting.

It was not until then that Issy saw that there were also leather bands around his feet. "What are you doing here?" He had followed her gaze. "You see? I can't move, I'm tied down, they've chained me, they're afraid I'll escape, it's as if I'm an animal."

Issy was shocked. She looked at the head of a tiger that hung on the wall behind him. It had murderous incisors, and she thought it looked a little like her grandfather.

"But I'll escape, I always manage to escape, they can't keep me here, not again, I'm not afraid, I won't tell them my name, not even if they cut out my tongue or shoot my eyes out of my head, like they did with the others."

Issy took a step backwards. The only manacled prisoners she'd ever seen were on the confrontational Amnesty

International posters that hung in the cafés near her school. Was it possible that her aunt and the butler had managed to handcuff him? Was he dangerous, and were they making sure he wouldn't escape? Or were there things happening in this house that had to be kept secret? Why was the door locked? Her father had explained to her that her grandfather's memory wasn't good, and she mustn't be surprised if he didn't immediately know who she was. But that he was being held prisoner and starved was something her father didn't know. She decided she would free him and help him escape. Or would it be better to wait until Aunt Charlotte came home and then confront her? Her grandfather was panting, visibly exhausted by his outburst. He brought the bottle to his lips and began to suck. Issy put down the pot, which she was still holding, and looked at the grey-haired old man. He was making loud sucking noises now. Although the wheelchair was positioned directly under the fan, his entire body was gleaming with sweat and the small bulb on the ceiling was encircled by tiny moths. Why didn't they go for walks with him? She wouldn't mind pushing the wheelchair, or cooking for him, she could make something he liked — she made great toasted cheese sandwiches. Maybe he'd like her to read aloud to him from a book or the newspaper. And she could ask the tailor to make a pair of trousers for him and she'd comb his hair. Old people who are forgetful sometimes enjoy singing children's songs, or she could tell him jokes and make him laugh. She'd never met her grandfather before, although she'd seen photos. She had always pictured him as tall and strong, and her father had told her that during the war he had performed acts of great valour in the jungle in Burma, and was the recipient of prestigious honours and awards. Her father told her that her grandfather could polish off a three-kilo leg of lamb all by himself, and knock back a whole bottle of whisky without getting drunk, and that he always wore black boots you could hear all over the house, and that all the servants — and there were close to forty of them — were terrified of him, and that in his entire life he had never shed a tear.

"Grandfather?"

He pulled the nipple out of his mouth and said, "Yes?"

"Did you shoot those animals?" She pointed to the heads of the animals on the wall behind him. She saw that he was searching deep in his memory, but in vain. Embarrassed, he shrugged his shoulders.

"Would you like me to read something aloud?"

"They've taken my glasses away."

"Who?"

"They." He gestured toward the wall opposite him.

Issy followed his forefinger but saw only a large nail in the wall.

"They, they, they . . ." Suddenly he was gripped by panic. He searched desperately for words. "They took . . . they . . . they . . ."

"What, Grandfather? What's the matter?"

He began to tremble violently and his head swung back and forth from left to right.

Issy put her hand gently on his shoulder. She jumped: his damp skin wasn't warm to the touch, but cold.

He was gasping for breath, and before she knew what was happening, she received a hard blow to her abdomen.

She jumped backwards and cried out in pain.

"It's you! You've got it!" His lower arms were waving in all directions. The bottle flew through the air and smashed into the large wardrobe. "You stole it. You're no better than the others. Filthy liar! A thief, that's what you are. A sneaky rat. Bowing and scraping, and giving me the old soft soap, but all the time conniving against me. I saw you. I'm not crazy. That would suit you, wouldn't it? You've robbed me of everything. I don't even have a pair of trousers to my name!" He looked around for something else he could throw at her, but everything was beyond his reach except for the steel pot. He grabbed it and threw it at the girl, spitting the words in her face: "Give it back! I want it back!" The empty pot landed on the floor with a crash. Issy was frightened out of her wits by his sudden fit of blind rage. She didn't know what to do.

"Witch, vixen, slut, whore, tramp!"

The door flew open and Charlotte stormed in. She was startled to see Issy standing there, looking as though she was about to burst into tears. She picked up the plastic bottle, automatically wiping the nipple clean as she walked over to the bed. "Hush now, Father, hush now. Everything's going to be all right."

"She stole my watch!" He sobbed and pointed to Issy. "My watch."

"No, she didn't, Father."

"Then where . . ." He pointed to the nail on the wall where the watch usually hung. "It's gone."

"No, Father, it's here." Charlotte opened her hand, revealing the large gold watch. "It was in the bathroom."

Issy looked from her aunt to the door of the bathroom and then back to the watch in her hand. She had no idea where the watch had suddenly come from, but she knew for sure it hadn't come from the bathroom.

The old man in the wheelchair began to cry, and Charlotte

hung the watch back on its nail. "Look, now everything is all right."

Tears ran down his cheeks as she put the nipple back into his mouth.

"Are you comfortable?"

Charlotte took a cloth and wiped the tears and sweat from his face. She patted his face dry, and then his forehead, shoulders, chest, and legs. Her hand went over the leather belt, checking to see that it wasn't too tight. She looked over her shoulder at Issy, who was watching in silence: her aunt, whom she had shortly before suspected of maltreatment, was down on her knees, lovingly drying her father's feet. "Sometimes he forgets that he can't walk," Charlotte said in a low voice. She felt the eyes boring a hole in her back.

"I thought . . ." Issy searched for words.

Charlotte knew what her niece thought and had no desire to hear it spelled out. Issy hoped that her aunt would never find out that she had been about to call the police and ask them to free her grandfather.

"Why don't you go downstairs? I'll be right there," Charlotte said softly.

Issy was glad to leave the dismal, gloomy room. On the landing, the dusty chandelier and the ticking of the clock brought her back to the present. She looked at the old clock and remembered one Christmas Eve when her father told her the story of her great-great-grandparents, who crossed the Himalayas in a snowstorm carrying the clock. For the first time, she believed the story, which according to her mother was just something her father had dreamt up.

Suddenly Charlotte heard that her father's breathing had changed. His cantankerous outburst had made way for a kind of wistful nostalgia. She looked into his face and saw that he was following her with a sad look in his eyes.

"May I ask you something?" she said.

The general nodded and pulled the nipple out of his mouth.

"Do you know who I am?"

"Yes."

"Who?"

"You never believe me."

"Sometimes it's difficult."

"Did you have the watch?"

"Yes."

"Why?"

"Because there's no more money."

"What about our pensions?"

"They don't amount to anything now."

"The savings account?"

"Empty."

"The box in the secret drawer of my desk?"

"Gone."

"Peter's lampshade?"

"Sold."

"All the stones?"

"Yes."

Father and daughter looked at each other. Charlotte had no idea how long the moment would last, but she knew that she would have to act quickly, while he had a lucid moment.

"All we have is this house, the clock, and your watch."

"Then we'll have to sell the house. It's a rotten house anyway: much too hot and the electricity keeps conking out."

Charlotte knew that at any moment he could slip back

into that intangible world that she was not a part of, so she opened the desk drawer and took out a piece of paper.

"It stinks, and I'm pretty sure there's wood rot, too. At night I hear the beetles gnawing on the rafters, the paper is falling off the walls, the water pipes wheeze, and it's a miracle that I haven't fallen through the floor yet."

She put a thick book on his lap and on top of it the piece of paper. While he went on running the house down, she put a pen in his hand. "Father, if you'll sign here, I can sell the house and see to it that you get a better room."

The general looked from the paper to his daughter.

Charlotte felt the drops of sweat running down her back. She'd never got this far before. During her last attempt, he had gone into a fit of rage when she produced the power of attorney, accusing her of collaborating with the Japs, while the time before that he had broken out in sobs, claiming that she didn't love him anymore. Once he'd cursed her and broken the pen in two, and another time he had simply fallen asleep, and when he woke up, the strange fantasies and delusions had taken possession of him again.

Calmly, he began to read the paper. Charlotte knew that she must not hurry him. The slightest encroachment upon his concentration could lead him to some inaccessible byway in his grey matter. She stood beside him motionless. Sweat ran in rivulets down her entire body, trickled into her eyes, made her neck itch. She looked at her father, the piece of paper in his hand, his lifeless legs, the dented chamber pot at his feet, the colourless wardrobe, and the stuffed animal heads on the wall, which had been ravaged by moths.

He coughed and said softly, "You did a good job of writing it down. Where do you want me to sign?"

She pointed to the bottom of the page. He muttered, "Better to do it quickly, otherwise this hovel won't be worth anything."

Mesmerized, she nodded and stared at the tip of the pen as he signed his name with a firm hand.

"Thank you." She took the paper and the book from his knees and the pen from his hand.

"Give that back."

"What?"

"That book."

"Do you want to read it?"

"What else would I want with a book?"

She handed him the book. He opened it and ran his eyes across the page. She saw that he was holding it upside-down.

1944 Burma

THE FIRST RAYS of sun creep through the dense layer of foliage that forms the roof. The wavering light reveals that the soldiers are still sitting in a circle, facing each other. In the middle of the circle lies the swollen, rotting body of the young soldier. Major Victor Bridgwater looks at the captain directly opposite him. Yesterday the man spent the whole day tearing the fabric of the trousers taken from the dead soldier's body into strips, which he used to bind up the feet of his three subordinates. Their feet were torn and bloody, and he wiped them clean before bandaging them. The captain's eyes are closed, but Victor knows that he's not asleep. No one is asleep. The atmosphere in the camp is restless. The Japs walk back and forth, carrying crates and sticks. Victor has no idea what they're preparing for, but it's clear that today is going to be different from the previous days.

FOR HOURS THE sun has poured down from high in the sky, torturing the men with its rays. Their thirst has remained unquenched. The pan of water that was shoved into the circle smells the same as the corpse lying in front of them — anyone who tried to drink it immediately puked it out again.

A whistle sounds. Japs come running from all directions. In the shadow of the trees, they line up in a straight row. Victor and the other prisoners remain where they are. There is another blast of the whistle and one of the Japs shouts something. They look at each other. Then the captain stands up. Like the others, he has been sitting on the ground for days, and getting to his feet is painful. One by one, the men stand up. The gate is opened and a small Jap with a stick walks over to the five British soldiers. He seems about to stop in front of Victor, but he keeps going until he's standing in front of the captain.

"*Name?*"

Peter hasn't used his voice in days. After the Japs caught on to their secret language, no one dared utter a word. They communicated by means of furtive glances. His tongue is stuck to the roof of his mouth, and his jaws are paralyzed by thirst. With his last bit of strength, he forces out an almost inaudible "Harris."

"You captain?" the man screeches.

Peter looks at the older British soldier opposite him, whose name and rank he doesn't know. The tattered remains of his uniform provide no clues to whether he is also a captain or perhaps even higher in rank. Peter remembers the day they arrived, when his first thought was that the man wasn't just a soldier. He held himself differently and radiated authority. But after Benjamin was shot dead and darkness fell, all of that was gone, and in the days that followed he remained huddled motionless, looking around nervously. "I cannot answer that question," Peter replies.

He feels a sharp jab in his back and he is ordered to walk in front of the Jap toward one of the huts under the trees. Inside there is nothing but a chair. The Jap man seats himself.

Torture is something Peter has always refused to think about. During his medical studies he learned that the human body is a highly vulnerable mechanism, and that even with the aid of the most advanced techniques and medication, not every patient can be saved. In New Delhi, where he works alongside the country's best physicians, they have only one goal, and that is to cure the patient. Not to shatter, burn, or desiccate. Not to twist, strike, or kick. Not to pierce, flay, and humiliate. After five hours in the hut, he is thrown back into the enclosure, next to the decomposed body of the soldier. A hoard of flies descend on him and lick his blood. When one of his men gets to his feet to help him, there's a shot and he falls to the ground dead.

PETER HASN'T SLEPT, but he has failed to notice that night is over. He feels how the sun discovers his body. He wants something to drink, no matter if it's poisoned or polluted. His mouth is full of sand, there's dust in his nose, it hurts to breathe, and his feet are on fire. He is convinced that none of his organs are in their normal place, and every square inch of his skin is black and blue. He cannot move. He drifts back into the night.

A Jap screams, "Stand up!"

Peter feels a kick in his side. He is dragged to his feet and they hang a heavy backpack on his shoulders. The smell of death and destruction pervades the camp. The couple of soldiers who until now were inside the enclosure are standing side by side. He can just manage to see his men through his bruised and swollen eyelids. They are staring at him in shock. He realizes that they have not been bashed about in the same way that he has. Then he sees that behind each of the three British soldiers there is a Jap with a gun trained at the man in front of him. He is the only one who doesn't have a gun aimed at him.

"Hunger?" The little Jap with the stick is now standing in front of him.

For Peter, hunger is a forgotten sensation. A luxurious notion that no longer enters his mind.

"Hunger!"

The diminutive Jap slams the stick into Peter's knee pits and he falls on his face in the sand.

"Stand!" he shouts. "Or all dead."

Peter manages to get to his feet, despite the heavy backpack.

"Eat!" the man shouts in Peter's ear.

Noise causes no pain either. Everything in him and on him is numb, anaesthetized. He doesn't understand how he is still able to stand. What does the man want from him? No one has eaten for days. Or had anything to drink. *If you're trying to starve me to death, you're too late,* he thinks. *I'm already dead.*

"You eat . . . everybody free."

Peter doesn't understand what the man means. What is he supposed to eat? And why? He doesn't want to eat. He's not hungry. *Go ahead, aim your gun. Then it'll all be over,* he thinks to himself.

The Jap faces him and gestures to the three men. He points to each of their terrified faces. Peter sees his comrades. They are all that's left of the group that lost its way. They still have the lengths of fabric that he made for them. They are all looking at him, imploring him. His glance goes to the older British soldier, the man who's never exchanged glances with anyone. But now those eyes are screaming in fear. What should he do? What is expected of him?

"Hand," says the little Jap. "Eat hand."

Peter sees the terror in the men's eyes. Is he supposed to eat their hands? He looks at the trembling, emaciated hands, hanging helplessly at their sides. They all still have their hands.

The Jap slams his swagger stick hard against his other hand. He raises his arm. For an instant Peter expects to see a stump, but his hand is still connected to his arm.

"Eat! Or man dead."

The Jap gives his men a sign. There are clicks, a sound Peter is all too familiar with.

"EAT! Now!"

Peter stares at his hand. As a throat surgeon he doesn't know much about hands, except that a hand consists largely of bones and tendons, not flesh. You couldn't eat a hand, not even if you wanted to.

A shot sounds. Alex, the young soldier first class with the stories about long-legged beauties, lies motionless on the ground. Peter sees that there is blood coming out of his ear. Two pairs of terror-stricken eyes plead with him. He wants to shout that he can't eat his hand, that he wishes he could but that he can't, that it's impossible, that even if they chopped his hand off, he couldn't eat it. Another shot sounds. Marcus, the lieutenant who knew dozens of Jap jokes and recounted them with relish, falls down dead.

The older soldier looks in panic as the man next to him slumps to the ground, and screams: "EAT!"

Peter lifts up his hand. He looks at it as if he's seeing it for the first time. Everything is quiet. Even the jungle forgets to make a sound. A smile appears on the Jap's face. Then, with his right hand, Peter brings his left hand to his mouth. He doesn't know where to start, how to start . . . he's never even bitten his nails. His fingers glide one by one through his mouth, searching for the weakest spot. He stops when he gets to the little finger. He bites into his own flesh. It is not his hand. It isn't even a hand. It's a chicken drumstick, the way his mother used to make them, pan-fried and with a nice brown skin. He can smell it. He can taste it. His mouth waters. He hears his mother ask if he wants another one, because it's his favourite dish. The bone is thicker than he's used to. He transfers it to his back teeth. The smell of the chicken is intoxicating. His jaws tense. He feels that he has to exert more pressure. His father laughs and tells his mother that she shouldn't spoil the boy. He hears the bone break. The juices run into his mouth. This is the most delicious drumstick he's ever tasted. He brings it to his mouth and tears off the skin with his teeth. His father begins to laugh hysterically. He falls forward and the voices cease.

1946 New Delhi ~

CHARLOTTE HANGS THE green silk evening dress that the maharaja's tailor made for her in the closet, alongside Peter's gala uniform. She felt quite proud when she walked into the huge marble hall on Peter's arm. Above her head the colossal chandeliers dispersed their twinkling light. Along the walls, beneath the paintings of the forefathers of the maharaja, stood the servants in their gold-coloured uniforms, bowing their heads low as they passed. Charlotte felt like a princess, and she had no idea why the wife of the maharaja made such a fuss because she was the first to see the newborn son. Peter had told her not to worry about it, since the maharaja had confided to him in private that it was the fault of his daughter Chutki, who should never have left Charlotte alone. But she finds it difficult to banish the shrieks of the nurse who held the newborn in her arms. The furious sobs of the mother who damned her son because she, a British subject, had seen him first. Nor does she understand why the servant she had taken on earlier that week refused to wash her clothes together with those of Peter, and always placed their shoes so that the toes were facing north.

"Those are the secrets of India," Peter says.

"No, it's superstition," Charlotte retorts.

"It's one of the things that make living in India so special," he says. "Nothing is what it seems, everything turns out differently than you expected." He walks over to where she's standing and takes her hand. His forefinger strokes her ring finger. "If my afternoon at the hospital goes the way I hope, then I'll be home early and we can finally buy our rings." He embraces her in an effort to banish her worries.

"You'd better go." Charlotte pushes him away. "Otherwise you'll be late and I'll never get my ring."

SHE CASTS A worried look at her watch. Peter should have been home by now. Perhaps an emergency has come in? Or the operation has lasted longer than expected? The newspaper is lying next to the chair, but she hopes he won't try to read it before they leave for the jeweller's. Her hand feels bare without a wedding ring, and the ladies at the club look askance at her ringless finger. Even among the servants she senses a certain disapproval. She reaches for the newspaper and impatiently swings her foot up and down. An article in bold letters on the front page catches her eye:

WAR HERO HONOURED

> Lieutenant Colonel Victor Bridgwater was this morning awarded the Distinguished Service Order, one of the highest military honours, reserved for soldiers who have displayed exceptional courage in defence of the British Empire during encounters with the enemy. Lieutenant Colonel Bridgwater received the award for his uncommonly brave opposition to the Japanese in the Burmese jungle.

Her father a war hero? What does she actually know about him? She has no idea what he did during the war, where he was stationed, or who his enemies and friends were.

Peter comes into the room, smiling. He kisses her and apologizes for being late.

Charlotte proudly presents him with the newspaper. "Look! My father is a hero."

Peter starts to read. She sees how he stiffens, how the smile disappears and a grey pallor comes over his face.

"What's wrong?"

He shakes his head. He tries to smile, but the grimace that appears on his face is bitter and hard.

"It's in the newspaper . . . ," she says with a questioning look.

The soft gleam in his eyes fades. His lips tighten.

"Then it must be true, mustn't it?"

He nods.

THEY'RE SITTING OPPOSITE each other at the table. Her plate is empty. His plate is untouched. She looks at his hands, on either side of his plate. They're twitching slightly. The absence of his little finger is something she has hardly noticed — until now. The wound is redder and swollen. It is as if something has taken possession of him. Something she has no knowledge of. She must write to her father, ask him what on earth happened during his time in Burma. Otherwise, she realizes, she'll never wear a wedding ring.

1995 Rampur ~

"I'M LOOKING FOR something small, more like this house." Charlotte stood in the middle of Sita's living room and looked around. Never before had she examined the house, which she knew so well, in such detail. The moment her father signed his name on the document, it was as if everything had changed. The barren trees were less barren, the heat was less intense, she had a biscuit with her tea, and even her lovesickness seemed less impossible. "Maybe I'll leave Rampur."

"Where would you go?" Sita was slicing a tomato, and the dal bubbled behind her, filling the house with a delectable smell.

"I don't know. Maybe a place where the sun doesn't always shine."

"Are you staying for dinner?"

"I have to get back. Donald's daughter is visiting."

"Yes, so I've heard. Everyone's talking about her. I thought: another guest for dinner. You won't forget to eat?"

Charlotte hugged the tiny woman whom she considered her mother, friend, and sister all at once.

"Mama?" called a cheerful male voice.

The two women stared at each other as if they'd both been stung by a wasp. The intimate atmosphere between them vanished. They both spun around with a jerk and looked at the door. Parvat came in, wearing his light-brown uniform with the gleaming metal buttons, kicked off his boots, but forgot to remove his yellow helmet.

"Aunt Charlotte!" he said in surprise.

He knelt down in front of her and respectfully touched her feet. Then he hugged Sita. Charlotte would rather have had a bear hug, too — his big body pressed against hers, so she could let him know how much she loved him. He opened the fridge in search of something to snack on, but his mother was already preparing a plate for him.

"You'll have to wait a bit for the *paneer.*"

"Are you staying for dinner, Aunt Charlotte?"

"No, I should be going. My niece is here."

"Yes, so I've heard. The guys at the station think that the wind started to turn when she got here. They say it's going to rain."

"Wouldn't that be marvellous!"

"They say she brings luck."

Could Issy really bring luck? Charlotte wondered as she climbed the hill leading back to the big house. It was true that her father had finally signed the power of attorney document, and that Hema went around whistling despite the suffocating heat, and that she felt younger than she had in years. Even the apple tree seemed to anticipate the arrival of the monsoon. She walked past the *mali*'s shed and turned the corner. At the bottom of the steps she saw a long line of parked cars, including the 1957 Ambassador belonging to widow Singh. The front door was wide open. Even from a distance she could hear the wrangling. She ran up the broad stone stairs two steps at a time, noticing the chips and cracks.

In the hall, halfway up the stairs, stood the wife of Nikhil Nair in a bright pink sari, visibly agitated and dripping with perspiration. From her elevated position she spoke to the women, gesturing in the direction of the closed door to the music room. Everyone nodded, and there was a forbidding mumble of agreement. In the hall Hema looked around in a panic, uncertain what to do with the tray filled with glasses of water. He finally picked up a glass and emptied it in one gulp.

"It's just like a real strike, isn't it?" said a voice coming from the drawing room.

Charlotte looked into the room. On the floor, next to the socket, sat Issy, surrounded by a pile of plugs and leads. She grinned at her aunt.

"Let's break open the door!" cried the wife of Nikhil Nair, waving her hands in the air.

"Has he run off?" squeaked the portly wife of the manufacturer of coconut oil.

"He's barricaded the door!" blared widow Singh, who was not asleep for once.

"We don't have to take this lying down!" screeched the wife of Adeeb Tata, who despite her expensive Parisian dress had also delivered a length of silk to the interesting tailor everyone was so taken with.

"My gold brocade dress . . . ," wailed the wife of Ajay Karapiet, who for several nights had dreamt of tripping the light fantastic in her black pumps.

Even the wife of Alok Nath raised her voice, although her contribution was drowned out by the desperate cries of the others.

Charlotte went to the door of the music room and pushed down on the handle, but the door did not open. She knew for certain that she had not given him the key. It was still on her own key ring, and since the last of the rubies on the lampshade had been sold, it was no longer necessary to lock the door.

Where are you? she called in her thoughts, but the ladies were making so much noise that she couldn't hear a thing.

The wife of Nikhil Nair beckoned her. Charlotte had no intention of obeying the summons, and remained near the door of the music room. She called: *Can you hear me? What's going on? Answer me!*

"We want the key!" shouted the wife of Nikhil Nair.

Charlotte strained to hear if an answer was forthcoming, and failed to see the furious looks launched in her direction by the portly pink woman descending the stairs. Taking steps that were far too big for her sari, the wife of the district director of the Eastern Indian Mining Company headed straight for her target. Her forehead was wet and circles of perspiration were forming under her arms. The ladies of the Tuesday-morning club made way for her.

Wheezing from the exertion, she stood before Charlotte and held up her hand. "Do you have the key?" she demanded.

"Of course I have the key," said Charlotte amiably. "This is my house and I have keys to all the rooms."

"Then open this door!"

"No, I don't intend to open the door. I've rented out this room."

"To a swindler!" she shouted back.

"Yes, to a swindler!" echoed someone from the back of the group.

"To the tailor who for weeks has been working day and night for all of you."

"The ball is tomorrow! We want our clothes!"

"And we want them NOW!"

"I still have to pick out my shoes."

"I don't know which necklace goes with my dress."

"I can't buy my earrings yet."

"I want to choose a new colour of lipstick."

"At the fitting my collar wasn't quite right."

"I can't remember the colour of my dress."

HE WAS ALMOST finished. The crushed mimosa leaves had been sewn into the hem of the dress destined for the wife of Nikhil Nair. The flowers of the teak tree had only been found early that morning and ironed into the shoulder pads of the blouse he'd made for the secretary's wife. He'd cut the leaves of the cinnamon tree into thin strips and sewn them into the seams of the gown he made for the painfully shy woman. The mixture of dried forget-me-nots and marigolds was destined for the dress of the woman who'd lost a son, while the bust of the wife of the coconut oil manufacturer was sprinkled with ground petunia seeds. All he had to do now was to sew the stamens of the wild orchid into the neck of the dress he'd made for the wife of Ajay Karapiet. He heard the pounding on the door. He tried not to listen to the chaos in the hall, since a mistake could have disastrous consequences for the wearer. He had shoved the cabinet in front of the door when he heard the women storming up the staircase. He was surprised when the manoeuvre proved successful. There were so many cobwebs behind the cabinet that it looked as if hadn't been moved in the last hundred years. In the hall outside, the shouting grew louder, and the cabinet shook from the blows that rained down on the other side of the door. Now and then he heard Charlotte's faint voice. He had to finish the very last seam. Like all the others, it was executed lovingly and with great precision.

CHARLOTTE STOOD IN front of the door with her arms outstretched. She was determined that they would not enter the music room, but she wasn't sure how long she could keep up the barricade. The perspiring women clearly had no plans to leave.

"We're going to call in the police," shouted the wife of Adeeb Tata, a distant cousin of the fabulously wealthy Ratan Tata. The fact that she had not yet paid for the fabric was conveniently forgotten.

"They'll arrest him and return our property," the wife of Nikhil Nair predicted. She held her arms close to her body, since the wife of Ajay Karapiet had whispered in her ear that she had sweat stains under her arms.

Charlotte searched desperately for a solution that would prevent things from escalating still further. "Have you knocked on the door?"

The women looked at each other. The wife of Ajay Karapiet shook her head, abashed. One by one, they all lowered their eyes. Except for the wife of Nikhil Nair, who couldn't bear being corrected. She mopped her brow and rapped briskly on the door.

The door swung open and Madan greeted them with a welcoming wave of his hand.

Even by the light of the lone bulb, the room was a fairy-tale palace. On the walls hung the most gorgeous gowns. The women were overwhelmed by the sight of such beauty. There were sighs of disbelief and admiration. Madan took the gold brocade gown from the wall. The wife of Ajay Karapiet began to glow with pleasure: it was as if she were already wearing the dress. With a flourish, he flung it onto the table, where it came to rest in graceful folds. Charlotte thought she saw the radiant woman perform a pirouette. They all held their breath. Madan took the tails of the skirt and folded them inward. The wife of Ajay Karapiet could feel his fingertips running across her skin. He wrapped the garment in crisp paper and handed it to her with a bow. She looked at him admiringly, and clutched the package tightly to her bosom. She was sure she could smell wild orchids.

Next Madan picked up the gown ordered by the woman whose husband owned the coconut mill. She, too, underwent a metamorphosis when she saw her dress: it made her bosom seem to rise upward and outward, becoming infinitely more attractive. He wrapped the garment in paper and presented it to her. She clasped it in her arms as if it were a newborn baby.

One by one, Madan brought the gowns down from the wall and wrapped them carefully in paper. Sometimes a moan or murmur was heard, or a muffled sigh of longing, but otherwise everything was deathly quiet.

Without a word, the women departed, anxiously clutching their new garments to their chests or hiding them in the folds of their saris, since no one wanted the others to see her gown beforehand.

They faced each other. Except for the cabinet, which was still at an angle, there were no traces of the recent turmoil. The sewing machine was on the table with his scissors beside it, and on a chair against the wall lay the pile of fabrics that had belonged to Charlotte's mother, carefully folded, with the scarlet silk on top.

To Charlotte, the fabric was as intensely ablaze as her heart.

To Madan, the material was bleeding as profusely as his heart.

"And that's the material you're going to use for my dress, right?" Issy was standing in the door opening and pointing to the red fabric.

Charlotte looked from Issy to the length of silk. Was this why she had risen at daybreak to mow the lawn, rejected suitors deemed unsuitable, reluctantly spent her childhood at boarding schools in the cold English climate, and been locked in a closet for sampling her mother's perfume? Why she had spoon-fed her father and wiped his bottom after he pooped, read edifying books forced upon her by Reverend Das, repaired and remodelled all her dresses until they wore out, turned penny-pinching into an art form, searched for her mother's hand in the folds of her skirt but seldom found it, sold her grand piano and made do with an imaginary keyboard, buried her husband next to her mother, written to her brother for years without ever receiving a reply, taken all the burdens on her own shoulders without ever a thank-you? Why she had allowed herself to be swindled by second-hand dealers who paid next to nothing because they knew she had to sell, listened to the eternal gossip dished up by the wife of Nikhil Nair so as not to be alone, run a household without the necessary personnel, devoted her youth to a man who was damaged by the war, refused invitations to parties because women didn't go to parties on their own, and after the one time she did go to a party, given birth to her child in a bleak convent in the Himalayas, so that no one would know about it, had a son who didn't know she was his mother, and for years spent every Monday afternoon playing with him like a doting auntie? Why she had never cried because a Bridgwater doesn't cry, suffered hunger pangs so that others could eat, rolled the carpet out and back up a thousand times so it wouldn't wear and become less valuable, cared for her father alone because he'd driven all the nurses crazy, lost her pension because no one told her that it would be frozen if she gave up her British citizenship, never known love and for that reason was the object of gossip and slander, cycled to the club in the heat, stopped smoking because people held that women shouldn't smoke, fallen in love with impossible, unobtainable men, which was why she had to lie to be believed, peered in from the outside because she didn't dare to enter, endured endless floods of abuse and tried not to be hurt, stolen from her father because he no longer understood her, and suffered guests she hadn't invited? Was that why she was resigned to the fact that everyone had forgotten her?

"No," she said, "the red fabric is for my dress."

1977 Hyderabad ~

THE RAIN IS pouring down. Madan doesn't like rain. People walk fast and don't give anything. In the past few years he's learned a lot about begging. And yet he calls himself not a beggar, but a tailor. All the money he doesn't need for food is set aside, so he can buy his own sewing machine. Whether he'll actually make it is something he prefers not to think about. Every morning he wakes up with the thought that it may be his lucky day. After all, he has already managed to buy a new spool with what he's earned by begging.

An umbrella comes sailing by — no doubt swept from someone's hands by the heavy rain — and he just manages to grab it. No one is looking for the umbrella, so he holds it above his head. Actually, he should try to find a more sheltered spot, since the rain is now bucketing down. He watches as the churning water seeks a path to the drains, which are becoming clogged by the accompanying rubbish. Madan crosses the street. The water comes up to his ankles now. He feels his slippers being snatched from his feet, but he grabs them in time, and wades farther in his bare feet.

The banknotes that he's collected in all these years are safely stored in three small plastic bags tied around his waist. There is also a piece of paper that says that he is looking for work, as well as the snippets of paper, now pasted together, that bear the address of Dr. Krishna Kumar. Not that he will ever go back there, but he cannot bring himself to throw the paper away. It is one of the few things from his past that he still has.

Madan walks into the alleyway where he's been sleeping, but the water is up to his knees. He sees that the piece of cardboard that had served as his bed has disappeared. A hard gust of wind snatches the umbrella out of his hands. He doesn't bother to watch it disappear, since the rain is now lashing him in the face. He was hoping to take refuge in the house where he was allowed to wash himself a few times, but he sees that the door is barricaded with sand sacks. The rain hurts, and the wind, which is becoming stronger and stronger, almost knocks him off his feet. *I have to find a place to shelter,* he thinks. He's afraid of the steadily rising tide of water gushing through the streets.

There are only one or two people battling the wind and rain, which are now increasing in force. His clothes are soaked through, and they slap against his body as the thundering power of the wind threatens to blow him away. On the other side of the street he sees a bowed old man clutching a small package. Suddenly the man is blown clear off his feet by the wind and disappears underwater.

Madan doesn't hesitate. Forgetting the wind, he takes giant steps over to the spot where he saw the greybeard disappear. Then something slides past his feet. The suction force of the water is enormous, and he's being pulled away. He bends down, feels around in the water, and pulls out a gasping and sputtering little man; the man is still holding the package in his hand. He weighs next to nothing, but Madan has to keep a firm grip on him so that the wind doesn't snatch him away. Madan throws him onto his back like a sack of flour. It takes all his strength to escape from the eddying maelstrom, but somehow he manages to reach the houses. He grabs one of the bars in front of a window and inches his way along, one step at a time. He finally discovers an open portico with a staircase. The water has now risen at least a metre. He climbs up the steps and lays the man, who is now coughing, on the floor next to him. Madan pats him cautiously on the back with the flat of his hand, for fear he might break.

After a bout of sputtering and coughing, the old man catches his breath again and is able to sit up alongside him. "I seem to have swallowed the wrong way," he squeaks. "I just hope it isn't damaged," he continues in a panicky voice. He tears away the paper, revealing an old book. "I must dry it. Now. Otherwise, the pages will stick together."

Madan motions toward the rain, which continues to come thundering down, obscuring their view of the street.

"But at least I've found it at last. It was missing for years."

Madan looks at the man next to him. There's something familiar about him . . . his voice? Or is it his hands? The nervous gestures . . . Then he recognizes him. He's much greyer and more stooped, and his face is full of wrinkles, but outside of that, he hasn't changed. It's Mister Patel. He wants to give him a hug. Never before has he been reunited with someone from his past, and he regards his old prison mate as family. Enthusiastically, Madan points to his face, but Mr. Patel is so flustered because his book is all wet that he doesn't notice. Then Madan takes the old man's hand in his own two wet hands, brings the gnarled old hand up to his forehead.

Mister Patel stops in the middle of his sentence. He stares, peers, screws up his eyes. Searches his memory.

Madan moves his lips, and gestures that he cannot speak.

"Son," whispers Mister Patel.

They're sitting next to each other on the stairs. The lashing rain is still bucketing down, and the wind is gaining in force. Mister Patel is silent. Madan has the book *Genetic*

Metamorphosis in Single-Celled Organisms on his lap. He blows gently between the pages before turning over the next one.

"Do you still pray?"

Madan nods.

"I don't. I'm afraid to."

Madan turns another page and blows onto a drawing of a paramecium.

"I should never have left you behind. I didn't even know who that man was. I went back, but you were gone. Where were you? Where have you been?"

How can Madan tell the old man about the years in Mister Chandran's weaving factory? Or his lessons on the hidden power of spices, flowers, and trees, his crush on Mister Chandran's daughter, his friendship with Subhash, the oiler, or the years he spent in Dr. Krishna Kumar's atelier? He pulls the new spool out of his pocket and shows it to Mister Patel.

"You're a tailor?"

Madan nods.

"Where?"

Madan stares at the rain, an army made up of millions of arrows boring into the ground. He understands Mister Patel, he understands why he left. He has never blamed him.

Mister Patel puts his arm around him. "Will you come home with me, my son?"

Then Madan also puts an arm around the fragile old man. Together they stare out at the rain.

1995 Rampur ~

MADAN SPREAD THE red silk on the table. The windows and shutters were open, but the sought-after cool of the evening failed to glide over the windowsill and into the room. Charlotte was sitting in the chair against the wall, watching him. Tiny droplets of perspiration gleamed on his forehead. Up until then he had seemed impervious to the heat. A measuring tape hung around his neck. Without taking her measurements, without even looking at her, he took the scissors to the fabric, like a slender boat slicing through the glassy surface of a lake. The scissors navigated, cutting lines and curves. The table was turned into a map full of red islands. Outside, crickets chirped, and in the living room Isabella complained loudly about her telephone, which was still giving her problems. Slowly Charlotte became aware of the distant sound of a fire engine siren racing past. Her heart missed a beat. She never knew whether Parvat was on duty or not. The monsoon would have to start pretty soon. Each successive day increased the chance of fires. Both trees and houses were dry as dust. There was not a drop of moisture in the entire city. The wood lice and other vermin that favoured clammy surroundings had buried themselves so deep in the earth that people were convinced they wouldn't reappear for at least a year.

We'll have to put the buckets outside. Then the rain will come.

Do you really believe that?

It's not just me . . . everyone believes it. Haven't you seen all the bowls and buckets?

She had seen the pots and pans in front of Sita's house and in the narrow streets leading to her house. She got up, still looking doubtful. But as she walked out of the house, she thought, *Why not? If only to ensure that Parvat does not die in a fire.*

THE LIGHT WAS on in the kitchen, but Hema was nowhere to be seen. On the shelf above the sink she found a stack of nested pans, and on the floor stood two bright green plastic buckets. She knew that he'd be upset if she borrowed a pan or bucket from his kitchen without asking, so she headed for the *mali*'s shed. Just as she was about to go in, Madan emerged carrying a pile of battered zinc buckets. He smiled and handed her one. She put it down on the ground.

No, no. You're supposed to invite them.

Who?

The rains.

He picked up the bucket and placed it on the crumbling pillar at the bottom of the stone steps leading to the front door.

Entice them.

He placed the second bucket on the opposite pillar. The architect had designed the pillars to bear statues, but the statues had never materialized.

And on the steps.

Charlotte remembered parties from the past, when a red runner was laid out on the stairs and there were two servants in blue tunics and gold-coloured berets on each step. They held plumes that flanked the approaching guests. Charlotte and Madan positioned their buckets with precision.

Yes! she heard Madan exclaim.

He ran back to the shed. There was an enormous clatter, and he emerged covered in dust and carrying another stack of pails, which they set out beside the path alongside the driveway, where torches had burned.

We're going to need more buckets, she thought, infected by his enthusiasm. More signs to line the desiccated borders, and coax the rain to break loose.

HEMA HEADED UP the hill, lugging two heavy jerry cans. He was pleased that he'd managed to buy water for the same price as yesterday, now that prices were going up almost by the hour.

From a distance, he saw the memsahib and the *darzi* running around with buckets. A huge smile appeared on his face, and the hill, which he had so often cursed, suddenly seemed as straight as an arrow. He himself hadn't dared to ask the memsahib, since he knew that she abhorred Indian superstitions, but the *darzi* had! Five years before, when the monsoon had been equally slow in coming, theirs was the only house in the neighbourhood where there were no buckets standing outside. The entire population of Rampur had been convinced that that was the reason the drought lasted a whole week longer.

Charlotte, who saw Hema carrying the heavy jerry cans, got the impression that he was upset. But she hadn't taken any of his pans or bowls. She saw him duck into the kitchen and feared that any minute he would emerge in a grouchy mood. Instead, he reappeared with the pile of pans and the two bright green plastic buckets, which he then began to place in a large circle around the kitchen.

She had no idea where he had found them all, and was amazed that there were so many objects in the house that could be used to collect water. But an hour later they were everywhere you looked: plastic and earthenware bowls, serviceable and leaky buckets, all the pots (including Hema's favourite pan and the deep-fat fryer basket no one else was allowed to touch), all the serving dishes and vases from the salon that hadn't been sold, plastic containers that had held plants, the fruit bowl, two watering cans (which were given a place of honour on either side of the door, like trophies), a cracked aquarium, a soap dish, a set of wine glasses positioned in a circle around the apple tree, a chalice that no one had ever seen before, ashtrays, jam jars, cans intended for old nails, a container for Dutch rusks that had been empty for months, a collection of rusty coal scuttles that had never been used, an aluminium mortar, a red wastepaper basket with an embroidered cover, the orange tub where the *mali* stored his herbicides, and his wheelbarrow, a colander lined with a piece of plastic, the feeding trough of a goat that had once lived on the property, the garbage cans that stood at the bottom of the path, the ash bucket without the ash, all the cups and saucers and mugs (including the one with Mickey Mouse on it), the beaker without a handle that Charlotte used for her toothbrush, a series of shot glasses that no junk dealer was interested in, a cracked toilet bowl . . . Charlotte had her doubts about the latter, but Hema and Madan figured the more the better. So she put the teapot, which had been glued back together, smack in front of the door.

They had just paused to catch their breath when Issy came out of the house — still complaining, and dragging behind her the cables she'd been fooling around with all evening.

"What on earth are you guys doing?"

"We've put all the buckets outside."

"Why?"

Confronted by her English niece, Charlotte suddenly felt quite foolish for allowing herself to be tempted by that idiotic Indian superstition. She began to redden.

"To entice the rain!" cried Hema.

Issy nodded quite seriously as she surveyed the colourful jumble of receptacles. She ran back into the house and returned with her grandfather's chamber pot. "He's wearing a diaper anyway," she said, when she saw the startled faces.

1977 Hyderabad ~

IT WAS ON the same day the violent rain and wind burgeoned into a cyclone, raging across the Krishna River delta, swallowing up villages and settlements, sweeping people along on a wave of churning water, destroying harvests, killing or carrying off ten thousand people, and making three and a half million homeless that, for the first time in his life, Madan found a home.

The tiny room is only big enough for two small tables; at one of them Mister Patel is working on his dissertation on native urban plants, and at the other Madan is using a third-hand Singer sewing machine that he was able to buy with the help of Mister Patel. On the shelf, next to the piles of books belonging to Mister Patel, there is a small box of thread, and when the door is open, there is just room enough on the floor to lay out a garment or cut fabric. Madan sweeps the floor three times a day and Mister Patel does the cooking. Although it falls far short of Dr. Krishna Kumar's atelier, to Madan it is the most beautiful workplace he has ever known.

The two men are completely absorbed in their work. Mister Patel enjoys the whirring sound of the sewing machine in the background, which calls up all manner of new insights, while Madan listens contentedly to the mutterings and sighs that accompany Mister Patel's writing, and that transport him into worlds he has never visited before. In the evening they shove the tables and stools against the wall, one on top of the other, roll out the sleeping mats, and lie down underneath, as close to one another as they were in prison.

This sheltered domesticity is in sharp contrast to the situation outside. The number of people drifting around without a place to sleep is growing by the day. All over the city, men and women sleep against buildings or among the carts on the street. They are searching for work, something to eat, and their missing loved ones. They have lost all their possessions, and some are barely clothed. Mister Patel's upstairs neighbour, widow Sethi, feels lonely and useless now that her last daughter has left to get married. She has decided to donate all of her late husband's clothes, her own leftovers, and everything left behind by her children to the homeless.

The sound of feet on the stairs is audible in Mister Patel's room. The long line of people extends from widow Sethi's front door, down the steps, past Mister Patel's door, and onto the street, right up to the baker on the corner. Everyone waits patiently.

Above their heads, the wooden floor creaks: the house has never had this many visitors at once. Mister Patel's sighs also sound different. When there's a knock at the door, he grumbles under his breath. He was just immersed in a difficult paragraph dealing with the pollen tube that leads from the grain of pollen through the pistel to the seed bud in the ovary, and he does not want to be disturbed. "Oh, Mister Patel, I'm so sorry to bother you, but it's an emergency! If I understood correctly, you have a tailor staying with you?" says widow Sethi. She is not as young as she used to be, and she's puffing slightly.

"This is my son. He's an excellent tailor," says Mister Patel, and shows her his new shirt.

"Oh! Your son! I didn't know!" Her shrill voice fills the room. "Could he possibly help me with these trousers?"

Madan gets up and goes over to where Mister Patel is standing.

"He doesn't look at all like you." She sees a deep wrinkle appear in Mister Patel's forehead, and she hastily adds, "But actually my Sarika doesn't look like me either."

Madan takes the trousers from her hand. Mister Patel sighs.

"I've pinned them — they're way too big — but the pins are so sharp and of course I don't want to prick anyone. As if those poor people don't have enough trouble as it is."

Madan motions that he's going upstairs with her. He hands her the pants, picks up his sewing machine, and ushers her gently out the door.

"Thank you, son," whispers Mister Patel, and returns to his books.

The stairs are populated by half-naked men, women, and children. Most of them are just sitting and staring in front of them; some have their eyes closed but are not asleep. Madan and widow Sethi have to crawl over them to get to the top floor.

The room is twice as large as Mister Patel's and a hundred times fuller. There are cupboards and cabinets overflowing with clothes and linens, and an array of baubles, idols, and other treasures. On and around the bed lies a display of the clothes she wants to give away. And in the corner that serves as a kitchen, there's such an assortment of plates and cups that it resembles a second-hand shop. In the middle of the room stands a shy young man wearing nothing but a torn piece of cloth around his hips. The man, who was a fisherman, has lost his family, his hut, and his boat, because his wife went to the market to sell the catch instead of him. He stands with his head bent. Madan sees at a glance that the trousers won't fit him, and points to the one table in the room, which is piled high with indefinable female garments.

"Does all that have to be moved?" sighs widow Sethi.

Madan nods. She begins by shoving the junk under her bed, where there's scarcely any room left. Madan observes the fisherman. It was not that long ago that Madan himself was living on the street and had nothing. Now he's holding his pride and joy, a Singer sewing machine, in his hands. With great care, he places it on the table. The widow hands him a stool and flops down on the pile of clothes on her bed. The fisherman is still staring at his bare feet. Madan removes the pins, turns the trousers inside out, and places them under the foot of the sewing machine.

"It's so sad, isn't it?" she says. "All these poor people who have nothing, absolutely nothing left. Look at this boy, a strong young man. . . . Suddenly he's lost everything, and when you're half-naked, it's not easy to find work, so that you're forced to beg. And then the line of people waiting at the door, I can't send them away while we've had wind and rain, but not the floods, I mean, and the waves, there was a leak, but that's nothing compared to what's happened to them. . . . I hope that you won't, I mean . . . er . . . you won't . . ."

Madan looks up inquiringly.

"You'll do it for nothing, won't you?"

Madan nods and returns to his work.

A little later he hands the trousers to the fisherman. He

looks at him expectantly, and widow Sethi turns her head away. The moment he pulls the pants up over his hips something happens. The man, who until then had stood shyly, head bowed, is suddenly a powerful young fellow who radiates energy. Even the grief that was etched in his features has softened. Widow Sethi blinks, and a smile appears on Madan's face.

"And now a shirt," she says with conviction, although a minute ago she decided to allow each person only one piece of clothing. She pulls out a white shirt that her husband always wore to the office.

Madan motions to the man to turn around, and looks at the shape of his shoulders and neck. Then he turns the shirt inside out and alters several seams.

When the man puts on the shirt, he looks like a hero in a film. Widow Sethi suddenly regrets that her youngest daughter has already been married off, for if she had met this young man earlier, he would certainly have been a suitable candidate. She doesn't want to let the fisherman go, and only after a cup of tea and repeated invitations to come by sometime does she finally allow the next person in line to enter.

The woman who walks into the room is painfully thin, with straight hair that hangs half over her eyes. She tells widow Sethi that she's lost her entire family, even her great-grandfather, and that all around the spot where her house stood there were bodies floating in the water. The bodies were so blue and swollen that they were unrecognizable, so she and other survivors from her village tried to cremate the bodies. The fire wouldn't catch because the wood was too wet, and in the end they tapped diesel fuel from a washed-up truck and doused the bodies.

Shocked, Madan listens to her monotone voice. She speaks without a trace of emotion, as if she were reciting a lesson. Widow Sethi has tears in her eyes, and she pulls one of her wedding saris out of the cabinet: a magnificent yellow silk, with gold embroidery. The matching blouse is too large for the woman's emaciated body, but Madan takes it in. He also shortens the sari and makes a hairband for her from the leftover material.

They hear the murmurs of admiration as she goes down the stairs. Widow Sethi hopes the fisherman is not too far away, since they would make a lovely couple. She calls the next person in line. It's another fisherman, who lost not only his entire family, his boat, and his house, but also all of his front teeth.

"Oh, Madame," he lisps, "can you make me just as handsome?"

Widow Sethi fears that not even the most elegant of her husband's suits would be enough to fulfill his request, but Madan bends over his machine and continues to sew.

The fisherman with no front teeth is pleased as punch with his new outfit. After his departure an atmosphere of unrest develops. It is rumoured that there are not enough clothes to go around, and that only people who have lost their entire family are eligible. Toward the end of the line, someone mentions that the benefactress is not only giving away clothes, but also filling their pockets with money. The people in line begin to push and shove. A young widow uses her elbows to work her way up one step, and two brothers who owned a small shipyard push a rival shipbuilder in the same situation straight off the stairs. He is thrown against a shy young woman who has never been touched by a man.

She begins to scream, which leads the other people in line to conclude that the handouts have come to a halt. Those at the very end of the line believe that is not only the benefactress putting money in the pockets, but also has promised them a job. The crowd of people on the street has swelled, and all of them are determined to get into the house. On the stairs, children are trampled underfoot or held high above the jumble of people. Widow Sethi tries to calm them, but when the next man leaves the house looking like a film star, the waiting mass squeezes past the widow and into the house, where they pounce upon the clothes and scour the cabinets in the hope of laying their hands on one or more garments.

Madan, focused on the fitted blouse he's taking in, is initially unaware of the upheaval on the stairs. When the people begin to charge into the room, his first instinct is to protect his machine. He bends forward and throws both arms around the Singer. But the destitute men and women are not interested in Madan or his sewing machine. They have just caught sight of widow Sethi's collection of saris. Greedy hands pull the colourful garments out of the cabinet. As more and more people crowd into the room, Madan feels the wooden floor begin to give way. He sees shirts and trousers being torn apart. He hears the screams and the creaking noises. He sees the cabinets start to topple. A cry of distress forms in his throat. He screams. The swarming mass of people suddenly fall silent, and they all look around in shock, searching for the roaring lion they expect to see. But there is only a man with a sewing machine in his arms.

Then they hear the clear sound of something cracking, and the floor caves in. Dust, splinters, scraps of wood, people, and clothes . . . everything comes crashing down. Madan hears a scream . . . a scream he heard once before, years ago in the prison, when Ibrahim the murderer grabbed Mister Patel by the throat because he didn't like his face.

THE CARS WITH their wailing sirens, a sound that has become familiar in recent months, arrive in front of what was once the house of Mister Patel and widow Sethi. There is nothing left but a few broken beams and a pile of roof tiles. All the clothes are gone, snatched up before the arrival of the ambulances and police cars.

Holding his sewing machine, Madan stares at the stretcher carrying the body of Mister Patel. His pen is still in his hand. The ambulance drivers are in no hurry. The sirens are silent. Madan wants to cry, but the tears won't come. He feels nothing. All he sees is the bloody face of the old man as he is shoved into an ambulance while the drivers discuss the final score of a cricket game. One of them picks up a piece of paper from the rubble and lays it over the disfigured face. Through a tear in the drawing of the paramecium, Madan can still see the terror-contorted mouth of the man he had come to call *Father.*

EVERYONE IS GONE, and a harrowing silence descends upon the street. Only Madan is left, standing in front of the collapsed house, with his sewing machine under his arm. He gazes at the closely written snippets of paper wafting away in the wake of their creator.

"Hey, you!"

Madan turns slowly in the direction of the voice.

In the door of the greengrocer's shop opposite the house stands the proprietor. He waves to him. "Come with me."

In front of the door there are large crates of apples. They're just as shiny as the apple he was given by Mister Patel's nephew. He hesitates, but then walks over to the shopkeeper.

"Don't you want his bicycle?"

Madan looks at him inquiringly.

"You're his son, aren't you?"

The man dashes into the shop and comes back with an old men's bicycle.

"Take it, please. It's been standing in the way for years."

1995 Rampur

THE MOON WAS almost full and shone down on the eager mouths of the buckets in the garden. There was as yet no sign of the clouds Charlotte was hoping for. However, it was not the heat that had kept her awake, but rather what had happened that evening.

They were standing at the bottom of the stairs, exhausted, when Isabella came dancing down the stairs with Father's chamber pot, belting out "Singing in the Rain" like a full-fledged Fred Astaire. She grinned at the invisible dark clouds overhead and made it clear that the "sun was in her heart and she was ready for love!" The old chamber pot became her dance partner: she paraded from one side of the broad, once stately stairs to the other, as if she were starring in a real musical.

Hema chuckled, Madan laughed his soundless laugh, and Charlotte found herself regretting that her niece hadn't paid them a visit before.

After the last sentence, the girl placed the chamber pot at

the bottom of the stairs, looked up into the sky, and called out in a loud voice: "Now you can piss as hard as you want!" She looked cheekily at the adults in front of her. "If it doesn't come now, then I give up," she said triumphantly, wiping the perspiration from her forehead.

"Thank you, Miss Isabella," said Hema, who was convinced that, as the "house on the hill," they had done more than their duty when it came to enticing the monsoon to burst loose. If the rain didn't come now, it wasn't their fault. "My name is Issy!" she called out, and made a pirouette. Charlotte didn't know if it was deliberately or by accident, but suddenly she stopped in front of Madan and pointed to his neck: "What did you do to your neck?"

Oh, it's nothing.

"It's nothing," said Charlotte, who could tell that he was startled by the sudden attention.

"Nothing? Look." Issy's finger pointed at the scar on his neck.

It's very old.

"It's very old," Charlotte repeated his words.

"How do you know it's old?"

Since Charlotte didn't actually know what her niece was talking about, she realized that she should have kept her mouth shut. Now, following Issy's glance, she looked at Madan's neck.

Madan wanted to turn away, but Issy stopped him.

"Did you have an accident?"

For the first time, Charlotte realized that the line on his neck was a scar.

"Is that why you can't talk?"

Embarrassed, Madan shrugged and hung his head.

Hema, who was not pleased to see the tailor suddenly attract the attention of his Miss Isabella, announced that the tea was almost ready, although he hadn't even started, and Charlotte diverted her niece's attention by asking her about her special telephone, since she felt it wasn't appropriate to discuss a person's handicap in his presence.

1952 Bombay ~

THE GLEAMING BLACK Rolls-Royce stops in front of their house.

"They're here!" Charlotte calls upstairs. There is no answer. She runs up the stairs. "Peter, they're here. Are you coming?" She goes into their bedroom, but he's not there, or in the bathroom, or in the lavatory. "Peter!"

Downstairs the doorbell rings. The servant opens the door and she hears their visitors entering the hall. She looks for Peter in the guestroom and the laundry room. The servant invites them into the drawing room. She hurries down the stairs and checks the sunroom opening onto the garden, the dining room, the kitchen, and the scullery. She even goes into the garden, to the shed, and the servants' quarters, but she can't find her husband anywhere.

"Welcome to Bombay," Charlotte says as she walks into the drawing room. "It's lovely to see you again. Couldn't your father come?"

"No, the minister of Public Works paid us a surprise visit. Father is hoping to build a canal, but he hasn't been able to get permission, and now it finally looks as if it's all going to work out." Chutki sits down on the sofa and begins to tell

Charlotte about the problems in the palace and the long journey to Bombay. Her baby brother, who's sitting next to her, looks around with interest. Behind them stand two nurses wearing white caps, one tall and the other short. Both are staring at the floor.

The boy has grown since she saw him a year ago, Charlotte thinks. She listens to his sister's stories, but her eyes are constantly drawn to the boy. There's something unusual about him, something she's never seen in a child before. She can't decide if it's his eyes, his smile, or his presence, but looking at him, a calm comes over her and she almost forgets her concerns about Peter.

"Would you like something to drink?"

"Juice," says the boy, and he begins to cough.

"We'd like tea," replies his sister.

The boy looks disappointed.

Charlotte rings and asks the servant to bring tea and a glass of mango juice. The boy grins in between bouts of coughing. The daughter of the maharaja is chatting away about the inconveniences of travelling by car in comparison with a train journey, when suddenly Charlotte sees a foot sticking out from behind the sofa near the window. A foot that she immediately recognizes. Chutki hasn't noticed her startled expression, nor have the nurses.

"We have a new grand piano," says Charlotte, and gets up. "Would you like to see it?" Chatting away, she succeeds in guiding Chutki and her little brother into the sunroom. The nurses do not budge from their post until Charlotte tells them that biscuits and tea are being served in the kitchen.

As Chutki plays various pieces on the piano, Charlotte steals back to the salon and kneels down by the sofa, where

Peter has taken refuge behind the curtains. Gently she strokes his back, and he begins to relax. "If you don't want to go through with it, I'll send them away."

"No." His reply is barely audible.

"I can say you're not feeling well," she whispers.

"I have to go through with it," he moans. "I owe it to the maharaja."

She draws the curtain aside. The sound of Chutki's unpractised piano playing is audible. Charlotte's hand slides through his hair. She sees the grey streaks that weren't there a while ago. He groans like a wounded animal with its leg in a trap. But she has no idea what part of him is caught in a trap. She cannot find it, no matter how hard she tries. "Can you stand up?" She helps him to his feet slowly, like a limp marionette. It's only then that she sees the little boy standing in the door.

"Did the doctor lose something?" he inquires in a worried voice as he fiddles with the gold chain around his neck.

"Yes," says Charlotte, "but luckily he's found it." She hopes that one day she will find out what it is that he has lost.

~

THE HOSPITAL CONSISTS of long, high-ceilinged corridors devoid of people. The sound made by the heels of the two nurses reinforces the uncomfortable sensation that came over her when they entered the building. Charlotte doesn't see why the operation has to take place now, why it cannot wait until tomorrow morning. But Peter is adamant. He's already called an anaesthetist friend who's a known cricket-hater, and with two extra nurses there to assist, it should be a piece of cake.

The elderly doctor at the first-aid station also agrees that there shouldn't be a problem. "I can guarantee that no one will fall ill before the end of the match," he jokes as he turns up the volume on his radio.

The enthusiastic voice of the cricket announcer echoes throughout the waiting room: "*India zindabad!*"

"I just hope Pakistan doesn't win," sighs the old doctor. "Then it could get extremely busy here." He closes his eyes, leans back in his chair, and listens to the game with rapt attention.

Peter, the anaesthetist, and Chutki are already in the operating room. Charlotte waits in the corridor. She toys with the gold chain the nurse took from the boy's neck when he was placed on the mobile bed. She has never waited in a hospital corridor before. Suddenly she realizes how a father-to-be feels when his wife is about to give birth to their first child. In the background, the radio commentary is audible, along with the cheering of the fans in the stadium.

"The doctor has changed," says Chutki, who sits down next to her and pulls her coat tighter around her.

Charlotte wishes she could say that things were improving, that it just happened to be a bad day. Although she can't remember when he last had a good day.

"Doesn't he want children?" Chutki asks cautiously.

Charlotte wishes she'd stayed home. She hates questions like this. Doesn't the daughter of the maharaja understand that there is no way she can raise the subject? She doesn't dare. She knows that she won't get an answer, that he'll roll into a fetal position, deaf and dumb to his surroundings.

All is quiet in the operating room. The anaesthetist and the nurses follow the hands of the surgeon, who performs the necessary procedures inside the boy's throat, intently and with great precision. He sees that there is more damage to the larynx than he had expected. He is happy that he found the strength to get up and to persevere. He sees that the boy's eyelids are quivering slightly. He casts a worried glance at the anaesthetist, who nods that everything is in order. Why are the eyelids quivering? Eyelids are not supposed to quiver. The patient must lie perfectly still. Otherwise he cannot continue to operate.

"Increase the dosage," he hisses.

"It's just right," says the anaesthetist.

Peter feels rivulets of perspiration running down his back. Can't his colleague see that the child is waking up, that life is returning to the boy's body, that he's not finished with the operation yet, nowhere near finished? His hands begin to quiver. The anaesthetist mumbles that everything is as it should be, that it's normal, that sometimes the eyelids do quiver. Peter grasps the scalpel in an effort to control his trembling hand. It is not normal, he's never seen it before, he knows that someone who is unconscious does not move. They're like the dead, they no longer feel anything. They rot away like cadavers, they don't feel pain when someone kicks them, they don't feel the bullets entering their body, they are devoured by insects and vermin, but they don't move, they cannot move.

The door flies open, the tall nurse calls to them to follow her, and Charlotte and Chutki are in the operating room before she's finished her sentence. The anaesthetist stares in desperation at the other nurse as she bandages the throat of the young patient, who is still unconscious.

Peter is standing between them, his whole body is trembling, and his eyes are focused on an imaginary horizon. "It went wrong," he murmurs, "the operation went wrong."

THE SHORT NURSE picks the boy up from the aluminium operating table. The tall one is crying. Chutki wants to know what happened, but no one will tell her. The anaesthetist pushes Peter out of the operating room and pulls the blood-stained sheets off the bed. Through the open door, the voice of the cricket announcer echoes through the corridor: he has lost his sense of decorum and he is spitting and yelling in his enthusiasm now that India is on the winning hand.

The nurses are busy transforming the Rolls-Royce into a makeshift ambulance. Chutki has shoved her baby brother in his bloodied shirt into Charlotte's arms and gone off in search of a working radio so that she can tell her father that the operation has failed. The anaesthetist sits across from her with a crestfallen face, and Peter is crouching on his heels at the end of the corridor. Charlotte looks into the boy's face. *Please, wake up,* she prays. *Stay alive.* She strokes his hair and looks at the bandage around his throat. Carefully she hangs the gold chain with the family's coat of arms around his neck. She tries not to touch the bandage. "It's going to be all right," she whispers. She is aware that the same feeling struck her earlier in the day, when he looked at her. There's something about this boy. She remembers the gossip that did the rounds of the palace . . . that the boy was doomed to lead an unhappy life because she — a white woman — had inadvertently been the first person to see him. She remembers the nurse's scream, the fury of the women in the *zenana*, and the reproachful glances. *Please, let it turn out all right.* She strokes him and gives him a kiss. *I would gladly give my life for you.* The boy opens his eyes. He blinks. He looks at her drowsily. She smiles at him. *It's going to be all right, everything's going to be fine.*

I promise. He smiles back at her. The stadium explodes. "*India zindabad!*" screams the reporter; the emergency-room doctor jumps up and dances around in a circle. It's all going to be all right. Then she sees that the bandage around his neck is turning red. The wound hasn't been sutured properly! She stands up and is about to call for help when the boy is snatched from her arms and disappears through the outside door, with the two nurses.

Chutki doesn't say a word to her as they get into the Rolls-Royce. The two nurses are sitting opposite them on folding chairs, like a pair of guard dogs. The boy is lying on the seat, with his head in his sister's lap. He's looking at Charlotte and he's still smiling when the door closes and the car drives off.

"Drive carefully!" Chutki barks to the chauffeur. She's furious with him. He couldn't be found because he was glued to a radio somewhere, like every other Indian in the city.

They turn into the deserted street that runs parallel to the stadium, and at that moment the gates open and throngs of euphoric fans burst forth, chanting, "*India zindabad! India zindabad!*" They pour onto the streets, numbering in the thousands. The chauffeur realizes that there's no way he can get through the crowd, and he starts to turn around. But Chutki orders him to keep going. The will of the maharaja's daughter is law, and he turns the wheel back, but the sea of people makes it impossible to move forward. They're waving, cheering, and whooping. Dancing, jumping, and singing. Laughing, screaming, and shouting: "*India zindabad!*" The people are delirious with excitement: India has beaten Pakistan! A man in a saffron-white-green turban — the colours of the Indian flag — celebrates by pounding on the roof of the Rolls-Royce with both fists. Although the car is well insulated, the blow reverberates alarmingly. The chauffeur starts honking his horn. Others hear the blows falling on the metal and join in. *"India zindabad! India zindabad!"*

"Make them stop!" Chutki screams.

The short nurse rolls down the window and a deafening cheers fill the car. She tries to stop the men, but they pay no attention.

The chauffeur sees in his rear-view mirror that Chutki is on the verge of panic. He gets out of the car and orders the men to stop.

"India zindabad! India zindabad!" The men continue to drum on the car roof. "Make them stop!" Chutki shrieks. Then she draws her coat tightly around her, opens the door, and jumps out.

The nurses, too, alight from the car, more to protect Chutki than to try to talk sense into the men.

The little boy looks around groggily. His throat hurts, but the cries of the men are so overwhelming that he sits up and looks out the open window.

"India zindabad! India zindabad!" a man shouts into the car and waves at the little boy.

Madan raises his hand and waves back.

"Come out and dance!" the man shouts, and he opens the car door.

Slowly the boy gets to his feet and slides down onto the floor of the car. Cautiously he crawls out. He turns toward the man who wants to dance with him, and spreads his arms wide. He sees his sister, with her blue coat, amidst all those big men. She has her hands in the air, too.

"Yes, dance!" the man calls out. "We won!"

Stumbling along on his little legs, Madan follows the

man: he loves to dance, just like his sisters and brothers. He loves the huge parties his parents give in the great halls of the palace. He watches as the dancing man in front of him disappears into the crowd. He totters after him. Madan Man Singh wants to dance with the others. Dance in celebration.

1995 Rampur ~

THE MOON MOVED languidly across the cloudless sky. It was not the screech of the owl or the warbling of the birds that was keeping her awake, not the heat or her thirst, not even the suspicion that she already knew the identity of the man she was in love with. It was the question she should have asked her father years ago. In her bare feet, she went to the nursery and opened the door. By the light of the moon she could see that he was lying peacefully on the narrow bed, with only the bands across his legs. He had been lucid when he signed the power of attorney. What must he have thought all those other times? He must have realized that they had tied him up. Did he understand, or was that the reason for all of his extreme outbursts of anger?

He was gleaming with sweat, even though the fan above him was revolving at full speed. The mosquito netting floated over him like a jellyfish. The anxiety that she often felt when she entered his room was absent. How could she ask him the question when even her own memories were slowly fading, making way for desires rather than reality? What would change if she knew? Would her image of him change? Could she forgive him, or would she end up hating him? She noticed that his fingers moved while he was asleep, as if he was trying to grasp something beyond his reach. His breathing accelerated. His arms moved, but his thin legs lay still. Was he still able to walk and run and jump in his dreams? Or did those memories also dim and blur?

His uniform was hanging on the cabinet door. Had Hema hung it there? She would have to take it down before he woke up, since he could not possibly go to the ball with her. He would be confused by all those people, and they by him. The Distinguished Service Order hung among the other forgotten medals. In the end, even heroism exists only in memory. He groaned softly. His hands relaxed. She could tell that he was drifting into a dreamless sleep. She didn't want to go to bed yet. She wasn't tired, although she hadn't slept for two nights. She took his uniform jacket off the hanger and put it on. The scent of fabric, the past, and mortality embraced her. Her hand caressed the coarse linen, the weathered seams, and the medal.

"Take it off."

She hadn't noticed that he was awake again.

"You can have it."

"I didn't want to wake you."

"I wasn't asleep."

The jacket slipped from her shoulders. "Take if off," he repeated.

She looked at him, trying to establish whether he knew what he was saying or was talking nonsense.

"You heard me, didn't you? Take it off!"

She opened the small metal pin on the inside of the uniform, attached to the cross that symbolized leadership and courage, and slid it off. The cross was heavier than she had expected and the corners were sharp; in the centre were a laurel wreath and a gold crown. She lifted the mosquito netting and handed it to her father.

"I told you it was for you."

"For me? Why?"

"You're his widow, aren't you?"

She gave her father a penetrating look. Had she heard correctly? Was he lucid or was he crazy? Did he mean that he wasn't a hero, but Peter was? He looked down. An owl screeched on the hill. The moon cast its light over father and daughter. She let the mosquito netting fall. It came down between them like the barred gate of a fortress.

Charlotte found her way back to her own room. She lay down on her bed with the medal in her hand and fell into a dreamless sleep.

"AUNT CHARLOTTE!" THE high-pitched, girlish voice echoed throughout the hall. "We're out of toilet paper again!"

At that very moment the telephone rang. Hema ran into the hall to answer it, but before he could do so, the doorbell rang. For a moment he hesitated, but then decided that if you don't know who is at the door, then it's a question of first-come, first-served. He put on his best telephone face, picked up the receiver, and repeated the sentence that memsahib had taught him years before. When he heard the voice of the wife of Nikhil Nair, he regretted not going to the door first.

Upstairs the clock struck nine. Memsahib was still asleep when he took her tea up at six o'clock, but the door of the nursery was open, so that he could hear the general singing his favourite song, about someone he'd see again. He didn't know where or when, but in any case it would be on a sunny day.

He had taken the tea back to the kitchen and finished it himself, since all night the heat had lain over him like a heavy blanket. Again, the doorbell sounded. Hema searched for some way to terminate his conversation with the wife of Nikhil Nair, but she continued to maintain that the table that the tailor had borrowed from her had to go to the club, because it was needed for the gala this evening. The fact that Hema didn't know where the tailor was, that the tailor didn't know that the table was on loan, and that memsahib was still asleep made little or no impression on the wife of Nikhil Nair. Against the background of her flood of words, he heard that the general was still in a good mood upstairs, for although Hema had locked the door, the old military man continued to sing the same song over and over. The doorbell rang again; this time it sounded louder and more insistent. If at that moment the young memsahib had not come into the hall with the mended teapot, he would no doubt have brought the conversation to a polite end, but he was so startled that someone else had taken over his work that he put the telephone down without saying goodbye, went over to the girl, and snatched the teapot from her hands. A splash of hot tea shot from the spout and landed on his hand. He gave a cry of pain that no one heard, because whoever was standing at the front door had his finger on the bell and was not planning on removing it until someone opened the door. With the teapot in his good hand, he opened the door with the injured hand.

"I came to pick up the table," said a boy Hema had never seen before. He had a small moustache and was tapping his foot impatiently against the doorstep. Both Charlotte and the general had taught him the rules that are part of a butler's training, but now Hema forgot everything. "The servants' entrance is at the back," he snapped, and slammed the door shut.

CHARLOTTE HADN'T SLEPT so soundly in years. And when she woke up, the medal was still in her hand. Her memories of the deceased hero were gradually displaced by an unsettling notion. Was the tailor the son of the maharaja? The little boy she had held in her arms in the hospital? The child who vanished in the commotion following the first cricket game between India and Pakistan? His photograph had been published in all the papers, but no one had seen him. The prince had scoured the country in an effort to find his son, but the boy seemed to have simply vanished. Prayers were said for him in temples, mosques, and churches, and astrologers and fortune tellers were approached, and the maharaja offered a gigantic sum of money if he was found. Was he here, downstairs, in her house? Or was it nothing but an idle hope, a way of reinforcing his right to exist, and thus give her love a chance? But it all squared with the facts: the scar, the loss of his voice, his age, the colour of his skin, and his resemblance to the maharaja. He had a family! She had to tell him, she had to call the maharaja. She didn't dare leave her room — if she went downstairs, he would immediately hear her thoughts. . . . She would have to find a way to approach him calmly, and ask him whether he could remember anything from the past. If he were able to read, she could have written him a letter. If they were far enough away from each other, he might not be able to hear her thoughts, but then everyone else around would hear her shouting. The only thing she could think of was to tell someone else first and then have that person ask him, but there was no suitable candidate. So she decided she would have to do it herself. She put the medal in the wooden box where for years she had kept the lone cigarette, returned the box to the drawer, and went downstairs.

THE NOISE THAT had awakened her had faded away. The house was filled with a serene calm. There was only the ticking of the clock and the squeaking of the stairs. She knocked on the door to the music room, and since she knew he could not answer, she gently opened the door, which creaked slightly.

The room was dark. The shutters and the curtains were closed. For a moment she thought he might have overslept, too. Except that he didn't sleep in the music room, but in the room next to the kitchen . . . when he did sleep. She turned on the light. The bulb wavered and her heart missed a beat. The room was empty; the table and the sewing machine were gone. The crimson dress hung on the wall, like a giant butterfly.

"Madan!" she called out, forgetting that the tailor didn't even know that that was his original name. "Madan, where are you?" She ran into the drawing room, which was also empty. She ran into the garden, and then the kitchen. There was no one there either. She found only a neat pile of sheets and a rolled-up sleeping mat in the room she'd had cleaned for him a few weeks ago. There were no other signs that anyone had lived there. She ran in the direction of the shed past the double row of pans and buckets. All that time, his bicycle had stood next to hers. It, too, had disappeared.

He regretted not taking along a big bottle of water. Cycling downhill was pleasant, with his shirt and his hair flapping, thanks to the speed of his descent. He zipped past the rows of buckets and cups, past the rusty sign at the bottom of the lane, unaware that it was a right-of-way sign, and crossed the road without looking right or left. The driver who was coming around the bend with his load of watermelons cursed him, but Madan was too far away to hear him.

He no longer understood himself. From the moment she had opened the door for him, her eyes half closed against the piercing sunlight, he had been lost. It was not only her beauty. There was more, once he had smelled her scent, heard her voice, looked at her. He had to pedal faster now, since the hill had become a stretch of flat road leading into town. Everywhere he looked, the houses and huts were encircled by bowls and basins. The droplets everyone was waiting for appeared on his forehead and his breath came faster. He would collect his money and leave town. He had to leave before the monsoon broke loose and the roads became impassable. Although he had been swept along on a wave of passion that was stronger, more intense, than anything he could remember, he must not want the impossible. It was not for him. He must forget her. Just as he had forgotten everything that lay in his past.

1954 Grand Palace ～

THE SHUTTERS ARE closed, and the maharaja and the maharani are sitting side by side, in silence. Their youthful, aristocratic features have been washed away by rivers of sorrow. They seldom talk anymore. And when they do, almost every sentence begins the same way: "What if . . . ?" The corridors of the palace are empty, and when a servant passes by, his head is deeply bowed and he makes no noise. Heavy black cloths hang over the paintings in the large hall and the fountains are dry. The birds that used to flock around the veranda of the *zenana* have disappeared. Like the women, who have retreated to their individual rooms or even left, in an effort to escape the atmosphere of perpetual mourning. The bed in which Madan slept until his disappearance has been moved to the maharani's room and, although it is much too small for her, she sleeps in it every night. The doctor has warned her that her bones will grow crooked if she continues to do so, but she is not interested in what the doctor has to say. In fact, she doesn't want to hear the word "doctor" ever again. Her daughter Chutki has been banished to a village in Rajasthan, on the edge of the Great Indian Desert. The two nurses, who had been in the service of the royal family for years, were thrown into prison without any form of trial. No doubt they will remain there, since everyone has forgotten them. Just as they have forgotten the chauffeur, who was so overcome by remorse that he refused to eat and died two months later.

The hand of the maharaja steals slowly toward his wife's black-gloved hand, which freezes under his touch. He must talk to her. Reports are coming in from the territories that the people are becoming rebellious. They say that the strict state of mourning that has been enforced for two years must come to an end, that it's time to start digging the canal. The women long to wear colourful clothes again, and the men have had enough of the ban on shaving and of the decree ordaining that every newborn boy must be named Madan.

"Mother of my children . . . ," he begins.

His wife moans. Her servant rushes to her side and starts to kneel down next to her, but the stern look in the eyes of the maharaja dissuades her.

"The time has come."

She begins to sob heart-rendingly. Her shoulders shake and she buries her face in her hands. The servant pulls out a lace handkerchief and hands it to the maharaja.

Clumsily, he presses it into the hand of his wife, who immediately brings it to her face. "On the first of the month I will proclaim the end of the mourning period," he says.

She winces and shakes her head. "We must find him. You know that. I put a curse on him," she sobs bitterly.

The maharaja conceals his sigh. He's had enough of his wife's superstitions. "Lift the curse," he says, unable to hide the exasperation in his voice.

"Lift it? A curse cannot be lifted." Now it is the maharani who sighs.

"Then change it. Say that if she dies, he will find happiness." The maharaja abhors the penchant for sorcery that his wife and his daughters display. He wants to shave off his beard, finish digging his canal, drink port, and go hunting again.

His wife closes her eyes devoutly and begins to hum a song he's never heard before. A high, shrill song. Then she presses her gloved hands to her heart and gazes at the only painting in the room that has not been covered. The painting is of Madan with a sabre that is almost as tall as he is. She calls out words that he has never heard, pulls off her gloves, and throws them at the wall. They fall behind the painting. She looks at her husband and says, "Open the shutters."

1995 Rampur

AT THE INSISTENCE of her aunt, Issy tried on the red dress. She had no idea why Charlotte was crying. There weren't that many parties in Rampur, and Grandfather had been singing cheerfully all day. Even the butler was in high spirits, after his accident with the teapot and the discovery that the tailor was gone. Issy herself was not in a good mood. She had hoped that the tailor would make a dress for her, preferably very short with a bare back. But she had to admit that her aunt's dress was quite lovely, considering it was designed for an older woman. She pulled it on over her head.

"You can keep it on. I don't want it anymore," her aunt said as she walked out of the room.

As soon as Issy zipped up the dress and felt it close around her body, she found it difficult to breathe. The fabric seemed to become tighter with every breath she took. She wanted to take off the dress as fast as she could, but no matter how hard she tried, she was unable to unzip it.

Hema, who had just arrived with the tea, gazed at the girl in admiration as she danced around.

"Help me!" she gasped. "Undo the zipper!"

Hema was shocked at such an impertinent request from a white girl. Surely she didn't mean for him to undo the zipper and run the risk of accidently touching her skin?

"Help me!" she shrieked.

Charlotte, who was in the hall, came running when she heard her niece's voice. She found her standing in the middle of the room, gasping for breath. She ran over to her and unzipped the dress.

Before Hema could beat a retreat, the girl had pulled off the dress and stood there in the middle of the room, wearing nothing but her panties.

"What a fucking dress!" she cried, kicking it away from her.

"Isabella!" Charlotte looked around for something to cover the girl with.

Hema shot out the door and, for the second time that day, the hot tea splashed over his hands. But this time he felt no pain, absorbed as he was in the spectacle of those firm young breasts.

Charlotte reached for the girl's T-shirt and held it in front of her as the door closed.

"Hema is a man!" she said.

"And I'm a woman!"

Charlotte picked up the dress and immediately found herself caressing the fabric.

"That dress is bewitched!" said Issy.

"Nonsense," she said dreamily. "It's just an ordinary dress."

"Then you put it on."

"No, I'm not going to the gala."

"I'm not talking about the gala. I'm talking about the dress."

Charlotte felt the soft folds of the silk glide through her fingers. It was just as she had imagined his skin would feel. Still holding it in her hand, she unbuttoned her worn housedress and slipped the garment on over her head. Charlotte slid into the dress like a snake crawls out of its skin. She put one arm through the armhole and glided into a space that was already familiar to her, while her other arm easily found its way. The crimson material flowed past her breasts, her belly, her back, and her hips. She couldn't tell whether it was her skin that drew the fabric to it or the silk that embraced her. It was not a second skin, but something much more intimate: it gave her the same strength as the bark of a tree, the same protection as the cocoon surrounding a larva, the same safety as the arms of a mother or the membrane surrounding the most delicious fruit. . . . She felt years younger, stronger, prettier, fuller, richer. The yearning in her heart was gone and the tears she had shed were forgotten. She knew that he loved her.

Upstairs the clock struck eight.

"Go to the gala . . . ," said Issy, who had noticed the transformation in her aunt. "I'm not in the mood."

But her aunt hadn't even heard her — Charlotte slipped on a pair of evening shoes and walked out the door without uttering a word.

Hema caught sight of his employer leaving the house in

her beautiful dress. She seemed to be floating rather than walking. He wanted to call out to her to wait, that he would call a taxi for her, but she danced off in the direction of the road. He overtook her, manoeuvring around the buckets and pans lining the driveway. At the gate, he jumped into the street, waving with all his might in order to attract a taxi, but they were all occupied by elegantly clad ladies and gentlemen on their way to the gala.

He heard a car horn, then a door flung open, and Mr. Nikhil Nair stepped out of his gleaming limousine.

"Mrs. Bridgwater . . ." It was several seconds before he found the right words. "May I have the honour?" He bowed deeply and held the car door open for her. Charlotte seated herself next to his wife, who was quite radiant in her new pink dress.

Before Hema had a chance to wish her a pleasant evening, the car drove off in the direction of the city, where all the streets were lined with bowls, basins, tubs, and anything else that was capable of holding water, leaving only a narrow corridor for traffic.

NOW THAT EVERYONE was gone, it was boring in the big house. Quieter and emptier than during the day. Even the butler failed to appear when she rang. After the car drove away, Hema went off to the neighbours' butler, to tell him about the breasts he'd seen. So Issy poured herself another cup of tea and tried for the umpteenth time to find the right cable to charge her mobile phone. That afternoon she'd found a pile of old cables and extension cords that everyone had apparently forgotten about. Maybe there was something there she could use.

She dropped the tangle of wires on the floor and pulled out one with dismantled scraps of copper at both ends. With a piece of sticking plaster she fastened one end of the wire to the rods of the plug that she would normally insert into the wall outlet. With great care — since she knew that electricity was dangerous — she put the two ends into the outlet. The tiny screen on her mobile phone lit up, and the symbol for "battery is charging" began to flicker. With a sense of accomplishment, she looked at her phone and said, "You see? I told you I'm perfectly capable of travelling on my own." She fell backwards onto the couch.

There was a loud bang. The bulb over her head flickered and then the power went out.

~

THE ORCHESTRA WAS playing a waltz. The large covered terrace had been cleared for dancing. There were torches at regular intervals around the perimeter, silver streamers that reflected the light hung from the ceiling. Ladies who were usually shy and preferred to sit in a corner now whirled around the dance floor. Those who'd always been considered fat were more slender than they had ever been. Those who had always been as thin as a rail had developed magnificent bosoms, while the most colourless individuals radiated a veritable joie de vivre. And for the occasion, the loudmouths who were universally disliked had a kind of poetic bonhomie about them. There was even a bewitching quality about the unbearable heat that held the entire city in its grip and intensified by the minute.

But the most beautiful of all was Charlotte, who whirled across the dance floor like an incandescent flower surrounded by buzzing bees. She laughed and danced with Mr. Karapiet, who kept telling her that he had never before seen so many beautiful women together in one place; she danced with Alok Nath, the goldsmith, who wanted to design a necklace for her because he found her beauty overwhelming. She danced with Adeeb Tata, a distant cousin of the wealthy Ratan Tata, who whispered in her ear that she was lovelier than any of the women he had met in Paris. She danced with the manufacturer of coconut oil, who said that he was intoxicated by her perfume, although she was not wearing any. And of course she danced with Mr. Nikhil Nair, who could not take his eyes off her, and even asked her for a second dance. She respectfully declined in order to avoid any possible discord with his wife. Charlotte was conscious of the fact that she was radiant, that all the festivities she had missed in the past were nothing compared with this one. The waiters went around with enticing delicacies on Wedgwood plates, some of which she recognized. But even that did not cause her pain. Just as the covetous glances in her direction did not embarrass her but made her feel happy.

"A cloud!" said the wife of Alok Nath. But as usual, no one heard her. She walked over to the edge of the terrace and pointed. Her husband thought she wanted to go home and, with a smile, he led her back to the dance floor. "A cloud," she whispered into the goldsmith's ear, but the music was too loud and the whisky had clouded his powers of observation. He saw only the eyes of his lovely wife and the whirling dresses of her friends. "There are clouds in the sky. Really and truly!" She forced the words from her throat. The police commissioner, who was whirling past, picked up the message and looked up at the sky. But he was circling so fast that it took him three full rounds before he finally saw the clouds.

"The clouds have come." His deep voice reverberated across the terrace.

The music stopped. Now everyone was moving toward the edge of the terrace. The moon had disappeared and the crowd of people pressing forward had to squint to catch a glimpse of the harbinger of the monsoon. They pushed and pointed, sighed with relief, and laughed at the buckets and their own superstition. The secretary of the club did something he'd never done before: he kissed his wife in public. She blushed and resolved to wear her dress more often.

"But . . ." The raised finger of Mister Nikhil Nair pointed to the colour differences in the sky. ". . . those can't be rain clouds."

All the men began to examine the sky. Wrinkles appeared on foreheads and the corners of mouths turned down.

Adeeb Tata, who enjoyed the most prestige as a distant cousin of the immensely rich Ratan Tata, turned to the excited partygoers. "Those are clouds of smoke." There was something denigrating in his voice, and the wife of the goldsmith, who deeply regretted having raised her voice, decided on the spot that she would never do so again, not even in an emergency.

"Oh no, not another fire . . . ," sighed the wife of Nikhil Nair.

Minister Das began to pray aloud, and in the distance they heard the whine of sirens. Charlotte thought of Parvat, hoping that it wouldn't be a large fire. The band struck up another waltz, and the dancers returned to the floor. The commissioner of police, who had never danced with a white woman before, shyly asked Charlotte for the next dance. Although the commissioner was a very good dancer, Charlotte's mind wandered. She thought of the candle in the drawing room that was sometimes left burning, now that the electricity was so erratic. She hoped that Isabella would blow it out before she went to bed.

The waltz music gradually merged with the sound of the sirens, which were becoming steadily louder. The band saw the dancers move closer and closer to the edge of the terrace, from which an orange glow was visible on the horizon.

She didn't know who had said it was her house, or whose car she jumped into. *Father! Hema!* she thought. *Isabella!* She felt a strange kind of relief when she remembered that Madan had already left. They were still some distance away when she saw that it was her roof that was on fire: a giant beacon high on the hill.

THE HEAT, WHICH for weeks had been unbearable, was nothing in comparison with the wall of fire that rose up in front as soon as she stepped out of the car. "Where is my father?" she called out. "And my niece! And Hema! Where are they? Where is everyone?"

Wherever she looked there were firemen wearing bright yellow helmets and carrying axes and ladders. They were all watching the flames shooting from the roof.

"Why aren't you doing anything?" she screamed.

The firemen looked at her in surprise.

"Because there's no water," said the old fire chief with the row of medals across his uniform.

"No water?! But the fire!"

"It has to burn itself out."

"But it's only burning upstairs!"

"It's our job to see that it doesn't jump over."

Charlotte looked around desperately. She didn't see the flattened buckets and pulverized teacups, crushed by the broad tires of the red fire engines, or the sofa and the rolled-up carpet that the firemen had salvaged. She ran over to the kitchen building and called Hema's name. On the countertop there was a jerry can half full of water. She grabbed it and ran back to where the firemen were standing. "Where is Parvat?"

"He's inside," said the old fire chief, and looked in surprise at the jerry can in her hand.

"Inside!"

"In the house. He's gone to get your father on the first floor."

Parvat had gone to Father, who was locked in his room and strapped to his bed. She didn't hesitate a second. She ran to the back of the house and slipped in through the servants' entrance.

The heat, which outside had been overpowering, was even fiercer inside. Next to the door hung Isabella's blue coat. Was she inside as well? She grabbed the jacket, throwing it over her shoulders for protection, and then opened the jerry can and doused herself with water. Then she opened the communicating door and stepped into the hall. It was as if she were being pierced by a thousand daggers. She gasped for air and shielded her face with her hand. She could hear the crackling of the wooden roof above her head. Through narrowed eyes she looked around. An unusual orange light shone on the bare space. On a narrow pillar stood the candle she had lit earlier that evening. The doors to the rooms were open and the few pieces of furniture had disappeared. She wanted to call the names of the people she thought were inside, but her hoarse cries were devoured by the seething air. She made her way through the thick, white-hot wall to her father's old study, where Isabella slept. The room was empty, and so was the bathroom. Where was her niece? Where was her son? Her father? Hunched down in an effort to escape the heat, she edged her way to the drawing room.

1935 Rampur ~

HER LITTLE BROTHER is lying on the sofa. He is crying. Charlotte looks around for Sita, but she's nowhere to be seen. The boy, still a baby, starts to cry even louder and waves his tiny fists wildly in the air.

"Shush now, don't cry, or he'll get angry." She picks him up and rocks him back and forth. He is heavier than she expected, and he's kicking his tiny feet. She has to hold him close to her chest so she doesn't drop him. "Shush now, I'm here with you." Very softly she begins to sing. A made-up lullaby about angels and fairies, about sunbeams and stairways to heaven, about little children and tears. The boy is quiet now. She rocks him back and forth, back and forth. Her head moves in time with the song.

He looks up at her with red-rimmed eyes and snivels: "Ma-ma."

She's about to smile at him and kiss him on the lips when she feels her father's swagger stick on her shoulder. He gives her a little tick, enough to make her look up.

"You're not a mother." His voice is cool.

1995 Rampur

THE DRAWING ROOM is empty. Where are they? Where is he? Is he upstairs? She wants to run up the stairs, but an unyielding wall of heat blocks the way. *I have to go upstairs, let me through!* she begs. It takes all her strength just to lift her foot and put it on the first step. She wants to call out again, but produces only a gurgling noise. She fights her way upward, through the invisible white-hot wall. The flames above her descend, devouring the dry wood of the walls, floors, and ceiling. The water she threw over herself has long since evaporated. Visibility, which was still clear near the orange glow shortly before, has made way for a penetrating fog that makes it impossible to breathe. She hears the clock start to chime its deep leaden voice. She stumbles up to the landing. She doesn't realize that she is crawling, that her knees are scraping the bare floor, that her hands are groping in the dark, or that her eyes are watering. She senses that the red dress she is wearing is protecting her.

The clock strikes for the second time. She finds the grooves of the nursery door, which is open. On hands and knees she continues her way, crossing the threshold she crossed so many times as a child, and entering the room where her life began.

The third stroke. She reaches the iron bed; the legs are white-hot and the mosquito netting has disappeared. Her hands go on searching. They find one of the leather straps, which dangles from the bed. But the bed is empty. *Where is her father? Where is Parvat? They must be here!*

The fourth stroke. Panicking, she opens her mouth, but the smoke sears her throat. She feels her way across the floor, searching for the tires of the wheelchair, which always stands next to his bed. *Where is it? Why isn't the wheelchair here?*

The fifth stroke. The smoke bores its way into her lungs, blocking her windpipe. She can no longer breathe, no longer see. Her arms thrash about. They must be there. It's been so long since he last asked to leave his room.

The sixth stroke. She bumps into the trunk where they used to keep their toys, and where Hema sets the general's tea tray down. She doesn't feel the pain, she must go back. Air! She has to breathe. She tries to stand up. She falls. She searches frantically for the door. Where is the way out?

The seventh stroke. She feels the doorsill, the door. But the hall, which before was filled with thick fumes, is now totally black. She coughs, and inhales the black smoke.

The eighth stroke tells her which direction she should crawl. The clock, which determines the rhythm of her days, fills the vacuum when no one speaks. It is her most faithful housemate, familiar with all her tears. It's calling to her.

Its ninth stroke. *No need to be afraid,* it says, *you're almost at the stairs, the way down, the steps your mother descended in her pale green dress, with the diadem in her hair.*

Its tenth stroke. The hour when the night with Madan began, the night that made her forget all the lonely nights she'd spent in this huge house. The dress he made for her embraces her.

It strikes eleven. The searing heat presses against her, ushers her into its hell, its heaven. Her legs give way. Her hands rest on the floor. Charlotte hears the large standing clock strike twelve.

ISSY PUSHES THE wheelchair up the path as fast as she can.

She should never have gone that far. It had been hard enough to get her grumbling grandfather down all those stairs. What possessed her to walk all the way down the hill as well?

"Faster, faster!" the general shouts.

Huffing and puffing, Issy manoeuvres the wheelchair up the hill between the rows of buckets. She keeps thinking about the electric wire she managed to connect to her mobile phone and then insert into the socket in the salon.

"Faster, faster," yells the general, clapping his hands.

Suddenly Hema appears between two fire engines. "General! Where were you?" He takes over pushing the wheelchair, but between the sand and the steep path, the going is much tougher than he expected. It has been years since he last went for a walk with the general. "Miss Isabella, all of a sudden you just disappeared!" he calls out. He is relieved, since he keeps thinking about the *beedi* he smoked on the sly behind the house.

"Faster! Faster! Get closer!" the general shouts. "This is the biggest fire I've ever seen!"

Issy stares in amazement at her grandfather as he shouts enthusiastically, and resolves never to tell anyone about the leather straps that confined him to his bed or the plug she stuck into the wall outlet.

~

MADAN IS SITTING beside his bicycle on the outskirts of the city. He cannot bring himself to leave Rampur, to leave her. At first he doesn't believe that the flames are real. He thinks that he's dreaming and that she is fired by the same passion as he is. Until suddenly the smoke appears: confused wisps reaching for the sky. Her house, it's her house! He jumps on his bicycle and races back into the city.

~

Parvat hears the clock on the landing strike twelve. He sees the smoke thicken through the glass window in his gas mask. The flashlight isn't strong enough to guide him. He enters the last room he has to check. He hasn't found anyone, yet the old man is always upstairs in his room. He knows that much from his mother. He cannot stay here any longer. The seat of the fire can travel faster than he can. His hands sweep across the last bed. It's empty except for the sheets. Then he feels something under the pillow. He pulls it out. It's a framed photo. He's about to toss it back onto the bed, but a sudden burst of orange light allows him to see it better. Although he has never seen it before, he immediately recognizes himself. It was taken long ago. He is still a baby, and he's being cradled in the arms of Aunt Charlotte, who is kissing him. A strange sensation shoots through his body. As if a tangled knot has suddenly come apart and the ends of the rope are lashing his body. Were the rumours he has heard true? He glances at the photo again. He wishes he hadn't found it. He doesn't want to know. He must forget what he saw. Parvat is aware that the clock has stopped chiming. He has to get out. He feels the fire coming closer. He throws the photo back on the bed and turns in the direction of the door, which he can no longer see. Feeling his way, he finds the door opening. He knows the stairs are to the right. He's familiar with the house, from all the visits to Aunt Charlotte when he was a child. His gloved hand glides along the balustrade. He doesn't have a second to lose.

As he is about to run down the stairs, his feet hit something. He recognizes the feeling: there is a body on the floor. He knows it wasn't there before. He quickly takes hold of the body, feeling for the head and the legs, and throws the fire blanket over it, smothering the flames. Above his head, the wood creaks. He hears and feels parts of the house crashing down around him. In one flowing movement, he picks up the body, swings it over his shoulder, and then staggers down the stairs. He has to get out. Away from the flames, away from the photo. He pushes against the heavy front door, but it won't budge. Behind him he hears the gigantic chandelier fall onto the once-gleaming white marble floor. He bangs on the door. He wants to shout, but with the gas mask on, he's the only one who can hear his call for help. Suddenly he looks down and sees the long white fingers hanging next to his leg: her thumb is long and her middle finger very short, just like his. He sees that her fingers are moving. Groping and searching. He gives the door a kick. *OPEN THE DOOR! LET US OUT!*

MADAN HEARS HER voice. *Come back! Come and get me! Come back!* He pedals up the hill as fast as he can, up the path flanked by shattered bowls and basins, past the silent fire engines. He throws his bicycle to the ground, heedless of his sewing machine on the carrier. He sees the firemen staring helplessly at the immense sea of fire, axes idle in their hands. Some of them are sitting despondently on the rolled-out carpet. He sees the two empty buckets on the columns next to the stairs. He sees the old man in his wheelchair, clapping his hands and shouting enthusiastic cries of encouragement, while an old firefighter with rows of medals on his chest looks at him with compassion. The handyman is comforting the sparsely clad niece, who is sobbing uncontrollably. *Come!* Her voice is despairing. *Come and get me!* He doesn't understand why no one is doing anything. *Why are they standing there, watching? They have to go in. She's still in there! They have to save her.* He sees portions of the balcony fall to the ground, blocking the front door.

Parvat wades through the flames that clutch at him, searching for the small side door. He advances through the burning debris, cradling her in his strong arms as tenderly as she held him in the photo. Tongues of fire lick hungrily at his legs. She must not die. Not now, not here, not in his arms. Then, surrounded by flames, he sees a figure approaching. He has no protective clothing. No mask. What kind of idiot has the courage to brave this sea of flames?

Madan wants to move forward, but it's impossible. The merciless flames force him back. He wants to fight, he feels no fear, but the scorching flames bar the way. The wall of fire is impenetrable. He no longer hears her voice, but he's certain that he did hear her, and that she called out to him.

Charlotte! he calls, without realizing that this is the first time he has spoken her name. *Charlotte, where are you?*

They emerge from the devastating curtain of flames. He doesn't recognize them. All he sees is a vague smudge, which seems to be moving, and the quivering contours of what might be a body.

They stagger outside. Away from the fire. Away from the house. Away from that raging hell. Parvat pushes Charlotte's limp body into Madan's arms and pulls off his mask. He sees how the man takes the woman in his arms. Embraces her. Kisses her. Embarrassed, the tall fireman watches the passionate caresses.

It's dark inside the wardrobe, the door won't open, even when I push, I smell the sweet scent of Mother's dresses, my hand brushes the soft velvet, I'm afraid, I know for sure they've forgotten me.

Madan's legs give way. The strength he had is gone. Charlotte's head sinks onto his lap. He strokes her face, her straight nose, her red lips, her long hair. He is crying. But it's not his tears that are falling on her face.

I hear the raindrops bouncing off the hood of the pram, my legs are bare, and my arms are uncovered, I don't know where they are, I'm outside, I'm alone, the rain is lashing me harder and harder, it hurts, I can't stop crying.

Above them, the sky breaks open. The drops plunge into the flames with a hissing sound. They're not afraid: in their millions they simply let go, allow themselves to fall, more and more of them, faster and faster. The rain rinses the soot from her face, and her translucent skin glows.

The tears carry me along, like a churning river, I am dragged into the jungle, I hear the rustling of the trees, I see the blood streaming down the trunks, I feel the fear of the silent column that plods along. Where are they heading? Where did they come from?

He closes his eyes and remembers Charlotte bending over him. Again he smells her scent. Again he hears the words she whispered then: *Stay alive!* She runs her fingers through his hair. He remembers the pain in his throat. She tells him that it's going to be all right. She kisses him. He opens his eyes and blinks. Through a haze, he sees that she is smiling at him.

We're dancing, our feet no longer touch the ground, our bodies touch only each other, we have no need for words, we have said everything, we have felt everything. The loneliness, the silence, and the fears have disappeared.

She looks at him, eyes wide open. Then her head falls to one side. A crashing bolt of lightning illuminates her broken smile. Above the hill, the thunder rumbles. The scent of jasmine rises.

Acknowledgements

THE FIRST PERSON I want to thank is Barbara Hershey, for the question that she asked me on the last day of filming *The Bird Can't Fly* and that ultimately led to this novel. I am also grateful to Nameeta Premkumar Nair, and to her family, friends, and assistants in Bombay, Chennai, Coonoor, New Delhi, and Shimla. During my investigative travels across India, they helped me find the right people and the right situations. My special thanks goes to Gopinder Vatsayayen in the foothills of the Himalayas, and Harmesh Rangaiah and his wife Rakhi in the hills of Coonoor, who arranged meetings that were decisive in determining the direction of this story. During my research I spoke with a maharaja, veteran soldiers, firemen, dozens of tailors, an elderly butler, retired servants, former nursemaids, street children, journalists, writers, and historians, as well as British citizens — and their descendents — who remained in India after independence was declared in 1947. I also visited former British clubs, palaces, orphanages, hospitals, workplaces, and a number of colonial villas. Nonetheless, all the characters and situations in this book are fictional: together they form a mosaic made up of the thousands of tiny pieces, which I discovered along the way.

I am also grateful for the help and hospitality of the former Dutch consul in Mumbai, Hans Ramaker, and journalist Rafique Baghdadi, who showed me what Bombay was like during the fifties.

In the Netherlands, my thanks go to Major General Germ Keuning and his network for providing the proper military terminology; Dick Plukker, who advised me on the correct Hindu terms; and Bargerhof Farm for the loan of its colourful pots and pans. My gratitude also goes to my four critical readers: Moniek Kramer, Helga Pranger, and my brothers Flip and Marc Schreurs — the latter also served as impromptu editor — as well as Linda Visser and Marleen Schoonderwoerd, who dotted the last "i"s and crossed the last "t"s. I thank my publisher Nelleke Geel, because she is different from all the other publishers in the Netherlands and a source of inspiration. But above all I thank my beloved, Adriaan Krabbendam, who read this book in serial form every day after dinner, encouraged me, and has been my editor for years.

About the Author

THREES ANNA is a writer and director of film and theatre. She is the author of five critically acclaimed novels, and her debut film, *The Bird Can't Fly*, premiered at the San Sebastian International Film Festival. She is currently working on the film adaptation of her novel *The Silent City*. She lives in the Netherlands.

About the Translator

BARBARA POTTER FASTING is an American translator specializing in fiction and literary nonfiction. Her previous translations include the novel *Unknown Destination* by Maya Rasker and *Disturbances of the Mind* by Douwe Draaisma. She lives in the Netherlands.

QUESTIONS FOR DISCUSSION

Waiting for the Monsoon by Threes Anna

1. What similarities and differences do you see between Charlotte and Madan? Between Charlotte and Victor?

2. In the opening lines of the novel Charlotte is compared to the electric lawnmower: "She was like the old Lloyds. For years it was the only electric lawnmower for miles around: the fact that it was still functioning was thanks to the brand and not to love." How does the last statement apply to Charlotte's life?

3. What does Madan gain from his friendship with Abbas?

4. When Victor announces that he plans to return to England Charlotte thinks, "He'll make it to London, and without a hitch, too." How true is Charlotte's assessment of her father?

5. Describe the relationship between Madan and Mister Patel. Do you think Mister Patel felt obligated to take care of Madan? Why do you think he made the decision to leave Madan with Chandan Chandran?

6. What is Hema's role in the book? How do other people react to him?

7. Why do you think Charlotte agrees to take Madan in? Do the ladies of the New Rampur Club influence her decision? Do they influence her in other ways?

8. Charlotte's great-grandmother Elizabeth Elphinstone whispers, "The clock is the future," as she crosses the Khyber Pass. What does the big grandfather clock symbolize for Charlotte in the past and present?

9. After giving birth, Charlotte tells Sita "From now on, this is your child." Why do you think Sita agrees to take the baby?

10. Victor says to Charlotte, "A true Bridgwater doesn't cry. Ever." What impact does this statement have on Charlotte throughout her life?

11. In what ways does Peter's war trauma impact his marriage to Charlotte? Why do you think he keeps this trauma from Charlotte? Why can't he move past it?